A WOMAN IN WINTER

To Amos.
With warm wishes.
There is no one I admire
more than you.

Vernon Sanders

I hope you can find time
to read the story.

Vernon

7/11/15

This book is a work of fiction. Any resemblance to actual events or persons, living or dead, is entirely coincidental.

"A Woman In Winter," by Vernon Sanders. ISBN 978-1-62137-712-2(Softcover).

Library of Congress Control Number: 2015907489

Published 2015 by Virtualbookworm.com Publishing Inc., P.O. Box 9949, College Station, TX 77842, US.

DEDICATION

To the Woman of my Dreams

Good night Ms. Calabash, wherever you are.

ACKNOWLEDGEMENTS

Writing book-length fiction is often a long and arduous process. The support of friends makes the journey sustainable. While there may be exceptions, most writers are bolstered by the advice and encouragement of others. Most important, he or she needs a sounding board that has a genuine interest in the story. I was fortunate to have those valuable resources.

A special thanks to Ralph Roughton, psychoanalyst and Duke classmate, who read the manuscript and offered innovative ideas. When the story stalled, as it did several times, he brought suggestions to the table which moved the narrative forward. I am grateful for Ralph's interest and participation in bringing *A Woman in Winter* to life. Thanks, my friend.

A nod to Jimmy Durante who helped put Calabash, North Carolina on the map.

A salute to Sammy Fain and Irving Kahal for the words and music to *I'll Be Seeing You,* a popular show tune from the late thirties, that provided the lyrical backdrop for this late-in-life love story.

A rousing round of applause for Sally Brady, my editor extraordinaire, who has shepherded me through four works of book-length fiction. In short, her contributions have been inestimable. I am grateful for her perceptive eye and considerable insight. It has been for me an exciting journey and Sally is the gifted guide who showed me the way.

OTHER BOOKS BY VERNON SANDERS

Poetry

This Small Ship, This Great Sea
Beyond the Mist and the Mountains
The Shadow of a Passing Cloud
Whispers in the Wind
The Glow of Ashes

Biography

To Chase the Sun

Fiction

When a Sparrow Falls
The Splendor of Light
A Boy's World, The Summer of '43

AUTHOR'S NOTE

Time and place have been noted at the beginning of some chapters with the hope it assists the reader. Since the novel's timeline is not linear, help may be needed to follow the chronological sequence. The story, with rare exception, takes place in Dallas (1984) and in Camden (2012). Crisscrossing the timeline does occur. Identifying time and location of critical chapters should smooth the flow of the narrative.

Wise men say, only fools rush in,
But I can't help falling in love with you.

Elvis Presley

Grow old along with me, the best is yet to be,
The last of life for which the first was made.

Robert Browning

PROLOGUE

Late May, 1969

WHEN SHE AWOKE, the knot was still there. Maggie lay in bed and massaged her stomach. It didn't help; no surprise. After all, she faced the most important day of her life. Maggie knew *anticipation* was enough to twist a sailor's knot beneath her rib cage.

Sitting on the side of the bed she felt the excitement; the time of departure had finally arrived; the seed planted during her junior year in high school when she was only sixteen. After a beating by an abusive father and the cold indifference of an addicted mother, she vowed to leave Rutledge with its Dairy Queen and one stoplight and not look back. Maggie was true to her commitment. She continued to work after school and on weekends at Rusty's Diner, save her tips and meager salary, enough cash to get out of town. She checked the schedule; the Greyhound bus made a two o'clock stop in front of Riley's General Store on its way to El Paso. Maggie settled on her time of departure: the day of her graduation. Almost eighteen and a high school diploma were valuable assets. She thought of Dell, her older sister. Lucky Dell, who had escaped the misery, by winning a scholarship to a branch of U. T. in Odessa. Their only living grandparent languished in a crummy nursing home in nearby Fort Stockton. Other than for a few casual friends, the small town in West Texas had nothing else to offer, nothing to hold her back. She let her eyes scan the small bedroom for the last time. There were memories here . . . none of them pleasant . . . some terrifying. She had plenty of reasons to leave, forever, the wood-frame house, weathered gray, that sat on a half-acre of parched land. Maggie figured her childhood was best forgotten.

Sunlight flashed through an open window. She checked the clock on the nightstand. The numbers blurred. Maggie rubbed her eyes and took a closer look: 7:15, enough time to dress, have a bowl of cereal and walk to school in time for homeroom. Cap and gown awaited her in the teacher's lounge. Flash Williams would be there to take the class picture, and then final instructions from Mrs. McBride, the school principal.

Maggie padded down the short hallway to the cramped bathroom. She heard her mother's light snoring, sleeping off last night's bender. Otherwise, the house was quiet. Her father, whom she loathed, had turned off the whirring attic fan on his way to work, an oil rig west of Rutledge. She hoped she'd never see him again. There were times, after a beating, that she dreamed of ways to end the madness. But when awake, Maggie knew the safest and wisest solution was to pack a suitcase and leave the "horrors" behind. The future beckoned. Once in El Paso, she had tantalizing options.

Her mother was still asleep when Maggie left the house. She crossed the narrow porch and down the tread-worn steps to a dirt path leading to the road. She stopped long enough to observe the only tree in the yard, a desert willow with its pink, trumpet-shaped flowers. She wondered how it survived the spring dust storms and the scorching summer sun, with roots buried in an arid earth. For some odd reason, she felt a kinship with the flowering tree and wished she could reach one of its blossoms. She would pin it in her hair and let its fragrance follow her throughout the morning. Maggie shook her head and looked up at the tree. "Just as well; it won't work anyway," she muttered, "I have to wear that stupid mortarboard."

The auditorium of Rutledge High was almost full as Maggie and her classmates marched single file, down the center aisle and onto the stage while the brass-heavy high school band played the ceremonial *Pomp and Circumstance.* The twenty-eight graduates sat in folding chairs, a semi-circle behind the podium. Mrs. McBride welcomed the guests and family members who had come to share this memorable occasion. Maggie smothered a snicker with her hand. Memorable, maybe, but more like a resounding "goodbye."

Maggie scanned the audience, only a few familiar faces. Beverly Mason and Eve Sinclair were two of her casual friends. She recognized their parents who sat close to the stage, puffed up and smiling. No signs of her family; none were expected. She figured her mother was still asleep, and her father was miles away. Dell had finished the semester at U.T., and already started a summer job in Odessa; no plans to come home again . . . ever.

The valedictory speech was a blur of words, Maggie's mind drifted, her legs restless. She looked at her watch and thought about the dusty Greyhound bus that would whisk her away in a few hours.

The Congressman, lean and bald, walked to the podium. The commencement speaker waved to the crowd and smiled broadly. She got that; a politician's smile. But when he opened his mouth, her mind shuttled back to Riley's, waiting anxiously for the El Paso Express. Maggie, in her mind's eye, looked up; a few wispy clouds in an azure sky, ideal weather, no travel delays.

"Margaret Ellen Wilson."

The name brought her back to the moment. She stood, walked to the front of the stage, shook the Congressman's hand and accepted the diploma from Mrs. McBride. Rather than return to her seat, Maggie kept walking, left the stage through a side door, dropped off her cap and gown in the teacher's lounge and hurried out of the building.

She returned to an empty house, took off her Sunday dress and put on blue jeans and a gray T-shirt. No jewelry, no accessories, only the Ladies' Timex, a Christmas gift from Dell. She packed a small suitcase and placed the money she'd saved in the pocket of her jeans. She opened her desk drawer and retrieved the note she had written earlier. Maggie read it one last time:

To my parents

I graduated from Rutledge High this morning. Where were you?

This is my notice: I'm leaving this house of horrors and won't be back. There's no love here; only abuse and neglect and nightmares.

Where am I going? Does it matter? Don't bother to look for me. I'll be 18 in a few days, eligible for a driver's license. I have a high school diploma and enough money to get me where I want to go. Perhaps in my new life I'll find the virtue of forgiveness. Then again, maybe not.

So long,

Maggie

She placed the note on her mother's pillow on the way to the kitchen. She made a peanut butter and jelly sandwich and washed it down with a glass of cold sweet milk. Maggie figured it should tamp down her hunger for a while. She walked back into the bathroom to wash her hands. A final look in the mirror, the reflection of fine features; an overhead light picked up the sheen of her natural blond hair. Maggie was voted *Miss Rutledge,* the prettiest girl in the school, and she had the yearbook to prove it. She knew her looks were an asset and one she intended to exploit.

Maggie went back to her desk and recounted the cash. Earlier, she had taken a milk bottle full of coins and dollar bills to the Central Bank where she received in exchange $230 in tens and twenties. The Greyhound ticket to El Paso cost her $40 which included the transfer to her final destination. And it wasn't Phoenix or Santa Fe or San Diego. She had read about the boom town and its flood of job opportunities. Maggie was on her way to Las Vegas, daydreaming about her new found freedom and with a fistful of money.

CHAPTER 1

Early May, 1972

FRED MARTINGALE, A PATENT ATTORNEY for one of the most prestigious law firms in Dallas, lived in an elegant section of Highland Park and hosted the perennial Kentucky Derby party. He only invited a hundred or so of his closest friends, but from Fred's point of view, as the youngest senior partner in the firm, he needed to keep a high profile. And it was a tax write-off.

As the spring afternoon wore on and the liquor flowed freely, Fred found himself huddled in a corner of the living room with his closest friend, George McCloud, and Benny Friedman, an orthodontist. George was moving up the ranks of the city's largest bank like a man possessed. After the race the conversation was serpentine, winding its way through subjects, arcane and current, finally settling on the upcoming Preakness. They all agreed Riva Ridge, the Derby winner, was a lock. However, the Triple Crown was problematic; Belmont's one and a half mile track was formidable, a distance few thoroughbreds had ever run. Benny reminded the others that it had been twenty-four years since Citation had won the last Triple Crown. He took a pen and envelope from his inside coat pocket and recorded the bets for the Preakness, only two weeks away.

Benny did business with the bookie. The others preferred to remain anonymous which was okay with Benny, who handled the under-the-table transactions with the stealth and discretion of a C.I.A. operative.

"Get Ward's bet," Fred reminded him.

Benny nodded. "I'll call tomorrow."

"Too bad he couldn't make the party."

"Yeah, one of his patients spiked a high fever and went bonkers," Fred explained. "Jeannie called to apologize."

They stopped and admired Emma Cotter as she rustled across the room in her champagne silk cocktail dress with its eye-catching décolletage. She turned the heads of most men unless they were nearsighted or the "juices" that generated the interest had dried up. So the reaction of Fred and his friends was no surprise.

"Where is Earl?" Fred asked. "I caught a glimpse when he and Emma arrived but I haven't seen him since."

"Probably ordering another drink," George said with a chuckle.

"You think ol' Earl can handle that?" Benny asked with a lascivious grin.

"I doubt it," George replied. "And what a damn shame."

Benny bolted straight up as if Emma Cotter sparked an idea that blistered him like the sting of a jellyfish. "Let's go to Vegas for a long weekend. Whata you say?"

"Where did that come from?" Fred asked.

"It'd be great fun. Play some tennis, roll the dice, see some great shows. Hey, how 'bout it?"

"No wives, I assume," George said.

"No wives. And we'll talk Ward into going."

"I'm game, but we need some lead time." Fred cuffed Benny's shoulder. "And you make all the arrangements."

Benny clapped his hands with delight. "It's a deal," he exclaimed, so loud that others in the room turned and stared. "Las Vegas, here we come."

Six weeks later

On a sultry Friday afternoon, Ward sat at the bar just off the lobby of the Dunes, one of the preferred hotels on the Vegas Strip. He sipped a Coke, chatting with Joe the bartender.

The friends had flown west for a few days of fun and games. They were all respected professionals in their mid-thirties; too young for the getaway to be described as a mid-life crisis and too old to be mistaken for a fraternity romp. Nevertheless, there were those back home, including one of the wives, who accused them of self-indulgent and jejune behavior.

"Whata you do for a living?" Joe asked.

Ward cleared his throat. "Well . . ."

"It's not a hard question," Joe insisted while rubbing his several chins.

"I'm a doctor," he said, finally.

"Really." Joe's response was frayed by surprise. "Thought maybe you were from L.A., you know, the movie business.

"Nope, not even close," Ward said. "Settled in Dallas eight years ago."

"Oh yeah . . . never been there but hear it's a nice town."

Ward nodded. "No regrets so far."

Joe refilled his glass with Coke and asked, "What kinda doctor?" The bartender wouldn't let it go. "You work on horses or humans?"

They both laughed.

Ward seemed to have Joe's undivided attention. It was four o'clock in the afternoon and pedestrian traffic through the lobby of the hotel was light. The bar itself, with the exception of Ward, was surprisingly deserted. The check-in desk, a long slab of black marble, was out of his line of vision but he assumed, at this hour, it was the hub of activity.

Out on the street, the temperature was a sweltering one hundred and five degrees; an incentive for any sane person to stay inside where air conditioning and iced drinks provided a comfortable setting, even for those dour-faced losers streaming out of the casino. Ward wondered why Benny Friedman, a tennis freak, chose a hot-weather month for the getaway, but since Benny had made all the arrangements, Ward was reluctant to complain. Fred had suggested warmer weather during the early May party, but this was over-the-top . . . insufferable.

The group had planned to play tennis during their stay, but even Benny agreed that either they make a 7 a.m. reservation or forego the plan entirely. A vote was taken and the results were unanimous: tennis was tabled.

The chance encounter occurred as the conversation with Joe, the bartender, took a more serious turn—the upcoming Presidential election and the possibility of returning Richard Nixon to the White House.

Ward felt something brush his right ear lightly. He turned and found himself staring at a face sculpted like a goddess with sapphire-blue eyes and long dark lashes. Before he could speak, she planted a moist kiss on his lips.

Nonplused, Ward braced himself against the railing. Out of the corner of his eye, he noticed that Joe, a man of considerable size, had disappeared like a puff of smoke.

"Hi," she said seductively. "My name's Maggie and for a hundred dollars, we'll go up to your room." The proffer was succinct and unconditional.

Ward collected himself, but his voice had a nervous edge. "Look, Maggie, I've never paid for it before and I'm not starting now." Considering the sudden and sensual nature of her invitation, he was rather proud of his response. In truth, Ward felt relief; he had not become tongue-tied in the presence of this beautiful woman and her unexpected offer.

With a subtle smile, she looked him square in the eye. "Don't kid yourself; you always pay for it, one way or the other." (After Ward's divorce in 1979, those words were validated, in fact, they became axiomatic.)

Maggie was persistent. She took his hand and carried it discreetly inside her low cut cocktail dress and rested it on her ample breast.

Ward pulled away and insisted he was not interested though the traces of ambivalence in his voice were hard to hide. While she was desirable, his conscience was sending him an unambiguous message. He struggled mightily to right the ship that was listing in meretricious waters.

"Have a seat," he said finally. "I'll buy you a drink."

She slid onto the bar stool next to him. Before Joe arrived to take their order, she placed her hand on Will's thigh and stroked it gently. "Are you sure?" she asked. "It's a real sweet deal. I'm yours for a whole hour . . . that is, if you're still breathing."

He caught the devilish gleam in her eyes.

Ward again removed her hand. "Look, Maggie, I won't lie and tell you I'm not interested. But there's a little voice up there—he stopped and pointed at his head—that keeps saying 'no'; can you understand that?"

She hunched her shoulders. "I guess," she said.

"Tell Joe what you'd like."

She gave the bartender a defeated look. "How 'bout a vodka martini?"

"Coming right up." As he turned away, Joe took an over-the-shoulder glance and shrugged. "Whata you expect? The guy's drinking a Coke."

Ward repositioned himself on the stool and rested one arm on the railing. 'Now, tell me about yourself. I mean, you're young . . . attractive . . . poised . . ."

She placed a finger against his lips. "You're really wondering why I'm here, right?"

Ward nodded.

"The answer is simple . . . the money. Where else could a twenty-one-year-old from a hardscrabble town in West Texas make a hundred grand a year . . . tax free?"

Joe sat her drink down and refilled Ward's empty glass.

During the next half hour, Ward peppered her with questions, which she answered openly. He learned a great deal about her profession, but she refused to talk about family; the subject was off limits. It made him wonder about those influences that shaped her childhood (traumatic, by inference), causing her to leave home as a teenager and head for the Nevada desert. Was she abused? Neglected? Or just rebellious? Ward could only speculate.

He tried to lighten the conversation. She laughed easily, which surprised him. He assumed that the rough-and-tumble life of a strumpet soaked up mirth like a sponge. While he may have been wrong, Ward pictured them as becoming cynical and insipid old women, many of whom aged much too soon. But he avoided comments or questions that were judgmental or smacked of morality. He remembered the Biblical injunction and had no intention of "casting the first stone."

Maggie finished her drink and slipped off the stool. "Gotta go. I'm a working girl. Remember?"

"How could I forget?"

"Thanks for the drink."

"My pleasure." He stood up and brushed her cheek with a kiss.

"I'm sorry we couldn't connect.

"Me too . . . maybe if it had been another time and another pla . . ."

She looked at Joe, who with folded arms leaned against the back wall of the bar. "A romantic," she said and nodded toward Ward. "They're rare birds 'round here."

"Take care of yourself," Ward said, as she walked away. There was poignancy in the parting.

"You too." The words trailed her across the lobby and out of sight.

"Best looking hooker in Vegas," Joe said.

"Don't doubt it," Ward conceded.

"What's your problem, Doc?" Joe sauntered over and spoke softly, almost a whisper. "The way she was lookin' at you with those big blues, I bet you woulda got a free pass."

"'You always pay for it, one way or the other.' Those were her words," he reminded the bartender.

During the last ten minutes, Benny, half hidden behind an imposing statue of Ramses II, had observed his friend's animated conversation with this comely stranger. He was unable to curb his curiosity after Ward placed the kiss on her cheek and waved goodbye.

Benny strolled over nonchalantly as if he were there by happenstance and threw his arm around Ward's shoulder. "What's that all about?" he asked.

"I'll tell you at dinner," he said, fishing a twenty from his pocket and placing it beneath his empty glass.

Joe reached over, handed him his tab and picked up the twenty, all in one motion.

Ward looked back as he turned to leave. "Keep the change." A sheepish grin. "I got my money's worth."

"Thanks." He lifted an empty glass. "See ya 'round, Doc."

Disappointed by having to wait for Ward's recounting, Benny looked at his watch and picked up the pace. "We'd better get a move on. Our reservation for the dinner show is in less than an hour, and we'll have to grab a cab since the Frontier's way the hell down the strip."

The group was collegial and enjoyed their three days together even though the blistering summer heat cancelled their tennis plans. That was a disappointment. So they swam in the mornings, played the five dollar tables, napped in the afternoons, placed bets in the book room on the Yankees and took in a dinner show in the evening. Benny drank too much but fortunately he was a cheerful drunk who stood and whooped it up during Wayne Newton's stirring arrangement of *The Battle Hymn of the Republic* and a foot stomping, banjo picking rendition of *Dixie*. In fact, there were times when Benny got downright boorish and Ward pulled him into his seat forcefully, cupping his mouth to quiet the Rebel yells.

Delta Flight #442 left McCarran's on time Sunday morning. Ward squeezed into an aisle seat, settled against the headrest and let his mind reel back to the group's second day in Las Vegas and his chance encounter with Maggie and her enticing blue eyes.

The advice was unsolicited. He gave it nonetheless. "Why not take your savings, get out of the business and move to Phoenix or Dallas or a small town in California overlooking the Pacific? You'll meet some nice man who truly loves you, get married, have kids, take vacations and travel around the world, to exotic places."

She had put up her hand . . . a stop signal. "You sound like a doting father," she said. "But I'm not ready to leave the business. Not yet." Ward knew he was not her "keeper," but he still hoped that she would turn her life around. After all, there was always a chance. But what were the odds? Ward laughed at himself; the Vegas mystique was obviously contagious.

Benny, in the seat beside him, was asleep and snoring with gusto—luckily muted by the drone of the plane. Ward smiled at this bit of comic relief, leaned back in his seat, and recalled the Friday night dinner at the Frontier. After his friends got a full report concerning the woman with uncommon good looks, he faced a barrage of questions. Ward countered: The answers were easy. While he didn't want to sound holier-than-thou, he explained that fidelity was at the heart of a solid and successful marriage. To break that trust would irreparably damage the relationship. (The irony of those remarks was yet to unfold.) Others might see it differently, he admitted, but for him it was a simple matter of conscience.

One thing was certain; he would never forget the encounter. Or her classic rejoinder: "Don't kid yourself; you *always* pay for it, one way or the other."

The plane landed safely and within hours the four friends, their pockets lighter but their spirits refreshed, had slipped back into their comfortable, ordinary lives.

As the seasons turned, Ward remembered those words many times. Often the recall resulted from a painful experience (like his divorce) which injured his pride, weakened his confidence and blew big gaping holes in his pocketbook. But he had been forewarned by a stunning young woman with startling blue eyes; a hooker in Las Vegas whose maxim should be a reminder to all men, everywhere.

When Ward returned to Vegas on other occasions, he especially remembered the blue-eyed young woman and her sage words. And he always felt a faint awareness of their meeting that summer of '72. Did he really want to see that face again? Ward wasn't sure, but regardless, the question was rhetorical. She had walked out of the hotel and simply vanished. A poem by Burns came to mind: " . . . *like the snow falls in the river, a moment white, then gone forever.*"

He hoped she was well and had discovered a better way. He hoped she had found someone special to love and to be loved by in return. Above all, he hoped that she had not waited too long to make that crucial choice. For Ward knew that in the larger scheme of things, this uncertain journey called life was like the Ferris wheel at the county fair. While exhilarating at times, it was in fact, a very short ride.

CHAPTER 2

Early December, 1972

IT HAD BEEN SIX MONTHS since she'd met him in the lobby bar of the Dunes Hotel. She could still see his face, but Maggie could not remember his name. Maybe he'd never used his name. She remembered the bartender called him "Doc," Well, she wondered, was he a dentist? A surgeon? Or maybe a Ph.D., like Brenda McBride, the principal at Rutledge High. It bothered her that the encounter had not faded from her memory like all the others. As a high-end call girl, her customers were easily forgotten; she made a point of it; a discipline she imposed on herself from the very beginning.

The bar was empty, the mid-afternoon slump. Maggie sat on a high-back stool, her purse on the seat beside her. "Hi, Joe."

"Where've you been, beautiful?"

"Around . . . like always. Missed you last time; musta been your day off."

"How 'bout a drink?" He leaned against the back bar and folded his arms. "Guess you haven't heard from Doc?"

Maggie shook her head. "Good memory, Joe." She gave the lobby a sidelong glance as if he might appear like an apparition. "But it's funny how well I remember our conversation . . . at least, some of it."

"The guy drank a Coke and bought you a vodka martini." He skipped a beat. "A Texan . . . from Dallas. Now why would I remember that?"

"I guess he made an impression . . . on both of us." Maggie shrugged and ordered a scotch and soda, hoping it, along with a couple of aspirins would relieve the growing discomfort in her stomach.

She heard the fizz when Joe opened the bottle of soda and filled a glass garnished with a lime wedge. "Any plans for the Christmas holidays?" he asked.

"Not really . . . working as usual."

"Frankie should give you some time off."

"Yeah, I suppose." She squeezed the lime and stirred it with a straw. "He's invited me and two of the girls for an early Christmas dinner."

"Three out of . . . what . . . thirty or so?" He rocked his hand as if it were only an estimate.

"Plus some part-timers as well, locals, I guess you'd say. But when a convention is in town he keeps every girl busy. Runs an efficient shop."

"And he has plenty of muscle." Joe flexed his biceps, a poor imitation of a bodybuilder.

"Frankie's father?"

"Yeah, Joe Agosto, his old man runs The Capri; a front for the Kansas City Mob."

Joe stopped long enough to serve a customer, a middle-aged male, well dressed and wearing a fedora. He had passed Maggie without a glance and seated himself at the far end of the bar. He ordered a beer, tipped his hat back and buried his face in a newspaper. Joe had noticed and wondered if he'd ever seen a man *not look* at Maggie.

The interlude gave Maggie another chance to consider her options. She checked her reflection in the mirror that covered the back bar. Her face, unlined and with perfect symmetry, looked the same as the day she got off the Greyhound bus. Regular workouts kept her body firm and fit. Monthly visits to Frankie's doctor were mandatory and ensured she was healthy and free of infection. After two years, she was in demand by politicians, celebrities, high rollers and the going rate was $1000 an hour, with a two-hour minimum. While Frankie took a big cut, it was still big money for a twenty-one-year-old and hard to walk away from. Still, the stranger had planted a seed and she had a healthy savings account, enough to start a new life.

Maggie took the last swallow of Scotch and checked her watch. She gathered her purse and winced, clutching her side as she slipped off the bar stool. She'd had tinges since yesterday, maybe a stomach virus. "Gotta go, Joe."

"What's the rush?"

"I'm still a working girl."

Joe waved her off. "Come back soon. Next time, the drinks are on the house."

She blew him a kiss and disappeared into the lobby.

The pain she felt the day before her visit to the Dunes had been mild, tolerable and seemed to come and go. Now, she was relieved her friend, Judy, had forgotten their plans for an early dinner. She scanned the lobby and checked the casino to be sure. No signs of Judy. Meanwhile, her pain grew more intense . . . unremitting. Should she go back to her apartment and get off her feet? Maybe a heating pad would help. The onset of nausea made her decision easy. She took a taxi to The Capri and used the house phone. Frankie picked up on the second ring.

"It's Maggie. I'm sick Frankie."

"What's the problem?"

"Pain in my stomach, low down. And it's getting worse."

"What else?" Frankie asked.

Maggie's voice was subdued. "I'm 'bout to throw up on Mr. Agosto's plush carpet."

"Okay, listen up . . . go to the nurse's station on the second floor, then ask Ms. Arnold to call me after her exam."

"Thanks." She hung up the phone, took a few deep breaths, and wiped the moisture from her forehead.

Waves of nausea rolled over her as she made her way to the bank of elevators. The second floor of The Capri was familiar; she had been there before. It was a warren of offices for administrative staff and hotel/casino executives. It also housed the large control room that monitored surveillance cameras scattered throughout the property. The nursing station was near the end of the south wing, which Maggie considered an interminable distance. She felt weak and feverish as she moved slowly down the corridor, small wobbly steps, using the wall for support.

A bell jangled when she opened the door. No one was in the waiting room. She dropped into a chair and vomited into a waste basket. The nurse heard the retching and brought a wet towel to wipe her face and clean the stains on her blouse. “Let’s get you back to the exam room and a comfortable bed.”

Ms. Arnold, matronly, with an easy smile, took Maggie’s vital signs. BP, 104/66; pulse, 88 and regular: temperature, 100°. The abdomen was tender; rebound in the right lower quadrant. Otherwise, the exam was unremarkable.

“Maggie, it’s probably your appendix. A ruptured ovarian cyst is possible, but unlikely. We need to get you to the ER at Sunrise.”

“Whatever.” A sharp stab took her breath away. “Better call Frankie.”

Physical pain was no stranger to Maggie. She had felt it many times at the hands of her father. While the pain became more intense, it was not unbearable and bore none of the emotional equivalents of her childhood abuse. She had learned to process pain stoically. The irony: it made her mentally tough. While the beads of sweat reappeared on her forehead, and spikes of pain made her grimace, there were no tears; no requests for medication. She knew the hospital was only a mile away and had a stellar reputation. She would get the best possible care; Frankie would make sure of that.

Ms. Arnold sat beside the bed and wiped Maggie’s face with the towel. She spoke softly . . . reassurances. “Speck, from Frankie’s office, is on the way. He’ll take you down in a wheelchair; a courtesy car will whisk you to Sunrise. Quicker than calling an ambulance.”

“May I have some water?” she asked.

Ms. Arnold shook her head. “Nothing to eat or drink. If it’s your appendix, it’ll need to come out.”

Maggie gave a deep sigh of resignation.

“Anyone else you’d like me to call?”

Maggie shook her head. “There’s no one . . .”

A blind covered the window, but sunlight slipped through the slats, bars of light on the tile floor. Maggie opened her eyes, groggy and unsure of the setting. It took her a few minutes to clear most of the cobwebs away. She was able to make a few observations: a hospital room, flat on her back, the side rails up, a bag of fluids hung from an IV pole beside the bed. She licked her lips; a dry mouth. With her free hand, she pulled up her hospital gown and felt the surgical dressing that covered her incision. Tender, but the pain was gone.

There was a knock on her door. A young man in green scrubs and a white lab coat pushed it open and moved to the bedside. "Hi Maggie, I'm, Dr. Tom Boles." He leaned in close, resting his arms on the side rail. "How are you feeling?"

Maggie dredged up a half-hearted smile. "Better than yesterday."

He took her hand; a gentle squeeze. "Sounds good to me . . . making progress."

"Are you my surgeon?" she asked.

Boles nodded. "I was on call for the ER."

Maggie's eyes almost closed, but she resisted the pull and tug of sleep.

Boles gave her hand another gentle squeeze. "Would you like to know about the operation?"

She looked at him with her arresting blue eyes. "Sure."

"We removed your appendix. The surgery went well, smooth as silk. That's the good news." Boles stopped long enough to see if she was awake and listening. Satisfied, he continued. "There was one unexpected complication."

"Like what?" The question had a nervous edge.

"First, a little anatomy." He took her hand, a touch of solace. "The appendix sits at the juncture of the small and large intestine, Sometimes a leak may occur through a swollen appendix. That's what happened to you; a small appendiceal abscess which, thank God, had walled itself off. And here's the best news: it had not spread any further; *peritonitis* may be a life-threatening complication. However . . ." He frowned, hesitant, before giving her more unwelcome news. " . . . you'll need an extended course of IV antibiotics."

"So, I'll be here . . . how long?"

“You’ll be the hospital’s guest for the next two weeks.”

A weary sigh “Whatever,” she said.

“Let’s check my handiwork.” He tucked the sheet and lifted the surgical dressing. Only a few cc’s of drainage. The incision was clean. He pulled the stethoscope from his coat pocket and placed it on her abdomen. No bowel sounds. A quick check of her heart and lungs.

“Everything ok?” she asked.

“The entire length of your bowel is paralyzed which is often the case after surgery. The gut will begin to move again in a day or two. Meanwhile, nothing by mouth. The IVs will provide all the fluids and nutrition you need.”

Boles reviewed the nurse’s notes that hung at the foot of the bed: a low-grade fever, adequate urine output, the WBC was pending.

“Get some sleep and I’ll be back this evening.”

“Thanks.”

“Any questions before I go?”

She shook her head. “Maybe later.”

Boles started to leave; then stopped short. “Oh, one other thing . . . I left a drain in the incision which I’ll remove tomorrow, the stitches in a week.” He opened the door and turned back. “Remember the old Johnny Mercer tune: *Accentuate the Positive?”*

“The Pied Pipers.” Maggie found few pleasures in her life, but music was one of them. And unlike her peers, her favorites were the big bands of the forties and the “Pop” artists like Sinatra, Como, Clooney and the Ink Spots.

Boles applauded; a show of surprise. “Remember . . . only *positive* thoughts; it’s a standing order. Now get some rest.”

Maggie closed her eyes and drifted on a narcotic cloud into a peaceful sleep.

Maggie left Sunset Hospital two days before Christmas. Dr. Boles had given her discharge instructions, including prescriptions and an f/u office appointment. While she had walked the hall outside her room twice a day, her legs were still weak and her gait unsteady. Speck arrived with a wheelchair and rolled her to the black DeVille parked at the front entrance. A ten spot trumped the No Parking zone. He helped Maggie into the back seat and returned the wheelchair to the floor nurse who had accompanied him. The taciturn Speck turned the ignition and drove away. Maggie knew any attempt to jumpstart a conversation with Speck was pointless, like blowing in the wind. So she rode in silence, which was okay with her. In a matter of minutes, he drove through the gates of the Desert Sky Apartments just off Tropicana Avenue.

Speck stopped curbside and turned off the engine. Maggie wrapped an arm around his thick neck as he carried her up the steps to the second floor. He dropped her gently on the landing and let her walk the rest of the way. She plucked the key from her purse and unlocked the door. Maggie stepped inside, Speck right behind her. She took a few steps and flopped in the easy chair grateful to be home.

Speck opened the curtains that covered the sliding glass doors and set the thermostat at 75 degrees. Light from a winter sun brightened an otherwise bleak sitting-room. Just the easy chair, an upholstered hickory rocker, a lamp table and a wall-mounted color TV. Two Ansel Adams prints hung on a side wall begging for color.

Maggie had rented the furniture and kitchenware for the apartment. At the time, it was a pragmatic decision since her cash reserve was limited. After the first six months, she could have bought her own furniture, but Maggie was comfortable and content with the rentals and chose to extend her agreement with Abby's on a month to month basis. She had seen opulence and its trappings at The Capri and other hotels. Who needs a marble bathtub, Persian rugs or stainless steel sinks? While Judy, more than once, had urged her to "brighten up the place," she preferred beige and taupe and grays—muted colors. Midnight blue may have been her favorite.

Maggie watched Speck as he moved around the apartment. Window locks were secure. The sliding glass doors that led onto a small balcony were latched. Her eyes followed him into the kitchen. He opened the pantry door; then stepped back, shaking his head.

"Something wrong?" she asked.

He returned to the sitting room and leaned on the back of the rocker. "You need groceries."

"Don't think I can make it to Trader Joe's."

"Don't worry, Frankie's got you covered."

"Thanks, Speck."

"See you tomorrow." A hand wave and he was gone.

Maggie slept for twelve hours. It was so good to be in her bed with clean sheets and down pillows. She checked the clock on the bedside table: 11:20. Maggie opened the curtains that covered the bedroom window; black clouds and the rumble of thunder. Rain began to splatter the glass and she thought of all those last-minute Christmas shoppers, none of whom were prepared for the weather. Understandable . . . it rarely rained in the desert. But it was not a problem for her; no gifts for anyone. Even Dell had drifted away—the last letter six months ago—although Maggie assumed her sister was still in Odessa.

A knock on the door brought her back to the moment. She put on her bathrobe and padded barefoot across the thin carpet. She cracked the door wide enough to see Speck standing behind a food cart. She slipped the chain out of its track and opened up. "Come on in," she said and stepped aside.

"Mornin'." Speck rolled the cart into the kitchen.

She watched him fill the fridge and stock the pantry.

"Frankie sent you Christmas dinner."

"Thanks . . . tell him that . . . will you?"

"Sure and give him a ring if you need anything."

"Oh, Speck," she called out as he turned to leave. "Merry Christmas."

"Yeah, you too."

Maggie stood at the open door and watched him go. Rain pelted his slicker as he loaded the cart and the plywood planks (which he'd used to negotiate the stairs), into the bed of the truck. She knew that Speck was an indispensable part of the business. While Frankie was only an *associate* (his father, Joe Agosto was a *capo* in the Kansas City hierarchy), he needed a loyal *soldier* to handle "certain delicate situations." Speck fit the bill.

Frankie had his faults, even a dark side, but he took good care of his own. Maggie knew it was the reason he had the most successful escort service in Las Vegas. Speck's delivery was Frankie's way of looking after one of his girls. Maggie admitted he was no Mother Teresa, but he was always there when she needed him. Never once had he let her down. If her decision to resign and move on with her life became final, she wondered how he would take the news. Her best guess: not well.

It had been four weeks since Maggie left the hospital. She had spent the time reading, listening to Percy Faith's Christmas standards, and watching her favorite TV programs. She took Dr. Boles advice, bundled up (Las Vegas was cold in January) and walked through the Desert Sky neighborhood. It became a daily ritual. Her legs got stronger and she was able to take the apartment's stairs two at a time.

After she completed her course of oral antibiotics, her appetite returned and she regained some of the weight she'd lost during her six-week ordeal. Maggie knew she had fully recovered, since for the first time she felt like her old self.

During this period of rest and recovery, she had spent time pondering her future. Even before her surgery, Maggie had considered a different lifestyle, moving in another direction. The money in Vegas was good, but she had saved enough to explore other avenues. A fresh start had its appeal. It had not happened overnight, like some mystical revelation. In fact, the process had been slow and deliberate. The appendiceal abscess and long convalescence were the tipping points that finalized her decision.

She planned to move out the end of January; only eleven days to make her preparations. There were bills to pay, notify the apartment manager and recover her security deposit. She would call Abby's about the furniture and kitchenware. Was there anyone with whom she needed to speak and say goodbye? No, no one, other than Frankie. Maggie knew he would be displeased, maybe a bit annoyed, but no reprisals. After all, there was no written contract, no verbal commitment, and during her three years she had made him a chamber pot full of money. Of course, that was the reason he would hate to see her leave, and hope she might return although Maggie knew that she, like every girl in Frankie's stable, was expendable.

Next week she would have the Chevy dealer service her black Impala. Maggie had checked with Triple-A about the twenty hour drive to Dallas. She also planned a stop at Goodwill since she no longer needed the expensive dresses and finery that hung in her "business" closet. The back seat and trunk of her car would hold, with room to spare, those things she planned to take on her journey across the desert.

No one knew her final destination. Why Dallas? A question she had asked and answered. It provided anonymity, which was essential. The Dallas-Fort Worth Metroplex had a plethora of colleges and universities, one of which she hoped to attend. It also offered the Arts, cultural amenities of a big city. Maggie considered Houston, but she wanted to be further away from Rutledge while still in the state of Texas.

In eleven days, she would make a fresh start.

She left the Desert Sky at daybreak.

The iconic glow of neon in her rear view mirror.

Maggie felt her heart skip a beat. A surge of exhilaration.

That feeling . . . when was the last time? She stopped to think. Maggie snapped her fingers. Sure, she remembered . . . it was the day she left Rutledge.

CHAPTER 3

Camden, Louisiana, 2012

HE HAD ALWAYS HAD A WOMAN in his life, that is, until two years ago. He was surprised by this feeling of vacancy, as if something was missing, like a hole in the heart. Did it need to be filled? Would a woman provide the answer? He didn't think so. But it was a question Carl Sweeny had asked himself more than once since his divorce. And there was this: he was only months away from crossing the Biblical threshold of three score and ten, a milestone which provided a few trifling benefits like senior citizen discounts. The liabilities, some of them serious, were always lurking. Although active and vital, he often wondered if the inevitable effects of aging had redefined his view of women and diminished his interest in forming another meaningful relationship.

By his own admission, Carl had always been connected to a woman. At the beginning, as far back as he could remember, it was his mother. She nurtured him, imbued him with a *moral imperative* and bestowed unrequited love. While his father was an honest, hard-working man, he relegated the responsibility of parenting to Carl's mother who came from strong matriarchal ancestry. She died at the age of 94 with her mental faculties intact and Carl hoped that he'd emerged from her salubrious gene pool. She had been his faithful friend and advocate for many years and her memory lingered, burned as with a branding iron, into the deepest recess of his heart.

Following the collapse of his second marriage, he sold his house and bought a new, stepless condo close to the Camden Country Club. The change of scenery only heightened Carl's feeling of detachment which had dogged him since the marriage ended . . . a fact that made no sense at all. He had been born and raised in Camden, well educated, with a law degree from Tulane and an MBA from Wharton. He returned to Camden and practiced law for forty years; the last decade as District Attorney of Richland and Moreland Parishes. After all, the relocation was only five miles across town; it was not as if he were moving to the West Coast or upstate New York.

It was a late morning in mid-February, and the weather was abysmal. Carl sat at his desk working on his 2011 tax return. Outside, a light rain began to fall chasing a foolhardy sparrow beneath the eaves of a neighbor's condo. Through a window, he watched dark swollen clouds surge overhead; in the distance, the growl of thunder. Carl felt that it was the perfect setting for his love fest with the Internal Revenue Service . . . damp and dismal.

It was this collision of life-changing events that caused him to wonder. Was a fast approaching birthday, the big seventy, responsible for this unsettled feeling? He could only shake his head, he wasn't sure. While most of life was spent, he didn't dwell in an actuary's world. Carl was a realist, and he could hear the clock ticking. Therefore, each day was a gift to be savored. In Cajun Country they called it l*agniappe*. So his feeling of *discontent*, still ill-defined, lingered like the darkness of an Alaskan winter.

Carl checked his watch and realized that he had five minutes to make his meeting with Ed Seymore. He stacked his papers and old tax returns on the back of his desk and lifted his lanky frame out of a cranky swivel chair. He washed his hands in the kitchen and threw cold water on his clean-shaven face. He brushed a full head of unruly gray hair with his hand and grabbed his keys, all in the same motion. It was a ten minute drive to the club, but there was no need to hurry since Ed was notorious for his late arrivals.

The rain had picked up and the wipers on his car scraped the glass, a reminder they needed to be replaced. He drove over the slick asphalt, leaving spray in his wake. Rucker Road followed the bayou, a serene body of water that meandered along the northern rim of Camden. He turned right on Forsythe, which crossed the dam and funneled into the entrance of the Country Club.

Carl looked forward to his meeting with Ed Seymore. The two men had been friends since their return to Camden in 1968, Carl, a law school graduate; Ed, an honorable discharge from the Army. Their friendship endured while Carl's marriages failed, both ending—to quote Mr. Eliot—"Not with a bang, but a whimper." Once retired, they played golf twice a week . . . weather permitting. During the winter months, they settled for an occasional lunch at the Club. Carl found his friend to be convivial company and when asked, offered sound advice. Ed's comments were always more constructive than that of family members, the marriage counselor, or even Father Jerome, the parish priest.

Because of the rain, golf games had been cancelled and the parking lot was almost empty. Beneath an umbrella that he had bought at the Dollar Store, Carl scurried across the parking lot and up the steps to the Men's Grill.

It was a large rectangle with the usual amenities: a mahogany-paneled bar, with brass railings and a big-screen TV. A mirror covered the wall of the back bar, lined with bottles of whiskey and multicolored liqueurs. The floor-to-ceiling windows provided a panoramic view of the fairways, which by spring would be lush and emerald green.

When he arrived, Carl was surprised to find Ed sitting at a corner table watching the noon news.

"Sorry I'm late," Carl said while crossing the room.

Ed half-rose from his seat and extended a hand. "No problem. I've got all afternoon. The wife's happy to get me out of the house."

"How is Edith?" Carl asked as he pulled up a chair.

"She's fine, thank God. Don't know what I'd do without her."

"You'd survive." Carl skipped a beat. "But it wouldn't be easy."

Ed pushed his cup aside and rested both elbows on the table. "I'm not so sure. Married over forty years and the older I get, the more dependent I've become." He surrendered a smile. "I've never cooked a meal or made up a bed . . . that is, if you don't count Army time."

"You're a lucky guy."

"Well, I've tried to do my part."

"Sure you have," Carl said. "You've worked hard, educated the kids, and given Edith all the love and support she needed."

The compliment caused Ed's cheeks to color. "Thanks for the kind words, but what about you?"

"Still feel a little lost, even though it's been three years."

"Lonely? Is that the problem?"

"No, not really." Carl looked out the window pensively. "It's hard to explain but it's akin to a feeling of separation, like a ship set adrift from its moorings."

Ed nodded and waited for more.

"I know it sounds crazy but that's the best I can do."

"Could be the move. You'd been in the old place a long time."

"But this feeling started long before I sold the house."

"How about the big birthday next month?"

Carl shrugged.

"Well, maybe you need a woman in your life."

"I've wondered 'bout that," Carl said. "But I didn't feel this way the first time around."

Ed grinned broadly. "Look, you were thirty years younger and near the crest of your career. I remember being a little envious; a gaggle of young women chasing you all over the parish."

"It's sure different now," Carl said. "The only one breathing down my neck these days is the I.R.S."

"Hey, Ed." It was a familiar voice from across the room.

Ed pushed his chair away and dropped his napkin on the table. "I'll be right back. Order me a bowl of clam chowder and a refill on the coffee."

CHAPTER 4

CARL ACKNOWLEDGED THE INSTRUCTIONS with a lazy salute. He turned toward the window and looked out at the brown desolate fairways; outside the rain had stopped. But as the weatherman predicted, the afternoon temperature dropped precipitously and it had begun to snow. While he watched the white flakes fall softly to the ground, he entered his brain's mysterious time machine that took him whizzing back into the distant past.

At the time, following the collapse of his first marriage, his friends meant well. They knew the severance was traumatic and had left him reeling like an Irishman on St. Patty's Day. Each had a name, someone he was sure to like. "Carl, you must call," became the collective mantra. As a result, he was caught up in a series of blind dates best described as pedestrian, and in some instances that assessment was charitable. None warranted a second call.

Carl worked long hours at his office in downtown Camden and any spare time was spent on the clay courts at the Country Club. He remembered it was the Friday after Labor Day; he left the office early and planned to meet Wiley Langston for their singles match. The September day featured cobalt skies and a scattering of fleecy clouds. A refreshing breeze carried the cool currents of autumn and brought sweet relief from the August heat.

Carl pulled into the parking lot at 4:30 and went directly to the men's locker room to change and retrieve his racket. Wiley was dressed and waiting. By way of a greeting, he waved his Yonex and held up a new can of balls. He ran a hand through a thatch of sandy hair while putting on his visor and heading in the direction of Carl's locker. "Hope you're ready for an ass whuppin'," he said with a poker face.

Carl stepped up on the bench in a comedic pose and looked around the room as if he expected to see one of the club's "A" players, even Blake Wilson, the Senior's champion. "I'm playing Wilson . . . is that it? And you have another game," he ragged good-naturedly.

Wiley dismissed the tease with a swish of his hand and sat down on the wooden bench that separated the two rows of metal lockers while Carl put on his tennis shoes. "I went to an insurance symposium at the Marriott during lunch today." Wiley had a way of switching subjects without a change of facial expression or even a cautionary phrase like, 'On a more serious note . . . ' or 'Regarding more important matters . . . '

"So?" Carl asked while tying his shoe.

"I met Jenny Anders at the luncheon. And she's a knockout."

"Have you forgotten that you're a married man?" Carl asked with a chuckle.

"I got the info for you, Dumbo. You can thank me later."

Carl wondered why his friends and even casual acquaintances felt a need to find him a woman. What was the motivation? Was it simply an attempt to be helpful? After all, he had experienced a painful divorce; a big gash that left him bleeding and wandering aimlessly amid an emotional maelstrom. So why shouldn't they help by replacing the lost woman with a surrogate or something more? Or was their reason more convoluted, moved by some perverse desire to be part of the drama, like the director of a Greek tragedy. Or not unlike a respectful gathering at the graveside, some of whom barely knew the deceased but were there to validate their "aliveness" and offer a sigh of relief that someone else was being lowered into the ground.

Wiley handed him a slip of paper. "Put that in your locker."

"Name and number, huh?"

"Yeah, I told her 'bout you," Wiley said with a roguish grin. "Some of it was even true."

Carl put the slip on the top shelf, banged the door shut and clicked the lock. "I appreciate the favor, but to be honest, this dating game is wearing thin. I'm thinking 'bout a sabbatical. A month at the beach . . . alone, a chance to clear my head and reorder my priorities."

"Just check out Jenny before you haul ass to Hilton Head." Wiley put an arm around Carl's shoulders as they headed out the door. "I promised her you'd call. Don't let me down."

"Let you down? Nah, I'd never do that . . . not in a million years."

Wiley ignored the *bon mot* and jogged to his side of the court. "You won't regret it. And be sure to invite me to your wedding," he yelled deliriously as he slapped a forehand across the net.

"You bet," Carl cackled. "Mr. and Mrs. Wiley Langston will be at the top of the list . . . Oh! And be sure to send a nice gift."

Carl waited a few days before he called Jenny Anders. After all, he had given Wiley his word. While Jenny did not sound wildly enthusiastic, she agreed to dinner on Saturday night. Yes, she vaguely remembered Carl's name; someone at the luncheon had mentioned it and asked for her phone number. Carl decided it would be a crippling blow to Wiley's ego if he were to learn that Jenny, in less than a week, had forgotten his name. So he filed it away for his own personal use should he ever need a verbal needle.

The first red flag went up when Jenny gave Carl her address. She rented a duplex on the south side of Camden, considered by many, to be the most undesirable section of town. He wondered why anyone, single and unattached, would choose to live in a neighborhood that carried such an unsavory reputation.

Jenny's duplex sent up the second red flag. It was a small wood-frame building with security bars on all the windows and double bolt locks on the solid oak front door, reminiscent of the city jail that he'd visited on occasion during his active legal practice.

Jenny herself, hoisted the final flag, informing Carl that she preferred to "drop in" on Sara Spangler's party rather than have dinner for two at the Camden Country Club. Carl shrugged indifferently and agreed to the change in plans. At least, he would save a few bucks; these dinners had become an expensive crap shoot.

As Carl drove across town, there were lulls in their conversation. Within five minutes, he felt disinterested; another ill-fated, blind date.

Either Wiley needed an eye exam or their perception of "a pretty woman" was as different as rocks and rubies. While Jenny's face was pleasant to look at, she had the legs of a linebacker and "full-figured" would be an apt description. But in all fairness, to paraphrase Shakespeare, "*Beauty is in the eye of the beholder.*"

Once they entered her friend's apartment, Jenny headed for a small group hunkered down near the bar and set Carl adrift amid a room full of strangers. He surveyed the room crowded with unfamiliar faces and filled with the music of Neil Diamond pouring from two speakers that flanked the color TV.

In a far corner of the room, he spotted a man all alone—leaning against the wall, almost lost in the shadows that covered his space. He held a drink in one hand and abstractedly massaged his chin with the other. The guy was a Steve McQueen look-alike, but his face was vacant and his shoulders sagged as if burdened by some invisible weight.

Carl stopped by the bar and mixed a drink before moving over to meet McQueen.

"Carl Sweeny. Thought I'd drop over and say hello."

"Charlie Barton."

"Are you from 'round these parts?" Carl asked.

"Arcadia." The loner was a man of few words.

"Nice town. I've got an aunt who lives up that way. Her name's Jane Wellman. Taught school for forty years." An attempt at affable small talk.

Barton shrugged and his face registered a zero.

"Just as well, the old spinster's mean as a snake." Carl was not going to get much out of the taciturn stranger.

Barton sipped his drink; the ice rattled against the glass.

"Divorced?' Carl's asked; the struggle for dialogue was like blowing on ashes in hopes of rekindling a fire.

"Yeah, 'fraid so."

"Well, you're among friends," Carl assured him.

Barton nodded.

"What are you doing these days?" Carl had almost exhausted his quota of questions.

For the first time, Barton looked up and caught Carl flush in the eye. "I'm trying to pick up the broken pieces," he said evenly.

Carl could not hide his surprise. It was the first declarative sentence that Barton had uttered.

Carl gave him an empathetic look. "No, I meant your line of work. Whata you do for a living?"

"Civil engineer." Terse without embellishment.

"Is your business in Camden?" he asked.

"Nope, downstate."

"Let me guess," Carl said in jest. "How 'bout New Orleans?"

Barton shook his head. "Baton Rouge."

Carl conceded. He could not kick-start a conversation. Talking to Barton reminded him of the Dairy Queen, slurping ice cream through a straw. So he gave the stranger a parting pat on the shoulder and wished him well. "Hope you can glue those pieces together."

Barton acknowledged the departure by lifting his half-filled glass.

Carl thought he saw a smile flicker across Barton's face. Or was it just the play of shadows on the wall beside him?

After two hours of mingling with strangers and listening to their frivolous chatter, Carl informed Jenny that he was leaving. She had a choice: he would take her home, or she could catch a ride with one of her friends. Needless to say, the evening ended badly. Carl wondered if he would ever learn. Or would it take a whack on the noggin with a two by four.

Later, when his head hit the pillow, Carl's last conscious thought before tumbling down into a dead-man's sleep took the form of a question: With a friend like Wiley Langston, who needs an enemy?

CHAPTER 5

ED RETURNED TO THE table full of apology. "Sorry that took so long."

"Hey, no problem but you may need to warm the chowder."

Ed tasted a spoonful and waved off the waiter who was heading for their table.

"Josh seems to be wearing a frown these days," Carl said.

"Well, as you know, he's chairman of the golf committee."

"A thankless job, if you ask me."

"There's a clique among the golfers who want to fire Charlie McInnis."

"You mean our ol' pro, Good Time Charlie?" Carl chuckled. "I'm not surprised. Webster had him in mind when he defined a sinecure."

"The problem is," Ed explained, "that Charlie has a coterie of friends that will go to bat for him. So Josh and his committee find themselves in the middle of a tug-of-war that could get real nasty before it's over."

"We've all got problems," Carl said as though he was reconciled to the ubiquity of human hardship—an affirmation that closed any further discussion of Charlie McInnis and the battle brewing from within the ranks.

After Ed tipped his bowl and spooned the last of the chowder, he swiped his mouth with the napkin and leaned back in his chair. "May I ask you something personal?"

"Sure." Carl pushed his chair back and crossed his long legs.

"What happened to your marriage?"

"Which one?" A hint of a smile.

"The last one, you jughead." Ed cradled his cup of coffee in his lap. "Glad you haven't lost your sense of humor."

"Yeah, well it's one of the few things that survived both shipwrecks."

"Tell me about them . . . both shipwrecks."

Carl looked at the neighboring tables and lowered his voice. "The first marriage was misguided from the beginning. It was destined to fail. The ghost of John Calvin presided over the ceremony—just kidding—but he should have. We were young and made a commitment for all the *wrong* reasons . . . simple as that."

"Remember the old tune, '*Love is lovelier/The second time around?"* Carl asked.

Ed nodded. "Sure I remember." He waved his arms as if he were directing his own dance band and sang; an Irish tenor, no less. *"There are those who'd bet, love comes but once and yet, I'm oh so glad we met, the second time around."*

"Very good, Ed." Carl could not withhold the proverbial needle. "But I doubt that Sammy Cahn had you in mind when he wrote those words."

"Sorry, I just got carried away," he chortled.

Carl continued, "Beth and I had survived the trauma of divorce. After a two-year courtship, we felt capable of making a rational choice . . . marriage for all the *right* reasons. For a long time, that decision seemed to be well-founded. While I can't tell you what happened or even when, we drifted apart."

"I don't know how it slipped away . . . so insidiously." Carl looked out the window as if the answer would be found among the snow-dusted trees that lined the fairways. "I think most of us want to know the reason for our failures."

"People change," Ed said.

"Explain." Carl wanted clarity.

Ed took the last swallow of coffee, placed the cup and saucer on the table and leaned in Carl's direction. "You're not the same man who married Beth. Nor is she the same woman. In the case of marriage, for some, the changes are complimentary. While for others, they have an erosive effect that over time undermines the relationship."

"I guess you're right. We weren't the same two people who'd fallen in love a long time ago."

Ed removed his glasses and cleaned them with his napkin. He held them up to the overhead light, then slipped them into his shirt pocket. "While those changes may be subtle, they're often magnified by aging and circumstances beyond our control."

"It makes sense," Carl said.

"Whether *change* is your answer . . ." Ed lifted his arms and shrugged, gestures that asked the rhetorical question: *who knows*?"

Carl looked at the keen eyes of his friend. "Maybe *you're* right . . . it's better not to have all the answers. Just put the past behind and get on with your life."

Ed lifted his water glass. "I'll drink to that."

Carl pushed his chair back and took a last look outside. It was still snowing. "Thanks for the consultation," he said lightly. "Send me a bill."

"By the way, Edith's cooking a pot roast Saturday night. And for dessert she's making her infamous bread pudding with custard sauce. You're invited."

"I accept."

"She said to tell you there might be a surprise as well."

"What's her name?" He tried unsuccessfully to keep a straight face.

"No clues. Come casual. Around 7 o'clock."

"I'll be there," he said. "And thanks for hearing me out."

By mid-afternoon, Carl was back at his desk with the intention of completing his tax return. He slipped a Sinatra tape into his portable player, leaned back in the swivel chair and propped his feet on the edge of the desk. While his window was glazed with the splattering of frozen snow, he watched, nostalgia-laden, as white flakes fell from a leaden sky. The sentimental sounds of *I'll Be Seeing You* floated across the room.

I'll be seeing you in every lovely summer day,
In everything that's light and gay,
I'll always think of you that way,
I'll find you in the morning sun and when the night is new,
I'll be looking at the moon, but I'll be seeing you.

Maybe Irving Kahal, the lyricist had him pegged. A woman in his life might assuage this strange and indefinable feeling that had become as unshakable as his own shadow.

Maybe Ed was right. He had changed; the revised version of Carl Sweeny.

Maybe Edith's surprise would be better than expected.

Although his grandfather clock was ticking, maybe Carl would find that singular woman. And sparks would fly.

Too many maybes, he'd had his chances. Too late, ol' boy.

But there was always the possibility, the slender thread of hope. And there was the show tune's reminder:

I'll find you in the morning sun and when the night is new,

I'll be looking at the moon, but I'll be seeing you.

Carl slid the chair across the hardwood floor and turned off the tape player. Outside it was still snowing; the wind picked up and whistled between the buildings. He pushed his tax documents aside and turned off the desk lamp. He lay on the sofa and closed his eyes. For some quirky reason, he thought of Jimmy Durante and a lopsided smile filled his face. "Good night, Ms. Calabash, wherever you are," he whispered and settled down for a long winter's nap.

CHAPTER 6

Camden, 2012

ED AND EDITH SEYMORE lived on Lamy Lane, a tree-lined street in an upscale neighborhood. The two-story was red brick; black shutters framed the windows. The house sat on a half-acre lot, its lawn of Emerald Zoysia had turned winter-brown.

Divided responsibility: Ed cut the grass and trimmed the boxwoods along the front of the house. Edith weeded the flower beds and pruned the lavender hydrangea, the hearty shrubs, which lined the side walls.

Carl turned into the driveway and switched off the engine. The night-sky was littered with countless stars and cradled a crescent moon. The snow had come and gone, leaving Camden with clear skies and winter's invigorating chill. He followed flagstones to the covered stoop and rang the doorbell. While he waited he heard a dog howl, a wounded sound. Otherwise, the deserted street was as quiet as a Trappist monastery.

Edith, the most vivacious woman he knew, opened the door and invited him in. A warm smile stretched the lines on her handsome face. After a hug, she hung his coat in the hall closet, then took his hand and led him into the family room. Ed looked up and waved him in. A woman he'd never seen before sat in an armchair close to the hearth and a crackling fire.

Edith leaned on the back of the rocker and made the introductions: "Carl Sweeney, our new neighbor, Margaret McFarland, a Texan no less."

The woman reached out, extending her hand. "My friends call me Maggie."

Carl was surprised . . . stunned . . . by this attractive woman. A Christie Brinkley look-a-like? Close, but even better; the lively blue eyes and silky blond hair made her captivating. He recovered quickly, accepted a warm handshake, and settled into the upholstered sofa.

"Welcome to Camden," Carl said. It was a stale greeting, but the woman took his breath away.

Edith handed him a glass of Chardonnay. "Maggie bought the Simpson house, just two doors down."

"What part of Texas?" Carl asked.

"Dallas." She sipped her wine and placed the glass on the coffee table. "I went to S.M.U., fell in love with the city and never left . . . until this recent move."

"Why Camden?" Carl hoped he didn't sound like an interrogator. Old habits were hard to break.

Maggie wore his favorite color: a powder blue cashmere sweater and pleated slacks. No jewelry other than a string of pearls. She pushed a strand of shoulder-length hair behind her ear and sat back in her chair. "To be honest, the move was a tough decision but the location was easy. I have a sister, Dell Strong, who lives in West Camden; a nurse at St. Francis. And my son, Sam, lives close by as well."

Carl looked at Edith as if she might preempt his question. But no help there. He turned back to Maggie and asked, "Your son, tell me more."

Her eyes glowed with a mother's pride. "Well, he's married and lives in Benton, an Instructor in the English Department at Colby College."

"Sounds like you had good reason to move to Camden."

"No regrets so far."

Edith refilled the wine glasses. "While all of you get acquainted, I'm going to see about dinner."

The conversation that followed was mostly idle chatter. Maggie mentioned her immediate neighbors; on one side, a married couple with a second home in the Ozarks and two elderly sisters, retired school teachers, on the other. While she had made a cursory introduction to both neighbors, she hoped to know them better.

Ed assured her that Lamy Lane was a friendly street. There were eighteen homeowners, all of whom he had met, either walking the neighborhood or at the association meetings.

When Edith called them to dinner, Carl realized Maggie had not asked him a single question; not a single inquiry about his work or family. So what? They had just met. It was possible he had unrealistic expectations about this first encounter. After all, she was pleasant and congenial, and smiled broadly when asked about her son. Sill, Carl wondered if he'd pestered her with too many questions. But when she looked at him, he felt a jolt, something he had not experienced in a very long time.

During dinner, Carl could not help himself. He was mesmerized by this ravishing stranger, someone he hoped to see again. Distracted, he nevertheless willed himself to look at Ed and recall their conversation at the Club. Did he need a woman in his life?

Edith had prepared a sumptuous dinner and was the catalyst for those awkward moments when conversation lagged. Carl considered her the impeccable hostess who put disparate diners in her comfort zone. She laughed easily: mirth, one of her most endearing virtues. Carl was more certain than ever that, without her, Ed would be lost; wandering aimlessly like a ship without a rudder.

Edith looked at Maggie, then at Carl. "Care for more coffee?"

Maggie shook her head. "Thanks, but two's my limit. Otherwise, I'll lie awake half the night."

Carl patted his stomach. "Best meal I've had since your last invitation."

Despite her protests, Carl insisted on walking Maggie home. While she was grateful, he need not be gallant on a bitter cold night. After all, it was only a short distance; just two houses down. She pulled her coat tight around her and folded her arms against her chest.

According to Carl, Lamy Lane was in the town's safest precinct. But Camden was not crime-free. While uncommon, bad things did happen. During his ten years as the D.A., he had seen it up close and personal. Of course, Carl would never admit the real reason for walking Maggie home, namely, he was captivated by her presence and wanted—no, needed—to see her again. It would be easier to make a connection if they were alone. When they reached the front porch, Maggie keyed the lock and cracked the door. She half-turned and looked at Carl. "Nice meeting you; thanks for the escort."

Carl jammed his hands into his coat pockets. "It's cold and I won't keep you." He blushed like a schoolboy. "May I see you again?"

He felt his heart skip a beat, knowing it was a make-or-break question.

"Sure, Carl. Why not?" There was not a speck of hesitancy in her reply.

"How 'bout coffee, Monday morning?"

"Starbucks?"

"The Twin City Mall; say, around ten?"

"I'll see you there." Maggie stepped inside. "Good night, Carl," she said and closed the door.

He heard the bolt lock click. The wall lights beside the door went out. For a minute, Carl stood on the dark porch and savored the silence. The exchange had been spontaneous, easier than he expected. Maybe he did need a woman in his life. Beneath the grandeur of heavenly lights, he walked away buoyant and with a bounce in his step.

CHAPTER 7

CARL ARRIVED A FEW MINUTES EARLY. Only one table was occupied; a young man, head down, eyes locked on his iPad. By ten o'clock, the work crowd had come and gone. He scanned the narrow room again. No sign of Maggie.

Carl stopped at the register and ordered a small coffee. He gave Sherry a warm greeting, paid with a credit card and carried the cup to the back of the room. Two Naugahyde chairs flanked a small wood table and a reading lamp. He settled into the one with a clear view of the front entrance.

Carl was ambivalent about the coffee date. On one hand, he'd experienced the misery of two failed marriages and had summarily dismissed the possibility, however remote, of another woman in his life. So, why was he doing this? After all, he was only two months shy of seventy and while viable, he accepted the inevitable attrition of aging. Or as Ed liked to say, they were both on a short leash. On the other hand, Maggie McFarland was more than a pleasant surprise. It was as if the ground moved and squelched any plans for the final laps around life's track.

What did he know about her, he asked himself? She had show-stopping good looks, a beautiful woman, even at sixty. (Edith was the informant.) Other than her appearance, he knew very little about the Seymore's new neighbor. It was a mistake he'd made in the past and once again he remembered the Bard's enduring reminder: *Beauty is only skin deep.* Maggie was that and more; she was magnetic, and it seemed she had drawn him into her orbit; a displacement over which he had no control. It was important to know who she really was; what lay beneath the ivory skin, the secrets hidden behind those startling blue eyes.

Carl checked his watch: 10:07. Still no sign of Maggie. He sipped his coffee and drummed the arm of the chair with his hand. An old man with a cane hobbled in, ordered a latte, and hobbled out. No one else came through the glass door. Carl checked the time again: 10:15. Had she forgotten? Unlikely, he reasoned, since she had accepted his invitation less than two days ago.

"Are you expecting someone?" Sherry asked.

Carl looked her way and tapped his watch. "At ten o'clock."

"How 'bout a refill while you wait?"

He liked Sherry, a recent college grad who was working at Starbucks until she could find a teaching job, preferably in one of Camden's private schools. "No thanks, I'm good."

Inherently impatient, Carl was glad he'd waited.

At 10:25, Maggie pushed the front door open and stepped inside followed by a gust of cold air. She spotted him and pointed to the counter where she stopped and ordered a coffee.

When Maggie left the counter, Carl caught Sherry's mime: *Wow!*

"I'm so sorry, Carl." She placed her coffee on the table.

"I knew you hadn't forgotten." He helped her remove her suede jacket. "I wondered if you were okay."

Maggie settled in beside him. "I was about to leave when the phone rang. An acquaintance from Dallas needed my advice." Maggie threw up her hands in a-what-else-could-I-do gesture. "I practiced clinical psychology for twenty years and I still get an occasional call from an old patient." She reached for her coffee. "So I listen and try to help."

"A psychologist? Tell me more."

"Are you sure?"

"Of course, I'm sure."

She reached across the table and placed a hand on his arm. "Be careful what you wish for."

Carl swirled the dregs in his cup. "I'll take my chances."

Maggie took a sip of coffee, hesitating long enough to organize her answer. "Okay, here's the short version: I got my master's in psychology, a thesis short of my Ph.D., and worked as an assistant to Dr. Dwayne Walker, head of the department. Did some counseling in Student Health, read class assignments, graded papers, and even some classroom instruction when Dr. Walker was out of pocket." Maggie pulled one leg beneath her and sighed. "Didn't pay well, so I took a second job . . . a waitress at a popular steakhouse." She looked down at her half-empty cup, her face clouded. "It's where I met Jack."

"Jack?"

"Jack McFarland, my husband."

Where was Jack? Carl wondered. Maggie had come to Camden alone. Was she divorced or a widow? Her downcast eyes and somber expression gave Carl the answer. While he wanted to know more about Jack McFarland, he chose to wait. His connection with Maggie was tenuous at best, and for now, he wouldn't put that connection in jeopardy. Perhaps another time, a more propitious time to ask those questions.

"More coffee?" It was Sherry's voice.

Maggie shook her head.

"No thanks." Carl waved her off.

Maggie regained her composure and finished the narrative. "There was an introduction, a Friday night at a wonderful restaurant, then a courtship and an eighteen year marriage. When Sam, our son was born, I became a stay-at-home mom until . . ." She looked up at the ceiling, trying to remember. " . . . I think Sam was eight, the third grade. With Jack's support and encouragement, I went back to work."

"Your old job at the University?

"No . . . no . . . I was a volunteer in a women's shelter. As a psychologist, I counseled hundreds of battered women and abused children. So much debility and despair. But my interaction, especially with the children, while often heart-wrenching, was at the same time rewarding."

"I'm sure it was," Carl said. "I know a little about the subject since I'm a member of the Board at OverReach, the only safe house within a hundred miles." Carl put his cup down and touched her hand lightly. "We need more Maggie McFarland's."

"Have you thought about OverReach?"

"Funny you ask since I met the Director—I believe her name is Alice Fogleman—at a social occasion a few days ago. No mention of OverReach. Just a brief social encounter, like two ships passing in the night."

Carl could not hide the pride; "I was on the committee that vetted Ms. Fogelman. She's very capable . . . a good decision on our part."

Carl heard the chair scrape the tile. The young man upfront, transfixed by his iPad, closed it down and stood up. The sound had gotten Carl's attention; probably a college student, who on leaving trashed his cup and paper napkin. The student stuffed his hands in the pockets of his pea jacket, the iPad under his arm and shoved the door open with his shoulder. The wind whistled; another blast of cold air swept through the room.

Maggie shivered and pulled her arms across her chest. "I'm from Dallas," she said. A trace of a smile. "Not use to your wintry weather."

An awkward silence followed. Carl took a deep breath and locked her in his gaze. "Maggie, I have a confession . . ."

"Go on."

"It may sound crazy since we were strangers only a short time ago." Another sigh of diffidence. "Look, I'm not very good at this; never was . . ."

"Don't apologize. Say what's on your mind."

Carl felt the heat in his cheeks. "Maggie, I find you attractive and intriguing. I'd like to see you again; maybe one night for dinner."

Maggie took a pen from her purse and wrote her phone number on a Starbuck's napkin. She handed it to Carl and said, "I'd like that."

He caught Sherry's eye as he pocketed the card. Another mime: *Good for you.*

CHAPTER 8

Dallas, May, 1984

MAGGIE MADE THE RESERVATION for Friday night at 8 o'clock. Arthur's was her favorite restaurant with its dark wood and crystal chandeliers. The menu featured a wide range of mouthwatering entrees. Chef Rizzo's own creation, Halibut with lemon-butter and crispy shallots, was her favorite. While Arthur's was one of the most expensive restaurants in Dallas, the Friday dinner was an extra-special occasion and called for good food, fine wine and a warm ambiance. It was neither a birthday nor an anniversary. But the evening at Arthur's promised even more excitement. A tantalizing surprise . . . for Jack.

She put the phone in its cradle and curled up in her lounge chair. From her bedroom window, she could see the swimming pool and the row of hybrid poplars that lined the back of the two acre lot. A worker, dark skinned and wearing a wide-brimmed hat cut the grass on a riding mower. A Mexican, she was sure, employed by Joseph's Lawn Service. Maggie wondered if the man in the straw hat was here legally, Doubtful, she thought, since there had been an influx of Mexicans looking for work.

It was a reminder of how far she had come; a psychologist during the day and a waitress in the evenings. She had taken the second job because it was necessary. Maggie needed the money, simple as that. While she still lived in her Turtle Creek apartment, the Las Vegas' savings were long gone. But she had spent her savings well, knowing that an education was her best investment. It was inconceivable that a waitress at The Rustler's steakhouse would meet a man like Jack McFarland. Serendipity? A chance encounter? Maggie didn't know or care. But of this she was sure, his invitation had turned her life upside down. Now, thirty years old and married for eighteen months: Cinderella, the glass slipper had fit; a fairytale come true.

She remembered how it happened. A busy Wednesday night at the steakhouse, two years ago. A man, mid-forties, well dressed, sat in a red vinyl booth in her service zone. While polite and well mannered, she felt his eyes, a stare, really, as if she was someone of interest. It was commonplace for men to stare—Maggie knew she was still attractive—even in a waitress' uniform, with little makeup and her hair pulled back and secured with a barrette.

Maggie had tried to erase her past. However, it had left a valuable legacy: to assess with precision the male persona. She was sure . . . well, almost sure . . . that this man, amiable and soft spoken, was a gentleman. When she returned to refill his water glass and remove the desert plate, he was gone. She picked up the leather check presenter and carried it to Marty behind the register.

"Hey, Maggie. It's for you," Marty said with an arched eyebrow. Smiling, he handed her the note and a paper-clipped business card. The note was printed in bold letters.

Please meet me for lunch this Saturday.

The Bistro at the Adolphus Hotel

12 o'clock

Jack McFarland

Maggie had more than her share of "meetings" with anonymous men. While this invitation was an enigma, the invitee had emitted positive vibes. She unclipped the business card; the script, black on white; was easy to read.

Jack McFarlane Investment Services

The Renaissance Tower, Suite 5811

Dallas, Texas 75202

The following morning, Maggie drove from her apartment to the University campus and parked in the faculty lot adjacent to the Gilmore Arts Complex. Her first appointment, a consultation—anger management—with a senior student and repeat offender, who had decked his roommate without cause, was at ten o'clock. She arrived early, hoping to speak with Dr. Walker before his eight o'clock class.

She entered Jackson Hall through a side door and took the stairs to the second floor. Dr. Walker's office was at the end of the corridor. The door was closed; a sign hung from a mini hook: *The Mind Is A Beautiful Thing.* Maggie put an ear to the door; not a sound. She tapped on the frame.

From within came a booming voice. "It's open!"

Maggie stepped inside, stood by the door. "Morning, Dr. Walker. Have you got a minute?"

Dwayne Walker sat behind a desk cluttered with papers and journals. A cold pipe rested in a porcelain ashtray. He removed his reading glasses and checked the wall clock above the door. He dropped a letter in his outbox and invited her in.

Maggie took a seat, inched the chair closer to the desk. She handed him the business card. "Do you happen to know Jack McFarland?"

She watched him study the card, the wheels turning.

He raked a hand through his gray hair and looked up. "I've never met Mr. McFarland, but I know of him. From colleagues, newspaper accounts . . . that sorta thing. Second hand, of course."

"He invited me to lunch," she said, shrugging her shoulders. "I'd like to know more about him."

"Lunch, really?" Walker leaned back in his swivel and loaded his pipe.

"I served his table Wednesday night at the steakhouse. He left a note . . . and that." She pointed to the business card on Walker's desk.

Walker lit his pipe and snapped the Zippo shut, replacing it in his coat pocket.

"Here's what I know: Jack McFarland has an impeccable reputation; highly regarded in the business community. Made a ton of money; a millionaire before the age of 30." He leaned back and blew a spiral of smoke toward the tile ceiling. "Oh, one other thing, McFarland's a steward in his church . . . a Methodist, I believe, and last year gave a million dollars to the University . . . Perkins School of Theology."

"Married?"

"I think I read . . ." Again, a look at the ceiling as if trying to remember the source. " . . . he never married."

Maggie showed her surprise. "Attractive, wealthy, respected . . . I wonder why not."

Walker fingered his paisley bow tie, put his pipe aside. "Who knows? Maybe he's waiting for the right woman."

Maggie stood up and replaced the folding chair against the side wall. "Thanks for the profile. Lunch with a millionaire should be interesting."

Walker looked at the clock and gathered his notes. "Before you leave some fatherly advice. Margaret, I'm sure any man worth his salt would find you fetching. I'm also sure there are hundreds of women in Dallas who would give their hairdresser to have lunch with Jack McFarland." A look of concern, almost a frown. "Just be careful . . . and circumspect." With that, he shooed her out the door.

The roar of the mower interrupted her reverie. She looked out the window at the expansive lawn of freshly mown Bermuda. The slant of an afternoon sun shaded the pool and the adjoining terrace. Maggie thought a swim and a large, cold glass of iced tea had its appeal. Another reminder: she had toppled her tea at The Adolphus and smiled at the memory. Jack had graciously offered his napkin, but a waiter appeared to wipe up the spill. Jack's good humor tamped down her embarrassment; no apology necessary. There were other dinners, a year-long courtship, a proposal (the old-fashioned way . . . on one knee . . . ring at the ready), and finally a June wedding at the Preston Hollow Methodist Church. Never in her wildest dreams, on that Greyhound bus to El Paso, could she envision her present circumstance. She had pinched herself more than once to be sure she had not fallen off the edge of a cliff into a world of fantasy.

Her Las Vegas experience was a deep dark secret. While full of remorse, it must never be disclosed. Maggie knew she was vulnerable; even a whiff of the past would cause her wonderful world to collapse like a house of cards. There was not a decent man alive, especially

Jack, who could accept what she'd done without revulsion and/or an overwhelming sense of betrayal. Forgive, perhaps, but never forget. Nor would their lives ever be the same. It had been ten years since her epiphany. So far, so good. And she would guard her secret with her life; with whatever was required.

She stood in front of the full-length mirror on the closet door, naked, the bikini in her hand. Her breasts were firm, her body lithe, a gym rat, at least three times a week. More often during the summer break. Still, she wondered, as she had many times before, how she had survived her call girl years with impunity. Reproachful, yes. Regrets, yes. But grateful that she came out the chute a whole person. The stigma would remain; an invisible scarlet letter. But she insisted, it was her secret and only her secret.

She stepped into her bathing suit and thought of the irony. In Las Vegas Frankie's rules were peremptory; she, an automaton. Only Jack brought her ineffable pleasure; her moans of ecstasy. Jack was tender and patient and, above all else, he loved her. In the white heat of passion, maybe, she wondered if that was the key to fulfillment.

Her beige beach hat and dark glasses were on a table in the sunroom. She put them on and took a paperback and a glass of tea poolside and settled into a mesh recliner. Not a breeze stirred, but she thought the weather was agreeable. How long would it last? She dreaded the sizzling heat of summer. But the weatherman has promised a cool evening; a light wrap would be needed. Perfect, for the occasion. Maggie felt the anticipation growing and she could see the joy, even a few tears on Jack's face when she broke her surprise. It was not a box wrapped with blue ribbon, nor a gift basket festooned with balloons, but only words, a revelation . . . a divulgence . . . and one that would change their lives forever.

Jack turned his '83 Mercedes 350 SL into the driveway of Arthur's Restaurant. He stopped curbside at valet parking. He took the ticket stub and led Maggie up the steps and through an ornate glass door. Andre, the maître d', stood behind a stand-up desk and welcomed them.

He checked his list of reservations and with a red pencil drew a line through "McFarland." Andre leaned down and, with the other hand, picked up two menus from a stack beneath the desk.

"This way, please."

They followed him across a thick burgundy carpet to a table in the far corner of the main dining room. He seated Maggie, gave each a menu and an obsequious bow. "Buzz will be with you shortly. Enjoy your evening at Arthur's." Another bow and he was gone.

"It's so beautiful," she said, pointing to the crystal chandelier hanging in the middle of the room.

Jack reached over and took her hand. "I love you, Maggie."

She felt the warm glow in her face. "And you're the best thing that ever happened to me."

Jack withdrew his hand and placed the napkin in his lap. "Now, about the fish . . ."

"The fish?"

Jack canted his head toward a tank of tropical fish which lined an entire side wall. "They brighten the room."

"How interesting, so many colors. Where do they get them?"

"A supplier, I suppose. Aquariums and koi ponds are big business."

The years in psychology had helped Maggie understand why she'd left her preference for dark colors at the gate of Desert Sky, No, the transition was not overnight. But as her new life unfolded, bright colors replaced the taupe and midnight blue, as if *time and change* moved in tandem. She looked at the dress she had bought for the occasion: a sheath silk, pale yellow, just above the knee. A sharp contrast to the browns and blacks that filled her closet at the Desert Sky apartment.

A young man appeared with a bottle of wine. He wore pressed khakis and a white shirt open at the collar. His name plate read Buzz. "A very dry Chardonnay . . . from California," He tipped the bottle, wrapped in linen cloth and half-filled their wine glasses. "I'll give you time to relax and enjoy the ambiance before you order." He placed the wine in a table-side cooler and hurried away.

"I ordered the wine when I made the reservation. If you'd rather have a martini. . . ."

Jack raised his hand, a stop signal. “No, no . . . the wine is fine.”

Maggie heard the music and looked around, but the speakers were well-disguised. Nat King Cole and the sweet sounds of *Unforgettable* wafted through the room. “My kinda music,” she said.

Jack chuckled. ”Nat King Cole . . . really? I’d never have guessed.”

“I’m full of surprises, huh?” *There’s one you must never know.*

“A woman of intrigue,” Jack said playfully. “The mystery only makes me love you more.”

Maggie felt her heart skip a beat. Too close for comfort, so she changed the subject. “How was your day?”

Jack stroked his chiseled chin. “Well, let’s see.” A contemplative pause. “Oh, the Governor called.”

“Is Leland in Dallas?”

Jack shook his head; brushed a hand through his brown hair. “Austin.”

“May I ask what he was calling about?”

“Another fundraiser. The Presidential election this November.”

Maggie sipped her wine, a moment of reflection. “Regan’s a cinch. And you’ve said the RNC has a mountain of money. So why another fundraiser?”

“Leland is a worry wart; he worries about his cholesterol, climate change, the Dallas Cowboys and, of course, the upcoming congressional race. While Tim Simpson is a political novice, he should win in a breeze, riding Regan’s coattails. But the party always wants more money. It gives the chairman more clout and satisfies a jejune need for security . . . like Linus’ blanket.”

“I think he’s disappointed you didn’t throw your hat in the ring. And I might add, if you were elected, you’d make the state of Texas proud.”

“Maybe in ’86,” Jack said.

Maggie knew that the RNC held her husband in high regard. His business success had been chronicled by the Dallas-Fort Worth newspapers and local television. While he’d never run for public office, he had star-quality . . . in appearance and communication skills, with a degree from Yale (Summa Cum Laude) and a certificate of attendance from the Harvard Business School. He would have the full support of the Governor and the politically-connected Bush family. While they had discussed his options on other occasions, she had no idea how it would play out. But Maggie had made it clear that no matter the decision, he had her full support.

Buzz appeared and refilled their wine glasses. “Are you ready to order?”

Maggie chose the halibut and Jack, the beef tenderloin, medium rare, and a house salad for the two of them. Neither opened their menus.

During dinner, Maggie talked about her job at the University. She was pleased that she had been granted faculty status, officially an Instructor in the Department of Psychology. Beginning in the fall, her job description changed. No longer Dr. Walker’s assistant but a full-time student-counselor.

Dinner was interrupted by Ed Beasley, one of Jack’s clients, who stopped by the table to say hello and remind Jack of his good fortune, marrying a woman with killer looks. Ed gave Jack a wink and slapped him on the shoulder for good measure.

Maggie cringed but accepted dutifully a kiss on the check. She smelled his garlic breath, relieved when he went away.

“Yucky,” she whispered.

“But a good heart and . . .” A flicker of a smile. “ . . . Ed’s a very good client.”

After a hearty meal, both passed on a desert and settled for a cup of espresso.

“Can I get you anything else?”

“No, but I have something for you,” she said

A long silence hung over the table. *Mona Lisa*, soft and smooth, spilled into the room from the hidden speakers. Buzz stopped long enough to refill their water glasses and leave the check.

“You wanna guess?”

Jack looked around his chair and under the table. “Nothing there.”

Maggie laughed at the pretense.

“Let’s see,” he said lightly. “You got a raise.”

“That too. But guess again.”

"I know . . ." He thumped the table. " . . . you heard from Dell, your long lost sister."

"Nope . . . give up?"

Jack waved the white napkin; a flag of surrender.

She folded her hands and placed them on the table. She looked at him with her arresting blue eyes. "I'm pregnant, Jack. We're having a baby."

He reached for her hands and folded them into his own. "Are you sure?"

"I'm sure. After missing a period and a week later, waking up with a queasy stomach, I made an appointment with Dr. Hancock. The pregnancy tests were positive."

"Maggie, I couldn't be happier." His eyes brimmed and he wiped them with his napkin. "I hope it's a girl and she looks just like her mother."

"I'm glad you're glad." She squeezed his hand and winked. "Let's go home and celebrate."

On the drive to North Dallas, Maggie was filled with joy and wonder. It had been an enchanting evening with a man . . . a good man . . . who loved her and would provide a strong paternal presence for their child. It was a dream come true—one she could not have foreseen twelve years ago leaving the back roads of Rutledge for an unsure future; one which was brightened by hope and filled to overflowing with great expectations.

CHAPTER 9

Camden, 2012

IT HAD BEEN A WEEK SINCE the coffee date at Starbucks. Carl dressed for the day, sat at the breakfast table with his cell phone, the napkin with Maggie's number and a mug of freshly brewed coffee. He checked the wall clock: 8:40. He picked up the phone, hesitated, and put it down. He felt the ambivalence swell in his chest. Was Maggie still asleep? Possible, though unlikely. Carl looked at the phone again, but decided to wait.

Since leaving Starbuck's, Carl had felt a compelling need to see her again. He had used his ample supply of self-restraint, waiting a week to make the call. The overwhelming attraction for this woman whom he'd met nine days ago was hard to explain and his attempt "to sort it out" was a futile exercise. By his own admission, it was crazy; the highly-charged emotional encounter was beyond "reason." So Carl would not resist . . . no, could not resist, riding the rush of emotion, like a big-wave surfer.

Carl replaced the napkin in his shirt pocket and carried the coffee mug to the bay window. His back yard was bleak. The lawn, once summer-green, was dormant. The two maple trees were leafless, their limbs stripped by winter winds. No sign of the sun and dark, angry clouds augured a cold rain, or even worse, sleet and snow. Neither the dreary tableau nor the prospects of more inclement weather could dampen Carl's euphoria.

He propped one leg on the bench windowseat and sipped his coffee. Why was Maggie so different from the other women in his life? He thought of Beth and tried to reconstruct their first encounter. It began in the workplace without the sizzle and pop that he felt on meeting Maggie. Beth worked for Chuck Moran as his legal secretary. Of course, Carl saw her "in passing," on most work days and if asked, would have described her as smart, trustworthy, and yes, attractive. Moran, the firm's managing partner, gave her high marks. "Irreplaceable" was the word he'd used. But it was a year before Carl invited Beth to join him at O'Grady's for an after-hours drink. A friendship segued into courtship, unfolding like the petals of a beautiful rose, and then another marriage that lasted more than twenty years.

Carl smiled at the analogy. Beth was a slow dance; Maggie the Jitterbug. But he found no satisfaction in the comparison. Yes, with Maggie it was sudden, but did it really matter? He would dismiss his inquiring mind and settle for *infatuation,* although he wondered if the word applied to a guy looking at seventy. But of this he was sure: Maggie, beautiful and bewitching, had jarred him out of his humdrum days and sparked his benighted heart.

Carl refilled his mug and carried it to his desk. He spent the morning replying to emails, paying bills and finishing his tax return. He rinsed his mug and put it in the dishwasher, grabbed his car keys and headed out the door. There were things to do: Kroger, the dry cleaners, and the post office for a roll of stamps. These menial chores were a part of living alone; he remembered Ed's words: *It comes with the territory.* While married, his spouse had run the errands, something he'd taken for granted. But following the divorce, he became the errand boy. Otherwise it didn't get done.

After lunch (a corn beef sandwich and a bag of chips), Carl checked the wall clock: 12:15. He pulled the napkin from his shirt pocket, picked up his cell and punched in the number. After six rings, the call went to an answering machine. Carl berated himself, he should have called earlier. He would try again . . . later.

On Sunday night, Maggie had carried her glass of wine into the den. She closed the plantation shutters and sank into her recliner. Her cell chirped; it was Rita again, in a state of panic. Maggie had trouble hearing because the young woman was sobbing and trying to speak at the same time.

"Rita, try and calm down. Take some deep breaths." She waited until the crying subsided. "Now tell me, slow and easy, the reason for your call."

"Ms. McFarland, he beat me again, punched me in the face." She tried to muffle the sobs with her hand.

"Rita, listen carefully. Go to The Shelter. They'll provide security and the medical attention you need."

"Randy said he'd kill me if I tried to run away." A loud gasp. "Honest to God, those were his exact words."

"We talked a few days ago . . . Monday, I believe. Remember?"

Another gasp as if she was out of breath. "Yes'um."

"I suggested The Shelter during our conversation. Remember?"

"Yes'um, but he made promises to change; took me to bed and made love to me."

"He uses you for his own pleasure, both the sex and the violence. Randy, at the very least, is a sociopath. We agreed on that during our counseling sessions at The Shelter. Now, do you really think he'll change? Does the leopard lose his spots? Not in a million years."

"I'm trapped Ms. McFarland. Don't know what to do or where to turn. It's why I called you." The sobbing began again.

Maggie stared at the blank TV screen, a moment of reflection. "Okay, here's the plan: I'll fly to Dallas in the morning. We'll work it out. May have to confront Randy . . ."

"No, no, no . . . he's apt to hurt you."

"Don't worry about me. I've handled a few Randy's in the past." She took a sip of wine and reached for a notepad. "Now, give me your home address and phone number. It's an early flight out of Camden so I should be there mid- morning."

"I think my nose is broken."

"Use ice to staunch the bleeding and we'll see a doctor tomorrow." Maggie started to close her cell, hesitated. "Where's Randy?"

"Probably visiting one of his beer drinking friends. But he'll come home half-loaded, apologize, and promise to make it up to me."

"So it's the calm after the storm?"

"Something like that." The sobs gave way to sniffles.

"Okay, Rita. Stay strong. I'll see you in the morning."

Maggie awoke early, dressed for comfort and the weather, packed an overnight bag and drove to the Camden airport. The Delta flight departed on schedule and flew non-stop to Dallas' Love Field. She used the time to consider the question: Why was she doing this? Well, Rita was in trouble; her life at risk. She had no family . . . no resources . . . trapped and no exit strategy . . . a Gordian Knot. Maggie wanted to help, maybe save a life. Easy to empathize when images of Rutledge, long repressed, broke to the surface.

She knew innately she was no "Good Samaritan." Altruism was not part of her DNA. An abused childhood and her years in Vegas had hardened her further. But Jack had softened her—at least at the margins—and as a mother, softer still,. Her years of counseling had broken down self-centered barriers by shining a compassionate light on the needs of others. She was surprised by the *good feeling* that arose from her wise counsel and simple acts of kindness. So the flight to Dallas was a mission, to rescue Rita and set her free. It was as simple as that.

After deplaning, Maggie went directly to the Avis counter. After signing the rental agreement, she borrowed a phone directory, jotted down two numbers on the Avis folder that she dropped, along with the car keys, into her purse. While waiting for the shuttle, she called the Marriott in Plano and made an overnight reservation; a second call to the sheriff's department in downtown Dallas.

The morning sky was overcast and there was a winter's chill in the air. Maggie buttoned up her suede jacket during the short ride to the Avis lot. She unlocked the Nissan and slipped into the driver's seat. The heater worked and she dialed the radio and found a classical music station. She had checked Mapquest before leaving Camden. Plano was about twenty miles from Love Field; with traffic, a thirty minute drive up US 75. She checked the dashboard clock and reset her watch. She had gained an hour: 9:15. Perfect timing. It should put her at Rita's front door around ten o'clock.

Plano was a bustling city, one that Maggie had seldom visited even though she had lived in Dallas for almost forty years. The business district, no problem, but residential areas were alien and she needed help. The Nissan had no GPS device; Maggie stopped twice for directions. With help, she found Mesa Drive and the house address, 623, on a street-side mailbox. A split level ranch, white stucco with a red tile roof, sat near the back of the lot.

Maggie parked curbside and walked up the driveway which fed into a detached garage. She made a mental note: the garage doors were closed. While she couldn't be sure, she figured Rita's husband was at work. A cement walkway led past border shrubs and dead plants to the front door. Maggie rang the bell and waited; the neighborhood was funereal quiet.

Maggie had a view of the dim-lit entryway through a sidelight. A shadowy figure appeared, turned the bolt and opened the door. Maggie was stunned. While she had not seen Rita for a year, maybe a bit longer, she expected a defeated look. But the face mirrored much more: despair and desolation. Makeup could not hide the bruises, and her nose was broken, dried blood beneath the nostrils. Once bright eyes were cold and lifeless. She had lost weight . . . skeletal, fragile as a glass doll.

"Aren't you going to invite me in?"

"Randy's here," she said, almost a whisper.

Maggie shrugged. "All the better."

Rita stood aside, ushered her into the living room. "I appreciate your visit; I really do. But are you sure . . ."

Maggie stood by the artificial fireplace. "Look Rita, You called last night, twice within a week. There was desperation in your voice. So, I've come a long way to help." She placed her purse on the mantle and folded her arms against her chest. "And from the way you look, I didn't get here soon enough."

"Don't get me wrong," Rita said. "I'm grateful you're here. But he's so . . . unpredictable," pointing to the back of the house. I'd kill myself if he did this to you." This time she pointed to her disfigured face.

"Why is he home?

"Called in sick."

"A malingerer?"

"Not really, but he got home at two this morning. I'm sure he'll have a hell of a hangover."

"If I remember our sessions at The Shelter, the fits of violence may occur when he's sober."

Rita leaned on the back of an armchair as if she needed its support. "That's true and the pattern hasn't changed. But alcohol is usually the trigger."

Maggie moved across the room and stood in front of a large picture window that overlooked a vacant front yard and the gloomy street beyond. The sky was darker than when she arrived, rain clouds hovered overhead, and lightning flashed from a thunderhead. Maggie thought of her English Lit course; Jane Eyre came to mind. And here, Mesa Drive was the perfect setting for a modern-day Gothic tragedy.

"Would you like something to drink?" Rita asked.

"I'd love a cup of coffee if it's no trouble."

"No trouble at all. Be right back."

Maggie used the time to consider the risks in her attempt to rescue a battered woman. She had planned to take Rita to Damon's for an early lunch and have a serious conversation about her marriage and the option to extricate herself from this destructive relationship. Monday was not a holiday; Randy would be at work. However, Maggie had read Burns' *To a Mouse*; a line she'd remembered: *The best-laid plans of mice and men oft go astray.* So she had made a contingency plan, ready for a confrontation while hoping it wouldn't happen. Despite the grim and unsettling prospect, she had to smile, pleased with her preparation. But she didn't know how the scene would play out. Randy, while in his own bed, could sleep the morning away. Even so, convincing Rita to leave the house was problematic. Why not leave a note for Randy: *Having lunch at Jason's Deli, Town Center Mall with a friend. Home by early afternoon . . . Rita.* Any reasonable spouse would appreciate such a message. But Maggie knew Randy was not reasonable—rather he was combustible—and the note would light the fuse. Maggie would have to use all her resources to get Rita to The Shelter and accomplish her mission.

Rita brought a tray and placed it on the coffee table. "Sorry I took so long."

"No apology needed." Maggie stirred sugar into one of the mugs and moved back to the fireplace. "Since Randy's home, we'll go out to lunch. Someplace quiet. You pick the spot."

Rita's pale face was somber. "Randy will be furious if he wakes up and I'm not here."

"Randy is an angry man and you're his punching bag." Maggie heard footsteps on the stairs. "You've got to disengage or you won't survive."

A big man appeared in the doorway, rumpled khakis hung low on his hips. Shirtless and barefoot. He was unshaven, and his hair tousled. "Who the hell are you?" he half-shouted.

Maggie looked him in the eye and fixed her stare. "My name is Margaret McFarland and I'm a friend of Rita's. We're going out to lunch since I'm only in town for a short time," she said evenly.

He looked at Rita who huddled on the sofa shaking visibly. "Why don't I know her?" he yelled fiercely.

"She's just an old friend." Tears trickled down her cheeks.

"Is friendship against house rules, Randy?"

"A smart ass . . ." He took three steps toward the fireplace.

Maggie extended both arms. "Don't touch me or you're a dead man."

Randy stopped short and let out a belly laugh. "What are you . . . 'bout 120 pounds?"

"Lee Clancy . . . you know the name?"

Randy's expression changed, grim and quizzical. "Yeah, the sheriff. What's to know?"

"Rocco Caruso . . . you know the name?'

"What is this . . . some kind of stupid guessing game?"

"Rocco's father was head of the Louisiana Mob. Rocco is still in the business, but at a different level. He owes Clancy a big favor."

Randy was hooked. "So, where's this going?"

Maggie drained her mug of coffee and placed it on the mantle. "Lee Clancy was one of my late husband's closest friends. I called him from the airport, gave him your name and address and explained the reason for my visit. He expects to hear from me by 2 o'clock; otherwise his deputy will look you up."

Randy looked at Rita with a smirk. “Stop bawling and get me some aspirin.”

Maggie went over and helped Rita off the sofa. “Go ahead . . . get Randy the aspirin, and your coat. It’s time for an early lunch.”

Dead silence hung over the room. Maggie gathered her purse and looped the strap over her shoulder.

When Rita came back from the kitchen, her hand trembled as she gave Randy the bottle of aspirin and a cold beer. She knew it was the best way to relieve his headache and tamp down his aggression.

Maggie helped Rita into her winter coat and led her to the entryway.

Randy swallowed three aspirin and swigged the beer.

Maggie felt the hateful eyes follow them through the front door and onto the stoop.

Randy’s rage grew stronger like a gathering storm and, with uncontrolled fury, he hurled the bottle at the fireplace. Glass shattered. “You sorry bitch, you ain’t heard the last from Randy Bynum!”

Damon’s, on Legacy Drive, was popular with the lunch crowd. It was a free-standing building adjacent to the Concord, a high-end development of multi-story parking decks and high-rise office buildings that housed major corporations, including Dr. Pepper, Pizza Hut, and J.C. Penny. The restaurant was only a few miles and a couple of traffic lights from Mesa. Maggie checked the Nissan’s clock:10:45. She hoped the drive-time would allow Rita to compose herself. They needed to have an important conversation about options and a life-changing decision, one that only Rita could make. The hostess at Damon’s honored Maggie’s request: the far corner booth. After seating them, she gave each a menu and said, rehearsed, “Your server will be with you shortly.” She turned abruptly and walked away, her short heels clicking on the tile floor.

“I’m not hungry,” Rita said.

"Eat something. You've lost weight since I saw you last."

Rita shrugged. "Not much of an appetite these days."

A waiter appeared, filled the water glasses, took their orders and promised to return.

Maggie looked at the young woman across from her, distressed by what she saw: the dark circles beneath cheerless eyes and the sunken cheeks. Her shoulders slumped like an old woman. A reminder of her grandmother who she'd last seen in the nursing home before leaving Rutledge. Maggie saw a dispirited Rita, only a shadow of her old self, lost in the pitch-black darkness of depression.

Maggie knew the meaning of these changes. While at a different age and in a different time, she had struggled against an "abuser" and survived. So Maggie had an insight that others might not have. Rita was on a "slippery slope" and unless she moved out of Randy's realm—out of his life forever—she placed her life in serious jeopardy.

Maggie finished her sandwich and pushed her plate aside. She noticed how little Rita had eaten; only half of a BLT, none of her French fries. Since nutrition was not an immediate concern, Maggie chose to eschew the subject. The Shelter would address that issue along with the broken nose should Rita return to the safe-house as a long-term resident.

Maggie straightened up and rested both arms on the table. "Look at me Rita," she said softly. "We need to discuss your next move."

Rita leaned against the corner of the booth and raised her brow, giving a barely audible "Okay."

"What I'm about to say is based on our earlier consultations, the recent phone calls and the brief exchange with Randy this morning." Maggie stopped long enough to assess Rita's reaction. Perhaps a question or a comment. But it was neither; only dead eyes and a vacant face.

"Rita, you have two choices . . . and only two. Do you understand what I'm saying?" She held up two fingers.

"I understand," she said softly.

"One, you can go home and live with Randy. You'll continue to be a battered woman. He'll slowly beat you to death and swear the final assault was an accident. Since you've never charged him with domestic violence, there's no police record, and he'll walk away a free man. In a short time, he'll find another woman who's persuaded by his promises and good looks, only to become his punching bag."

Maggie waited for Rita's reaction.

She was still as stone against the booth's corner post.

A long silence.

"And the other?" Rita asked.

"I'll take you to The Shelter where you'll be safe and cared for . . ."

"Randy will kill me . . ."

"The Shelter is a safe-house. Security is a top priority. Randy will never get past the front desk. Besides safety, you'll live there, room and board, receive counseling and medical care until you are fully rehabilitated . . . a whole person again."

"Then what? He's still out there."

"When you are ready, you'll be given a new identity, similar to the FBI's witness protection program and transported to another state. Arrangements will have been made for a job, a condo and a car. Oh, I almost forgot . . . a driver's license. A bank account will be set up in your name, and a sizable deposit will keep you afloat for three months. After that, with the job, you're on your own. Independent and with the resolve to avoid the mistakes of the past." She looked at Rita, who for the first time managed a faint smile. "Rita, it's your choice, your call. Which will it be?"

"I still worry about Randy," she said.

"Don't! He'll never find you. Me? Well, it depends . . . if his rage morphs into revenge . . ." Maggie shrugged. " . . . who knows?"

Rita bit down on her lower lip and sighed heavily. "I can't go home. He'll kill me for sure."

"Good decision," Maggie said. Her cell phone chirped. She dug it out of her purse and checked caller ID. "Hello, Lee."

"Just checking. You okay?"

"I'm fine, Lee. Thanks for calling."

"Anything else I can do?"

"As a matter of fact, there is. I'm taking Rita Bynum to The Shelter by way of the local precinct here in Plano. She looks like she went three rounds with Sugar Ray. So we'll file assault charges against her husband. It would expedite the process if you would call the Captain of the Eighth Precinct and give him the background."

"No problem, Maggie. Glad to help."

"There is one other thing. While her complaint and battered face will jail Randy overnight, he'll be out by morning. Rita won't testify at a preliminary hearing; too traumatic. But it'll buy time for her to go home and pack some clothes and a few keepsakes."

"Tell you what . . . one of my deputies will pick her up this evening and provide escort."

"Thanks, Lee. You're a good friend."

"Jack McFarland was a man who meant a lot to me. Still can't believe he's gone."

"I know, Lee. It's been ten years and my heart has yet to heal."

"Take care, Maggie, and call if I can ever do anything. And I do mean anything—for you or your family."

She thanked him again, said goodbye and closed the cell.

It was late afternoon when Maggie got back to the hotel. She called Delta and reserved a seat for the morning flight to Camden. She was weary having spent two hours at the police station and a like amount of time admitting Rita to The Shelter—a process that included a frank discussion with the Administrator.

She opened the mini-bar and mixed a Stoli and tonic, then a phone call to room service. She ordered grilled halibut and a Caesar salad, too tired to eat out. Maggie kicked off her shoes, settled in the lounge chair and savored her drink. It was an opportunity to assess the spur-of-the-moment flight to Dallas and, more importantly, the Plano experience—which was brief but eventful. Maggie thought she could sum it up: she had saved a life, a good thing. But she may have knocked down a hornet's nest and released its fury. It was easy to think of Randy in those terms. One thing she had learned in Rutledge and validated in Vegas and confirmed as a counselor: there were bad people everywhere; some psychos, some villains, some pure evil. Randy fell somewhere within the spectrum.

In a moment of whimsy, she thought of Carl. It had been a week since their morning meeting at Starbucks. Maggie wondered why he had not called. While their time together had been limited, she liked Carl and had spoken to Edith, who gave him a five star rating. According to Gloria Kahlil, her across-the-street neighbor, Carl was indefatigable as a District Attorney in the pursuit of justice, even-handed in its administration and admired parish-wide for operating an efficient and cost-effective department. She wondered if Carl had called while she was away. Maggie hoped he had and hoped he'd try again.

CHAPTER 10

CARL LEARNED OF MAGGIE'S TRIP after the fact. It explained why his six phone calls on Monday went to an answering machine. Now he understood why her house was dark when he drove by Monday night. There were plausible reasons for her absence. With his background in law enforcement, Carl knew that an adult missing for a day was little cause for concern. An overnight stay in Benton with her son and daughter-in-law? Visiting a relative whom he knew nothing about? A getaway to Vicksburg with its civil war exhibits and a night at Harrah's with its table games and a grand view of the river? None of it made any sense without telling someone. He had spoken to Imogene and Pixie, Maggie's elderly next door neighbors, but neither sister was helpful. Carl started to call Dell, but changed his mind. He remembered Maggie's lament: Dell was a stranger, a broken connection when her sister left for Odessa and never came home. After Maggie moved to Camden, the two sisters made an effort to reconcile, but forty years of separation was insurmountable. They settled for civility, an occasional conversation.

He was relieved to hear from Edith, who had seen Maggie pull into her driveway around noon. Why had he worried like some starry-eyed romantic? Carl knew the answer; despite the inanity of it all, he was falling in love with Maggie McFarland.

Mr. Cool (that was a joke) waited until mid-afternoon to call, curious to know where she'd been.

Maggie checked *Caller ID* and picked up on the third ring. "Hello, Carl."

"Where have you been?" He realized the question was boorish and probably none of his business. "Scratch the question . . . just worried. Hope you're okay."

Maggie laughed. "I was out of town, Carl—a spur-of-the-moment decision."

"Glad you're back. Just worried . . . think I just said that."

"I had my cell phone . . ."

"But I only have your home number, the one you gave me at Starbucks."

"My mistake. Why don't you drop by, say, around five? We'll have some refreshments and I'll tell you about my trip. Unless you have other plans?"

"I'll be there. Can I bring anything?"

"Nope. Come casual. See you at five."

It was almost dark when Carl turned into Lamy Lane. He longed for spring and daylight saving time. He missed his golf game, even though his high handicap was a source of stubborn vexation. While the Club's course was playable on some days, it was not worth bundling up and enduring the wretched weather. Carl had taken a college course in Greek mythology and remembered the god of the cold north wind and harbinger of winter. He cursed the purple-winged *Boreas* for his confinement and the faint feeling of melancholy that disappeared like magic with the first sighting of a red-breasted Robin or—to borrow from Wordsworth—*a host of golden daffodils.*

Carl knew that at seventy, the glass was almost empty. He tried to make the most of every day despite the dreary landscape, hoping soon to put his overcoat and heavy sweaters in the cedar closet. But Easter was a month away and only then would a nascent spring appear among the pink azaleas and flowering dogwoods.

Carl turned into Maggie's driveway and cut the engine. While he wasn't keeping score, their first meeting on that cold February night dwarfed the season's downside. Fortuitous? Absolutely. He had met someone special, someone who brightened the drab colors of the season. He could only hope for a connection. After all, it had only been ten days since the Seymore's dinner. For Carl, that evening was exceptional—a sudden attraction that defied reason. She radiated warmth and allure, even an air of mystery. But he knew she was someone special . . . *this woman in winter.*

He followed the brick walkway to the porch and rang the bell. A gentle breeze stirred the wind chime in a nearby poplar tree. Darkness claimed the neighborhood; a ceiling light came on. Carl felt her tug when she peeked through the sidelight, turned the bolt and opened the door.

"Come in, Carl," She took his trench coat and hung it over the back of a chair. He followed her into the den, dry wood crackling in the fireplace. He stood with his back to the hearth and warmed his hands. "It's good to see you, Maggie. Last night this place was dark and locked up tighter than Dick's hatband."

Maggie could not suppress a smile. "I'm glad you came by, but I'm only sorry I didn't give you both phone numbers."

"I just overreacted. Sometimes the old prosecuting attorney reappears and takes charge."

"How about something to drink?" she asked.

"What are you having?"

She leaned on the back of her easy chair. "I'm not the queen of the kitchen, but there's homemade pound cake in the fridge and I brewed some Irish coffee." Maggie tapped the top of the chair with the tips of her fingers. "By the way, when will this artic winter ever end?"

"Easter . . . it never warms up until then."

Maggie did the math. "Another . . . what . . . five weeks?"

"Yep, 'fraid so."

Maggie brought the refreshments into the den and placed them on the glass-top coffee table. "Help yourself; it'll warm you up."

Carl picked up a steaming mug and a slice of cake before sinking into the cushioned chair. "Very good," he said after sampling the cake. "I'm not kidding, it's really good."

"Hope it hits the spot. As I said, I'm no Paula Deen. Never spent a lot of time in the kitchen."

Carl was anxious to hear about her recent trip. "So what prompted your flight to Dallas?"

"Remember Starbucks?"

"Of course, it's only been a week."

"I was late, delayed by a phone call . . . remember?"

"It was a client from The Shelter who called for advice." He tapped his temple. "Good memory."

"Her name is Rita Bynum, lives in Plano, Texas. I counseled her for about six weeks as an outpatient, right before I retired. Recently her problems escalated; she panicked, needed to talk with someone. I guess she felt comfortable with me."

"Let me guess," Carl leaned forward and placed his mug on the coffee table. "You got another call, Sunday night, from the same woman who sounded so desperate that you took a morning flight to Dallas. Is that about it?"

Maggie nodded. "Rita is a victim of domestic violence. Randy, her husband is, at the very least, a sociopath and mean as a snake. I'd urged Rita during those outpatient visits to leave Randy and take refuge in The Shelter, which would provide her security and a long-term disposition. But he's so intimidating; threatened to kill her if she ran away. Said he'd find her and cut her throat from ear to ear." Maggie grimaced. "Those were his exact words. So Rita put up with the abuse and never filed a police report. To make matters worse, she feels isolated, trapped. No family, no money, nothing . . . so I get a call." Maggie stopped long enough to sip her coffee. "I made the trip to save Rita Bynum. Simple as that."

"How 'bout your own personal safety? Weren't you worried, at least a little?"

"Not really. My objective was to get Rita to the safe house and I had a contingency plan if Randy interfered."

"And he did." Carl read the expression on her face.

Maggie told him of the unsettling encounter with Randy Bynum. She was satisfied that Rita was safe, assured of a fresh start, and that Randy would never find her. "But he probably knows where to find me," she said without a trace of angst.

Then Maggie described his rage; the threats that followed her down the driveway. She was sure Randy would never forget her intrusion, even if and when his anger cooled. He was a mad dog, cruel and vindictive and would never let it go.

Carl crossed his legs and drained the mug. "It sounds like you saved one life but in the process put your own at risk. In my experience, these loonies are unpredictable; he may forget his vendetta, then again, maybe not."

Maggie refilled his mug and added scraps of dry wood to the fire. "Carl, as you know, risks are an unavoidable part of daily life. Crossing the street or drinking and driving are risks people take every day. While I don't underestimate Randy Bynum, I'm prepared. Pepper spray in my purse; a .38 in my nightstand."

"The gun . . . you know how to use it?" Carl figured it was a dumb question.

Maggie gave him a look of amusement. "I'm licensed to carry a concealed weapon. During our courtship, Jack insisted I take the State-set instruction course which included a professional instructor and qualifying at a firing range . . . a fifty-round minimum. And, of course, a photo, fingerprinting, and background check."

"You're within the law here since the state has reciprocity with Texas." Carl patted his stomach and reached for another piece of pound cake. "Too good to pass up. Compliments to the chef."

"Carl, it's only a cake. But I'm glad you like it."

He washed it down with a swig of Irish coffee. "How about home security? I didn't see a keypad by the front door."

Maggie shook her head. "But I have secure window locks and bolt locks on all the doors. While it may not be impregnable, it's close."

"If you give me the address, I'll call an old friend with the FBI. He'll check their database and see if Bynum has a record. The more we know about Bynum . . . well, all for the better."

Maggie went to the kitchen and jotted down the address on note paper. She handed it to Carl and settled back in her easy chair. "How did you like my neighbors?"

"Imogene and Pixie?"

Maggie nodded. "Sisters, retired schoolteachers, both in their early nineties. Neither has lost a neuron," Maggie said tapping her head.

"I had the impression the sisters were worried when you didn't come home last night. While it was dark, only the porch light, I saw consternation among the wrinkles."

The conversation moved from the Dallas trip to subjects more casual and comfortable. Carl talked about his frustrating golf game, surprised to hear that Maggie carried a 10 handicap. Jack had encouraged her to take up the game, which she did to please him, only to find she really loved the game. Carl was pleased; something in common, an interest they shared.

The den was warm, embers glowed in the fireplace. Maggie's cell phone chirped. She reached for her purse and recovered her cell. She held up one hand, a semaphore, which said to Carl, "Just a minute."

Maggie opened the phone. "Hello."

"Are you the bitch I'm looking for?" barked the loud, baleful voice.

She looked at Carl and mouthed, "Randy."

"Who's calling," she asked evenly.

"Don't play games with me," he growled.

"Then why are you calling?"

Carl moved up to the edge of his chair. While he could only hear one side of the conversation, he could fill in most of the blanks. He saw her eyes narrow, her jaw set; firm and resolute.

"I have a message. So listen up . . ."

"I'm listening," she interrupted.

"You made a mistake, a serious mistake, sticking your nose into my affairs."

"You are a violent man, Mr. Bynum; you abused Rita on countless occasions and almost killed her. You're also a coward, Mr. Bynum. Pick on a man; someone your size." She stopped and laughed, "It'll never happen."

Carl was shocked by her effrontery. His hands sent the message: *Tone it down.*

"I don't wanna hear any goddamn sermon. I want Rita back. You put her away and you can bring her back. Two weeks, you sorry bitch, then I'm coming after you."

"You might like to speak with Sheriff Clancy before you make the trip."

"Fuck Clancy!"

"Don't forget Mr. Caruso, Randy. Should anything happen to me, your ass is toast. So think twice before you do something stupid."

The line went dead. Maggie closed her phone and let out a deep breath.

Carl reached over and took her hand. Not a trace of a tremor. No fear in those blue eyes. "Maggie, you are an amazing woman."

She looked at him, her gaze intense. "I've dealt with a lot of "sick" men in my life and it doesn't help to subjugate yourself. In fact, it only fuels their aberrant behavior. While my connection with Sheriff Clancy in Dallas may slow him down, I don't think it will change his plans. He is consumed by vengeance. Since Rita is no longer available, I've become his intended victim; the one responsible for moving Rita to The Shelter, out of his life forever." Another deep breath. "No, he'll come. I'm sure he'll come."

He held her soft hand for the first time and didn't want to let it go. But he knew it was the proper thing to do. Just holding her hand meant something to him. A nearly seventy-year-old . . . is that crazy? He only knew that the evening with Maggie, while only a few hours, had reinforced his feelings (yes, his yearning) for her—this woman whom he met by chance—a Godsend for an aging idler.

They sat in silence and watched the dying embers. Finally, Carl stood up. "I've overstayed my welcome."

"Don't be silly," she said walking him to the foyer.

Carl grabbed his trench coat and put it on. "How 'bout dinner Saturday night? The Rendezvous, best restaurant in Camden."

"I'd love that, Carl."

A chaste kiss on the cheek and he was out the door.

On the drive home, he chided himself. He had forgotten to tell Maggie to "lock up tight," although he knew a reminder was a waste of breath. And this: he felt ten years younger—rejuvenated—now that there was a woman in his life.

CHAPTER II

Dallas, May, 1984

THE GREEK REVIVAL, with its elegant Doric columns and louvered shutters, sat regally amid an enclave of high-end homes in Preston Hollow. It had been custom-built for Jack McFarland and a gift for his beloved Maggie. On their New Orleans honeymoon, they took the tour of plantation homes along River Road. Oak Alley, with its archway of live oak and only a stone's throw from the Mississippi, was their favorite. Maggie was enchanted; the "oohs" and "ahhs" betrayed her usual, zipped up emotions. Jack saw her smiles as they walked across hardwood floors and beneath high ceilings. Then and there he made the decision. While he could not replicate the tree-lined archway, Eli Elliot, the best residential architect in Dallas, could draw a likeness of Oak Alley, but with all the modern amenities.

Maggie sat by her bedroom window with a cup of tea. The sun had cleared the back row of hybrid poplars, its light glittering on the pool's surface. She remembered Jack's prediction: fast track; eighteen months. At the time, she said, "Impossible." Jack grinned and flashed that look of confidence.

He was a remarkable man who loved her and lavished her with kindness. While her feelings for him ran deep, Maggie worried that her role in the marriage was not reciprocal. She tried her best to be caring and considerate; the "good wife," and for Jack that seemed to be enough. She had pinched herself more than once thinking it must be a dream having come so far in such a short time; from a bleak and cheerless town to a stately mansion with servants at her beck and call, from abuse and abasement into the arms of a warrior with a gentle soul. And, most improbable, she was an expectant mother; the news filled

Jack with elation and it also tightened the golden strands that entwined them. She wondered if it was too good to be true; if it were a dream or if she'd drifted into a world of fantasy. But she was awake . . . wide awake.

Earlier in the week, Maggie parked in the faculty lot and despite a queasy stomach, climbed the steps of Jackson Hall. She padded the length of the corridor, hoping Dr. Walker was available. His office door was closed; a sign hung from the mini hook: *A mind needs books/As a sword needs a whetstone.* She knocked, louder the second time. A student wandering the hall gave her a lustful look. She ignored him and put her ear to the door, but heard nothing. Maggie checked her watch: 10:50. She wondered where he could be since students were between classes.

Maggie felt a tap on the shoulder. "Looking for me?"

"Hi, Dr. Walker. Got a minute?"

"You bet." He opened the door and with his cold pipe pointed to a folding chair near his desk.

Maggie chose to stand; she knew he had a class at eleven.

Dr. Walker hung his tweed blazer on the back of his chair, fiddled with his bow tie and dropped into his swivel. "Good to see you, Margaret. What brings you to Jackson?"

"First, the sign." She half-turned and looked at the door. "Didn't recognize the quote."

Walker lit his pipe with a match and dropped it into an empty Coke can. "George R.R. Martin, screenplays, that sorta thing. Not exactly a household name."

Maggie stepped closer to the desk. "The reason I'm here, Dr. Walker, since you need to know . . ."

"Uh oh. Bad News?"

"Not really." But Maggie could not conceal the joy that overflowed into her face and shaped a blissful smile. "Good news, really. I'm pregnant."

Walker laid his pipe in an ashtray, folded his hands on the desk. "I should have guessed. That angelic glow is a giveaway. Congratulations, Margaret."

"Please keep it a secret. I've only told Jack, no one else."

Walker crossed his heart. "You have my word."

"I'd like to work into my third trimester if that can be arranged. You can use the time to find another student counselor."

"Maternity leave is a given," he said. "But we'd like to have you back."

"Thanks, but I plan to retire; become a full-time mom."

Dr. Walker checked the wall clock and stood up. He pocketed his pipe and scattered the papers on his desk until he found the notes for his lecture on *An Introduction to Neuropsychology.* "Stay as long as you like. You have done a stellar job and you'll be missed. Give Jack my congratulations." He grabbed his coat and put it on, all in one motion. "Gotta go."

Maggie finished her tea, but she was still on the edge of nausea. She closed the shutters that blocked the sun and put on her terry cloth robe. The big house was quiet as a wake. Dora, the housekeeper, was off on Saturday and Jack had an early meeting at the University. The Derby party was at four and she had no appointments at Student Health. Most of the day was hers, with a few exceptions. She didn't expect Jack any time soon. Probably a long meeting, since the trustees were recently informed of the sanctions imposed on the football program for recruitment violations. The penalty: three years' probation. She had picked up bits and pieces of the story from their conversations and, while she was neither an authority on football nor even a fan, she knew cheating spelled *trouble.* The NCAA continued to snoop around for other recruiting violations while rumors swirled state-wide of a "pay for play" program that if true, invited the "death penalty." Jack told her that he and some of the trustees knew nothing of these infractions and were now in the process of finding ways to control the damage and restore integrity to each and every athletic department. She hoped Jack and his allies on the Board could stop the bleeding, but her cynical side said otherwise.

Maggie, barefoot, took the stairs to the kitchen. The shutters were open flooding the room with sunlight. She made a slice of cheese toast and another cup of tea. She found the note paper, folded once, when she sat at the breakfast table. Maggie pushed her cup aside, found her reading glasses and picked up the note.

Should be home before lunch. I'll stop by the deli and pick up sandwiches and cold slaw. Afraid the football program is in serious trouble. I guess I was naive or didn't pay attention as it was happening. I'm embarrassed and, of course, share some of the blame. Look forward to the Martingale's party. Have you picked a winner? You might consider Swale. the favorite, out of Seattle Slew. And this: no one in the whole wide world could love you more . . . Jack

Maggie held the note close to her heart. "Jack, the romantic. You should have been a poet or a lyrist writing love songs," she said as if he were in the room. She refilled her cup, dropped in a fresh tea bag, and stood by the window, bathed in the morning light. The nausea had subsided. She wondered if it was the note or that slice of cheese toast.

Dr. Hancock had given lecture 101 on her recent visit. Morning sickness might last for 12 weeks, then again, maybe not. Every woman was different so it was hard to predict when it would end.

Maggie drained the cup of tea and headed up the stairs to dress. She spent little time on her hair and makeup. That could wait for the Martingale party. Just shorts, T-shirt with a mustang stenciled across the front, and scandals. The weather was warm, and it was only the first week of May. While she dreaded another sizzling Dallas summer, she was grateful if Dr. Hancock's due date was in the ballpark and her last trimester fell during cooler months. Maggie picked up her purse, hooked the strap over her shoulder and hurried to the garage.

Fred Martingale lived in a sprawling contemporary of glass and stone in one of the toniest sections of Highland Park. Maggie checked the invitation as they turned onto Hillcrest, a four-lane to Highland Park and only a few blocks from St. James Place and the Martingale residence.

"We're late." Maggie held up the card. "Starts at 4 p.m., says so right here."

Jack checked the dashboard clock: 4:15. "A little, but not by much. The race starts at 5:30; plenty of time to make the rounds."

Maggie stuck the invitation behind the sun visor. "Let's not stay too long after the race. Promise?"

"I'm with you. Besides, I have two tickets for the symphony. Thought you would love the program: Beethoven's 5th, Ravel's Bolero and Shubert's' 8th."

"Oh Jack, I'm thrilled. The 'Unfinished Symphony' is one of my favorites."

Jack nodded. "By the way, you look stunning . . . as always."

"It's just a sun dress, but I like the pastel colors."

A quick look over. "Heck, you'd look good in a bag lady's dress."

Maggie shook her head in disbelief. "You, the hard-nosed business mogul with a soft side, a *bona fide* star gazer. Where did that sentimental streak come from?"

Jack shrugged. "How's the hat?"

The white straw with a yellow band and narrow brim rested in her lap. "It's not fancy, but it'll have to do."

"I gather you're not into bird nests and flower gardens."

Maggie shook her head vigorously. "They remind me of that silly mortar board with the tassel that I had to wear at my high school graduation."

"It'll come in handy if we ever go fishing." A sly grin.

"Now for that, I'm all in."

St. James Place, from one end to the other, was lined with cars. Jack turned into the sweeping driveway and left the car with a young black man in a white jacket. Valet parking was worth a Hamilton.

They passed through a courtyard with its fountain of tempered glass. Maggie noticed the goldfish swimming in the fountain's pool and remembered the enchanted evening at Arturo's. Through the heavy glass door, they could see the entryway and a long congested hallway. Before ringing the bell, the door opened as if on cue, and Fred Martingale, all smiles, welcomed them to the party.

"Jack, glad you could make it." He gave him a firm handshake, canted his head slightly. "This must be the Mrs. McFarland I've heard so much about."

"This is Margaret. Guess you could say I got lucky."

"My friends call me Maggie," she said, extending her hand.

Fred's face was more animated than usual when he took a longer look at Maggie and the colorful sun dress with the scooped neckline. "I've heard good things about you, Maggie." He gave her hand a gentle squeeze before letting go. "And your husband here is the patron saint of 'good causes,' and the poster boy for the entire Metroplex. Tia and I . . ." He stopped and looked around as if his wife might be hovering nearby. " . . . are honored to have you here. Please join the party. There are plenty of refreshments. Enjoy yourselves." Fred half-turned and pointed to the drone of voices behind him.

Jack took Maggie's hand and led her through the chattering crowd (Mint Juleps flowed freely) to the glass-enclosed porch. At each end was a portable bar; bookends for a long table filled with enough food to feed the neighborhood: mounds of sliced tenderloin, tomatoes stuffed with goat cheese, avocado eggrolls in a sweet cilantro sauce, and exotic appetizers neither of them recognized. Calorie-laden deserts filled a side table only a few steps from the smorgasbord.

They took their small plates and drinks into the living room, (Maggie had a Coke over ice in a Collins glass, and Jack stuck to a tried and true Johnny Walker Black with a twist.) Jack nodded to passing acquaintances and lifted his glass to someone across the room. Maggie felt uncomfortable amid a horde of the Metro's finest (and wealthiest), but Jack knew many of them. Some were business connections—the reason they were here—and as the obliging wife, she was pleasant, well-mannered and suffered in silence.

They sat on an upholstered bench close to the marble fireplace. When they finished eating, Jack took her plate and stood up. "I need to speak with John Jeffrey, a fellow trustee at the University. John and I are up to our necks in . . . well, a mess. " Jack rolled his eyes. "Be back in a couple of minutes."

"Before you go . . . who are the two men?" she asked pointing to a large ficus tree. They were standing beside the ornamental in such a way that both could see her. However, the younger one had been staring at her between bits of conversation. Maggie was not offended; men stared at her all the time. But she felt uneasy, a little edgy. The handsome face with the staring eyes looked faintly familiar, but she could not place the face no matter how hard she tried.

"The one with gray hair is Sterling Rawson, a neurosurgeon, at Parkland Memorial, the hospital that received a lot of notoriety following the Kennedy assassination. The other is Ward Mitchell, an invasive cardiologist and one of the best in the Metroplex." Jack leaned down and kissed her cheek. "Be right back."

Maggie placed her empty glass on the mantle and leaned against the wood-panel wall. She folded her arms and tried to be as inconspicuous as possible. When she looked up, only the younger one stood beside the ficus tree, still watching her. Maggie as a high-end call girl and later a psychologist had learned to read a man's body language and facial expressions. His stare was neither a tease nor an enticement; rather it was as if he knew her, a puzzled look, trying to decide.

Finally, the fog lifted, she remembered, and the memory startled her . . . the lobby bar at the Dunes Hotel. She didn't know his name, but Maggie was sure he was one and the same. Maggie felt the panic, her heart begin to pound. He was the one person who could destroy her, everything she had achieved and cared about.

Maggie scanned the room, but no sign of Jack. She had no way of knowing when he might come back. But she felt an irresistible need to break the laser-stare of the man beside the ficus tree. She reached for her glass on the mantle and walked back to the porch. She ordered a refill and huddled in the far corner. So much to think about. Maggie remembered the encounter as if it were yesterday. He had turned down her proffer, bought her a drink and gave her some unsolicited advice—as if he were a benevolent uncle rather than a good-looking guy. He was in his mid-thirties and referred to as "Doc" by the bartender. She had left the Dunes still shaking her head over the rejection and the *Dear*

Abby advice she'd received. The splash of Bacardi rum in her Coke seemed to tamp down some of her panic.

She slowed her breathing and tried to clear her mind. The odds were good that he recognized her. "What should she do?" she asked herself. Maggie knew there was only one viable option: talk to him and beg for his silence. She left her glass, half-empty on a side table and returned to the living room. It was no surprise to Maggie that he stood beside the fireplace expecting her to return.

"My name is Ward Mitchell. Don't think I introduced myself in Vegas."

A wave of silence washed over her. Finally, she found her voice. "Doc is the only name I remember."

"Well, that part is true. But please call me Ward."

"How did you recognize me?" Maggie had recovered her composure; spoke softly, not to be overheard. "It's been more than ten years."

"Maggie, I'll never forget you as long as I live."

Her brow wrinkled. She bit down on her lower lip. "Ward, no one must know. No one must ever know. It would destroy my marriage and more than that, humiliate Jack beyond words."

"You're secret is safe; a solemn promise, as God is my witness."

Maggie looked him in the eye and locked her gaze. "I'm grateful for your . . ."

"Grateful? How so?"

"What you said that afternoon. I took those words to heart, and they were part of the reason for my turn-around and to move my life in another direction. You're a part of what I've become, and I can't thank you enough."

"I like to think I saw something special during our brief encounter. Now you are married to a good man; one of the best." Ward searched the ceiling. "What's the word? *Vindication.* That's it . . . I feel vindicated."

Maggie relaxed, her pulse slowed. She felt confident Ward would keep her secret. "There's something else I'd like you to know."

"More surprises?"

"I guess you'd say that. It was part of your narrative that summer afternoon." She felt compelled to share with him her secret. "I'm pregnant."

Ward clapped his hands lightly. "That's wonderful, Maggie. I'm so pleased for you and Jack. And you know what?"

She was hesitant to ask.

"One day you should tell your story." Out of the corner of his eye, Ward saw Jack heading their way.

"Maybe when I'm as old as Methuselah and the brain is still functional."

"In any event, consider me your friend."

Jack wrapped an arm around Ward's shoulders. "I see you've met my wife."

"A real pleasure, Jack." He stepped away. "And nice meeting you, Maggie."

A wave and he was gone.

Jack put ten dollars in the bowl. It was the price to play. Before post time, a hat with each of the entries passed through the crowd. Maggie picked Life's Magic, a filly. Swale won going away. Jack took her slip and tore it into little pieces. "Win some; lose some," he said cheerfully.

"We'll get 'em next year," Maggie added.

The McFarlands thanked the Martingales for a delightful afternoon. Jack handed the stub to the valet, who jogged down the street and brought the car around. On the drive home, Maggie revisited her meeting with Ward Mitchell in Las Vegas. It had been more than a decade, so there were only fragments of memory, but enough of them to recount the role it played in her transformation. She had expressed her gratitude at the party. It had poured out of her like a gusher from one of the wells west of Rutledge. She also felt her secret was safe. Ward worked in a world of confidentiality, a patient's medical record. He had also made her a solemn promise, one she believed he would keep and take to his grave.

Maggie broke the silence. "Is Ward married?"

"Divorced, four or five years ago."

"I'm a little surprised. He seems like such an attractive and decent man."

"She left him with two kids . . . for another woman."

A gasp. "You're kidding?"

"Nope, and he'd just gotten some bad news from his doctor."

Maggie didn't ask, but she wanted to hear more.

"A lesion on the back of his scalp, a melanoma. The good news was that his occipital lymph nodes were negative and he was treated with a wide surgical incision. While it was a harrowing experience, the prognosis is good. And fortunately Ward has a lot of hair, which hides the scar."

"Poor guy," Maggie mumbled.

Jack turned into the driveway and parked in the padded turn-around. He glanced at the clock. "Need to leave in an hour if we're to make the symphony."

"Wash my face and a change of clothes . . . that's it. I'll be ready."

"You know what, Maggie?"

"What, Jack?"

"You are an astonishing woman, Maggie McFarland." He pulled her toward him and planted a kiss on her perfect lips.

CHAPTER 12

Dallas, June, 1984

CHARLIE CHEN, MID-FORTIES, moon-faced and with a slick of black hair, lived in La Bajada, a small neighborhood in West Dallas. His house, wood frame with stucco siding, sat on a small lot, more dirt than grass. The 1800 square feet was more space than Charlie needed, but it was paid for. However, he had often thought about moving closer to his place of business, a dry cleaner, in a strip mall across from the University. And he was comfortable here. The neighbors were mostly Latinos, but he had melted into the mix and while he kept a 9 mm. Glock in his dresser drawer, security was not a concern. No bars on the windows and only a bolt lock on the front door.

Charlie parked curbside and picked up the mail. His steps were deliberate as he mounted the porch steps and unlocked the paneled door. It had been a twelve hour day; they all were, except Sunday, and he was weary. Charlie dropped the mail on the kitchen counter and made himself a gin and tonic. The fridge was almost empty—only some left over moo shu pork and the bottle of Schweppes tonic water. Maybe later, when he was hungry. He turned up the air conditioning and carried the mail into the den. With a heavy sigh, he kicked off his shoes and slipped into his favorite easy chair.

He skimmed through the small stack of letters—all bills and promos. But a thick envelope got his attention and he felt his heart skip a beat. It was postmarked "The Blue Lagoon" and Charlie knew before opening it that the mailing spelled trouble. *Serious trouble.* While his business was profitable and he had made some wise investments, his luck at The Blue Lagoon had turned sour and he was over his head in gambling debt. He conceded that baccarat was an addiction, and he'd tried to limit his trips to Vegas . . . maybe two or three times a year. His last visit a month ago was a disaster; more losses than he could cover. He spoke to Mario, the casino manager, and asked for an extension—assuring him he could sell assets and pay off the debt. Because he had been a reliable guest in the past, Mario honored his request . . . one month, not a day longer. But if he failed . . . well, it was frightening.

He could sell the house but where would he live? He could sell the business, but its income stream paid the bills. His stock portfolio was almost depleted from earlier losses. He tried to think of other solutions, even those that crossed the line. He looked at the envelope and felt a cold sweat under his arms and creeping down his back. He had heard the terrifying stories; a final resting place in the Nevada desert.

Charlie knew the history: The Las Vegas strip was built and operated by the Mafia. Glitter and glass on the outside; darkness and deadly reprisals on the inside. In 1966, only eighteen years ago, the eccentric Howard Hughes moved to Las Vegas and within two years, bought five hotels and casinos. While it was not his intention, he changed the culture of the city. Corporations moved in, bought up valuable properties, and displaced the Mafia as the dominant player in the city. Small casinos like The Blue Lagoon remained independent, which Charlie knew was a euphemism for *The Mob.* Why not stay at The Stardust or The Dunes which were under the corporate umbrella? Charlie had asked himself that question countless times. He'd had a run of good luck at The Blue Lagoon during his early visits to Vegas and was too superstitious to change. They comped everything and gave him a generous line of credit, treated him like royalty until he couldn't cover his losses. "A big mistake," Charlie mumbled as he opened the envelope.

He dumped the contents into his lap, copies of markers which he had signed. A note was attached: Your total is $120,000; you have another thirty days to pay in full; otherwise, expect a visit from the *Snowman.*

Charlie's hands began to shake; he had heard about the albino, the fiendish hit man, who handled unfinished business for Mario and his Associates. He couldn't spend a lifetime looking over his shoulder, even with the Glock holstered in his belt. A handgun would not deter the elusive *Snowman.* Nor could he run and hide even if he left the country. The Mob had a long reach; they would find him. Charlie had to settle up with Mario or all bets were off.

On Sunday morning, Charlie dressed, picked up the morning paper and left the house. A sunny day, not a cloud in the sky, a warm 85 degrees. The street and sidewalks were deserted. A church bell tolled in the distance. While Charlie was not a believer, he respected St Marks, which served a large swath of West Dallas, including his Catholic-heavy neighborhood. The church's soup kitchen fed the indigent and provided an oasis from the sweltering summer heat.

He keyed the ignition and the Datsun 510 roared to life. He made the drive from Sylvan Avenue in West Dallas to the affluent community of Highland Park, with its resident-celebs and high-priced homes, in record time. Sunday traffic was light. He parked near the end of the strip mall and walked past his shop, the paper tucked under his arm. *The Java Joint,* a coffee house, two doors down was crowded as usual. Charlie ordered a small coffee and carried it to a table by the window. He started to open the newspaper, but he had too much on his mind. A restless night and dreams of a scowling Mario and markers falling from the sky like snowflakes. Instead, he concentrated on the line of faces, most of them young, waiting for their caffeine kick-start. Charlie saw a few that were dog-tired, leaning on the counter, needing relief, he was sure, from their Saturday night hangover.

Charlie sipped his coffee and tried to think of a solution to his problem. He took a pen from his shirt pocket and a napkin from the dispenser; he'd make a list. Deep in thought, he tapped the pen against the top of the table. Nothing. Zip. Zero; he drew a blank. "Wait a minute," he mumbled. Something outrageous came to mind. He could rob a bank, but on reflection Charlie wondered if he had lost a marble or two and drifted into the Land of Oz. He was no Bonnie and Clyde, legendary outlaws, born and raised in West Dallas. He didn't think he could pull it off, even a small community bank on an off-the-beaten-path, but then again, desperate men do foolish things.

Charlie drained his cup and went back for a refill. He noticed the woman in front of him, well dressed and a little older than most of the others. First, he saw her in profile as she placed her order. He thought maybe he'd seen her before. He got a good look when she turned and walked away. The face was faintly familiar. It nagged at him. He asked himself again, "Where have I seen her before?"

Charlie returned to his table and his eyes followed her out the door. Suddenly it hit him like a Tyson sucker punch. . . . Las Vegas. She was as attractive as when he last saw her more than a decade ago. He let his mind wander into the past; one of his best nights at the casino . . . over fifty grand. At the time, with a fat bankroll, Charlie felt entitled to a little extravagance. Two thousand bucks for two hours of fun and games with one of Frankie's girls. She said her name was Maggie, and it was a night he'd never forget.

Candice Barrett (Charlie called her Candy), a retired school teacher, was part owner of *The Java Joint.* She saw Charlie frequently since he came in once or twice a day for coffee. They often spoke, and a casual friendship evolved. She knew little about his personal life other than he was born and raised in San Francisco, visited an uncle who lived in Dallas as a teenager and never went back to the West Coast. While Candice thought it was odd, she didn't pry and Charlie never mentioned his family.

Standing near the register, she saw him wave. Having gotten Candy's attention, he picked up his cup and headed her way. She assumed he wanted another refill.

"Hi, Charlie. What's up?" She reached for his cup.

"Morning, Candy." He looked at his half-filled cup. "I'm good, but I have a question."

"Shoot."

"The attractive woman in the pink dress who just left . . ." He pointed at the door of tinted glass. " . . . you know her?"

"Sure I know her . . . Margaret McFarland . . . married to one of the wealthiest men in Dallas."

"No kiddin'"

"Not your typical socialite either," Candice said.

"How's that?"

"She needs to work like I need coffee."

Charlie chuckled. "What kinda job?"

"She's an instructor at the University, the Department of Psychology."

"No kiddin'."

"So what's with the curiosity?"

Charlie shrugged. "I admire beautiful women . . . always have. It's why I'm here every Sunday . . ." An extended arm swept the room. " . . . all these good looking chicks and the best coffee in town."

She slapped the air playfully. "Get outta here; got work to do."

"See you tomorrow, Candy. And don't take any wooden nickels."

A dismissive wave and a come-back-to-see-me smile.

He retrieved the newspaper and walked to his office.

Charlie sat at his desk invigorated and savored the possibility. Maggie, the Las Vegas hooker, and Margaret McFarland, the noblewoman, one and the same. He was sure of it. From newspaper accounts, her husband was rich and respected; rumored to have political ambitions. Charlie wondered how Maggie had made the seamless transition from a high-end call girl to a psychology instructor and patron of the arts. He drained the cup and tossed it into the trash. He knew the sixty-four dollar question was his lifeline: How much would Mrs. McFarland pay to save her marriage, job, and respectability? To keep her past buried like those dead men in the Nevada desert; to sequester her deep dark secret? How much? He was about to find out.

CHAPTER 13

Dallas, the following Friday

MAGGIE LEANED BACK IN her office chair and took a few deep breaths. She heard the door close; her last appointment. She would see Brenda once a week for three months. It was a court order, part of Brenda's sentence for shoplifting. Maggie knew that many considered it an *infraction or petty offense* (something less than a misdemeanor), when in fact, for some, shoplifting became as addictive as drugs and alcohol. As Brenda's student-counselor, she felt a grave responsibility but wondered if she was too "wrapped up" in the student rather than maintaining a professional relationship. Maggie was sure her empathy fed her feeling of exhaustion at the end of the day. Perhaps the pregnancy played a role, but she didn't think so. The morning sickness disappeared after eight weeks as Dr. Hancock had predicted, and she felt replenished following a good night's sleep.

She rested her head against the chair-back and remembered the plans for the evening. Just the two . . . no, the three of them. "*Jack and me and the baby makes three,*" she crooned softly. Some mood music and Dora's pot roast with all the trimmings. The anticipation of a quiet night at home generated a wave of renewal that lifted her out of the chair. Maggie checked her purse; the car keys were there. She looked briefly at the charts on her desk. The dictation could wait until the weekend when Jackson Hall was vacant, quiet as a snowfall. She locked her door, padded down the stairs to the first floor and out the side entrance, a short walk to faculty parking. She felt a blast of hot air on opening the car door. No surprise; it was a Dallas' summer. She keyed the ignition, turned on the a/c and waited. No need to hurry. While only a few miles to Preston Hollow, Friday afternoon traffic moved at a snail's pace. "Patience . . ." Maggie mumbled, " . . . is a virtue." The drive home would put the maxim to the test.

Maggie plodded up the stairs to her bedroom, plopped into her lounge chair and kicked off her loafers. Jack had called; he would not be home for another hour, enough time for her to rest and hopefully recover from the fatigue of a heavy schedule. A few deep breaths before drifting down into a shallow sleep.

She awoke with a start. Was Jack home . . . downstairs? She looked out the bedroom window; shade and shadows covered the backyard. Maggie hurried to the head of the stairs. "Jack, are you home?" She called again; still no answer, only a faint echo, her voice bouncing off the high ceiling. Relieved, she undressed on the way to the bathroom, took a quick shower; no makeup, only her lip gloss, and a dab of perfume behind each ear. She pulled her hair back in a ponytail, held in place with a silver clip. She put on a summer dress, pink with lavender piping at the edges of the fabric. Satisfied, after a quick look in the mirror, she went downstairs and followed the hallway into the kitchen.

Dora had prepared the meal and set the table before leaving for the weekend. Maggie put on an apron and tossed a green salad; there was little else to do. She put a Morton Gould tape in the cassette deck, which relayed music into the dining room. She stepped outside and cut three blooms from a flowering plant of Gold Lantana. She put them in a crystal vase and placed it in the center of the dining room table.

Dora had made a pitcher of ice tea and left it in the fridge. Maggie poured herself a glass and stood by the kitchen window. Should she worry? Jack was compulsive, always on time. He had said an hour, but it had been almost two. She called his cell, but Jack had turned it off. That, too, was unusual. So she sipped her tea and waited. In a matter of minutes, a flash of light from the driveway. In her mind's eye, the garage door opened. Now she could put worry aside. But Maggie was still curious. There had to be a reason.

Maggie dimmed the lights and lit the table candles. The Orchestra's string section, with its rich, sustaining sound, drifted through the dining room. After Maggie had taken her seat, Jack reached for her hand and as always, said the blessing; short and to the point.

It was something she'd never done, but she went along because Jack's "religion" was important to him and he was important to her. Like the strong chin and his high-octane motor, it was who he was, a part of the total package.

"How was your day?" he asked.

"Long and tiring." Maggie tried to conjure up a cheery smile. "Would you like a glass of wine?"

He shook his head. "The tea is fine."

"No need for you to climb on the wagon. I'm the one who's pregnant."

Jack chuckled. "What's good for the goose is good for the gander . . . or something like that."

The roast was so tender Maggie cut it with her folk. "You want to hear about Brenda, my end-of-the-day consultation."

"Maggie, I'm interested in everything you do. So sure, tell me about Brenda."

"What I'm about to tell you is in the public record, so I'm not betraying a confidence."

"I wouldn't expect you to. Not the honest and upright Maggie McFarland."

She gave him a dismissive finger wave. "Brenda is nineteen, a sophomore, from a well-to-do family in New Orleans. She is attractive, carries a 3.8 GPA, active in her sorority, and an avid swimmer. Set the state breaststroke record during her senior year in high school." Maggie stopped long enough to push her plate aside. "Why would a young woman with looks, smarts, and talent get caught up in this web of illegal activity? A bracelet,—cosmetic jewelry from Target of all places—and two Club Room golf shirts from Macy's. Stuff she didn't need and, if she did, her father would have bought it for her."

"Here's my take," Jack said, reaching for his glass of tea. "She gets a *kick* from shoplifting; a *high* like a back alley junkie. There's the tension before the theft, an adrenaline rush during the steal and a feeling of exhilaration after the theft. Shoplifting is a crime, but I bet your Brenda doesn't feel a speck of remorse."

Maggie shrugged. "We'll know about that after a couple of sessions. Meanwhile, she needs help. Maybe counseling will be a step in the right direction."

Jack buttered one of Dora's homemade rolls. "She'll be a challenge. I'm sure those who do it for the *thrill* are the toughest to treat."

"We'll see," Maggie said and left the table. She returned from the kitchen with a pitcher of tea and refilled their glasses. She replaced the pitcher on the sideboard and took her seat. "Were you tied up with a client?" She tapped the face of her watch.

"Had to go by Parkland. Remember Ed Beasley . . . you met him at Arthur's?"

"A little over-the-top; how could I forget?" The cheek kiss and the garlic breath were indelible reminders.

"His mother, who lives alone, fell and broke her hip. She was out for a walk and tripped on the curb. A neighbor spotted her and called 911. She was rushed to Parkland and will have surgery tomorrow." Jack hesitated and looked at Maggie, her eyes gleaming with candlelight. My goodness, she's beautiful, he thought. Married for more than a year and she still takes my breath away. "Now where was I?"

"Mrs. Beasley, a broken hip."

"Of course, Ed's a friend and an important client, so I stopped by the hospital to speak with Ed and wish Mrs. Beasley smooth sailing."

The phone rang in the kitchen. "I'll get it," Maggie said.

Carrying her glass of tea, she backed through the swinging door and answered the wall phone. "Hello."

"Hi, Maggie."

"Who's calling?" A wave of apprehension swept over her.

"An old acquaintance." The voice was calm; the tone civil.

"I'd like a name."

"Not necessary. Just an acquaintance. We met in Las Vegas . . . hmm, say ten years ago."

Maggie felt a second wave of discomfort, this one larger and menacing. She sensed where this was going and leaned against the wall for support. "So why are you calling?"

"You were one of Frankie's girls and I was a client."

"Oh, no." Maggie felt the tears trickle down her cheeks.

"Here's why I'm calling. I read the papers. You're married to a very rich man with high-level business and political connections. And you, Maggie, are his helpmate and enjoy a high-society lifestyle." The voice went silent for a few seconds before adding, "Don't think you want your face stuck on the front page of the *Dallas Morning News*."

Maggie said nothing. The shock waves began to subside. She tried to focus . . . to think. Her face on the front page of the paper . . . well, the fallout would be an utter disaster; her life in ruin.

"You can buy my silence . . ."

"How much?" she asked.

"One hundred and fifty thousand will seal my lips; a drop in the bucket for your old man."

Maggie gulped and slid down the wall until she was sitting on the floor.

"What guarantee do I have that you won't come back for more?"

"Trust me."

"Why would I trust a thief?" Maggie managed a cackle.

The retort was loud, frightening. "Because you have no other choice."

Jack stuck his head in the door. "Are you okay?"

She looked up, contrived a smile and mouthed, "A student."

He respected her privacy and went back into the dining room and poured himself another glass of tea.

Maggie knew the phone line was open, she could hear the breathing.

"No one will believe you. Ever think of that?"

"Should that be the case, I have the picture."

Maggie said nothing.

"Yeah, the Polaroid. Our night together, the picture, topless of course, cost me another five hundred bucks. But I was on a roll at the tables and wanted a souvenir." A chuckle. "I get the money and you get my silence and the picture. Good deal, huh?"

Maggie knew she had a losing hand. How could she raise the money without revealing her secret? She needed time to think; to find a way out of this morass. Meanwhile go along, learn all that she could about the blackmailer. "OK, when and where? Remember it takes time to raise that much money and nothing happens on the weekend."

"I'll send the details. Check your mailbox next week, addressed to you and marked 'personal.'"

"If I have a question or there is an unexpected delay, how can I reach you?"

"You can't."

Maggie listened for background noise, but there was none. She assumed he was inside, probably at home, sitting in his den, his feet up on an ottoman. A cool customer was her best guess. "A final question, humor me: how did you know I was in Dallas?"

"Coincidence. Call it unlucky, whatever. I spotted you at a strip mall several weeks ago. At first I wasn't sure, but 'pretty sure.'" Went home and dug out the Polaroid picture. And there it was . . . a match. Just couldn't forget that beautiful face. Put two and two together, and that's where we are." The phone line went dead.

Maggie took some time to compose herself before getting up and replacing the wall phone. Another secret that must remain hidden whatever the cost. She dabbed her eyes with a paper towel and smoothed out her dress. After taking a deep breath, she went back to the dining room, circled the table and placed a kiss on Jack's cheek. "Sorry, but I may have made myself too available."

Jack shook his head. "If a student is comfortable calling you, that's a compliment" He pointed his folk in her direction. "You should be flattered."

"Just don't want my feelings to interfere with the objective."

"Too many teachers at the college level are just doing their job. They lecture and leave. Hoping for tenure. No personal touch." Jack leaned toward her and said, "The way you care about students like Brenda is a good thing and makes you an exceptional counselor."

Maggie felt she was sitting beneath the Sword of Damocles held in place by a frayed and slender cord. It took a concerted effort for Maggie to hide her angst. She had compounded the threat of blackmail by lying to Jack about the phone call. She wanted to drop the subject, afraid that he, with his inquisitive mind, would want to know more about the "troubled" student. She knew the best way to close the door on that subject was to open another one.

"Are you ready for some desert?"

"What's on the menu?"

"Dora's custard pie."

Jack patted his stomach. "Calories I don't need, but how can I turn it down?"

Maggie headed back to the kitchen. "A slice of pie and a cup of espresso, coming up."

They spent a quiet evening together. There was discussion of the upcoming Republican National Convention to be held in Dallas. The city was busy putting on its best face. And only two months away. Ronald Reagan, seeking a second term, was unopposed. Maggie asked about his role in the Convention. Jack admitted he was involved, but as an operative and speech writer for Vice President Bush. He preferred to stay out of the spotlight since his interest in running for political office had waned. "They're already giving it plenty of press," he said, opening the afternoon paper.

Maggie's mind was elsewhere. It was hard to focus. The phone call, earlier in the evening, trumped all incoming messages. She turned on the color TV; switched stations since it was almost time for a rerun of C*heers,* one of her favorite programs, and she needed a good laugh. But even the light-hearted comedy could not block out the threatening phone call.

The grandfather clock in the entryway chimed ten. Jack yawned and folded his paper. "Think I'll turn in."

"I need to load the dishwasher. No Dora tomorrow. But I'll be up in a few minutes."

After cleaning the kitchen, she turned off the lights and slowly climbed the stairs. She was spent, as if she had run a marathon; weary, but wide awake.

When Maggie came out of the bathroom, Jack was asleep, snoring softly. Slivers of moonlight slipped through the plantation shutters. She climbed into bed, her body pressed against his and closed her eyes. Sleep would not come, not even close. She had too much on her mind. Maybe a glass of wine would help, but she had pledged to avoid anything that might compromise the pregnancy. Maggie stared at the dark ceiling and considered her problem. There seemed to be no solution. She asked herself the salient question: how can I raise the ransom without exposing my past? If she sought help, whether it was Jack or the FBI, she'd have to explain her request for the money. It was not a viable option; she would never give her secret away. Well, could she fabricate some other explanation? None Maggie could think of. Why else would she, married to wealth, need that kind of money and in a lump sum? She answered her own question: it was rhetorical. She felt locked in, nowhere to turn, no way out.

Maggie tried to put the subject aside and get some sleep. She decided any plan, if there was one, should wait until she got the mailing from her "acquaintance" which she assumed would provide more details. After the turn-around, the start of a new life, she promised to defend her secret, no matter the cost. Maggie felt that commitment would soon be tested. How far would she go? She knew the answer to that question: whatever was necessary to conceal the past. She thought of the .38 stashed in her closet and hoped it was a last resort.

She turned on her side and rearranged her pillow. The name came unbidden, like a flash of lightning . . . Ward Mitchell; he knew her secret, someone with whom she could discuss the phone call. Maggie needed a sounding board, a confidant. After she received the letter and digested the message, she would call Ward and make an appointment. His office in the professional building beside Parkland Hospital ensured privacy and avoided the risk of being seen together in a public setting. Ward's name was like a sedative. Her eyes grew heavy, her mind slowed, as if his image had put on the brakes. It was only a matter of minutes before Maggie dropped down into a restless sleep.

CHAPTER 14

Camden, 1968

NO ONE WOULD MISTAKE SATURDAY nights in Camden with the boisterous and carnival atmosphere of New Orleans. No jazz bands or girlie bars that lined the narrow streets of the French Quarter. No Fat Tuesday's or Pat O'Brien's or a Bourbon Street crowded with revelers partying well into the night. The contrast to Camden was striking. The stores on Main Street locked the doors and turned off the lights at nine o'clock; pedestrian traffic disappeared into parked cars or boarded the city bus. Only the restaurants and fast food outlets were open until the witching hour. It was as if the moon had sent beams of light over Camden and bedded it down for the night.

Carl had known Chris Markos, a casual friend, since high school. Like most of his classmates, they had gone their separate ways after graduation. When Carl returned to Camden with a law degree, he was surprised to hear that Chris never left Camden, skipped college and opened a small cafe in West Camden.

Several months after he arrived, Carl left his law office before noon and drove across the river, planning to have lunch at the cafe and renew his acquaintance with Chris Markos.

Parking was at a premium. He found a metered spot a block away, dropped three quarters into the coin receptor and chose to walk the shady side of the street. Inside the Kando Cafe, he stopped and looked around. The dining room was spare, a dozen or more tables, most of them filled. Along the north wall was a lunch counter, not an empty stool, and behind it, the kitchen. Standing near the checkout counter, Chris picked up a menu from the stack and headed his way.

"Hello, Chris." He extended a hand.

"Carl . . . Carl Sweeny, what are you doing here?"

"I came by to see an old friend. Heard some good things about the Cafe." Carl looked around the small dining room with its no-frills decor. "Thought I'd check it out."

"What brings you back to Camden?"

"Finished law school in '66, spent last year at Wharton, then came home and joined Kelly and Moran. Just gettin' started; if you need a lawyer, look me up."

"You handle divorces?" Chris asked with a loopy grin.

Carl nodded. "Sure, you got a problem?"

"Maybe . . . I'll let you know."

Carl took the menu and followed Chris to an empty table. "When did you get started?"

"I went to work at Tilly's right out of high school. Got a job as a waiter, kept my eyes and ears open. Wanted to learn all I could about the restaurant business. After five years at Tilly's, I'd saved some money and Mr. Harbuck at the Richland Bank gave me a good-faith loan; enough to get started."

Carl scanned the room again. "Good crowd. It looks like you made a wise business decision."

"I learned the secret for a successful operation at Tilly's." He counted them with his fingers: "A good chef, good service, reasonable prices and most important, Tom Tilly was ever-present, greeting customers and providing oversight."

"Sounds like you've found your calling."

Chris nodded. "But I dream of something bigger and better."

"Like what?"

"I want to build a five-star restaurant in Camden. I've already picked out a lot on Louisville, just below the car dealerships. "

"A darn good location."

"It's probably ten years away, but I can tie up the land with some good terms."

"Remember, if you need a hot-shot real estate attorney . . ."

They both laughed.

"I'm calling it *The Rendevous* and making the best chef in New Orleans an offer he can't refuse."

"Why does a good Greek like Chris Markos open a French restaurant?" Carl asked airily.

"I conducted an unofficial poll . . ."

"And?"

"French over Greek . . . four to one."

"Good luck, Chris, Keep dreaming big."

A young waitress, neatly dressed in uniform, moved toward the table. "Sally will take care of you. Enjoy your lunch. It's on the house."

"Thanks, Chris, and don't forget if you need a good lawyer . . ."

Chris took the business card and dropped it in his shirt pocket. "You'll probably hear from me before long." He turned and headed back to the check-out counter.

Card ordered the "lunch special" and marveled at Chris's success, the Camden High senior voted *less* likely to succeed. (The student newspaper, *The Fish Wrapper,* conducted the poll, not the official yearbook.) He was sure Chris would make it happen.

Camden, March, 2012

Carl sat at the kitchen table with his mug of coffee and the morning paper. He looked out his bay window hoping for signs of spring. There were none. Frost covered the lawn and a March wind stirred the maple trees, which were bearing new leaves early. A plucky sparrow flitted across the backyard and took refuge beneath the roof's overhang. A winter sun had cleared the horizon climbing with precision into a powder blue sky. Carl looked at the wall phone, but it was too early to make dinner reservations at *The Rendevous.* The restaurant opened for lunch so he would make the call at noon. Instead, he phoned Ed about a spur-of-the-moment golf game. The club gave them a 10 o'clock tee time; he would call the restaurant at the turn. And of course he would phone Maggie, who was always on his mind.

Carl unfolded the Saturday paper; the story was on the front page. He was shocked and saddened. Had he not told Maggie that Camden was almost crime free? But Carl knew that on rare occasions, bad things happened to good people. But who would want to harm a gentle soul like the Reverend Rhea Joslyn? He'd met her when she served as an associate pastor at the Camden Methodist Church. Gifted and charismatic, the Bishop gave her a challenging assignment: form a new church (from scratch) on the southside of Camden with its impoverished neighborhoods. By the third year, the Southside Methodist Church had seven hundred members and a sanctuary of brick and stone, stain glass windows and seating for twice the membership. He knew it was made possible by the hard work and unflagging devotion of this young woman who possessed an evangelistic fervor. A zealot who singlehanded uplifted these blighted neighborhoods with a spirit of compassion and good works. Carl read the newspaper article and from his experience in the D.A.'s office, he could visualize how it probably happened.

On Friday evening, Rhea drove to a small wood-weathered house with blue shingles on Poker Road. She had received a dinner invitation from the Franklins, an Afro-American family and members of her church. It was an opportunity to enjoy a home-cooked meal and an after-dinner coffee. She stayed longer than she'd planned since there was still work to do at the office.

It was dark when she drove into her parking space. No outside lights. Rhea killed the engine, turned off the headlights and got out of the car. Fearless to a fault, she went through a side door and flipped the overhead light in her office. She locked the door before settling into her swivel. She needed to clear the clutter from her desk since Saturdays were reserved for visiting the hospital and nursing homes. And there was always this: a final revision of her Sunday sermon. It was an important time in the life of her church, the holiest of seasons; Easter fell on April 8th, only a month away.

A rapping sound. She wondered if it was the wind or maybe her imagination. She went to the window and peeked through the blinds. The sharp angle prevented her from seeing anyone who stood in front of the door.

The knock came again, louder, repetitive.

Rhea went to the door. "Who is it?"

"Help, please. I'm in trouble."

A man or a woman? Rhea didn't know. The words were muffled by the wood, but she got the message. She turned on the outside lights and opened the door.

A man, lean and disheveled, with shoulder-length hair partly concealed by the black ski mask covering his face, took a step inside. He wore jeans, a T-shirt, and a grimy Levi jacket. He gave off a scent of danger; gloved and holding a gun.

"Move," he said. "Get back in your chair."

Rhea did as she was told. "What do you want?" she asked evenly.

"Shut up and listen". He opened the coat closet; Rhea's jacket and a few office supplies. He looked around the room with haunting eyes as if someone might suddenly appear.

Paranoid, she thought. Not good.

"I know you keep money here. Let's have it." He moved closer to the desk and waved the gun in her direction.

"I have some cash in my pastor's fund which I keep in my desk drawer."

"Let's have it." This time, louder and more acerbic.

"May I ask you a question?"

The outside lights filtered through the window blinds. Obviously agitated, the intruder stepped back to the door but couldn't find the switch.

"Drugs, is that why you need the money?"

"None of your goddamn business. Now hand it over." This time he extended an arm, the gun in her face.

Rhea opened the bottom drawer of her desk and tossed him the bank bag. "There's about seven hundred dollars; it's all I have. So take it and go." It was an order, not a plea; her voice strong and confident. Rhea wondered if a show of strength was the right tactic but there was little time to consider her options.

He unzipped the bag and sifted through the bills; mostly twenties, a few fifties, a couple of hundreds. After closing the bag, he looked at the preacher who sat calmly in her chair, fingers steepled beneath her chin.

"You think you're something special, don't you?"

Rhea didn't answer but his perturbation was palpable, filling the room.

“Yeah, that’s it . . . you think you’re an angel . . . God Almighty’s angel . . .” He kicked the front of the desk with his boot; the wood shattered. The gun went off, a bullet in her chest.

Rhea slumped forward, her head on the desk, blood seeping from the wound.

The killer tucked the money bag beneath his arm, hurried through the wash of outside lights and disappeared into the midnight darkness.

“How was your golf game?” she asked as they turned onto Louisville, a busy four- lane, east-west highway.

“We’ll never learn. Still too cold, even if you bundle up.”

“How many holes before you surrendered?” Maggie kidded.

“Nine—and that was a struggle. But Ed defied the weather and shot his handicap.”

“And you?”

“Let’s just say it was not a pretty sight.” Carl laughed and turned off the highway and into the circular drive of *The Rendevous.* He stopped at valet parking. A young man in uniform opened Maggie’s door and handed Carl a ticket. They followed a brick walkway to the front entrance, well lighted and covered by a forest green awning.

Chris Markos greeted them; Carl made the introductions. The owner led them to a table in a quiet corner. Carl had given Maggie background; Chris, fresh out of high school, had a big dream and with perseverance and a little luck, fulfilled that dream. Carl had described the small cafe in West Camden which he’d visited on his return home to join the law firm. He also mentioned a recent issue of Gourmet magazine that gave *The Rendevous* a five-star rating and the number one ranking among restaurants in North Louisiana.

Maggie looked around. It reminded her of Arthur’s in Dallas sans the fish tanks and the piped-in classical music. But the plush carpets, handsome wall covers and elegant table settings made for delightful dining. In the center of the large room was the restaurant’s signature: a fountain of polished rock which spilled into a koi pond with underwater lighting. Again she thought of Arthur's; the fish theme was the same, but the arrangement was different. "It's lovely, Carl."

Chris stopped by their table with two menus and a bottle of California Merlot. "Compliments of *The Rendevous.*" He winked at Maggie and said, "I think he got it right this time." He opened the bottle and filled their wine glasses; a pleasant fragrance wafted over the table. "Your waiter will be with you shortly." Chris half-bowed, kissed the back of Maggie's hand and disappeared into the crowded room.

Maggie gave Carl a quizzical look. "What did Chris mean by you're "getting it right?"

Carl thought about her question and took some time to frame a proper reply. "He sees a beautiful woman, well-mannered and soft-spoken. Chris knows my marital history, so he makes an off-the-wall assumption. I think it was more about you, a compliment, rather than me."

A waiter appeared, filled their water glasses and promised to return.

Carl looked at Maggie as she studied the menu. Just the sight of her caused his heart to speed up, even skip a beat. She was magnetic, mesmerizing, and much, much more; those arresting blue eyes . . . God help me. It was something he didn't expect to happen at his age, but it had; he had fallen madly in love with Maggie McFarland.

He felt her hand on his. "Carl, are you alright?"

He looked at her, locked his gaze. "I couldn't be better."

During dinner, Carl asked Maggie if she had read the morning paper. She had not. He was sure that Maggie, who moved to Camden a short time ago, knew nothing about Rhea Joslin. He summarized the newspaper's account: the break-in, the armed robbery, the clean getaway. His voice cracked when adding: Rhea Joslyn was in critical condition.

"That's unbelievable, Carl. Thought you said Camden was a safe place to live."

"I did, but I hedged when I said *almost* crime free.

Maggie sipped her wine. "So who found Reverend Joslyn?"

"She'd had dinner with Bertha and Jesse Franklin, who live near the church. Rhea had forgotten her scarf, which Bertha found during a late night clean up." Carl stopped for a moment and pushed his plate aside. "I guess it was reflex that caused her to look toward the church.

The outside lights were on. They were never on at that time of night. Bertha knew something was wrong. Jesse was asleep, but she shook him awake. The two of them drove the short distance to the church; the office lights were also on. They felt the panic when the door to the pastor's study was unlocked. But once inside their hearts sank. Rhea's head lay on the desk. Jesse checked the carotid and felt a weak pulse. Bertha found her jacket and covered Rhea's blood-stained blouse. Jesse picked up her and carried her to his car. He gently placed her in the back seat, her head cradled in Bertha's lap. The Franklins knew they could get her to St. Francis with dispatch, faster than calling 911.

Maggie shook her head. "Who would do something like that?"

"During my ten years in the D.A.'s office I asked that question many times. I finally came up with a simple answer . . ."

"Which is . . . ?"

"Since Cain and Abel, there has been this timeless struggle between good and evil."

Maggie sipped her wine; her brow wrinkled. "If there's a God, the creator of all things—and I'm still searching for Him—why put evil in the world in the first place?"

"Free will," Carl said.

Maggie shrugged; a bemused look.

"I believe God chose not to make man an automaton. Rather he is free to choose; thousands of choices that shape a life and define his behavior. But the kicker is this: choices have consequences. The man who robbed and shot Rhea Joslyn did it for one of two reasons. He is either mentally ill, in which case the justice system will cut him some slack, or he is consummate evil and, if caught and convicted, will face the death penalty."

"While we're on the subject, this came in today's mail." Maggie took the envelope from her purse and passed it across the table.

Carl noted the postmark: Fort Worth, Texas. He removed a greeting card from the envelope that read "I'M THINKING OF YOU." The script was superimposed upon a cartoonish elephant, his trunk scratching his head. Inside it read, "Always remember, I'm thinking of you." It was unsigned.

"Randy Bynum." Carl passed the card back to Maggie.

"Who else? Must've mailed it right after I left Dallas." Maggie sighed. "Guess he means business."

"It worries the heck out of me. I wanna help but there's not much I can do other than alert the Camden police department and the sheriff's office to be vigilant. An old friend, retired FBI, checked their database and turned up zip, zero. His record is clean. High marks from his employer: *Direct Energy* is headquartered in Plano.

"What about a picture?"

"I'll have the sheriff call your friend, Lee Clancy, and see if he can get a copy of Randy's driver's license from the county DMV. The crime lab can do wonders with a small photograph . . . blow it up . . . touch it up . . . a reasonable facsimile."

"I appreciate you doing that, Carl."

"You're special, Maggie. But I guess you know that. "If anything happened to you, I don't . . ."

"Carl, don't worry. I'm a big girl and will take all the precautions."

The waiter approached the table with the dessert menus.

Maggie shook her head.

Carl waved him off.

"Coffee?"

"Let's go back to my place and have coffee," Maggie said. "Build a fire and get comfortable."

Carl looked at the waiter. "The check, please."

"It's on the house, compliments of Mr. Markos."

Carl gave her a what-can-you-do look before reaching for his billfold. He took out a twenty and handed it to the waiter.

The dinner was delicious and the wine went down easy, but the conversation had turned grim, their mood somber. It was time to leave. Carl decided to hold the final bit of bad news . . . Rhea Joslyn had died that afternoon. Maggie took the morning paper; the murder of Reverend Joslyn was front page news. No need to lengthen the dark shadows that Rhea and Randy Bynum had cast on their Saturday night dinner.

It was only a ten-minute drive from Louisville to Lamy Lane. Carl parked in the driveway and followed Maggie into the house. He started a fire by adding a layer of kindling on pine logs. The dry wood crackled and burned; smoke drifted up the open chimney.

Maggie brought a tray into the den and placed it on the coffee table. "Everything's there; sugar, cream, Sweet and Low. It's not Irish coffee, but it'll warm you up".

They sat on the sofa, in opposite corners, facing each other. The fireplace provided a warm and cozy ambiance. Maggie had dropped a cassette, Tony Bennett, into the tape player; *I left my heart in San Francisco* . . . soft and mellifluous.

Carl turned pensive. He had so much to say but was unsure of himself. Was it the right time and place? He sure as hell didn't want to screw it up. He took a sip of the hot coffee and burned his tongue. Not a good start, he thought, although it seemed to fuel what he wanted to say.

"I'm worried about you, Maggie. The note from Bynum is troubling. He is unpredictable and poses a real threat."

"Carl, I understand the risk and . . ."

"Sheee!" He reached across the sofa and placed a finger against her lips. "I'm worried about you because you mean so much to me." Carl dropped his eyes to the floor searching for meaningful words, not maudlin sentiment. "I know that Jack still owns a big part of your heart, but if there's room for another . . ."

"Carl, it's only been a few weeks. I enjoy your company, our friendship. But let's give it some time. Okay?"

Carl nodded. "Guess I've gotten more impatient with all the birthdays piling up."

Dulled by the Merlot and the warmth of the fire, both grew drowsy. Finally, Carl stood up and covered a yawn. He looked at the clock on the mantle. Almost midnight. "Better go, it's getting late." He gave Maggie a hand and lifted her off the sofa.

"Thanks for a pleasant evening." On tiptoe, she took his cheeks in her hands and placed a kiss on the lips. "Good night, Carl, sleep well."

The kiss was unexpected and left him momentarily speechless. "Lock up tight. Remember Bynum is out there somewhere, we just don't know when or where."

She gave him a hug and a nudge out the door. "Call me next week."

He waved good night. It was already in his plans.

CHAPTER 15

Dallas, June, 1984

ANOTHER EARLY AWAKENING. Maggie had not slept well since she had received the Friday night phone call. It was dark outside; the digital clock on the dresser with big red numbers: 5:25. She slipped out of bed and put on her robe. Jack was still asleep when Maggie left the room and tiptoed downstairs to the kitchen. She made a pot of coffee and waited by the window for it to percolate. She opened the plantation shutters; only a sliver of moon and the contrail of a falling star. She could see the faint outline of the pool, but the hybrid poplars were cloaked in darkness.

Maggie filled her coffee mug and sat at the kitchen table. There was a ribbon of crimson on the eastern horizon, the arrival of dawn, and she had a front row seat. But Maggie's mind was on other things. During the weekend she was obsessed with the threatening phone call; she had thought of little else even though she knew it was a waste of time, at least until she got the letter. Fortunately, Jack worked most of the weekend and didn't notice her introspection.

It was Monday, another work day, five appointments beginning at eleven o'clock. Maggie wondered if she could stay focused with desperation and worry, pressing distractions, hanging over her like ominous storm clouds. But she wouldn't complain since it was her decision to work until the Christmas break, well into her third trimester.

Maggie could not believe this was happening. Cinderella, that fairytale come true, was in serious jeopardy. She felt the tension in her shoulders crawling up into her neck, a prelude to a punishing headache. She found the bottle in a kitchen cabinet, shook two Tylenol into her palm and washed them down with a swallow of coffee. (It was the only over-the-counter analgesic that Dr. Hancock had approved.)

It had been twelve years since she left Las Vegas. Suddenly, she had a flash of memory. "Frankie . . . Frankie Agosto," she murmured. Could he be of help? There were a lot of unanswered questions. Maggie had read and heard of the new construction and dramatic changes that had made Las Vegas more than a gambling mecca but a family-friendly destination as well. The Capri had been sold to a corporation listed on the New York Stock Exchange and the Kansas City Mob moved its operation to the Caribbean. Maggie wondered if Joe Agosto had made the transition or even if he was still alive. She figured Frankie stayed in Vegas; probably moved his office from The Capri to a free standing brothel on the outskirts of town. She bet he was still in business, an escort service with the best product in Vegas.

Maggie sipped her coffee and watched the sun brushstroke low-lying clouds coral-pink and primrose yellow. Maybe she'd give Frankie a call, if she could find him. Maggie sighed and leaned heavily on the table. She wasn't sure that Frankie, while smart and cunning, could resolve her dilemma. And even if he could, what would be his incentive? He was annoyed, even a little angry, when she told him of her decision to leave Las Vegas. Maggie drained her mug and placed it in the sink. She decided to forget Frankie. There were too many variables. And while Frankie knew her Vegas secrets, he didn't know about Dallas and her life-changing experience, and she didn't want him to know. Only Ward offered even a thread of hope. But first things first: the letter. The postman delivered the mail mid-afternoon. Dora always placed the mail on the Queen Ann gaming table with its cabriole legs, in the entryway. Maggie needed to retrieve the letter before Jack got home .Then again, if her "acquaintance" mailed the letter Saturday, it might not arrive until tomorrow or even Wednesday.

Maggie's last appointment on Tuesday was at three o'clock. She ended the session at 3:45, anxious to get home and check the mail. On Monday, in a rush, she had almost rear-ended a Plymouth Horizon at a busy intersection. Maggie scolded herself. "Pay attention!" Anyway, it was wasted effort since the letter from her "acquaintance" had not arrived. Maybe today, she thought, as she slowed down and focused on driving. An accident would only exacerbate her present state of discontent. And why hurry? If the letter is there, it won't disappear; it has neither legs nor wings. The cartoonish image of a flying letter made her snicker.

Since Dora left around 4:00 and Jack wouldn't be home until after dark, another meeting at the University, she would have privacy. Maggie hoped the letter was there, it was a propitious, uninterrupted time to read and study the missive and reconsider her options.

She left her car in the turn-around and took the steps to the veranda. Maggie unlocked the front door and went inside. Dora, as usual, had placed the mail on the gaming table. She dropped her purse and keys on the table and shuffled through the day's delivery. Her heart skipped a beat when she found the envelope marked PERSONAL and addressed to Maggie McFarland. No return address. It was postmarked Arlington, Texas. Mailed on Sunday.

She tore open the plain white envelope and removed the single sheet of tablet paper. Still standing, she examined the note. No salutation. Typed, large capital letters. It was unsigned. Maggie sat down beside the gaming table, her back to the wall, and with a sense of foreboding, read the letter:

> THERE IS A PAY PHONE NEAR THE CORNER OF PRYOR AND STONE. WALGREEN'S IS ACROSS THE STREET. BE THERE WHEN I CALL. MONDAY NIGHT . . . 8 P.M. BRING THE MONEY. ALL 100'S IN AN ATTACHE CASE. FURTHER INSTRUCTIONS AT THAT TIME. BE THERE. THIS IS NOT A GAME.

Maggie re-read the note and dropped it in her lap. She leaned her head against the wall and tried to consider only the facts. She had six days to raise the ransom but "how" was the question. Jack would give her the money in a heartbeat, but her past would unravel before his very eyes. Maggie felt like she was in an English maze, and every path led to an impenetrable hedge. She had made an appointment to see Ward Wednesday afternoon. It was a long shot, but maybe he could pull a rabbit out of his hat. At least, he was someone with whom she could share her seemingly inextricable dilemma.

Maggie picked up the letter and put it back in the envelope. Had she tainted the evidence? Were the blackmailer's fingerprints on the letter? Was the postmark or note paper a clue? The questions were moot since any investigation would disclose her sordid past. So, there would be no investigation. She would only show the letter to Ward; no one else. Maggie crossed the porch, down the steps and back to her car. She placed the envelope in the glove compartment and locked it. Safe enough, she thought, until the meeting with Mitchell.

Maggie had a Wednesday afternoon cancelation. It was a relief since her personal problem was a distraction, as it had been all week, and that was unfair to her "troubled" students who needed her undivided attention. The break in her schedule also allowed Maggie to make a leisurely drive to her four o'clock appointment. In light traffic, ten minutes, maybe fifteen easy, from the University to the professional building off Harry Hines Boulevard. It was just enough time to cool the car parked in the faculty lot since mid-morning beneath the blistering heat of an unforgiving sun.

Maggie took the short walk from visitor's parking to the front entrance of the handsome building of brick and glass. Inside, she checked the wall directory; Ward Mitchell M.D. Suite 1100. She crossed the terrazzo floor to the bank of elevators and waited with a knot of strangers. She felt the butterflies and wondered why. There was no need to be nervous. During their two encounters (the lobby-bar at the Dunes Hotel and the Martingale Derby party) Ward had been amiable and respectful, qualities Maggie had found in very few men; and a subject on which she had become an authority . . . the hard way.

She stepped off the elevator on the top floor and to her right was suite 1100, the names of six doctors imprinted on the glass. An elderly gentleman held the door for her while holding his hat and a prescription in his free hand. Maggie thanked him with one of her "knock-out" smiles. She went to the reception counter and spoke to a neatly-dressed woman with gray hair, cut short, and makeup which could not hide the wrinkles. *Millie* was on the name plate pinned to the pocket of her blouse.

"Hi, I'm here to see Dr. Mitchell."

Millie checked the appointment book. "Have a seat, Mrs. McFarland, he'll be with you shortly." Just as Maggie took her seat, a young nurse in scrubs waved her back and led her down a long corridor to the office of Ward Mitchell. She ushered Maggie inside and closed the door.

"Hello, Ward. Thanks for seeing me."

"Oh, Hi Maggie," he said, and pointed to a wing-back chair. "Please have a seat."

With his good looks and athletic build, Ward Mitchell could have been the poster boy for the AMA, or the cover of GQ magazine. Maggie had assessed his good looks a long time ago. It was the reason she'd chosen him that afternoon in the Dunes lobby-bar. Now in his mid-forties (only a guess), he looked the same, fine features perfectly placed in a well-chiseled face. "A nice view," she said tipping her chin toward one of the windows.

"Top floor suite with a panorama, but you pay for it, one way or the other." Ward shaped a smile. "Sound familiar?"

"My gosh, how do you remember our conversation eons ago?"

He leaned back in his chair, hands behind his head. "Guess you made an impression," he chuckled.

"I'm in trouble, Ward."

He gave her a puzzled look. "Millie said it was personal. Go ahead, it will go no further."

Maggie removed the letter from her purse and dropped it on the desk. "The phone call came Friday night. The caller recognized me at a strip mall, or thought he did; claims he has a picture of me during a night in Vegas. He wants big bucks to keep quiet. Otherwise he'll sell the picture and the story to the newspaper, knowing it would destroy my marriage, maybe run me out of town and damage irrevocably Jack's business and political aspirations."

Ward read the note twice before slipping it back across the desk. "You only have five days to meet the deadline. What about the cash?"

Maggie shook her head. "That's the problem. Jack would gladly give me the money but I would have to give him the reason for my request." Maggie took a deep breath and let it out slowly. "I feel trapped, Ward."

"When you talked to the caller, I assume it was a man. Was there anything distinctive about his voice . . . you know, like an accent?"

"It was a man, no accent, a baritone; just sounded like your average Joe."

Ward got up and went to the window, his back to Maggie. He stood there, quiet and contemplative.

Maggie watched him and waited. His mind was engaged.

He came back to his chair and leaned forward, both arms on the desk. He looked her in the eye, unblinking. "Maggie, as I see it, you only have one way to go."

Maggie extended her arms begging for an answer. "Which is . . . ?"

"Jack . . . you must talk to your husband."

"No! No! Ward, are you crazy. I can't." she half-shouted, covering her face with her hands.

"Listen to me, Maggie, it's the only solution."

Her eyes brimmed. "I can't tell Jack," she said shaking her head. "I'd rather die."

"Hear me out," Ward said. "Okay?"

Maggie wiped her eyes with a Kleenex and nodded.

"First, if you don't meet the blackmailer's demands . . ." He stopped and pointed to the letter resting on the desk. " . . . you'll be exposed."

Maggie said nothing.

"Second, if there were ways to raise the money, say a bank or family or friends, you would have to give the reason for the loan. Bottom line: exposure."

Maggie dropped her hands in her lap, her eyes at the ceiling. Despair had drained the color from her cheeks.

"Third, do you have a savings account?"

Maggie nodded again. "But only what I've saved from teaching. Jack insisted I set up my own account and use it as I pleased. There's less than twenty thousand in that account, way short of bailing me out."

Here's the heart of my proposal: Pick the right time and place to make your confession. Be truthful, but minimize the details. You made a mistake trying to survive, just a teenager; made some foolish decisions and were guilty of bad behavior that you deeply regret. So ashamed, you kept it hidden. But you had an epiphany and turned your life around. You can't expunge the past Maggie, it's part of your history. The best approach is head-on." Ward stopped long enough to see the skeptical look on her face. "Jack is one of the finest men I've ever met. As you know, he is deeply religious and he'll forgive you. I'm sure of it. He may even love you more. Explain the Friday night phone call and let him read the letter. I'll bet the mortgage that he'll give you the money, provide whatever support you need and keep your secret until the day he dies."

Maggie walked to the window, her mind reeling from Ward's advice. The sun was still high in the sky and glinted the glass. Plenty of sunshine; mid-June, one of the longest days of the year. But she was oblivious to the weather, even the pristine landscape that lay before her. Maggie was consumed by the feeling of entrapment but buoyed by the possibility of extrication. That is, if Ward was right and if she had the courage to face Jack McFarland and find the magic words that bought her forgiveness and redemption.

She came back to his desk and gave him a kiss on the cheek. "Thank you for your kindness and your valuable time. No one will ever know the depth of our friendship. I would not be standing here were it not for our chance encounter at the Dunes a long time ago and the advice, a sermonette, really, which turned my life around."

Ward half-stood, his hands on the desk. "You're a beautiful woman, Maggie, and from the things I've heard about you, Jack is a lucky man. I am your friend and want to know how all of this plays out. Please keep me posted."

"I will," Maggie said and reached down for her purse. She stopped at the door and turned back. "Send me some positive thought waves, Ward, that somehow I'll find the right words." With that, she left the office and closed the door behind her.

CHAPTER 16

The following Monday

CHARLIE CHEN WALKED INTO Walgreens ten minutes before nine o'clock. No one at the checkout counter, the drug store was soundless. Once inside, through the glass front, he could see the pay phone on the opposite corner. Despite a light drizzle, he had a perfect sightline and enough illumination from the street light. He saw no foot traffic on Pryor or Stone, only an occasional car with headlights that cut the darkness. Charlie turned around and spotted a telephone beside the register, but he had yet to see a clerk or customer. Should someone appear and look at him inquiringly, he'd point outside, as if waiting for the rain to stop.

Charlie checked his watch: 8:55. He knew that Maggie McFarland would have a logistical problem raising the cash in less than a week without giving up her secret. He hoped she had been successful since his life depended on it. Thoughts of the *Snowman* were terrifying and, as always, sent a shiver down the length of his spine. Charlie saw the irony: his life depended on the guile and resources of a hooker bought and paid for a dozen years ago. "Thank the gods that be for the Polaroid," he mumbled.

He saw a car park across the street, lights on, the engine running. The driver got out of the car carrying a satchel and entered the phone booth. Charlie pulled the 3x5 from his shirt pocket; still no sign of a clerk. He picked up the telephone; the line buzzed while he checked the numbers on the card and punched them in.

"Hello." It was a woman's voice . . . on the first ring.

"Have you got the money?"

"Yes," she said calmly.

"The picture is behind the phone box. I put it there fifteen minutes ago."

"I've got it."

"Leave the money in the booth and drive away. I'm watching you as we speak. So do it my way and you'll never hear from me again. Otherwise, it will get messy. Understand?"

"Yes."

"Now go." Charlie placed the receiver in the cradle and quickly moved to the front. He watched her leave the phone booth without the satchel and drive north on Stone until her taillights faded into the darkness. He stepped outside and looked in all directions. The streets were lifeless. He crossed the street and picked up the leather case. The drizzle had become a pelting rain as he ran to his car parked in an alley behind the stores on Pryor. Charlie keyed the ignition and breathed a sigh of relief. He knew his plan was faulty; a dozen things could have gone wrong. But there was one sure thing Charlie could count on: Maggie McFarland would never betray her past.

It appeared she had come alone to deliver the money. No one had followed him, although his journey was not complete. Maybe it was his lucky day; maybe Yinglong, the Chinese god of rain was smiling on Charlie Chen.

Charlie drove down Pryor and onto the expressway. He checked the dashboard clock, plenty of time to make his 10:20 flight to Las Vegas. He pulled into long-term parking, shut down the engine and, for the first time, opened the leather case. It was filled with one hundred dollar bills. Charlie didn't bother to count the banded bills; he was sure it was all there. He opened the glove compartment and combed through the clutter until he found his round trip ticket. He picked up the leather case and carried it into the terminal.

Charlie walked along the concourse to gate 7. The flight from Atlanta had deplaned, and boarding for Las Vegas had begun. He sidled through the waiting area to a pay phone and put in a call to Mario Rossi. The sound of quarters pushed into the receptacle tumbled into the coin box and reminded him of the slots at The Blue Lagoon.

It was almost eight o'clock in Nevada and Charlie was sure the casinos were busy, even on a Monday night. A hotel operator answered the call. "This is The Blue Lagoon; how can I help you?"

"This is Charlie Chen, a Gold Rewards card holder. I need to speak with Mr. Rossi."

"He may not be on the property, but I'll check."

"Thank you, ma'am." Charlie used the time to check the departure gate. The business and first class passengers had boarded.

The phone clicked. "Mr. Chen, hold on and I'll transfer your call."

"Hello, Charlie. Where you calling from?"

"Dallas, but I'm on my way to Vegas. My plane is boarding as we speak."

"Why the late night visit, Charlie?" he asked, his voice raspy.

"I'll explain everything, Mario. Just be there. I have the money,"

"Good to hear, Charlie. A helluva surprise."

"Gotta go." Charlie hung up the phone, grabbed the satchel and hustled to the gate. After a stewardess scanned his boarding pass, he followed the jet bridge to the cabin door. When Charlie reached his aisle seat, he ignored the overhead bin and held the leather case in his lap. He had made a plan but it carried monumental risks. But so far, so good. It was no time to make a mistake. He tightened his grip on the leather case as Delta Flight 323 lifted off heading west.

Mario returned to his office from the second floor after a chat with Gino, his nephew who was in charge of the surveillance cameras. Barry McBride was waiting, his considerable bulk wedged into a cushioned chair. Mario stopped by the wet bar and poured himself a scotch on the rocks. He turned his head as if it were on a swivel. "Care for a drink?"

The big man shook his bald head. "Started my diet yesterday." He patted his protruding stomach, which stretched the seams of his extra-large sports shirt.

"Yeah, Mac, I've heard that before," he said in a sing-song voice. "Hope you get serious before you have the big one." Mario slapped his chest with an open hand. "Bam! Just like that . . . you're gone. Pushin' up daisies in a casket, custom-made, so's room 'nough for your fat ass."

"Nah, it's in the genes. My papa weighed three hundred pounds and lived to be ninety. Died in the nursing home, fell out of Clare Beaumont's bed with a smile on his face." A bellow of laughter; his belly shook like a tub full of Jello.

Mario settled in his desk chair, sipped his scotch and lit a cigarette. He looked at his accountant and detailed Chen's story. "He's holding some big-time markers. Called from Dallas a couple of hours ago; heading here to pay up." He squinted at the wall clock "Should arrive before midnight, our time."

"How much moolah?"

"A hundred and twenty thousand big ones." Mario began to cough, a violent paroxysm that turned his face purple. Finally, the bolus of thick mucus broke loose; it rolled around his mouth before he spit the plug of sputum into the wastebasket beside the desk. He took a sip of Scotch and another long drag from his cigarette as if they were cough suppressants.

"Disgusting, makes me wanna puke."

"Be my guest. But remember, Fatso, you're here for only one simple reason . . . to count the money."

McBride ignored the caustic comment. "My uncle Everett was 58 years old when he turned up his toes. Smoked until the day he died. Emphysema, couldn't breathe. Terrible way to go." McBride, with effort, rearranged himself in his chair and leaked a smile. "Did you know that fat men outlive smokers?"

"Look McBride, I don't need a goddamn lecture on the side effects of smoking." He held up the glass in one hand, the cigarette in the other. "I'm addicted, simple as that. So mind your own business."

McBride held out both hands defensively. "Just stating facts and didn't even mention the big "C." But don't worry; I'll say some nice words graveside before they stick you in the ground."

Before Mario could respond, the office door opened and Charlie Chen, holding a leather case, waited for an invitation.

"Come in Charlie. Glad you beat the deadline." He pointed toward McBride. "Meet my accountant; he's here to count the money."

McBride grunted as he struggled to his feet. He shook Charlie's hand and took the leather case.

"Have a seat, Charlie." He canted his head toward McBride who had moved to a table in the far corner of the room and turned on a desk lamp. "I hope it's all there."

"It's all there and more." Charlie had not counted the cash but the case was full of banded bills and he was sure Maggie McFarland had met his demand. "How 'bout a drink?"

"Help yourself." Mario lit another cigarette.

"And a room . . . for the night. I have an early morning flight to Dallas."

"No problem." Mario picked up the phone and made the reservation. "Stop by the Premium Members office and pick up your key."

Charlie poured himself a gin and tonic and took a seat beside the desk.

He was in no mood for conversation; here, only to be scratched from the *Snowman's* hit-list and a quick turnaround time.

"How does a guy who runs a small business in a strip mall come up with the big money? Rob a bank? Win the lottery?" Mario ribbed.

"Does it matter, as long as you get your money?"

"It's none of my business, right, Charlie?"

"Something like that." It was hard to hide his vexation. It had been a long day; a long flight; lots of stress and he didn't need to be teased or interrogated.

A lengthy silence and a thin mist of smoke hung over the room. McBride lumbered across the Berber carpet and placed the open case on Mario's desk. "It's all there . . . and more."

"How much more?" Mario asked.

One hundred and fifty thousand, all in hundreds."

Mario's brow furrowed. "Well done, Chen. But why the excess?"

Charlie leaned on the front of the desk, his brown eyes fixed on Rossi, the man who had made the death threat and put a bull's eye on his back. "As I said before, does it matter?"

Mario shrugged.

Charlie picked up a pack of hundreds, shuffled them like a pack of cards and looked at McBride. Two . . . three thousand?"

"Three thousand in each band of bills," the fat man said.

Charlie's eyes went back to Mario. "I'll take two packs to cover expenses. You keep the rest. Consider it interest on the debt."

Mario tossed a second pack to Charlie and latched the leather case. "I think we're finished here. Don't forget your key."

"Not quite. There was a note inside the case." McBride handed it to Mario.

It's for you, Charlie. But let me read it:

Don't come back for more.
It would be a fatal mistake.
You're not the only one with a camera.

"Sounds like extortion, Charlie, and your pawn, somehow, got your picture." Mario crushed his cigarette in a metal ashtray. "Better watch your step."

Charlie shrugged and left the office without another word. He wished he could fly home tonight.

It had been two days since the payoff. While the ordeal had taken an emotional toll, Maggie had work to do. Summer school was in full swing and even though the campus was more subdued, student counseling was available and active. Referrals from the dean's office and from municipal court judges knew no season. Admittedly, there were fewer appointments, but she was in her office each day of the week. Yesterday was an exception. Maggie had rescheduled her two Tuesday sessions in order to visit Dr. Hancock. While she had no overt symptoms related to the pregnancy, she wanted to be checked and reassured. Could inordinate stress—she'd had more than her share of it—cause a miscarriage? She wasn't sure, but it was better to play it safe. Of course she disguised the real reason for her visit; instead she expressed concern about a light discharge. After the exam, Dr. Hancock convinced her that the symptom was common in pregnancy and put her mind at ease. Both mother and baby were fine.

She left Preston Hollow mid-morning and drove to the University, past Jackson Hall and into the faculty parking lot. Maggie took the stairs to the second floor and stopped by Dr. Walker's office. She knocked. No response. The sign was there hanging from its hook with another pithy axiom: A MIND IS A TERRIBLE THING TO WASTE. Now she remembered: Dwayne Walker had left the country, a three-month sabbatical as guest lecturer at Oxford's Magdalen College. She went to her office, sifted through the mail, but found nothing of importance. There was plenty of time to stroll across the quad to her consultation room, an appendage of student health.

Maggie leaned back in her chair and wondered about Jack, something that had consumed every waking moment since her confession. She had taken Ward's advice and admitted her mistakes years ago, only a teenager. While short on graphic details, she did not hide the truth. The words came out haltingly and with a racing heart. She waited, fearful of recriminations. But Jack had only said, "Go on." She recounted the blackmail letter, the amount of the ransom, the drop site and the devastating consequences to both of them should she fail to comply. He smiled, one she would never forget if she lived to be a hundred. Maggie expected anger or torment or alienation, but saw only that smile. Maggie was incredulous; she couldn't believe his benevolence and fought back the tears.

"I love you, Maggie," he said softly. "The past is forgotten; we live only for today and the days that follow." He reached over and took her hand. "I'll get the money. Don't worry. Our secret; we'll be fine."

Lunch with Kit Emerson, an instructor in the English Department, and the afternoon counseling sessions were a blur as she drove home, her mind consumed with thoughts of her husband. Her gratitude swelled in her chest until she thought it might explode. Two questions must be answered. Did she deserve his forgiveness? The past aside, had she done enough for him to receive absolution? Then, where does Jack's grace and goodness come from? Maggie imagined ten men, similar to Jack in age and background. How many would have said, "We're in this together?" She answered her own question: Not one.

While she had expressed her gratitude in myriad ways, at the risk of redundancy, she would thank him again and probe the secret of his unmitigated mercy. She had heard sermons on the subject when she had accompanied Jack to the Sunday morning church service, but saw little of it in real time. Maggie knew the questions seared her own heart, since she would never be able to plumb the depth of Jack's love.

When Maggie got home, Dora was in the kitchen putting the final touches on the evening meal: chilled gazpacho and egg salad pinwheel sandwiches, along with pickles and chips. A pitcher of iced tea was already in the fridge. It was a change-of-pace kind of meal but ideal for the sweltering summer weather. Dora had also made a peach cobbler, knowing that a generous serving topped with a scoop of vanilla ice cream was one of Mr. McFarland's favorite deserts.

Maggie licked her finger after swiping the inside of the bowl. "Dora, you're the best cook in Dallas County."

Dora was a small woman with unblemished mocha skin and lively umber eyes.

"Thank you, Ms. Maggie. I tries my best."

"Jack and I are grateful for all you do. This is a big house, and you keep the place humming."

"I sho 'preciate that," she said. The compliment bowed her neck, those dark eyes on the floor.

Maggie looked at the wall clock. "Jack won't be home until after six. Think I'll take a shower and clean up." She tugged at her short sleeves and grimaced. "Yuk, I sweated right through my blouse."

Dora straightened up and carried the bowl to the sink. "It's summertime, Ms. Maggie, and we's got three more months of this devilish heat."

After dinner, Maggie loaded the dishwasher and put leftovers in the fridge. She passed the kitchen window; daylight had faded imperceptibly into a purple dusk. The phone rang; Maggie was momentarily startled. She picked it up! A wrong number. And a stark reminder of the blackmailer's call, only twelve days ago, with all of its ruinous possibilities. It had been a hellish nightmare, not the least of which was the fear of putting her pregnancy in jeopardy. She refilled the two glasses of iced tea and backed through the kitchen door.

The den was their favorite room. A large Matisse print in a gilded frame hung above the marble fireplace, an amenity they only used two or three times during the winter months. An upholstered sofa of soft velvet and a beveled glass coffee table fronted the hearth. There were two book shelves with Jack's eclectic collection of biography and fiction, including the complete works of Tolstoy, Graham Greene, and C. S. Lewis, his favorite writers. Hundreds of books, all arranged alphabetically by authors, was a gold mine for Maggie, who had become an avid reader during college. A color TV occupied empty shelf space.

Jack sat in his favorite easy chair, reading glasses perched on the end of his nose. He held a small calculator; a loose-leaf notebook rested in his lap. The TV was off, the room quiet. He was going over the final draft of a speech he was to make on Friday at the noon meeting of the Dallas Chamber. His subject: The financial impact on the Metroplex following the November election; Regan versus Mondale.

Maggie placed his glass of tea in a crystal coaster on the lamp table beside his chair. "I'm sorry to interrupt . . ." She sat on the arm of the sofa, leaning in his direction. " . . . but I have a question, a very important question."

Jack closed the notebook and placed his glasses in his shirt pocket. "Maggie, I'm never too busy to answer your questions. So what's on your mind?"

"I've thanked you countless times for your grace and forgiveness. There are few men in the world as charitable as you. I changed my life; left the dark past behind. I'm so grateful that knowing about those early years, you can still accept me, the genuine Maggie McFarland." She slipped down onto the sofa and placed her glass on the coffee table.

Jack got up from his chair and eased into the sofa beside her. He wrapped an arm around her shoulder and asked, "Now, about that question?"

She rested her head on his shoulder, her eyes on the vaulted ceiling. "Where does it come from, Jack? Your gift of forgiveness? Is it something you acquired, or is it part of your genetic template, like those brown eyes and broad shoulders?"

"Probably some of each. I was fortunate to have parents who gave me a moral compass; read bedtime stories, many of them from the Bible. My mother loved to read me the parables of Jesus and explain their meaning. Her favorite was The Prodigal Son, a father who forgave his wayward and profligate son and welcomed him home with tears of joy and open arms." Jack stopped long enough to relish the memory. "I was only five or six years old, but I remember her words. *We are closest to Heaven when we forgive.* Even as a young child, I understood my mother's message. How much parenting feeds into a child's character and conscience is debatable, but surely it plays a significant role. As a psychologist, you know better than I about the subject."

Maggie thought about her early years—an abusive father and a callous, indifferent mother. She had never heard a bedtime story or the simple words, "I love you." No wonder she couldn't get rid of those impenetrable emotional barriers. Was she capable of loving someone? Or had the trauma of those early years suppressed the will, even the inclination, to surrender her heart unconditionally? She looked at Jack and analyzed her feeling. There was respect and caring and gratitude, the ineffable pleasure in their "togetherness"; she was fully committed, and that was enough. Then an admission: a show of affection did not come easily, but she made the effort knowing its importance in nourishing the relationship. Were the words *love and affection* interchangeable? A game of semantics? Not really. She was sure love set a higher standard. Perhaps unknowingly, she had it; felt it deep within. Yet without a frame of reference, she could not define it, or with certainty attach a name to those deep-seated feelings of the heart. But they were there . . . for Jack.

Maggie gave him a kiss, stood up and reached for her glass of tea. "I'll let you get back to work," she said, nodding to the notebook which lay in the empty chair. "I have an early appointment tomorrow, so I'll say goodnight." She leaned over the back of the sofa and kissed him again.

"Sleep well, and remember how much I love you."

Maggie took the stairs to the bedroom, his words echoing sweetly, wondering as she often did how her life, once benighted, had changed so profoundly. How did it happen? She wasn't sure; nor did it really matter. It was reality, no doubt about it. She stopped on the top step and for the first time, offered a simple prayer: "If there's a God up there somewhere, I'm forever grateful."

CHAPTER 17

CHARLIE TOOK THE EARLY BIRD from Las Vegas to Dallas. He deplaned at 10:05, bypassed the baggage carrousels and went directly to his car. Good timing; workday traffic had thinned. Despite a steady rain, he drove to West Dallas in record time. He had a plan: clean up, change clothes, and head for Highland Park. No time for lunch; he needed to open the cleaners. Coffee and a pastry from the *Java Joint* would have to suffice until he closed the shop for the day. He knew that customers were surprised, and some irritated, to find the cleaners closed on Tuesday morning, but there was nothing he could do about it. The ransom and the payback in Vegas had been his top priorities. However, customer concerns spawned a sense of urgency to get the cleaners open for business.

Charlie unlocked the front door and went inside. He turned on the lights and went to his desk. He needed to deposit the six thousand dollars, but it would have to wait until Wednesday morning. While Chad Pomroy, his banker in West Dallas, knew of his trips to Vegas, he always arched an eyebrow when handling a large deposit, all in hundred-dollar bills. Charlie wondered why Pomroy cared, since the amount was below the ten-thousand dollar threshold in which the bank filed a Currency Transaction Report to the IRS. In the meantime, Charlie put the cash in the top drawer of his desk and turned the key.

Charlie felt an oppressive fatigue from stress and loss of sleep. On the other hand, he was buoyed by immense relief. He had paid his debt and removed himself from the hit list of the brutal Snowman. Did he feel any remorse for what he had done? Charlie looked ruefully out the glass front of the cleaners. He nodded abstractly and murmured, “A little, I guess.” But it was easy to rationalize. He had to find the money somewhere, and McFarland had plenty to spare. It wasn't some nefarious scheme for a roller coaster thrill or for some previous grievance. The blackmail was necessary because his life depended on it. Otherwise, he would sooner or later have been a dead man. He planned to put the past few days behind him, stay out of Vegas, channel every ounce of energy and effort into his business and keep his nose clean.

The note in the leather case was a minor worry. So McFarland had a picture of him. So what? It was a rainy night when the transfer took place. A clear picture . . . doubtful. Could the photograph identify him? Maybe . . . maybe not. But the note had implied it would be used only if he came back for more. No need to worry about the picture. He had no intention of blackmailing Maggie McFarland again.

The bell jingled when the door opened. "Morning, Charlie."

Stewart Apple was tall, stoop-shouldered, and wore a USPS uniform. He dropped the mail on the desk.

Charlie picked up the only letter and tossed the promos in the trash. "Thanks, Stew. Hardly worth the trouble."

Stew tipped his hat back and wiped the sweat from his forehead. "Guess it's a cheap way to advertise."

"By the way, how's the back?"

"Better; couple of aspirin and I'm good to go, at least for a few hours."

Charlie gave him a thumbs-up. "Glad to hear it."

Stew shook his head like a man with an insolvable problem. "Climbing in and out of that Jeep don't help the back none. But I can't quit; too much invested, almost twenty years." An afterthought: "Sure wish the damn thing was air conditioned."

"File a complaint," Charlie said lightly. "Send it to old what's-his-name in Washington, the Postmaster General."

"You gotta be kiddin'." A behind-the-back wave and Stew was out the door.

Charlie did not recognize the return address on the letter: Lloyd and McLain LLP, 1708 West Ohio Avenue, Midland, Texas, 79701. Could it be about his uncle, the only person he knew in Midland? He let his mind tumble back into the past. It was five years ago that his uncle met Patti Wang, a school teacher in Midland, who was visiting friends in Dallas during her summer break. His uncle was so enamored with Ms. Wang that he closed his bank account, cleaned out his safety deposit box, deeded the house to his nephew, and on a whim moved to Midland. Charlie assumed Lin had made a wise decision since he rarely heard from him. In fact, only at Christmas; a greeting and the assurance that Patti was wonderful and he was the luckiest Chinaman in Texas. Charlie made an extrapolation: Since there was no mention of marriage, they must be good friends or something more; probably living together. When his uncle left Dallas, he took his savings and stock portfolio with him. So Charlie wasn't concerned about Lin's finances. His uncle had worked all his life, lots of experience; and if the money ran out, which was unlikely, he'd find a job. And he had a fallback position; he could always come home.

Charlie opened the envelope and removed a single sheet of paper. The letterhead in bold script: a Midland law firm. He felt uneasy, moved his chair closer to the desk, and read the missive:

> Dear Mr. Chen,
>
> I regret to inform you that your uncle, Lin Chen, died on Friday, June 22nd of a pulmonary embolus, confirmed at autopsy. The site from which the clot arose was the pelvic veins, but the cause of his venous thrombosis was not determined. While the coroner was perplexed—your uncle was only fifty-four years old—he signed the death certificate.
>
> Mr. Chen retained our firm to draw up his last will and testament two years ago. He left a sizable estate, having invested in fifty acres in the Permian Basin. A lucky strike, a gusher, made him a wealthy man. After taxes, expenses and debt retirement, the estate is valued at one and a half million dollars, to be equally divided between Ms. Patti Wang and Mr. Charles Chen. Your share will not be available until the will moves through the probate process. As Mr. Lin Chen's executor, I see

no delays or discomfitures along the way. Regarding funeral arrangements, Lin Chen asked to be cremated and for Ms. Wang to scatter his ashes in the creek that runs along the northern rim of the Basin. No memorial service or marker of any kind. Please call me if you have any questions or concerns.

My condolences on the loss of your uncle, a level-headed and likeable man.

Raymond Lloyd

Charlie leaned back and stared at the ceiling. There were no tears, but he felt a genuine sadness, the loss of someone he cared about and to whom he owed so much. When he left San Francisco, only fifteen years old, he never looked back. He flew to Dallas to visit an uncle who was divorced and childless. Uncle Lin knew about his dysfunctional family and suggested that Charlie live with him. He acknowledged that it was one of the best decisions of his life. Lin was more than an avuncular figure; he demanded respect, dished out discipline while providing the guidance and support that a teenager needs. Looking back, Charlie characterized the relationship as warm and congenial. There was no show of affection, but Charlie believed Lin cared about him and had defended him in times of need. During his adult years, Charlie felt the ground shift; sure, they remained friends, but important connections were broken and the road divided. While they shared the same house, their interests and priorities differed. It could not have been more explicit than Lin's decision to follow Patti Wang to Midland and for five years remain incommunicado. Only a greeting card at Christmas.

Two customers interrupted his reverie. One left six dress shirts with button-down collars; the other picked up his dry cleaning. Charlie gave each a warm greeting and small talk, and though a struggle, spoke of the weather and asked about their families. Banalities, really. But Charlie believed a friendly engagement was good for business.

He went back to his desk and read Lloyd's letter again. For the first time, he grasped the size of his inheritance. The number jumped off the page. Seven hundred and fifty thousand dollars. His uncle had owned a restaurant for fifteen years. He sold The Mandarin House, the best Chinese restaurant in West Dallas, in 1977 despite the recession and still walked away with both pockets full of money. The Mandarin House had provided a modest income stream, and Charlie considered his uncle a better than average businessman. However, the return on the Midland investment was pure luck, like stumbling into a gold mine or winning the megabucks lottery. He was sure luck played a role in his own good fortune—a runaway who landed in Dallas, learning a "business" at his uncle's restaurant, winning a college scholarship and raised by Lin Chen; not as a nephew, but as a son. There was an element of luck each step of the way.

The inheritance, a godsend, would allow him to open another dry cleaner. He had already selected the site, but the deal was on hold until Chad Pomroy, his snotty banker, got the loan approved. Now he could tell Pomroy to take the loan and shove it . . . sideways. His inheritance would allow him to move ahead unimpeded and with alacrity. Lloyd said the will was plain vanilla and probate was routine, not a problem. So he gave the new location a name, Grace Cleaners, in memory of his grandmother. Of course, Charlie needed a full-time manager, someone honest and dependable. He planned to place a want ad in the Sunday paper.

Charlie slapped the side of his head when he realized the money had another dimension. Had his uncle's death occurred, say, two weeks earlier, there would have been no blackmail, and he would not be a felon with the risk of exposure. Charlie squeezed his eyes shut. "Wow!" he mumbled. "Talk about irony."

Mid-afternoon, he posted a sign: Back in 10 minutes. He locked the door and walked on hot cement, which he felt through the soles of his sandals. An hour earlier, the sun had broken through the rain clouds and steamed the sidewalk. Beneath blue awnings, he past *The Pizza Parlor* and *Flo's Florist* and opened the glass door to *The Java Joint.* Only one table was occupied, a student with his nose in an open textbook. He looked at the table by the window, a reminder of the Sunday sighting and that seminal moment when he'd hatched the plan.

Candice leaned on the register and assembled a smile. "You don't look so good."

Charlie shrugged. "I'm good, just not sleeping well."

"My coffee should pep you up."

"And a slice of that lemon pound cake."

Candice handed him the cup of steaming coffee and the pastry on a small paper plate. “Why don’t you go home and get some rest?”

“I’m okay,” he insisted, and lifted the cup of coffee in affirmation. “This’ll tide me over.”

“By the way, you remember a couple of Sundays ago and the lady in the pink dress?”

“Oh yeah, Mrs. McFarland.”

Charlie felt a jab of apprehension. “So what’s with the good-looking chick?”

Candice could not camouflage her curiosity. “She and Mr. McFarland were here early this morning and asked about you.”

“Really!” A look of surprise. He remembered the note in the leather case: *You are not the only one who can use a camera.*

“They seemed disappointed your place was closed.” Candice topped off his cup with fresh coffee. “I had the impression they wanted a conversation.”

Charlie knew what they wanted to say: *Keep quiet; keep the money. If you slip up, it’s a long way down.* He was sure McFarland had contacts that stretched far beyond the state of Texas, probably someone as capable as the Snowman. Not to worry, Charlie reassured himself, he would keep his mouth shut.

“Still wonderin’ what the McFarlands wanted to see you about.”

“Who knows? Maybe he wants to leave some dirty laundry.”

Candice pushed the air away with both hands; a goofy grin, “Get outta here, and get some sleep. It’ll put you in a better mood.”

“It’s irony, Candy. That’s all it is.”

“Irony?”

“Yeah, look it up.” With cup in hand, he left the coffee shop.

CHAPTER 18

Camden, March, 2012

THE SHERIFF'S DEPARTMENT and the district attorney shared a three-story brick building, adjacent to the Richland Parish Courthouse and with a scenic view, across South Grand, of the Ouachita River. It was officially the Charles H. Howard Building, to honor the previous Camden mayor. However, because it sat beside the courthouse, it was referred to as The Annex. For Carl the visit was homecoming, since he had served a decade as the D.A., long hours in a corner office on the second floor. Nothing had changed since his retirement, other than the completion of a parking deck behind the office building.

He turned off Calypso Street and onto a cement apron that led to the entry for metered parking. He took the entry ticket and waited for the gate-arm to open. He found a vacant space on the first level—a lucky break—and followed a covered walkway to the Annex.

He spoke to Spook Swanson at the security desk, the name acquired when Spook was nine years old. (Carl had heard the story more than once.) Chauffeured by his mother, Spook won the double-dog-dare of classmates to walk through Riverside Cemetery alone on a moonless Halloween night. Spook kept the name as if it were a badge of honor. After some friendly banter, Carl headed for the sheriff's office at the end of the corridor. He pushed open the glass doors and walked into the reception area.

Half-standing, shuffling papers on her desk, Rose Marie Rainey looked up and showed surprise. "Carl Sweeny, haven't seen you in a month of Sundays."

"Hello, Rose. I thought you'd retired."

"Gettin' close," she said. "I've been behind this desk twenty years come next October."

Carl noticed the changes; more gray in her hair and a little heavier . . . ten pounds, maybe more. Middle age had granted her no favors. "Don't put it off. Take the time to do other things."

"That's the plan. I've got a long list."

"Don't let the sheriff talk you out of it. He can be pretty convincing. Stick to your guns."

She shook her head. "Six months and I'm outta here."

"Is Bailey available?"

"Go on back, Carl. He's in his office."

Bailey Grant was in his second six-year term as the sheriff of Richland Parish. He had won reelection in a landslide. His notoriety soared when he took down a gunman who attempted to rob the Camden Community Bank three years ago. While shots were fired, no bystanders or bank employees were injured. The residents of Richland Parish admired his effective leadership and, of great importance to the electorate, his efforts to maintain a working relationship with the Camden Police Department; one that in the past had been splintered by petty jealousies and the overlap of authority. Since criminal activity often crossed geographical boundaries, it was for the *common good* to have the departments work together, rather than at cross- purposes.

Before his retirement, Carl had been in this office on countless occasions. He always thought the office reflected the sheriff's persona: modest and unadorned. No hanging pictures or paintings; only a wall clock, black numbers on a white face, no artifacts on the desk or side table. Beige industrial carpet covered a wood plank floor. No fancy window dressings, only Venetian blinds to tame the sun. *Austere* was the word that came to mind. *Frugal,* a close second. Carl had searched for color before, but without success; it was the perfect setting for an old black and white movie.

Carl knocked on the jamb, walked in and closed the door behind him. "Hope I'm not interrupting anything important."

"Hello, Carl. Have a seat." He closed his copy of *Sheriff Magazine* and pointed to a cane-bottom chair near the desk. "What brings you back to your old stompin' grounds?"

“Need a favor, Bailey. Figured you’d help an old pal.”

The sheriff, tall and sinewy, leaned back in his swivel, hands behind his head. “Let’s hear it.”

“First, I need to tell you about a woman who moved to Camden recently. Her name is Maggie McFarland, and she’s an endangered species.”

“Is she a friend?” Bailey asked with a twinkle in his eyes. “Or something more?”

Carl leaned forward and looked directly at the sheriff. “After my divorce five years ago, I promised myself ‘never again.’ My two failed marriages were enough, and I had other interests to fill my days. Didn’t think I needed a woman in my life. That is . . . until I met Maggie, dinner at the Seymores’. You know Ed and Edith?”

“Sure, nice folks.”

“Well, simply stated . . .” Carl hesitated and patted his chest. “ . . . Maggie stole my heart.”

Bailey moved up in his chair. “Sounds serious, Carl.”

“It was unexpected, right out of left field.”

Rose Marie tapped on the door, opened it, and brought two Styrofoam cups into the office. “I thought some fresh coffee would pep you up.” She handed Carl his cup. “I remember the way you like it: one sugar and a dollop of cream.”

“What’ll you do without her, Bailey?” he asked rhetorically. Carl looked at Rose Marie and winked.

“I don’t know. She’s made herself indispensable.”

“You’ve gotten a couple of phone calls, Sheriff. Nothing urgent. Buzz if you need me,” she said and left the office.

“Where were we?” Bailey stirred his coffee with a plastic spoon. “Your romantic interest and concern for her safety. Right?”

Carl nodded. A long look out the window, sunlight sparkling on the river. He came back to the moment and recounted Maggie’s story and how her work as a counselor at The Shelter in Dallas had created the crisis. While she had saved a young woman by the name of Rita Bynum from a destructive marriage, the husband was enraged and vindictive. The threat was clear: return my wife or I’ll come after you . . . meaning Maggie. Carl stopped long enough to sip his coffee. “The

Shelter's attorney handled Rita's divorce filing. Then after weeks of counseling and rehab, Rita was given a new identity and a new address, somewhere out west. Mr. Bynum will never find her. So, Maggie became the object of his anger and avowed vengeance."

"Bynum . . . the husband?"

Carl nodded again. "Randy Bynum." He slipped a 3-by-5 across the desk. "Name, address, phone number. "

"How can I help?"

"Do you know Lee Clancy, the sheriff of Dallas County?"

"We've met, of course, at the annual Association meetings"

"We need a picture of Bynum which Clancy will be happy to get through the DMV. The sheriff was a long-time friend of Jack McFarland, Maggie's late husband. Would you call Clancy and make the request?"

"Sure. Not a problem."

"Randy has already begun to stalk Maggie by mail. It won't be long before he makes his way to Camden."

"A picture would be helpful."

"It leads to my second request . . ."

"Which is . . . ?"

"I hope your deputies, along with Captain Graves and the police department, will be on full alert. My feelings for Maggie aside, I believe Bynum is a serious threat."

"I'll call Clancy and get the picture. The lab will blow it up, and beneath the name: A PERSON OF INTEREST. Bynum's face will be everywhere. I'll personally carry a copy to Ray and give him the inside scoop. Just remind your friend to take all sensible precautions."

"I've done that and more, but she's fiercely independent and absolutely fearless. It's another reason to worry." Carl stood up and dropped the empty cup in a wastebasket beside the desk. "Appreciate your help."

Bailey reached over the desk and extended his hand. "I'll let you know after I talk with Clancy."

"Thanks, my friend."

He passed Rose Marie on his way out. "Good coffee," he said and waved goodbye.

Late Wednesday morning, Maggie got a call from her son, Sam, an instructor in the Department of English at Colby College. He needed advice; urgent advice. Would she drive to Benton and meet him at the Student Union Building, say, around four o'clock? Of course, she told him. It was only a short drive, and the weather was postcard perfect. No need for details; she would get them upon arrival.

Maggie fixed a glass of iced tea and made a pimento cheese sandwich. It seemed like a good idea, since she'd only had her morning coffee and no plans for dinner. Maybe she and Sam could go to her favorite restaurant in Benton . . . *The Place Where Louie Dwells*. She had been there only twice but remembered the saloon doors, the dim-lit room, the haze of smoke, and old Rufus, who played jazz on a stand-up piano—the best she'd ever heard. Maggie also remembered tapping the table with her spoon as Rufus banged out the Bourbon Street Blues to a boogie beat. Any meaningful conversation with Sam had to occur before they pushed past the swinging doors into a room filled with a cacophony of sounds; noise, really, not the least of which was a piano player swaying on his stool, a cigarette dangling between his lips and running the keys.

Maggie decided to call Carl before leaving. Better to let him know about her trip to Benton before he formed a one-man search party, as he did the last time. She punched in the number, which went to his answering machine, and left a brief message with assurances that she would return home, although the time was indeterminate. She planned to have dinner with Sam, who at 6-foot-4 and 220 pounds was more befitting a Mafia Don's bodyguard than a bespectacled college instructor. And besides, the .38 was in her glove compartment. Talk later.

Maggie put on her dark glasses and keyed the ignition. She left Lamy Lane at three o'clock; a calculated drive time of forty minutes. She checked her gas gauge, which was three-quarters full; more than enough. After crossing the Louisville Bridge, Maggie picked up I-20, which ran through the heart of Benton. No one would call it a scenic drive. A bit monotonous, Maggie thought. There were long stretches of pine forests, a couple of country churches with their attendant cemeteries, and exit ramps leading to gas pumps and convenience stores.

Maggie let her mind drift to the earlier phone call. Sam's voice had a nervous edge. Maggie didn't probe; she knew it was important and presumed it was a call for help, or for professional advice. She would get the reason for his request soon enough.

Maggie was proud of Sam, even as a boy, always studious and motivated to excel. She was sure his good looks and ambitious bent were right out of his father's gene pool. She could not hide the broad smile or hold the applause when Sam received his advanced degrees from Columbia University. At the time she considered his three years in New York City a bonus . . . an education unto itself. While Sam wanted to become a writer (not a journalist), he was married and needed a job. She recalled the short story he'd submitted to *Esquire* while still a graduate student. Its acceptance was a pleasant surprise, and he could use the check for two thousand dollars. Maggie didn't understand the intricacies of the academic network, but she assumed Sam's short story, read by chance, impressed the head of the English Department at Colby, who contacted Sam and set up an interview. With his impressive resume, the college made him an offer on the spot—an instructor in the Department of English, teaching a course in creative writing and two courses in twentieth century fiction. One, American: Steinbeck and Fitzgerald; and one, English: Greene and Du Maurier. Maggie was surprised that Jane, his wife, was agreeable until she realized the move to Benton would place them thirteen hundred miles closer to Jane's mother, a relationship that had already caused a rift in the young marriage. Maggie wondered if the mother-in-law had intruded again, prompting Sam's wounded call for help.

Colby was a small liberal arts college founded before the Civil War; the oldest college west of the Mississippi River. Despite a sterling academic reputation, growth was stunted by a modest endowment and a bland location. Benton was neither a typical college town nor part of an urban mix, both more appealing to young people than a small, humdrum southern town.

Maggie left the Interstate and took the surface streets to the gates of Colby College. She parked in a lot behind the dining hall and followed the brick walkway to the student union building. Inside, she spotted Sam, his back against the refreshments counter. He greeted her with a hug and ordered coffee, which they took to a corner table.

"How are you, Mom?"

"I've made the adjustments. A move is always a little unsettling, but it was a good decision, closer to you and Dell."

"Why not Benton?" he asked.

"Camden gives us a little space. I don't need to hover over you and Jane like her mother."

Sam started to comment but changed his mind. He would get to that subject later. "How is Aunt Dell?"

"I've only seen her once since I moved to Camden. She's busy, still working as a floor nurse at St. Francis." Maggie's eyes roamed the room in reflection. "You know, Sam, she's four years older, and as kids that's a significant spread and may account for the 'wide divide' that separates us. Funny; it was never about sibling rivalry. Rather it was sibling indifference." Maggie stopped long enough to sip her coffee. "When I moved to Camden, Dell and I had a heart-to-heart and agreed to try and breathe some life into our kinship. An occasional phone call, a birthday dinner . . . that sorta thing." Maggie rocked her hand. "We'll see."

"This is my second year at Colby and I have yet to receive an invitation from Aunt Dell. So your aloof relationship with her comes as no surprise."

Maggie looked around the room, which was almost full. Most of the tables were claimed by students interacting at the end of a school day. Maggie counted three tables of bridge, a popular pastime, but there may have been others. Foot traffic streamed though the SUB, a shortcut from the science building to the women's dorms. It was different from her college years, at least as she remembered them; older than the average coed and with less idle time. She had gotten a job as a waitress in a Turtle Creek restaurant the first week of school, since she knew the money from Vegas would not last forever.

Maggie refocused on her son. "You called for a reason."

Sam loosened his tie and unbuttoned his collar. "First, thanks for coming. I'll give you the short version."

Maggie held up her hand. "Take your time. I'm in no hurry."

"Several weeks ago, I received an email from Dr. Mark Masters, chairman of the English Department at Tulane. They need to fill an assistant professor's position and wondered if I was interested. An interview could be arranged at a mutually convenient time. I talked to Jane, invited her to go along. But she was totally indifferent; she had been to New Orleans and once was enough. So I went alone. The interview went well, and I was offered the position."

"What were the incentives to leave Colby?" Maggie asked, swelling with pride.

"I've mentioned a promotion to assistant professor; plus a substantial increase in salary and benefits, a housing subsidy, oversight and contributor to the *Tulane Magazine,* grant money to support my work in progress, and limited teaching responsibilities to give me more time to write."

"And . . ."

"I'm honored to be asked, but I am truly ambivalent."

"How about Jane, her reaction?"

"Chilly. Cold as an Eskimo's nose. She was not going to New Orleans. End of discussion."

"You suppose her mother put in her two cents' worth?"

"No doubt about it. If Gertrude has her way, she'll gut the marriage." Sam took a deep breath and sighed. ""What would you do, Mom?"

"First, some advice about Gertrude and her relationship with Jane: Don't take her putdowns personally. It would be the same if someone else—anyone else—married her daughter. She'd try to undermine the union. The woman is a narcissist who wants to possess Jane under the guise of 'mother love'. In my experience as a clinical psychologist, it's a mental disorder, so pathologic that it's impossible to treat. As for the job offer, I would stay at Colby. The college has a fine reputation, and Benton, while a bit staid, is a nice town. Jane is happy here, and you have no financial worries."

Sam arched an eye, a quizzical look.

"Your father put your inheritance in trust until you reached the age of thirty. He wanted you to start out and make it on your own, the progenitor of self-esteem and self-reliance. You've done that, and he would be so proud." She reached across the table and took his hand.

"Invest wisely and your future is financially secure. And finally, if I were writing the great American novel, I'd rather do it here. There are fewer distractions and more writer-friendly surroundings. New Orleans worked for Tennessee Williams and Anne Rice, but it's not the haven for most aspiring young writers."

Sam nodded. "Okay, it's settled. I'm staying. Tomorrow I'll send a letter to Dr. Masters with my decision." Sam looked at his watch. "How about an early dinner?"

"Louie's?"

Sam grabbed his coat, which hung on the back of his chair. "Good choice; the best in Benton."

It was almost dark when they left the restaurant. There was a nip in the air and a scattering of stars winking overhead. They agreed the dinner was good, but Rufus alone was worth the price of the meal. Sam drove his mother to her car on the Colby campus. The sidewalks and common areas were deserted as usual on Wednesday nights, but lights burned in dorm rooms, the Regal Library, and in the steeple of the Brown Chapel. It was pitch black and deadly quiet in the parking lot behind the dining hall. Sam unlocked the car door, handed her the keys and helped his mother into the driver's seat. "Thanks again for coming, and for your sage advice," he said before closing the door.

Maggie rolled down her window. "It was good to see you, Sam. When you have a chance, drive to Camden and see my new home. Meet Pixie and Imogene, my ninety-something neighbors who seem to know everything that happens on Lamy Lane. I call them the 'gossipteers.' Bring Jane along; she's always welcome." She put the key in the ignition and turned on her headlights. "I also have a friend I'd like for you to meet."

"Good for you, Mom. Is it something serious?"

Maggie looked at Sam through the open window. "Just a good friend, and we've only known each other for a short time. But I find him attractive and I enjoy his company." She laughed as she started the engine. "I'm afraid he's ahead of the curve . . . time will tell."

Sam bent down and kissed his mother on the cheek. "I've saved the best news for last, something to carry back to Camden."

"Do I get three guesses?"

"Not necessary . . . are you ready?"

"I'm sitting down," she said eagerly.

"Jane is pregnant."

"Oh, Sam . . ."

"Six weeks, and the baby is fine."

There was excitement in Maggie's voice. "I remember when I told your father I was pregnant. While it was too early to know the baby's gender, he said, 'I hope she looks just like you.' Those are my sentiments, Sam, but more important, if it's a boy, I hope he'll emulate his father and grow into the kind of man you've become."

Sam banged the roof of the car. "Drive carefully."

Maggie drove out the gates of Colby College, back on the Interstate, her joy overflowing.

When Maggie got home, she was dog-tired, but relished the evening with her son. The news of Jane's pregnancy was an exciting and unexpected bonus. In the southwest parishes, Cajun country, they called it *lagniappe*. When Maggie went into the kitchen, the red light blinked; a message from Alice Fogleman on her answering machine. It was a request: Could Mrs. McFarland drop by OverReach on Thursday at her convenience? The director of the woman's shelter wanted to speak with her in person, and she would be available the entire day. Mrs. Fogleman left a phone number in case Maggie had questions or if another day was preferable.

Maggie thought about her schedule: an exercise class at the Preston Gym at nine o'clock, and the offer to take Pixie and Imogene grocery shopping at eleven. There was nothing else on her calendar until the Rhea Joslyn funeral Friday morning. So, there was no reason she couldn't meet with Alice Fogleman in the afternoon.

She deleted the message and poured herself a glass of wine before making the rounds and checking the locks on all the doors. It was a promise she had made to Carl, a security check before retiring for the night. She removed the .38 from her purse and placed the revolver in the top drawer of the bedside table. After a tub bath, she put on an extra-large golf shirt Carl had given her. No elastic or bindings or buttons; just loose-fitting, soft cotton, and comfortable. Maggie grabbed her Russo novel and slipped into bed. She had just fluffed the pillows and gotten settled when the phone rang. She groaned and looked at the clock; it was after ten. She bet it was Carl.

Maggie took a deep breath and picked up the receiver. "Hello."

"Hi, Maggie, it's Pixie."

"Are you okay? And Imogene . . . ?"

"We're fine. I'm calling to report an intruder."

"A what . . . ?"

"Tonight I bundled up and sat for a while on the back porch. It's screened, you know . . . to keep the damn bugs out. And during the summer, those pesky mosquitoes big enough to pick me up and carry me to who knows where."

Maggie laughed. She was always amazed that the two old gals had razor-sharp minds and an uncensored sense of humor. "You mentioned an intruder . . . go on."

"It was after dark and your lights were off. But it was a clear night, lots of stars and a big fat moon. Enough light to see someone in your backyard . . . as they say in the movies, 'casing the joint'."

"Pixie, are you sure? Night shadows can play tricks on the imagination."

"Imogene brought me a cup of hot chocolate and we both saw the intruder step away from the windows and check your back door, which was locked, of course. Couldn't give you any other details . . . too dark. The mystery man—I figured it was a man—rounded the house a couple of times, and then he was gone. Kinda scary, Maggie, so lock up tight."

"Thanks for the heads-up, and I'll see you and Imogene at eleven tomorrow. Don't forget your grocery list."

"We'll be ready. Goodnight, Maggie."

CHAPTER 19

The following day

CARL HAD A LOT ON HIS MIND. He sat at the kitchen table and savored his morning coffee. A light rain splashed the bay window and a March wind raked the leafless maples. Dark clouds hovered overhead, a perfect backdrop for his troublesome ruminations.

Randy Bynum was out there . . . somewhere, malevolent, with an insatiable appetite for revenge. Carl knew that many times anger, even red hot rage, will cool over time. However, his professional instincts sent him a different message about Randy Bynum, who got his kicks by taunting and teasing; the sadist's game of inducing fright and panic over weeks, even months, before extracting deadly revenge. Of course, Bynum misjudged Maggie McFarland, who was tough as shoe leather and immune to the psychotic tactics he had begun to employ. She was fearless, not a craven bone in her body, which Carl knew was often a precursor to carelessness. Maggie failed to see the fine line between valiant and foolhardy, a blind spot which added to his concern for her safety. At the risk of repetition, often an irritant, he would remind Maggie of imminent danger and the importance of vigilance and sensible precautions. Meanwhile, he had put law enforcement, both city and parish, on full alert and had been assured by Bailey Grant of their cooperation.

Yesterday, Carl had meant to ask the sheriff about the investigation of Rhea Joslyn's murder. Newspaper accounts were sketchy. A reporter from the *Crier* had spoken with Bertha and Jessie Franklin, the first to find the body, but they were unable to shed any light on the thief who fired the fatal shot. There were also interviews with distraught church leaders, all of whom were charter members of Southside Methodist. The paper published their names and reactions; a common thread ran through all of them. Money was the motive, but to harm Rhea Joslyn was unthinkable. She was the kindest and most caring human any of them, black or white, had ever known; a woman who unaided, at least in the beginning, had built a vibrant church, and by sheer determination and door-to-door visitation had improved the plight of several poor and deprived neighborhoods. At the time of her death, the support of these neighborhoods was still an important part of the church's outreach. The paper indicated that no one mourned her loss more than the residents of those deprived and disheartened areas of South Camden.

Carl wanted to become a part of the investigation. Since he no longer had the authority, he would have to fly "under the radar." Rhea's funeral was tomorrow at eleven. The church would overflow with members, clergy, and the curious. He was sure Bailey Grant would be there. Carl planned to corner the sheriff before he left his cruiser and ask the questions he meant to pose yesterday. As for today, he'd drive to the Southside and visit the Franklins. There may have been questions the police failed to ask. Carl felt a surge of excitement, drained his mug of coffee, and headed for the bathroom to shave and shower.

When Carl left the house, the rain had stopped, leaving behind an overcast sky and a bitter cold morning. He had lived in Camden most of his life, and years ago he had decided March, weather-wise, was the most unpleasant month of the year. During the winter, the town usually got a light dusting of snow; just enough to excite the children. He could only recall two heavy snowfalls, six inches or more, which made the roads a hazard and closed the schools and most of the shops on side streets. Both of those snowfalls had occurred during mid-March, a bleak happening that the locals referred to as the Ides of March.

Carl opened the garage door, turned on the car's heater and kept the motor running. He went back inside and refilled his mug with hot coffee. The *Camden Crier* was still on the kitchen table; another in a series of articles on the life and times of Rhea Joslyn. The last paragraph was an official announcement of the Friday morning service:

Bishop Ben Oliphant presiding; arrangements handled by Vickers' Funeral Home; condolences online were welcomed.

Carl zipped up his fur-lined jacket, got into his Acura TSX, and backed into the street. He headed south on Riverside Drive, a lightly traveled two-lane that tracked the river. After crossing Main, he picked up South Grand, the most direct route to South Camden and Poker Road.

Carl was sure the Franklins were home. Earlier, he had called the reporter at the *Crier* who had done the initial interview and requested a profile. The Franklins were in their early sixties and had retired early—Bertha, an elementary school teacher and Jessie, a mechanic at Ryan's Chevrolet. They were frugal; always had been. The reporter expressed surprise on learning the Franklins had no debt, a bank box full of CDs, and their employee health insurance coverage until Medicare kicked in. The reporter concluded admiringly that meticulous planning had allowed their early retirement.

Poker Road was rutted asphalt in need of repair. He suspected the reverend had spoken with the mayor, urging his Department of Streets and Parks to fill the pot holes. Carl believed Rhea Joslyn had leveraged her good works into political action in the form of voter registration; a sizable faction the mayor would not ignore. Game-changers like Joslyn were rare, and her death created a yawning vacuum. Carl wondered if it could be filled. Doubtful. Politicians often forget their promises when the air was out of the balloon. Only more pot holes on Poker Road.

The Franklins' residence at 561 was easy to find. A white wood frame house with blue shingles sat in the center of a small lot, which was graced with beds of purple pansies and English daisies, a colorful counterpoint to the brown grass and gunmetal sky. He assumed Mrs. Franklin had the green thumb.

Carl parked in the driveway—two cement strips from the street to the metal carport, cover for the Franklins' Ford sedan. He turned off the engine, climbed out into a cold drizzle and made his way up the steps to the front door. He noticed the wicker porch furniture, four glazed terracotta pots filled with cineraria and asparagus fern. Carl rang the bell and waited. It had started to rain again . . . a downpour.

A handsome woman, her skin the color of mocha, opened the door. She wore a house dress, and a wool sweater hung on her narrow shoulders. The visitor looked vaguely familiar. She had seen him before; maybe a picture . . . the newspaper. “Can I help you?”

“Mrs. Franklin, my name is Carl Sweeny, former district attorney for Richland Parish.” He pulled out his wallet and showed her some identification. “This is an unofficial visit, but I’m looking into the recent homicide at the church and wanted a few minutes of your time.”

Bertha unlatched the screen door. “Come in, Mr. Sweeny, have a seat.” She pointed to the upholstered sofa abutting the back wall of the small living room. “Could I get you something to drink? Just made a fresh pot of coffee.”

The fragrance wafted down the short hall and into the living room. “I’d sure like a cup, if it’s no trouble. A little sugar if you have it.”

“Make yourself at home, Mr. Sweeney. I’ll be right back.”

Carl thought the woman had survived twenty-five years of fourth graders remarkably well. The face was unlined, her step was lively, and only a few streaks of gray in her hair.

Bertha handed Carl his coffee and sat across from him in a slip-covered chair. “Jessie should be home soon. A down-the-street neighbor called about an hour ago; said he was having car trouble and wondered if Jessie would take a look.” Bertha stopped and grinned. “My man is so good-hearted he can’t say no.”

Carl cleared his throat and set his cup on the coffee table that held copies of *Popular Mechanics* and *House and Gardens.* In the middle was a black bible, the King James Version. He leaned forward, elbows on his knees. “Mrs. Franklin, as you know, the death of Reverend Joslyn is a terrible loss for all of Camden, but especially the Southside where she was an activist and advocate, bringing hope and good will and Christian charity to the poor and disadvantaged. Her influence on behalf of her flock extended to City Hall and, I’ve heard, all the way to the marble corridors of the State Capitol. A community center was in the works. Upgrading the two schools was a top priority. The mayor promised road repairs this summer. She had big plans to make the Southside a better place to live. It is a loss beyond measure.”

Bertha Franklin nodded and wiped her eyes with a tissue.

"I know you and Mr. Franklin have spoken to Detective Moody and a reporter from the newspaper. Perhaps you've thought of something else since those interviews."

Bertha shook her head. "We talked with the police, answered some questions, and passed on others . . . since we arrived after the shooting. Reverend Joslyn was barely alive, face down on her desk, blood seeping from her chest. Jessie felt a weak pulse in her neck, which gave us some hope. The police asked about the crime scene but we weren't much help, since we just wanted to get the Reverend to the hospital."

"Homicide swept the entryway and office for prints, fibers, and the like. Nothing evidentiary turned up. The gun was a .22, no casing. At autopsy, Dr. Swanson described the path of the bullet . . . through her heart and lodged in the bony spine. The investigation is stymied in that no one saw the shooter or heard the shot. And Rhea Joslyn didn't have an enemy in the world. Captain Graves did an extensive background check to be sure. Maybe someone held a grudge; a long-forgotten vendetta." Carl threw up his arms. "Nothing. So where does one start to find an assailant with so little to go on?"

"He stole the money," she said.

Carl picked up his coffee and cupped it in his hands. "You're right. We know two things: money was the motive, and the shooter knew—or it was a lucky guess—that Rhea kept a 'pastor's fund' in her office. She probably handed over the cash without resistance, so why pull the trigger?"

She dabbed her eyes again. "Crazy, sick, evil . . . take your pick."

Carl shrugged; his expression grim. "Maybe all of the above."

Bertha snapped her fingers, as if a light had come on. "Let me show you something." She got up and hurried out of the room.

Carl listened to the heavy rain pelt the windows. He remembered Ms. May Coker, his high school history teacher, had spent a whole week on the assassination of Julius Caesar and the prevailing political winds which transformed the Roman Republic into an Empire. Camden, on a smaller scale, had experienced a modern version of that tragic event. The rain pounded the blue shingles. Carl let out an audible sigh. Would the month of March ever end?

Carl could not avoid his mindset, formed during ten years in the D.A.'s office. He had asked himself some relevant questions and probed for answers, like a good prosecutor. Who would rob a preacher on a Friday night in her church office? Why not a convenience store or an ATM? Was it random . . . the shooter rode by the church and saw the office light on? Carl thought that scenario was unlikely. Highly unlikely; he was not a fan of coincidence. Okay, then did the shooter know Rhea Joslyn, or know of her? And that a bag of money was stashed in her desk drawer? If that were the case, the shooter was local, not an out-of-towner; maybe attended a worship service, then took his own tour of the place. Or he got the information from some other source; say a family member, or at a bar during an alcohol-saturated conversation. Carl had considered another mystifying question: Why kill Rhea Joslyn? The shooter could have tied her up, taken the money and fled. No one believed the preacher offered any resistance. So why shoot the woman? Carl put himself in the shooter's shoes and in seconds, the only logical reason popped into his head: He wanted to avoid identification. Perhaps Rhea had seen the shooter's face and she knew him, or had seen him before. Then again, his face may have been covered. Was there reason enough to pull the trigger? Possible, if he were on drugs or having a psychotic meltdown. But were drugs in the equation? Did Rhea say the wrong word, or was it a facial expression, even a smile that tortured a twisted mind? Release the brakes and the gun goes off. Carl had drawn two conclusions: The shooter was "local," and a drug habit demanded money. Drugs may have pushed the shooter over the edge of sanity and into a madhouse. While only theories, they were angles worth pursuing. Since Carl was out of the loop, he would have to tread lightly, but he hoped to share his thoughts—his conjectures, really—with Graves and Grant.

Bertha returned to the living room clutching a small object in her hand.

Carl moved up to the edge of his seat.

"Jessie picked this up when we were in the church office, right in front of the desk. Tell you the truth, Mr. Sweeney, we were hardly thinking straight and just forgot about it during our interview with Detective Moody."

"What is it, Mrs. Franklin?"

She unfolded her hand, palm up.

"An arrowhead," Carl said, bemused.

"We weren't playing detective; Jessie just happened to see it." Bertha turned up the thermostat. "It's a little chilly in here." She buttoned her sweater and sat back down.

Carl examined the arrowhead; black flint and sharply pointed. "You said it was on the rug in front of the desk?"

Bertha nodded. "The shooter must have dropped it when he pulled the gun from his pocket."

"I don't suppose Reverend Rhea collected arrowheads?"

Bertha shook her head. "No hobbies. The woman was too busy with the Lord's work."

"How about visitors, or someone who needed her advice or counsel? I bet there was a lot of traffic in and out of that office."

"Lester, the custodian, cleans her office every day, usually late in the afternoon. Vacuums the rug, empties the trash . . . that sorta thing. If that arrowhead was there earlier, ol' Les would've found it."

Carl turned the arrowhead over and over, as if some magical inscription might appear. He stopped the turning and handed the artifact to Bertha. "Have you ever been to the Indian mound off Old North Road, between here and Farmersville?"

"I planned a field trip for my fourth graders one year, but the principal vetoed the plan. It seemed like a good idea; a history lesson the kids would enjoy and always remember."

"When I was a boy, my friend Billy Folkes and I used to hitch a ride to Clayton's General Store. From there we'd walk through a pine forest until we reached the river. We knew the Indian mound was in the neighborhood." Carl's eyes lit up as he reveled in the memory. "We'd spend half a day looking for arrowheads, then climb to the top of the mound for a great view of the river."

"I think the state made the mound a historic site."

Carl nodded. "When Mr. Clayton died, oh, ten or so years ago, the family sold the place . . . about thirty acres . . . to a developer, who turned it into a trailer park with cement pads and an access road that ended in a cul-de-sac less than a hundred yards from the Indian mound.

But the park was private property and those who wanted to visit the Indian mound had no choice but to take the long way around, the same trail I took as a boy, through the state-owned pine forest."

Carl stood up and checked his watch. "I've taken up too much of your time, Mrs. Franklin." He looked at her hand holding the arrowhead. "I think we should give that to Captain Graves. Would you like me to do that?"

Bertha lifted herself out of the chair and handed him the arrowhead. "Please, and with my apologies for the oversight."

She walked him to the door and onto the porch. Sheets of rain obscured the road. "Would you like to borrow an umbrella?"

"No thanks, I'll just run for it."

"Jess will regret missing your visit."

"Give Jess my regards." Carl zipped up his jacket and turned to leave. He stopped short and said, "Sometimes, Mrs. Franklin, an observation gets lost in the shock of a gruesome discovery, but for some odd reason pops up later. Please keep me posted."

"We'll do that, Mr. Sweeney. And be careful on those steps. We don't need a broken hip."

Carl snapped the pocked of his jacket, securing the arrowhead, and hurried to the Acura. He was soaked by the time he was in the car. He turned up the heat before backing down the cement strips to Poker Road. The windshield wipers were no match for the cold rain lashing the glass; the road barely visible. Carl pulled into a BP station on South Grand and decided to wait it out.

He revisited his conversation with Bertha Franklin. Had he learned anything that might assist in the investigation of Rhea Joslyn's murder? He had the arrowhead, which may have been dropped inadvertently by the shooter. Then there was the Indian mound, a landmark he had not thought about for years, and its close proximity to a rundown trailer park. Was there a connection? Or just unrelated bits of information? Three dots; could anyone connect them? He didn't think so, but he would leave what he'd learned with Dray Moody, Camden's only homicide detective.

CHAPTER 20

MAGGIE PICKED UP IMOGENE and Pixie at eleven o'clock, as promised. It was still raining and the sisters wore their rain gear—matching, of course. She watched them navigate the front steps, holding on to each other, and shuffle along the sidewalk to the car. Maggie opened the door and helped them into the back seat. She had called earlier and suggested they wait for better weather to do their grocery shopping, but Pixie would not hear of it. "It's only rain, for heaven's sake. Don't think we'll melt. See you at eleven." Maggie was amazed at their mobility and hoped, if she lived as long, to have their uncanny balance, their iron will. No walkers or wheelchairs for the Painter sisters.

Kroger was much closer to Lamy Lane, but the sisters insisted on Safeway. The seniors' discount on Thursday pulled them in like honey bees to spring flowers. Maggie stopped at the front of the supermarket, beneath the overhang, and helped them disembark. She rolled a grocery cart inside the store and instructed them to hold on and stay put until she parked the car.

"She's worse than a damn drill sergeant," Pixie said to her sister.

"Hold your tongue, Sis. She's doing us a favor."

The two nonagenarians hung onto the handle of the cart until Maggie reappeared. "Got your list?"

Imogene nodded.

"Then let's get started."

Off they went, with Pixie leading the way.

After a light lunch and a short nap in her recliner, Maggie felt refreshed; a full recovery from her role as chauffer and guardian.

Grocery shopping with Pixie and Imogene was never routine; better described, she thought, as an adventure. But Maggie thanked her lucky stars—despite the wretched weather, she had gotten them home safely and unloaded the groceries. Her reward: a kiss on the cheek from Imogene and a word of advice from Pixie. "Be careful, Maggie. Last night, someone was messin' 'round your place."

"I'll be careful. It's a promise." She gave them both a hug and dashed through a driving rain to her car.

The rain had stopped, finally. As Maggie drove east on I-20, she saw an ephemeral rainbow with its arc of pastel colors and remembered its meaning, one of Jack's favorite Bible stories. She hoped he was right; the rainbow was a promise, the rain was over, only bright sunshine for Rhea Joslyn's funeral. Maggie took a second look, but the rainbow had vanished.

OverReach was a mile past the airport and north of the interstate. It was a brick Colonial painted white, a gift from A. B. Armstead, one of the wealthiest men in Richland Parish, and renovated to meet the needs of a women's shelter. Maggie took a long look as she approached OverReach. It was a handsome building with stately columns and a wide veranda.

On the drive to the shelter, Maggie thought about Alice Fogleman's open invitation. She had never met Ms. Fogleman, although Carl had given her high marks as director of OverReach. Maggie knew the reason for the phone call; the shelter needed another counselor. Why else would she have called? And who gave her Maggie's resume? She wondered if it had been Carl.

After getting her postgraduate degrees, Maggie joined the University's Department of Psychology as an instructor, and served as the student counselor for three years. With Jack's encouragement, she became a stay-at-home mom, but when Sam was eight she signed on at The Shelter with favorable hours so she could pick Sam up from school every afternoon. Maggie worked there for eighteen years. She had honed her skills during those two decades of counseling, and after her retirement, she retained her membership in the American Psychological Association and renewed yearly her subscription to *American Psychologist.* While she had moved to Camden to be near Sam, and hoped to cultivate a civil relationship with Dell, she had no intention of working again. She had looked forward to making new friends and committing her time and resources to worthy charities. With her credentials, Alice Fogleman's phone call was no surprise. A job offer? Well, it was a decision she'd have to make. Part time, possibly? But it sounded as if the director needed a full-time replacement. She would soon find out.

Maggie parked out front, a space reserved for visitors. She followed the sidewalk to the front steps, crossed the veranda and pulled open the heavy oak door. Maggie's first impression: the reception area was spare, not unlike The Shelter in Dallas. Two chairs in a far corner and a drop table with an accent lamp and a Tiffany shade. The walls were polished wood panels without pictures or other adornments. A young woman in a pink smock sat behind the reception desk, her laptop open. Her name tag read Madeline. She closed her computer and pushed it aside. The greeting was formal, much like a recording. Maggie had expected a warm welcome from the receptionist. After all, OverReach was a charitable entity similar to The Shelter. Helping victims of abuse and violence was its raison d'être.

Maggie was fascinated by Madeline's appearance; not model-worthy but interesting, flaming red hair cut short and green cat-like eyes. A scattering of faded freckles on her cheeks. But it was a vacant face, and she wondered if it could construct a smile. She made a mental note of this first encounter.

Maggie tucked her hands into the pockets of her jacket. "I'm Margaret McFarland, and I'm here to see Ms. Fogleman."

Madeline removed a key from her desk drawer and stood up. "She's expecting you. Please follow me." She keyed the lock of the security door that opened into the twelve thousand square foot interior. Madeline led her down a long hallway, past offices and consultation rooms, to the back of the building.

Alice Fogleman stood at her office window with its scenic view of the bayou, listening to the faint roar of a motor boat speeding downstream.

Madeline made the introductions and left the room.

Ms. Fogleman closed the door and walked back to her desk. "Thank you for coming," she said, and pointed to an armchair.

"Curiosity, I suppose," Maggie said.

"I'll get right to the point," Ms. Fogleman said. "We've lost one of our counselors and are in dire need of a replacement. You have been highly recommended."

Maggie wanted to ask "by whom?" But she had second thoughts. "Tell me about your charter. I assume it's similar to The Shelter in Dallas."

"We are a safe haven for battered women. While there are other causes for abuse, domestic violence tops the list. As you know, depression is often an integral part of the syndrome, and we have an on-call psychiatrist who works in concert with other staff members. We believe counseling is the essential part of treatment, both individual and group therapy. Right now, we are short-handed. That's why I called."

Maggie thought Alice Fogleman was well-spoken and appeared younger than she had expected. Mid-thirties, if she had to guess. She wore a pants suit but no jewelry; only her wedding ring. "What about your service area? It must extend well beyond Camden with a population of how many . . . maybe thirty thousand people?"

"We serve women within a radius of a hundred miles. OverReach is one of only two shelters in North Louisiana."

"So why am I here?" The question was pointed, sharper than Maggie intended.

"Would you consider coming on board?"

Maggie shook her head. "Full time . . . no, but I might consider three days a week." She hesitated and rearranged herself in the chair. "But it sounds like you need a forty-hour-week professional."

"We'll take twenty hours. Of course, salary would be adjusted accordingly."

"Not a consideration," Maggie said without pretension. "I'll get compensation from the good I may accomplish."

"Really? Are you sure?" Nonplussed, she could not conceal her surprise. "We are well funded."

"It's not about money," she said. "But I'm curious. Where does your support come from?"

"Some help from the state, a little from the parish, but most of it comes from the Armstead foundation. We are heavily endowed by Mr. Armstead and his family."

"What's the connection?"

"About fifteen years ago, his daughter was the victim of domestic violence. A battered wife. She wanted out of the marriage. A heated argument, the way they often start. Then, as usual, it got physical. Brad, the husband, threw her around like a ragdoll and hit her head, a crushing blow on the corner of a table. She had an intracerebral bleed and died two days later, despite heroic efforts by the neurosurgical team at St. Francis. Brad was tried and convicted of second degree murder with the intent to kill or do serious bodily harm. In Louisiana, the judge hands down the sentence, not the jury. Brad got a hard-ass judge who gave him life without parole at the state prison in Angola. Doubt he's survived that snake pit."

Maggie stood up and put on her jacket. "I'll talk with Carl this weekend." She buttoned up and reached down for her purse. "I believe you know Carl Sweeny."

Fogleman nodded vigorously, an affirmation. "A board member, and one of the finest men in Camden."

Maggie stashed the compliment, adding it to her perception of Carl Sweeny as she moved to the door. "You'll hear from me Monday."

"I hope you'll join us. And thanks for coming by."

"My pleasure." Maggie walked down the hall, past Madeline who was lost in her laptop, and out the front door into a bright, sunny afternoon.

CHAPTER 21

THE ACURA TURNED ONTO South Grand and breezed past the courthouse on the way to Rhea Joslyn's funeral. Friday morning featured cerulean skies, only a few wispy clouds. The day was windless and a bit warmer. From her seat, Maggie had a clear view of the river sparkling with sunlight. She thought of the rainbow . . . a promise kept.

"I met with Alice Fogleman yesterday."

"How did that happen?"

Maggie recounted the phone call and a brief summary of their meeting. "She offered me a job."

Carl kept his eyes on the road. "The Board learned of Ms. Roundtree's resignation at our last meeting. She was one of the best, the consummate professional. Alice spoke to the Board and expressed a sense of urgency in filling the vacancy. She was authorized to use whatever means necessary to find a replacement, including FirstFind, an employee search company in Little Rock."

Maggie turned in her seat and looked at him in profile—clean shaven, a patrician's nose. "Was Ms. Fogleman's invitation your suggestion?"

"Are you implying a conspiracy?"

"Something like that."

Carl raised one hand, feeling her stare. "I'm guilty."

She reached over and stroked his cheek gently with her fingers. "I thought so."

"You would be such an asset to OverReach. I didn't think it would hurt to ask." A shoulder shrug. "I told Alice to make the offer, but no hard sell. I made that very clear."

"Would you like to know my decision?"

Taken aback, Carl pulled off the road, kept the motor running. "Of course I wanna know. You just met with Alice yesterday."

She laughed at his look of incredulity. "I'm signing on . . . part time, three days a week."

"What changed your mind about, uh, un-retirement . . . is that a word?"

"I don't think so." Maggie chuckled. "Last night I had a glass of wine, sat in my easy chair and thought back over those many years of counseling and remembered how much satisfaction came from helping others. I miss that, and Ms. Fogleman's concession, part time with flexible hours, was too good to turn down. Really, it's the best of both worlds. I'll call her Monday."

Carl gave her a fist bump and then drove back onto South Grand. The dashboard clock read 10:25. In the distance, they could see the steeple of the Southside Methodist Church, the sun glinting off the gold cross.

Bailey Grant planned to attend the service and had said as much. Carl hoped he arrived early. He felt the arrowhead in his shirt pocket. Was it part of the answer as to who killed Rhea Joslyn, or an incidental and meaningless discovery? Carl wasn't sure, but he wanted to talk with the sheriff and give him the artifact.

The homicide occurred within the Camden city limits, the jurisdiction of the police department. Carl knew the boundaries of authority: he should give the arrowhead and his "unofficial" opinions to Ray Graves. However, Carl had a strong rapport with Bailey Grant. After all, they had shared the same building and worked countless cases together during his tenure as the district attorney. The feeling for Graves was not the same; a good chief, but the chemistry that bonds a friendship was missing. Carl reasoned—really a rationalization—if the trailer park and the Indian mound, both outside the city limits, were pieces of the puzzle, then the sheriff became a part of the investigation.

The church had a spacious parking lot which was almost full, although they were a half-hour early. Carl pulled into the lot and spotted the Ford Crown Vic next to the border fence, sitting on a patch of dead grass beneath the naked limbs of a towering white oak. He circled around the asphalt lot and stopped in front of the church. "I'll park and speak to Bailey. Save me a seat."

"Think the Seymores will be here?" Maggie asked, getting out of the car.

"Possible . . . check it out."

Maggie shut the door and climbed the steps to the church's narthex.

Carl watched her go, graceful and comely; my, how she had enlivened his life and brought bright colors to his drab landscape. He never dreamed of falling in love again; not at his age. But he had, and fallen hard. Carl shook his head at the *improbable* happening again. He looped around the asphalt lot, refocused on Bailey Grant, and found a parking place near a back aisle. He locked the car door and headed for the Crown Vic.

Bailey saw him coming and got out of the car. In deference to the deceased, he was out of uniform; just a black suit and bolo tie. He tipped his Stetson back and leaned on the door frame. "Mornin', beautiful day." Sunlight filtered through the gnarled limbs of the oak. "Just what Rhea would've ordered."

"I was worried, since we've had so much rain. Should've listened to Maggie."

"How's that?"

"She saw a rainbow yesterday and said it was a good omen." Carl pointed skyward. "Something about ol' Noah and the flood."

"I'm not a church-going man, but I've heard the story. If I've got it right, the rainbow was a sign, a promise really, that the rains would end and God would never flood the earth again."

"Well, the rain stopped . . . for Rhea." Carl moved off the asphalt as cars poured into the lot. "I have something for you." He removed the arrowhead from his shirt pocket and handed it to Bailey.

The sheriff looked at it as one might inspect a rare coin or an antique brooch—held it up to the light, rubbed the grayish-black patina, then looked at Carl and shrugged.

"I paid the Franklins a visit yesterday." Carl held both hands in front of his chest defensively. "I know . . . I know, it may have been over the line, but I saw no harm in a friendly visit."

"Dray Moody spent a lot of time with the Franklins and came up empty." Bailey shook his head as he reexamined the arrowhead. "Did the Franklins give you this?"

Carl nodded. "When they went to the church office on the night of the shooting, Jessie found the arrowhead on the rug right in front of the desk. He picked it up and put it in his coat pocket. Just luck; they weren't looking for anything. Too scared and in a state of shock. Rhea was motionless, her head on the desk and blood on her shirt. Jessie found a weak pulse in her neck and acting on instinct rushed her to the hospital. Neither can describe anything in or around the office of evidentiary value."

"I wonder why they didn't mention the arrowhead to Dray."

"I asked that question. Ms. Franklin said the police made Jessie nervous, got real jittery during the interview with Dray and the arrowhead just slipped his mind."

"I'll give this to Ray. It's his investigation."

"Look, Bailey, that was my intention, for you to pass it along." Carl moved closer, leaned on the front fender. "Remember the Indian mound on Old North Road?"

"Sure. You think this came from there?"

"Possible. And it's close to Trappers, that seedy trailer park."

"We've had to arrest a couple of drunken deadbeats who live there; a drug bust about a year ago." Bailey frowned at the memory. "The developers of Trappers went belly up and the bank is trying to unload an onerous liability. I remember the remark about Paula Jones, from one of Clinton's boys: 'Drag $100 bills through a trailer park, there's no telling what you'll find.' Trappers makes his point."

"The arrowhead, the Indian mound and the rundown trailer park may mean nothing, but Ray needs to know."

"I'll talk with him Monday." His face lit up with the possibility. "If there's a connection, the location puts me in the game."

Carl straightened up and tapped the face of his watch. "Guess we'd better go. Almost starting time."

Carl walked through the narthex and into the crowded sanctuary. Folding chairs along the back wall were filled. The balcony overflowed into the stairwells. He scanned the nave, looking for Maggie. He found her only after she turned toward the exit doors and spotted him. A wave got his attention.

The organ played the prelude as Carl maneuvered down a side aisle and squeezed into the seat beside her.

He pointed discreetly toward the organ. "What's he playing?"

A whispered exchange. "An old hymn, *Abide with Me.*"

"Sounds familiar."

"The composer, Henry Lyte, died of tuberculosis three weeks after putting the words to music."

Carl looked at her, amazed . . . speechless.

She leaned close to him. "It was Jack's favorite hymn and, always curious, he wanted to know its history. Whatever he learned, he shared with me."

Carl straightened up as the bishop approached the pulpit. The prelude ended, but his thoughts of Jack McFarland lingered. He had heard enough during the past few weeks to believe that Jack, with whom Maggie had lived for twenty years, was a modern-day version of Thomas More or Thomas a Becket. What chance did he, Carl, have to win Maggie's affection? She would make comparisons; it was just human nature. Would he measure up? Probably not. Jack McFarland had set a high bar, wildly successful in business and a gentle, generous, Godly man. His own career had spanned more than forty years, and he walked away with an unblemished reputation and few regrets. Carl considered himself an honorable man who cared deeply for Maggie. He hoped and prayed that would be enough.

After the bishop's opening prayer, the church choir sang a stirring rendition of *How Great Thou Art,* Rhea Joslyn's favorite hymn. Three short eulogies followed and carried a common theme: Rhea Joslyn was a woman of compassion and commitment. She was the embodiment of Christian service, helping those in need and bringing hope and change to beggared neighborhoods. Her legacy was more than a stately church;

it was her Christ-like spirit which reached out to the sick and the disabled and the disadvantaged. While Reverend Joslyn would be missed, her legacy had a life of its own.

The bishop, with gray hair and robed in black, stood tall behind the altar railing. His remarks were brief. "Rhea will never be forgotten." He let his arms sweep the sanctuary. "Her presence is here, the church she built, and in a hundred different places; all those lives she touched. Once again, she's heard the words of Jesus, the book of Matthew: 'Well done, good and faithful servant.'"

The choir sang the Halleluiah Chorus as eight pall bearers carried the bronze coffin down the center aisle, through the narthex and into the waiting hearse. The bishop gave the benediction and dismissed the gathering.

Carl drove Maggie home and reminded her of their reservation at The Rendezvous. He'd pick her up at 6:30 for an early dinner. Neither was sure they would feel like eating, since the funeral service, sad and pensive, had taken their appetites.

Maggie reached over and squeezed his arm. "See you later."

He waited until she was in the house before backing into Lamy Lane and driving away. Bynum was still out there . . . somewhere.

Carl heard the wall phone ringing when he entered the kitchen. He took off his coat, dropped it on the counter and picked up the receiver. "Hello, Sweeny here."

"Carl, this is Bailey. Meant to tell you this morning, but time ran out."

"It was a squeeze," Carl conceded.

"Well, the service was fitting and a well-deserved tribute to Reverend Joslyn."

Carl reached in the fridge for a bottle of water. "So what's on your mind, Bailey?"

“After you left the office Wednesday, I called Dallas and got Clancy on the first ring. Couldn’t have been nicer. He’ll get Bynum’s picture from the DMV and have his lab touch it up and make the enlargements. He’ll send a hundred copies, Fed Ex, overnight, should get the package Monday morning.”

“Sounds good,” Carl said. “I think I mentioned Clancy’s affection for Jack McFarland, which spills over to Maggie. He wants to help if there’s a way. Maggie called him when she was in Dallas several weeks ago to rescue Rita Bynum, her former patient. So the sheriff’s acquainted with the husband and his history of domestic violence.”

“We talked about that. He’ll try to keep tabs on Bynum and help in any way he can.”

Carl held the phone against his shoulder and uncapped the water bottle “Be sure and leave a stack of pictures with Graves. He has the resources to saturate Camden with the posters.”

“I plan to do that. We’re meeting Monday afternoon. Need to give him the arrowhead and the highlights of our morning conversation. I hope he’ll issue a ‘Bynum alert’ and make sure every man and woman in his department has the picture and understands Bynum’s a serious threat. Meanwhile, I want to work with him on the Joslyn murder. We’ve shared responsibility before, always amiably; shouldn’t be a problem.”

“Thanks, Bailey. Keep me posted.” Carl hung up the phone and took a big swallow, half emptying a bottle of Evian.

The Rendezvous’ parking lot was half empty. But it was early, not yet seven o’clock. Dusk settled soft as feathers over the town, along with a stubborn March chill. The warm-up Friday was either a godsend or a tease. He turned into the driveway and left the car with valet.

Chris Markos was standing behind the reservation desk. Carl was not surprised to receive open arms and warm greetings.

Markos picked up two menus from beneath the desk and led them past the rock fountain to a corner table near the back of the room. He seated Maggie and handed each an open menu.

“May I get you something to drink?”

"A glass of red wine for me," Maggie said.

Carl nodded. "Same here."

"Jason will bring your wine, a full-bodied cabernet sauvignon with the subtle flavor of blackberries."

"Sounds good to me." Maggie gave him a winsome smile.

""We trust your judgment," Carl said. "I'm no wine connoisseur, that's for sure."

Chris looked at Carl with a roguish grin. "I'm glad you had the good sense to bring this beautiful woman with you." He winked at Maggie. "Enjoy the ambiance." His eyes swept the well-appointed dining room before walking away.

Carl put his menu aside. "Are you hungry?"

Maggie frowned. "The funeral put a damper on my appetite. I've been thinking about Rhea Joslyn all afternoon. She was a woman of mettle who changed lives for the better and transformed some of Camden's blight. To me, it compounds the tragedy when the victim is so vibrant and vital. And I'm sure, in the case of Rhea Joslyn . . . irreplaceable."

"Well, Ray Graves has his hands full," Carl said, shaking his head. "The investigation of Rhea's murder, the 'Bynum alert', and other police matters will strain his resources. It sure helps to have a working relationship with the sheriff's department."

Maggie reached into her purse for the envelope and passed it across the table.

"It came in the afternoon mail."

It was another cartoonish greeting card. On the front was depicted a funny-looking kangaroo with sad eyes and an empty pouch. Beneath the marsupial were the words: I'M MISSING YOU. Inside, a blank page and four words in large block letters: BUT NOT FOR LONG. Like the first greeting card, it was unsigned. Carl checked the envelope, which was postmarked Shreveport.

He replaced the note in the envelope and held it up. "Let me take this to Captain Graves."

"My fingerprints are all over it."

"Along with the postman and a few others. No, it's not about fingerprints. Ray needs to know the game Bynum is playing; that we're dealing with a psychopath who is unpredictable and fueled by vengeance."

The waiter appeared with a crystal carafe. He poured each of them a glass of deep red wine. "My name is Jason, and I'll be serving you." He unfolded Maggie's napkin and handed it to her. "Are you ready to order, or would you like more time?"

"About five minutes," Carl said.

Jason placed the carafe in a table-side ice bucket and disappeared.

Maggie had debated whether or not to tell Carl, since it would only add to his layers of worry. On the other hand, he was her friend and, more than any other, wanted to keep her safe. She placed the napkin in her lap and sipped the wine. "Maybe I should have mentioned this sooner."

Carl interrupted. "I'm listening."

"I believe Bynum is in Camden, or he may have come and gone."

"Theory or fact?"

Maggie gave him an account of the Wednesday night intruder. "Pixie insisted, and her sister agreed, someone was doing a little reconnoitering. If Bynum drove from Dallas, he could have mailed his creepy card from Shreveport on his way here. In Pixie's words: 'to case the joint'."

Carl's eyes floated toward the ceiling, the lines in his brow deepened. "I worry about you, Maggie. We know he's out there, but where? And we know he wants to hurt you, but when? If I had to guess . . ." Carl hesitated and his eyes narrowed, almost a squint. " . . . Bynum is back in Dallas and will continue this game of cat and mouse."

"You think Lee Clancy could scare him off?"

Carl shook his head and looked at the fountain, water cascading over polished rocks. "Bynum is obsessed, and Clancy's warning won't frighten him or change his plans. He'd use the confrontation to his advantage: an opportunity to plead ignorance. He'd simply tell the sheriff he was angry when Ms. McFarland engineered Rita's disappearance. But his anger had cooled and he simply couldn't believe anyone would want to harm the lady, who was just doing her job."

"You think he's really that smooth and self-assured?"

"Absolutely," Carl said firmly. "During my tenure as D.A., I learned a lot about psychopaths, up close and personal. An example: they can change faster than a nervous chameleon—one minute charming your socks off, the next ready to put a knife in your back. Or as some wise man said, 'What you see is deception; it's not what you get.'"

Jason reappeared and refilled their wine glasses. He waited while Carl and Maggie checked the menus and gave him their orders. A half-bow and he was gone.

"Did you read Capote's *In Cold Blood?"* Carl asked.

"Saw the movie when I was a teenager. At the time, Dell was a junior at U. T. Odessa and came home for some reason. May have been Mama's birthday. She later admitted it was a mistake. Our parents were raising hell, feuding as usual, so Dell drove the two of us to the movie in Fort Stockton.

I remember it was pretty gruesome."

"Those two punks . . ." Carl scratched his head. " . . . forget the names, but they were perfect examples of the psychopath; affable and even generous at times, but they could turn on a dime, blowing away the Clutter family with a 12-gauge shotgun."

"I think Jack would have put them in a different category."

Carl shrugged. "Such as . . . ?"

"Consummate evil."

"Yeah, that too."

After finishing their meal, Maggie's cell phone chirped. She opened her purse and removed the cell. A frown morphed into a smile when she heard the voice.

"Hi, Mom. Hope I'm not interrupting anything important."

"Not at all, Sam. Just having a casual dinner with Carl, the friend I mentioned Wednesday evening."

"Just some good news, Mom. Dr. Rowe, the president of Colby, called me into his office this morning; quite a surprise, a promotion to assistant professor beginning in the fall. Apparently they'd heard about the Tulane offer and weren't sure of my decision. Dr. Rowe said, 'We want to keep you at Colby.'"

"That's great news, Sam. I'm so proud of you."

"Since we'd talked about the Tulane offer, I thought you'd be pleased."

"Oh, I am . . . proud as a peacock. And Sam, my friend Carl is sitting here patiently. I want the two of you to meet." She looked over at Carl with those engaging eyes. "Pay us a visit. Bring Jane."

"We'll do that, if I can get my wife out of Benton."

"Thanks for calling and sharing the good news."

"Take care of yourself, Mom."

The goodbye was almost a cliché, but she was glad Sam didn't know of the Bynum threat. He couldn't solve her problem and it would only add to his worry list, which included Jane's pregnancy and a meddling mother-in-law.

"You too. Bye." Maggie closed the cell and replaced it in her purse.

Carl pushed his plate aside and sipped his wine. "The message must have been special. You lit up like a Christmas tree."

Maggie mentioned the promotion. "I meant to tell you earlier, but with so much happening . . ."

"That's pretty remarkable, an assistant professor."

She reached across the table and took Carl's hand. "I also failed to mention that Jane, his wife, is pregnant."

"A grandmother. Wow! How does it make you feel?" He squeezed her hand gently.

"Wonderful, Carl, really wonderful." Happy tears trickled down her cheeks.

Chris appeared tableside unnoticed. "Is everyone okay?" A frown as he handed Maggie a fresh napkin.

"Sorry, Chris. A little preoccupied. It's been an emotional day," Carl said.

"How 'bout some dessert? Coconut cream pie is Chef Broussard's specialty."

Maggie dabbed her eyes with the napkin. "Next time, Mr. Marcos."

"Ask Jason to bring the check."

"Monette has it at the register." Chris helped Maggie out of her chair. "Come back soon."

When Maggie got home, she set the alarm and locked the front door. Carl had insisted on the security system and had called the owner of Ace Security to get it done, installation the very next day. Maggie was impressed with the timely response and figured it was a favor to Carl. The owner of Ace was either a casual friend or connected in some way. And there was this: in a town the size of Camden, a long-time resident with name recognition like Carl Sweeny, well, he moved to the head of the queue. It was less apt to happen in Dallas or in any large, sprawling metropolis. Maggie flipped the lights and trudged wearily into her bedroom. She closed the door and locked the deadbolt, another of Carl's security measures.

Maggie undressed, considered the golf shirt, but put on flannel pajamas (the March chill was relentless) and sat on the side of the bed. She transferred the .38 from her purse to the bedside table (the safety was on) and turned off her reading lamp. Exhausted, she slipped into bed beneath the counterpane and took a few deep breaths. At the time, she had not realized the emotional drain of Rhea Joslyn's funeral. And there was the second card from Randy Bynum, which put her on edge. It was not panic or even fear, which Bynum had intended, but there was a sense of unease and the need to be observant, darting eyes, a glance over the shoulder. She was sure, predicated on her training and experience as a psychologist, Bynum would not back off. There would be a confrontation; she just didn't know the time or place.

Maggie remembered the feral eyes and the high color in his face, the way Bynum appeared the day she drove Rita away. Recognition was not a problem unless he'd devised a clever disguise, which was unlikely since he worked for DIRECT ENERGY, a Plano supplier of natural gas with a no-nonsense dress code. So she kept the pepper spray in her purse, along with the .38 which she had been trained to use. She was neither feckless nor afraid to fire the weapon if her life was endangered.

Maggie rolled on her side and let her mind drift back to the drive from Louisville Avenue to Lamy Lane. Only a short distance and quiet all the way. Carl walked her to the door and gave her the usual reminders. The two glasses of wine emboldened him . . . a little. A goodnight kiss. It was the first, but rather cursory. No endearments. No embrace, only a shoulder squeeze and a promise to call. As always, he waited until she was safely inside and heard her thumb-turn the lock. Actually, she would have liked something a little more . . . romantic. But Maggie understood his strategy: slow and easy. After all, he had expressed openly his feelings for her—falling in love, which at his age was stunning . . . but true. On the other hand, Maggie had only admitted friendship. Nothing more. An uneven playing field.

While her body begged for sleep, her mind would not retreat from the subject spinning in her head like the wine whirling in her glass at the Rendezvous. How much did she care for Carl? Perhaps more than she'd been willing to admit. She was comfortable with Carl and enjoyed his company. But there was always Jack, embedded in memory, who had set the precedent . . . sky high. She knew it was unfair to hold Carl to those stratospheric standards. On her back again, she made a mental list of Carl's positive traits; he was attractive, with a strong jaw and a full head of hair. Only some wrinkles around the eyes and a little sag beneath the chin betrayed his age. He had retired with his integrity intact, or so she had been told by the Seymores and others. As a litigator and district attorney, he had earned the respect and admiration of his peers and the people of Camden. She would add: kind, soft-spoken, a Southern gentleman. And he was her friend and cared deeply about her wellbeing. What the heck was she looking for? Maybe that was the problem; she wasn't looking. But Carl had generated interest, more so than any other during the ten years of her widowhood. Friendship would have to do for now. She knew the passage of time would bring clarity and resolution. It was Psychology 101: A relationship cannot survive stagnation. It must move, like the flow of a river winding its way to the sea. But the river may merge with another; say, the Mighty Mississippi, or conversely dry to a trickle beneath the blistering sun of passivity. But there is always a chance, if it keeps moving, to reach the inviting arms of the ocean. It was a journey she wanted to continue. Maggie knew her mental exercises were foolish, time wasted; for in the final analysis, it was a matter of the heart. Assuaged, she closed her eyes and dropped like a rock into a serene and restorative sleep.

CHAPTER 22

Camden, March 15th

Dray Moody had been a member of the Camden police department for ten years; a street cop promoted to homicide seven years ago by Captain Ray Graves. Since the town had few serious crimes. Dray was also assigned a desk job with administrative duties. An honor graduate of the police academy in Baton Rouge, Dray's scores on cognitive function and raw I.Q. were at the head of the class. The test results impressed Graves, who at year-end reviewed all of the personnel files and decided Moody walking a beat was a waste of talent.

Dray was in his mid-thirties and unmarried. No social life. There were rumors. Graves neither asked nor cared. Dray's service record was impeccable. The detective's life revolved around his job and the support of his invalid mother, whose stroke had left her badly impaired. They lived in a modest three-bedroom ranch on Ryder Road with a ramp for the wheelchair that Dray had built himself. The location provided convenient access to the hospital and its free-standing rehab facility; City Hall, and the police department just across the street.

Dray had inherited his father's height, well over six feet, and the sandy hair thinning at the crown. Clean shaven and well groomed, he had a special affinity for cashmere sweaters worn during the cooler months, each day a different color. There were no Izods or Ralph Laurens hanging in his closet, only Club Room cashmere. His signature, along with tasseled loafers polished to a high shine. While his looks were ordinary, no threat to Hollywood's "pretty boys," there were women in Camden who would give up their country club membership for his (depending on the light) violet-blue eyes.

Dray remembered (how could he forget?) the night his father died. He was a junior, second semester at Colby, when the phone call came. Mrs. Howell, the dorm's house mother, awakened him. He tried to shake the sleep from his eyes as he stumbled down the hall and picked up the phone. The Moodys' next-door neighbor, her voice choked with emotion, urged him to come home as soon as possible. He asked all the scary questions, but only got evasive answers; non sequiturs. He imagined several scenarios that prompted a call at 3 a.m. but none placated his dread, the gut feeling that something unthinkable had happened to one or both of his parents. Dray dressed quickly while his roommate slept. He found his keys and billfold in the dark and took the stairs to the parking lot. A cold wind was like a slap in the face, but it got him fully awake. He started the old Ford Falcon which he had bought from Shelly Ford's second-hand lot with savings from summer jobs and his father's help. When he got home, he learned the devastating truth; his mother was disconsolate, her tears flowed unchecked. He pulled a chair next to her bed and felt the tremors in her hand. Dray laid his head next to her and wept.

Dwight Moody owned a pharmacy on Howell Road in West Camden. It was dark, a Saturday night, when the gunman came in and made his demands. Had his father offered resistance? Possible. Dwight had survived the fiery hell of Viet Nam and had the medals to prove it. So, yes, Dray thought his father may have tried to disarm the thief. If so, a mistake. Shot and killed for bottles of Percodan and dextroamphetamines. No witnesses. No casings or prints. The trail fizzled. After fifteen years, the homicide rested in the "cold case" file.

At the time of Dwight's death, his mother, a piano teacher, slipped into the black pit of depression. Since Dray had no siblings, he dropped out of college and returned home to provide encouragement and comfort. A year passed before his mother, with the help of antidepressants and Dray's steadfast support, clawed her way out of the black hole and returned to teaching. Shortly thereafter, Dray submitted his application to the Police Academy. Those who knew him understood his reason: law enforcement was the surest means of vindication.

It was early Thursday afternoon when Dray left the department and drove up Old North Road, officially State Highway 463. He put on his Ray-Bans and moved his visor to counter the glare from a bright sun in a "high sky." The four-lane road ran past fields of freshly planted cotton, forests of short-leaf pine, and an obligatory gas station and convenience store. Dray thought he'd caught the first glimpse of spring when he past Pillsbury's dairy farm; golden strands of forsythia entwined around wooden posts. He let out a deep sigh of relief; it had been a long winter.

Dray tried to focus on his mission: reconstructing the Monday meeting with Captain Graves and Sheriff Grant. He'd heard a lengthy discussion of the arrowhead, the only piece of hard evidence which was found in Rhea Joslyn's office by Jessie Franklin on the night of the murder. There was a consensus: the shooter had inadvertently dropped the arrowhead. If it had been there earlier, Lester, the church's custodian, who had cleaned the office that very afternoon, would have found it. Dray was impressed with Mr. Sweeny, who without invitation had catapulted into the middle of the investigation. He remembered clearly that it was Carl Sweeny who raised the improbable connection (admittedly a long shot) with the Indian mound and the trailer park. While problematic, Captain Graves felt it was worth a visit to Trappers, with orders to ask questions and get a feel for the tenants who made a crummy trailer park their home. Dray left the meeting thinking: *sometimes the obvious is overlooked.*

Dray believed the most important piece of the puzzle was the link between the shooter and the preacher. "Just plain old common sense," he said half-aloud. Dray was sure the shooter had a connection with the church—somehow, someway—or he knew someone who did. A friend? A relative? Overheard in a bar, or the pool hall in West Camden?

"A random robbery," Dray mumbled. "No way." A liquor store or even a fast food joint, but not Joslyn's office. It didn't add up. The thief had to know Joslyn kept money in her desk, and if logic followed, it meant a connection of some kind existed.

Dray was so caught up in his musings, he almost missed the turnoff to Trappers Trailer Park. At the entrance, a sign weathered gray by the elements issued a warning: NO TRESPASSING. He crossed a bridge of packed dirt and gravel that spanned a culvert onto rutted asphalt, a private road in disrepair. He drove slowly, a hundred yards or more, avoiding the pot holes, dead-ending in a cul-de-sac. A row of trailer homes, twenty or more singlewides, sat on fifty-foot lots, their fronts slotted east. It was obvious to Dray that these were not mobile homes, but trailer-rentals, placed for permanence on a cement pad. On the first pass, Dray only counted one unit that appeared well kept. He gave the renter high marks for yard care and the blue hyacinths growing along the sides of the trailer. He noticed the deck, which he was sure the tenant had built: pine railing and floor planks, brick steps leading to the front entrance. Vinyl siding had been added to each end of the trailer, and there were curtains in the windows.

He circled the cul-de-sac and drove back, slower still. At least half the units were vacant. *For Rent* signs hung in the dirt-glazed windows. Shut up tight, patches of dead grass, the yards overrun with weeds and windblown trash. While the occupied units didn't look much better (no *Southern Living* awards), Dray saw light and/or movement inside, no *For Rent* signs in the windows. A motorcycle beside the trailer was also a giveaway.

Across the asphalt road, there was a clearing choked with brush and bramble, which backed up to a forest of pines. In the clearing, mid-way down Trappers Road, was a metal shed which housed a coin-fed washing machine and dryer, both bolted to the floor, and a vending machine that dropped soft drinks and snacks rattling into a tray. The place had the look of abandonment, and Dray wondered who at the bank was in charge. At the very least, someone collected the rent and restocked the vending machine. But it was obvious the lender had no interest in upgrading Trappers Trailer Park or investing in a marketing campaign.

After several trips up and down the asphalt road, he clearly remembered his earlier official visits. Dray had been part of the drug bust a year ago, and on another occasion he responded, along with a sheriff's deputy, to a 911 call—a woman's cry for help; domestic violence. This visit was different; an investigation rather than a police action and an arrest. Still, he had a feeling, vague and ill-defined, like an itch in the middle of his back which he couldn't get his hand on. Since Mr. Sweeney may have intuited something others could not see or infer, Captain Graves, with so little else to go on, ordered Dray to check it out. Interview tenants. Get a "feel" for the place. He would start with the tidy trailer and its skirt of blue flowers.

He left his car in the clearing, near the laundry shed, and crossed the road. Only a few feet away, a rabbit with startled eyes scampered into the high grass. Dray bounced up the brick steps and crossed the wood-plank deck. He stood in the shade of a blue awning and knocked on the front door. On both sides of the entrance were pots of bright red geraniums. While waiting, he buttoned his blazer and popped a BreathSavers in his mouth.

A woman, older than his mother, cracked the door. "Yes?"

"My name is Dray Moody, a detective with the Camden police department." He scrolled his badge, eye level, across the crack in the door. "May I speak with you?"

Dray heard the chain slide along its track.

"Come on in, Detective."

He stepped inside the cramped singlewide. "I appreciate the courtesy."

"I'm Bernice Majors." She pointed to a sofa with floral slip covers. "Have a seat."

The woman sat in a narrow hard-back chair, legs crossed, hands folded in her lap.

Dray thought Ms. Majors looked older than his mother, early seventies maybe, still attractive. The gray hair was cut short, boyish-like, and the clear denim-blue eyes belied her age. Nice teeth, ivory white; he figured she was neither a smoker nor coffee drinker, probably never had been. A few wrinkles, which disappeared when she smiled. Dray bet fifty years ago, she had a pin-up figure and the face of the poster girl for Pepsodent toothpaste or Clairol shampoo.

Dray leaned back on the sofa, unsure of himself. As a homicide detective he had done his share of interviews, but for some reason, he felt out of sorts and not sure where to begin. He had seen a folded copy of the *Camden Crier* on the TV table and assumed Bernice Majors had read an account of Rhea Joslyn's murder and the funeral, with its overflow crowd and heartfelt eulogies of praise and applause.

Dray found the opening and cleared his throat. "Ms. Majors . . ."

"Bernice, please."

He acknowledged her request with a thin smile. “Bernice, I’m sure you know about the recent tragedy at the Southside Methodist Church.”

Bernice nodded. “I find it hard to believe.”

“As you probably have surmised, investigating a homicide in Camden is my responsibility.”

“I understand . . .” She hesitated a beat. “ . . . but why are you here?”

“The shooter left nothing of evidentiary value behind. Our forensic team made sure of that. However, the couple who discovered the body found an arrowhead in front of the preacher’s desk. “

“An arrowhead!”

“Yes’um, an arrowhead. Do you know anyone in the trailer park who collects arrowheads?”

She fiddled with her necklace, a gold cross on a delicate chain. “Sorry, Detective, I only know a couple of tenants; an old couple next door, and Mrs. Galloway, an elderly widow, three doors down.” The chair creaked when she leaned in his direction. “Care for something to drink?”

“No thanks.” He moved to the front of the sofa. “So those are the only folks you know?”

She gave him an affirmative nod. “For what’s it worth, there are two, maybe more, potheads who live near the cul-de-sac.”

“I saw a motorcycle next to one of those trailers.”

“It belongs to one of them. I’ve seen him ride by several times during the day and wondered if he had a job. Couldn’t be more’n twenty-five. No helmet, long hair flying in the slipstream, buckskin vest, tattoo on his arm; right out of the sixties. Reminded me of that old movie . . .”

“Easy Rider.”

“Yeah, that’s the one.” Bernice let out an exasperated sigh. “And at least once a week, they have wild pot parties and music blaring so loud you can hear it all the way to the bridge. Wouldn’t be surprised if they were selling dope right here in Trappers. Might explain how you survive without working; either that or food stamps.”

“I’ll talk with the sheriff, since these alleged stoners are on his turf. He’ll send a deputy to check it out. Even if he can’t find a stash without a warrant, he can nail them for disturbing the peace. Give 'em a no-nonsense warning, which may or may not quiet them down."

"I appreciate that, Detective. And tell the sheriff I'll be happy to talk with his deputy when he's out this way."

Dray removed a small notepad from the breast pocket of his blazer and reviewed his notes. "The Indian mound . . . ever walk over there?"

"Years ago, but not lately."

"Since we have so little to work with, only an arrowhead, could it have come from the Indian mound? I guess there's no way of knowing. It doesn't light up and share its provenance. I mean, it could have come from a hundred different places; you can even buy them online. So a link between the two is a stretch, but a possibility, though pretty remote."

Bernice put on her sweater, which hung on the back of the chair. "Sure you wouldn't like something to drink?" she asked while heading for the kitchenette.

"No thanks, I'm fine."

Bernice opened the fridge and picked up a can of Coke. She popped the tab and returned to her seat. "Where does Trappers fit in your scheme of things?"

Dray held up both hands. "No offense, Bernice. But the trailer park has a shoddy reputation. Its proximity to the Indian mound probably means nothing, but it's still in the mix of speculation."

"*The Crier* reported money was the motive. True or not?"

Dray nodded. "We know nothing about the shooter, but robbery, which went awry, was the motive. Joslyn kept a bank bag in her desk drawer and used the money to help members in need. For example, a parishioner was in a short-term financial bind or a church group needed some help to finance a weekend retreat in the Ozarks. Church records indicated she had about seven hundred dollars in her desk drawer on the night of the murder. As you can imagine, the bank bag and the cash were stolen. So, yes, money was the motive."

Bernice took a sip of Coke and looked at Dray with inquiring eyes. "Why kill the poor woman?" she asked dolefully.

Dray shrugged his shoulders. "We don't really know. Maybe she refused to give him—I assume it was a man—the money; maybe something she said was a tripwire and made him angry; maybe the gun went off . . . an accident. Until we arrest the shooter, we'll not know for sure what happened on that fateful night."

Bernice shook her head. "Everything I've read about the woman was glowing. She helped so many people. An advocate for the poor and needy on the Southside. Earl Crow, who writes a column for the newspaper, called her a saint . . . high praise, indeed."

"Why do the good ones go so young, while so many of the 'bad guys' live to a ripe old age?" It was rhetorical and Dray didn't expect an answer.

"You may have stumbled onto something that could be useful in your investigation." She stepped to the window and pointed down the asphalt road. "The sheriff needs to interrogate those potheads. They not only use the stuff, but I'd bet a hundred bucks they sell the stuff. Maybe one of those stoners is desperate enough to kill the preacher for money . . . maybe a customer, maybe another stoner from West Camden." Again she flipped a thumb in the direction of the cul-de-sac and added, "Only a theory."

"Are you sure you haven't done police work in the past?" he ribbed.

"Street patrol when my son was in grammar school. That's the closest I've come."

Dray checked his watch and replaced the notepad in his coat pocket. He folded his long legs and lifted himself off the sofa. "Thanks for your time, Bernice, you've been most hospitable." He handed her his card. "My phone numbers are there. Please call if you should see or hear anything of interest."

Bernice put the card in her sweater pocket. "Glad you came by, Detective. I don't get many visitors; spend most of my time alone, but I've made the adjustments."

"Well, your place looks awfully nice; can't say the same for the rest of Trappers."

"I'm fortunate to have a grandson who comes by once a week and tends to the yard and take me grocery shopping. Don't know what I'd do without him."

Dray had other questions—about her family, personal questions—but decided to hold them in abeyance, should there be another time. As he stood on the deck and said goodbye, the roar of a motorcycle raced down the asphalt.

"See what I mean?" Another vexed look. "Drive safely, Detective."

CHAPTER 23

Camden, Friday, March 16th

RHEA JOSLYN HAD BEEN ON Maggie's mind since the funeral a week ago. While she had never met the preacher, the testimony of so many made it clear that she was a woman whose commitment and compassion were immeasurable. Maggie had asked Carl for more insight and background, but he was unable to fill in the blanks. He admitted their paths had crossed briefly several times in the past, but his store of information was limited and unable to expand on the *Crier's* accounts of Rhea's life. Maggie's most pressing question was simply this: Whose influence set Rhea on the path of selflessness and good works? Was she born with altruism embedded in her DNA? Or did she, like the Apostle Paul, have a *Damarcus Road* experience? They were the same questions she had asked about Jack McFarland, who, while not a man of the cloth, lived a life of nobility and benevolence, leaving a legacy of goodwill and generosity. She still carried those sweet memories of Jack, like the lingering refrain of an old Rogers and Hammerstein song.

She had made the admission and asked the question more than once. For many years, Jack had possessed her heart. Was there room for another? There had been other suitors after his death, but at best, each was only a weak shadow—nothing more—of the man who gave her unrequited love. At least Carl had cracked the door; a pleasant surprise. But could he open it further? She still wasn't sure.

Maggie put on her flannels and crawled into bed. She turned off thoughts of Rhea Joslyn and replaced them with those of Carl Sweeny. It had been a "fun night" out—hamburgers, fries and a soft drink at The Blue Light, a movie at the Paramount, *The Help* (her choice, not his) and a stroll down Main Street, holding hands like teenagers, to Starbucks for a cup of espresso. Once she was home, Carl gave her another goodnight kiss (this time with feeling). She grabbed the lapels of his jacket and kissed him again. "Goodnight, Carl."

He keyed the lock for her, his spirits inflated. As usual, Carl waited beside his car until she was safely inside and had locked the door before he drove away, humming that old Sinatra tune.

The phone rang and awakened Maggie from a sound sleep. She picked up the receiver. A sluggish, "Yeah."

No one spoke. But she heard the breathing. Or thought she did. Then a click and the line went dead. She sat on the side of the bed and tried to clear her head. Had she heard something? Or was it her imagination? Could it have been phantasmagoria? Or had she been dreaming? Maybe simple confusion. Maggie believed she was half-asleep during that brief period of not more than ten or fifteen seconds. Now wide awake, she put on her robe and padded a bit unsteadily into the kitchen. She poured herself a glass of milk and sat at the breakfast table. A swatch of moon-glow filtered through the window above the sink, a ghost light in the darkness. She leaned across the table and squinted at the wall clock—2:35—then sat back and considered the possibilities. A wrong number made the most sense. But the heavy breathing stoked her memory of Charlie Chen's phone call a long time ago. Naturally, the image of Randy Bynum appeared; a crystal-clear, overblown photograph in her mind's eye. Maggie took a swallow of milk and drummed the table with her other hand. It had to be Bynum, she convinced herself; playing his game, as Carl had described it, of cat and mouse. Meanwhile, there was little she could do to change the dynamics that Bynum had set in motion. He was bent on vengeance and a confrontation seemed inevitable, even though the Camden police, thanks to Lee Clancy, had posted Bynum's picture all over town. Of course *persona non grata* meant nothing to Bynum, who could avoid recognition with a clever disguise or carry out his crazy/evil (take your pick) objective in the dark of night.

Maggie moved to the window, bathed in moonlight, and leaned on the sink. Was there any benefit in tracing the call? She knew Carl had the contacts and could make it happen. But Bynum was not stupid and would have used a pay phone, never his cell or a landline. Would she feel any different, maybe relieved, if the call was a wrong number? Probably not. Regardless, the chase was on; she was the pursued and sooner or later, as with any contest, even the most deadly, there would be a winner and a loser.

Maggie, steadier now, went back to her bedroom, opened the drawer of the night table and removed the pearl-handled .38. She double checked the safety before polishing the gun with the hem of the sheet. The house was a fortress with every security measure imaginable. Carl had seen to that, and she had kept her promise, which morphed into a compulsion, to bolt the doors and set the alarm. But Maggie had no intention of becoming a prisoner in her own home. Outside . . . well, added risks. Bynum could be anywhere at any time, despite the flyers and "Bynum alert." She would be careful and circumspect. While he had the edge, she had better than average intuition and 20/20 (without glasses) vision, and—Maggie held up the gun, the silver barrel glinted in lamplight—a weapon. "I'll use it without compunction to defend myself," she muttered with a grim expression. She replaced the gun in the drawer, turned off the table lamp, and slipped back under the comforter. Sleep might or might not come easily, which was okay, since she had a lot on her mind.

The next morning, Edith picked Maggie up at 11:45 as planned; lunch at Renee's Tea Room on Riverside Drive with its sweeping view of the Ouachita, its banks covered with lush vegetation. Maggie put the disquieting phone call aside as they left Lamy Lane beneath azure skies and the sprouting of daffodils, the prelude to a long-awaited spring. While Bynum's threat was ever-present, she intended to enjoy her time with Edith, who had befriended her and introduced her to Carl Sweeny. As she recalled, almost in disbelief, the Seymores' dinner had been only a month ago. "Only a month?" Maggie asked herself. "So much has happened, is it possible?" The reality took her breath away.

During the drive to the Tea Room, Edith handed Maggie a clipping from *Jes Ramblin',* a weekly column in the *Crier*; news and gossip of local interest.

Maggie dug her reading glasses from her purse and slipped then on. She unfolded the clipping and read the vignette:

A year after the untimely death of Almar "Al" Jorgensen, his widow, Renee, bought the once-stately Victorian home on Riverside Drive, which was weather-worn, victimized by neglect and sorely in need of repair. Mrs. Jorgensen made a major commitment to restore the old lady to her former imposing self. The interior was redesigned, a staircase with mahogany railings and balusters; bedrooms, baths, and study on the second level; a commercial kitchen, a small office and the dining area on the first floor. Hardwood floors buffed to a high shine replaced shag carpet, which had trapped dust mites and flakes of human skin like half-penny nails to a magnet. Six Drysdale watercolors graced the dining room walls with warm colors and a pleasing visual experience. It is no surprise that Renee's Tea room, which features fine dining and attentive service, has become a venue of choice for many of Camden's *bon vivants.*

Maggie returned the clipping. "This town has some remarkable women. I'd like to meet Mrs. Jorgensen."

A young waitress appeared and took their order. She filled their water glasses, smiled dutifully and sidled between tables back to the kitchen.

After scanning the room, Edith shook her head. "I don't see Renee, but we'll ask on our way out."

Once they were seated, Maggie took a long look at her friend and wondered if something was wrong. Edith was not her usual convivial self. *Languid.* Her easy smile was missing; so was the sparkle in her hazel eyes. Unlike the Edith of old, she had lost her contagious laugh. *Subdued.* There were lines in her face Maggie had not seen before. *Worry lines.* So should she ask? As a psychologist, Maggie knew that sometimes sharing a problem was helpful. But she would frame her question carefully.

"Edith, you look a bit . . . melancholy, not your usual cheerful self. If it's a private matter, I understand. But if I can help in any way, please . . ."

"It's Ed," she said.

"What about Ed?"

A tear slipped down her cheek. Edith wiped her eyes with the napkin.

The waitress brought cups of hot tea; the interruption allowed Edith time to regain her composure. "He went to see Dr. Cooper for his annual physical. Felt fine. No complaints. We went back for reports and were shocked to learn his PSA was elevated."

Maggie hunched her shoulders. "The acronym?"

"It's the blood test for prostate cancer."

Maggie didn't have the context, but she had heard somewhere that most men with prostate cancer did pretty well. But Jack's pancreatic cancer had taken malignancy to another level, and his oncologist had little to offer. Chemotherapy would buy a few months, but the side effects were brutal, and Jack chose to forego chemo and enjoy the quality time that was left. Only four months and he was gone. Maggie stayed close, often at the bedside, attentive and in her own way suffering vicariously. It had been ten years since her tragic loss, but the treasured memories of their time together were there and always would be. And why not? Jack had given her infinite love and so much more. As a young waitress at Rustler's Steakhouse in Dallas, the gifts of grace and forgiveness from any man were unfathomable—and yet Jack had bestowed them lavishly; no strings attached during their courtship and twenty years of marriage. For the transforming changes in her life (there were more than a few), he deserved the credit. *Her man for all seasons.*

"Dr. Cooper repeated the blood test with the same result." Edith took a deep breath, a sigh of dejection. "He referred us to Dr. Brice Greene, the urologist who did the biopsy, which unfortunately confirmed our worst fears."

Maggie stirred a pack of Splenda into her cup of tea. "From what I've read, there are treatment options. Right?"

Edith nodded. "Dr. Greene took us through the process step by step. He said the pathologist can grade the aggressiveness of the tumor cell and give it a number between 2 and 10 . . . the lower, the better. Ed's score was four."

"So that's a positive?"

Edith nodded again. "With age and general health factored into the equation, Dr. Greene gave Ed a pep talk, very optimistic. He laid out the options: surgery, irradiation or regular surveillance. Each had a downside, and he asked that we read the brochure he had given us earlier. Bottom line: Ed's profile allowed him to choose one of the three alternatives.

"Before leaving the office, Dr. Greene gave Ed some 'common sense' advice. 'Take a week and think it over. Read the material I've given you. Call if you have questions. A final caveat: do not talk to friends or family about the problem. It will only create angst, maybe downright confusion.' It must be human nature, since these folks always tell you the worst case scenarios; the awful things that happened to Uncle Will."

"Have you made a decision?" Maggie asked.

"We talked about the various treatments options at length. Ed decided, after a few days of our back-and-forth, to go with surveillance."

"Which means. . . . ?"

"He checks his PSA every six months and hopes and prays it remains stable. Should there be a spike in the number, then the other options are back on the table."

The waitress reappeared with their soup and finger sandwiches. "More tea?"

Maggie politely waved her off. "It sounds like a sensible decision, Edith."

"It was Ed's choice, but I'll do the worrying. The week before the blood test, my anxiety will rise sky-high." Edith fully extended an arm to make the point.

Maggie reached across the table and took her other hand. "If I can ever do anything to help, please let me know."

After the women finished lunch, Maggie reached for the check. She left cash and the check on the table. A final look around. "I still don't see Mrs. Jorgensen."

Edith pushed her chair back. "We'll catch her next time. And it'll be my treat."

The Schulze Building (named in honor of a former city judge) on Wood Street, across from the hospital, housed the police department and the city jail. The courtroom and judge's chambers were on the first floor, along with the city attorney and other administrative offices. While the Schulze, a two-story brick rectangle, was five blocks from the courthouse, modern technology had abridged the distance between the sheriff of Richland Parish and Camden's chief of police. It was in part responsible for their effective partnership, while many law enforcement agencies in towns like Camden were at odds with each other rather than working in tandem.

Dray Moody pulled the unmarked police car into the parking space. It was Saturday morning; the sun had just cleared the horizon. He crossed the terrazzo and took the stairs to the second floor. Captain Graves' door was closed, but near the landing he noticed the break table with the coffee maker, its red light shining. Dray looked around and saw no one; he checked his watch: 7:30. He had missed the captain yesterday but assumed he'd made the morning coffee and imagined a Do Not Disturb sign on his office door. But he had a report to give Graves, and with only a few notes from his Thursday meeting with Bernice Majors, he was afraid his account would be incomplete. He stepped forward with a cup in one hand and tapped the doorframe with the other.

"Come in!" The voice was unmistakable . . . deep bass, authoritative.

Dray opened the door and stepped inside. When the captain didn't look up, he settled into a chair near the desk and waited. He had learned the hard way, years ago, that it was unwise to interrupt the captain when he was in the middle of "something." He guessed it was a personal letter or an official report of some kind, since he noticed a scatter of mail on the desk, which was usually uncluttered and spotless. *Compulsive.* Dray figured habits formed during twenty years in the Army were ingrained like zinc and copper in a brass bowl.

Ray Graves had gray hair, crew cut since his Army (Military Police) days. The steel-blue eyes were laser-like, always probing, penetrating. While not a big man, he had kept his military bearing. A daily three-mile run along the river kept him fit and trim. The old saw made the rounds in the department: *You can take the man out of the Army, but you can't take West Point out of the man.*

Dray knew the story: After discharge as Brigade Commander at Fort Leonard Wood, a dozen years ago, he returned to Camden, his home town. Still in his prime, his mid-forties, the City Council offered him his current job. He deplaned and hit the ground running. Most of the folks in Camden wondered why he didn't take a break . . . a vacation, a few months of R-and-R. The Council had said as much; the job would still be his. Dray never heard the real reason but figured the captain found the greatest pleasure in his work.

Graves pushed the paper aside and reached for his coffee. "Sorry I was out of pocket yesterday. That twenty-four hour virus really nailed me."

"When I came in, the whole department was abuzz. Sergeant Redmond said you spent the day on the crapper and to leave you alone." Dray tried to hide the grin with a hand to his face. "Actually, the sergeant's language was more colorful, so I cleaned it up a bit."

"Thanks, Moody," he said and sipped his coffee. "Now, tell me what you learned at Trappers."

"The place is a pig sty. Looks like something out of post-Katrina."

"That bad, eh?"

Dray nodded. "The developer, an out-of-towner, cleared out. The Camden City Bank is not a proud owner, nor is it inclined to manage or improve the property. Guess they're hoping with Old North Road, now four-lane all the way to Arkansas, traffic will pick up and they can unload the trailer park. They send someone to collect the rent and restock the vending machine once a month . . . that's it."

"Anyone recognize the arrowhead?"

"I talked at length with a Ms. Majors, who lives in the only tidy trailer; I mean the only one. A nice deck, flowers in the yard, neat as a pin inside and out."

"Did the arrowhead mean anything to her?"

"No, but she understood the reason for my visit, since Trappers is so close to the Indian mound."

"Was she aware of Ms. Joslyn's murder?"

"Absolutely. Smart lady. She volunteered information about the potheads living at the end of the road, who she believes are more than users and thinks we ought to check it out." Dray finished his coffee and trashed his cup. "Oh yeah, she wants to file a complaint: disturbing the peace. Apparently these stoners have wild parties with loud music and motorcycle races down that asphalt road. She considers them a menace to anyone who wants to get a little exercise, and the noise level—her words—would wake the dead."

"I'll call Bailey and fill him in. Trappers is in his jurisdiction. I'll ask him to get a warrant and pay the potheads a visit. Maybe one of them has an interest in arrowheads."

"Ms. Majors would be grateful if we can just quiet them down."

Graves leaned back in his swivel, his eyes closed. "Where does the investigation go from here?"

It was a pose Dray had seen many times before. *Contemplation.* Not to be ignored.

"I've got a couple of leads. Let me check 'em out and get back to you."

"It's been a week since Rhea Joslyn was gunned down. We have motive . . . the money, but nothing else. If you read the newspaper, the police department is clueless. And bad publicity stirs the pot. We're already getting lots of e-mails and phone calls from concerned friends of Reverend Joslyn, most of them church members, asking questions about the investigation and implying that we are not doing enough. Della Doss in P. R. handles all the inquiries, but it's driving her bonkers." Graves hesitated and ran a hand through his flat top. "Do you need some help, Dray? A call to my friend Roger Blackstock, who heads the CID (criminal investigations division) of the State Police, will get a prompt response. They'll jump in with both feet . . ."

"And take over the investigation," Dray said glumly and gave Graves the look of a mendicant. "Give me another week, Captain. I believe a local cop will be more effective than the State Police. They make most of the folks around here nervous and, like the Franklins, less likely to speak freely."

Graves read Dray's face like a book. His homicide detective had a few leads and wanted to work them. He also knew Dray was fully committed and had the record to prove it. No one from Baton Rouge would outwork or outthink Dray Moody. “Okay, another week; keep me posted.”

“Thanks, Captain. You won’t be disappointed.” With that, a handshake and Dray was gone.

CHAPTER 24

Friday, March 23rd

CARL STOPPED AT ROMERO'S for takeout, since Maggie suggested they spend the evening at her place rather than another restaurant. If he would pick up lasagna, the one loaded with ricotta cheese, and a mixed green salad, she had a chilled bottle of Pinot noir and chocolate ice cream in the freezer.

She had learned early on that chocolate of any kind, even his cereal—chocolate toasted oats—was Carl's weak spot. She remembered Jack, when it came to food, he had his own Achilles' heel . . . cheese. Melted cheese on an English muffin was a breakfast favorite; a grilled cheese sandwich was a lunchtime staple. Dora had prepared macaroni and cheese so often, Maggie was sure she could have done it blindfolded.

Carl placed the bag on the passenger seat and drove away, the medley of lights on Louisville reflecting in his rear view mirror. He embraced Maggie's stay-at-home suggestion. An evening together, just the two of them, filled him with anticipation, and her family room was the perfect backdrop for Maggie to unwrap her gift.

Carl had seen it in the window of Reuben's Jewelry on Main Street, and it stopped him in his tracks. It may have been the angle of the sun on the glass that brightened the sparkle of its rich green color. An emerald, oval in shape, encircled by diamond accents. He remembered the trivia from Ms. Coker's history class: it was Cleopatra's favorite gemstone. And it was Maggie's birthstone. He stood on the sidewalk awash in sunlight and argued with himself. He wanted the ring for Maggie. But was the ring an inappropriate gesture? After all, they had known each other for only a short time, but long enough for him to know he was in love with this captivating woman.

He didn't want to send the wrong message, causing her to back off, when the relationship was moving in the right direction. Small steps, to be sure, but enough to lift his spirits. He would call it a friendship ring—innocuous enough, and without a romantic inference. Carl knew love was a potent gift-giving catalyst; a need to please the one you love. A metaphor, perhaps, for the giving of one's self. He understood the reason for his decision and satisfied, he went inside to negotiate the deal with Paul Reuben.

On the short dive to Lamy Lane, he felt the excitement of seeing Maggie again. It had been a week; the Friday night movie and hamburgers at The Blue Light. He had called her mid-week, only a brief conversation in which Maggie insisted she was fine and there had been no messages from Randy Bynum. But Carl wanted to be close to her, smell the scent of her hair, and feel the soft touch of her hand. But he tried to show restraint, which was not easy. He had prided himself during his professional career in maintaining calm, even during the fiercest legal (and domestic) storms. . . . *self-control* . . . but not so with Maggie.

Fortunately, the weather had warmed a bit—the low sixties—and he channeled his need for her to the golf course. Ed Seymore was an ever-ready playing partner who always insisted on lunch in the men's grill, activities that consumed much of the day. And there were errands to run, including getting his tax return to Jim Egle at H&R Block. He promised himself: first thing Monday.

Carl parked in the driveway and picked up the package, which Paul Reuben had gift-wrapped in white paper and bright green ribbon. He rang the doorbell and waited. The street was quiet; nightfall claimed the neighborhood. Carl could see light through the transom window. He wondered if the doorbell was broken and rapped on the door. Maybe Maggie had lost track of time, or God forbid she had fallen and couldn't get up. Carl shook his head, trying to shake out the adverse options. He had always been curious: Why, in the most pleasant circumstance, did the mind often conjure up the worst case scenarios? Maggie was the psychologist; he would ask her for an analysis.

He heard the bolt turn; the door opened, Maggie held the cell phone to her ear and waved him in with her free hand.

"It's Edith," she mouthed.

Carl placed the small package on the mantle. There were only a few scattered ashes in the fireplace, the final reminder of a wicked winter.

Maggie, on tiptoe kissed his cheek, while holding the phone against her ear. She stepped back and shrugged as if to say, "There's nothing I can do."

Carl nodded as if he understood and stepped into the kitchen. He placed the bag of lasagna and salad in the fridge. He took the bottle of wine to the counter, removed the cork, and half-filled two crystal glasses. Carl handed one to Maggie, took the other into the family room, and sank into his easy chair.

"Whew," Maggie said and dropped the phone in the pocket of her slacks. "Edith is good company, but she can talk your ear off."

"Ed has mentioned that more than once," Carl chuckled.

"I meant to tell you we had lunch at the Tea Room last Saturday. Edith was not her usual chatty self. Apparently Ed has a health problem, and she's worried to death. This latest call was to apologize for her 'woe is me' attitude."

"I've talked with Ed, and as you would expect, he's taken the news in stride. Ed's one of those eternal optimists who believes in fairy tales and happy endings."

"Oh, I almost forgot." Maggie went to the glass-topped side table which held the CD player and a ceramic vase filled with yellow daffodils. She picked up a compact disc and removed the sleeve. "I went into Annie's Antique Shop the other day, just browsing, and was surprised to find several stacks of CDs, 'oldies' from the fifties." Maggie waved the CD in his direction. "I only bought one, but you may want to go by Annie's and see for yourself." She held the disc head-high. "Some of your favorites: Jerry Vale and *We've Only Just Begun;* Ernie Ford and *The Tennessee Waltz,* and much, much more." She dropped the disc into the tray, pushed it into the player and keyed the start button. Vaughn Monroe and his Big Band sound, *There I've Said It Again,* filled the room.

Carl felt his heart strangely warmed. Maggie had done this for him; she knew it was his kind of music. He tried to reign in his intense pleasure, accept the CD graciously, all the while hoping her gift was meaningful; another small step toward fruition. He looked at the small box on the mantle but decided to wait and give it to her later, a more propitious time.

"Any news on Reverend Joslyn?" she asked, carrying the wine to her striped accent chair.

"I talked to Bailey Grant a few days ago. While the investigation is still in the preliminary phase, he and Graves are in agreement on a couple of things."

"Which are . . . ?"

Carl placed his glass on the coffee table and leaned back. "They believe the arrowhead Jessie Franklin found on the night of the murder is worth investigating. Maybe it's only a keepsake or an amulet. Or maybe it's like a Rosetta stone with a story to tell."

Maggie curled her legs beneath her. "Arrowheads are easy to come by."

"True, but it's the possible connection to the Indian mound that has their attention." Carl reached for his glass, held it chin-level and took a deep whiff. "Blueberries."

She swirled the liquid emitting its fragrance and nodded.

"Grant sent Dray Moody, his homicide detective, to Trappers, that rundown trailer park on Old North Road."

"What's a trailer park got to do with anything?"

"It's near the Indian mound, and Moody made an interesting discovery."

"More arrowheads?" she asked wryly.

Carl shook his head. "The place is a hotbed for stoners who may be dealers as well as potheads."

"Okay, so Grant and Graves have an arrowhead, the Indian mound and a neighboring trailer park in which drugs are used and sold." Maggie paused for effect, her finger drawing a line in the air. "Now connect the dots."

Carl conceded the conundrum with a shrug. "Bailey and one of his deputies plan to pay the stoners a visit . . . with a warrant. Wondered if I'd like to come along."

"And you said . . . ?"

"Absolutely! He'll deputize me, and I'll dust off my old Glock 17."

"Carl, it's your decision, but remember, you're no longer on active duty . . . and never a cop. Why not let the sheriff and his merry band of deputies handle the druggies? It could get out of hand, always a possibility, and put you at risk."

"I'm comfortable with Bailey in charge. He may be the best sheriff in the state. Don't worry, we'll be fine."

Maggie got up and went into the kitchen. "While I'm tossing the salad, well, you said there were two areas of agreement."

Carl turned in her direction and crossed his legs. "Both Bailey and Grant are certain that either directly or indirectly, the shooter knew the preacher kept cash in her office. The Pastor's Benevolence Fund was no secret, since gifts to the church were listed in the Sunday bulletin and the church's weekly newsletter."

Maggie put the plates of lasagna, right out of the microwave, on the kitchen table along with bowls of salad and a basket of Italian bread. "It's ready, Carl. Bring your wine."

After they were seated, Maggie pushed a wisp of hair behind her ear. "Where were we?"

"Rhea's benevolent fund which she kept in her desk drawer."

"You don't need Einstein to figure it out," Maggie said lightly. "The thief had inside information. Or why else would he rob the church office, rather than Zack's liquor store or the 7 Eleven?"

"Both Grant and Graves believe it's where the investigation should go full bore. Detective Moody has taken a tough assignment. The church has thirty charter members. He will interview all of them one-on-one, hoping for a valuable lead. Maybe one . . . just one . . . of the charter members will drop a name, a person of interest. Moody will remind them of possible connections: a drug addict, a gambler, a crazy, or someone full of spite aimed at the preacher, although that seems unlikely."

The phone rang. "I'll get it," Maggie said.

She cupped the speaker with her hand and looked at Carl. "It's Sam."

"Take your time, I'm busy," he said with a devilish grin, cutting his lasagna, the cheese oozing over sheets of noodles.

It was a short conversation. Carl heard the phone click before he had cleaned his plate.

Maggie leaned on the back of her chair. "He wanted to share some exciting news."

"A good report from Jane's OB-GYN?"

"Nope. Early in the week, Dr. Wagner, head of the English Department, asked if he might read the first fifty pages of his novel."

"I guess Sam didn't have much choice."

"None at all, but he reminded Dr. Wagner it was only the first draft."

"So the good news . . ."

"The professor called Sam this afternoon, having critiqued the first four chapters, and said all the right things. He also gave him the name of an old friend, Troy Sturdivant, an agent in Manhattan whom he had already called, and the agent wanted to see the fifty pages as well." Maggie could not conceal a mother's elation. "It's his passion, Carl, and Dr. Wagner's final comment—*it's really good*—gave him such a lift, he had to call his mother."

"When can I meet Sam?"

"Soon. We may have to visit Colby, since Sam has trouble getting Jane out of Benton."

Carl pushed his chair back and picked up his plate and salad bowl.

Maggie gave him a gentle shove. "Stay put, dessert is on the way."

Carl unlocked the door and walked onto the deck, which ran half the length of the house. The back yard was dark, no heavenly lights; rain clouds had moved in. Only dim lamplight from the screen porch of Pixie and Imogene. He wondered how Pixie had seen the intruder; maybe it had been a clear night, star-strewn and a gibbous moon. It was probably Bynum, and he would be back. Carl was sure of that.

Maggie tapped the door to the deck. "Your dessert's ready."

Carl returned to his seat and looked at a super-serving of his favorite dessert . . . chocolate ice cream. And beside the bowl was a paper plate filled with fudge brownies.

Maggie handed him an envelope before slipping into her chair. "I thought you might like to read my note to Sam, in light of our earlier discussion. I can only share this with someone special."

Carl felt his heart accelerate. Not 'I love you' or even words of endearment, but 'someone special' was getting close. He felt the warmth in his cheeks and the slight tremor in his hand as he reached for the envelope. He slipped the note from its cover and shifted his chair to improve the angle of light.

Dear Sam,
I was walking the mall a few days ago
and happened to see these words painted
on the window of *Set the Table*. So unusual
it caught my attention.
And so we float
Across the sky, moored to nothing
But our dreams
Dream big, Sam, and may all your dreams come true.
Love,
Mom

Carl took a moment to choke back his emotion before replacing the note in the envelope and handing it to Maggie. He looked deep into those mesmerizing blue eyes. "Sam's a lucky guy," he said wistfully.

After dinner, they sat on the sofa in the family room, Carl's arm around her shoulder. The conversation was casual and comfortable. Maggie kicked off her shoes and curled up close to him. Nat King Cole and the new Jerry Vale CD provided the entertainment. A hard rain arrived, as predicted by the weather service, and battered the windows. Sleep beckoned as the wine's effect kicked in. Carl awoke bleary-eyed, checked the clock on the mantel—11:05. He also saw the package tied with green ribbon, which he had almost forgotten.

He felt her nestled against his chest, asleep. Carl kissed her forehead and stirred her awake. "It's late, so I'd better get going."

Maggie straightened up and rubbed her eyes. She massaged the stiff muscles in her neck and shoulders, then started to get up, using his knee as leverage.

He pulled her back gently. "I have something for you."

"Sorry I left you," she said like a repentant child. "It must have been the wine."

"Don't go anywhere." He stepped to the fireplace, picked up the package and brought it back to the sofa.

"What's the occasion?" she asked with eyes full of surprise.

Carl chuckled. “It’s not your birthday, and it’s not Christmas. I just wanted you to have it.” With heart-racing excitement he watched her untie the ribbon and tear off the wrapping paper.

A gasp when she lifted the lid from the box. “Oh, Carl, it’s gorgeous. And my favorite color.”

“I know jewelry is not a big item, but emerald is your birthstone and when I saw the ring at Reuben’s Jewelry, I couldn’t resist.”

She slipped it on her ring finger, the right hand. “Thank you, Carl, it’s beautiful.” With great delight, she looked at the ring. “And it’s the perfect size.” She pulled him down onto the sofa and wrapped her arms around him with a kiss that almost took his breath away.

“Look, Maggie, the fact I care deeply about you is no secret. As I’ve said before, I hope that over time, our relationship will grow and the feelings will be mutual. The ring carries no obligation; it is simply a gift of gratitude for enlivening my life, when I had accepted the indolence of aging and a belief that I could never love again. So should someone ask, call it a friendship ring, or an ‘occasional’ ring, or. . . . call it whatever you like.”

“You’re a dear, sweet man, Carl Sweeny.”

“If nothing else, it’s a memento of our time together. Now, I’ll let myself out.” He stopped at the door and turned around. “And don’t forget our tee time Sunday. I’ll pick you up at one.”

“The Seymores joining us?”

“A foursome; and bring your ‘A’ game. The way I’m playing, we’ll need it.”

Maggie sat for a long time after the front door closed and admired the vivid green of the emerald. She had read somewhere that Jackie Kennedy’s engagement ring was an emerald encircled with diamonds. Was her emerald an omen of love in the autumn of life? The possibility put a time-will-tell smile on her face. She admitted the relationship had taken on new dimensions since the Seymores’ dinner on that cold wintry night. A casual acquaintance had segued into something more. Slowly, like bare roots turned by a growing season into a fragrant flower. Unexpected, an invasion of her heart.

She knew Carl loved her—he had said as much—and he’d accepted the disparity in their relationship graciously while hoping for more. Maggie looked at the ring and made a heartfelt admission: while she was not ready to surrender, at least not yet, she had moved closer, much closer to a man who two months ago was a total stranger. It had been more than thirty years since she had felt this way—The Rustler's Steakhouse in Dallas—feelings that were now bubbling up to the surface.

CHAPTER 25

MAGGIE AWOKE WITH A ghastly headache. Too much wine, too little lasagna. She lay in bed and massaged her neck, thinking about the emerald ring and the enjoyable evening with Carl. It may have been the best time she'd had since the move to Camden. She swung her legs over the side of the bed, hoping her head would not explode. As the remnants of sleep dissolved and the positional vertigo faded, she remembered her appointment with Mrs. Fogleman at 11 o'clock. Maggie could see splinters of sunlight sneaking through the Venetian blinds. But first things first: she needed two Advil and a hot shower.

The trip to the kitchen was full of resolve; never again would she have that extra glass of wine. After swallowing the pills, she drank a second glass of water (hydration was helpful) and checked the wall clock. She made a pot of coffee; no time for Starbucks. She had an hour and a half before the OverReach appointment, with twenty minutes needed to negotiate I-20 and the surface streets. She prodded herself to get moving. Holding her head steady with both hands, she padded back to the bedroom and gritted her teeth as she pulled the extra-long golf shirt over her head, which felt the size of a watermelon. It was only a few steps into the shower, where she let the hot water play on the back of her neck.

After ten minutes of wet heat, she stepped onto a bath mat and dried herself with a white fluffy towel. She dressed quickly; no makeup other than lipstick that matched the floral fabric of her dress. No jewelry other than her watch, a ladies' Rolex. She considered the emerald ring, but dismissed it summarily; much too elegant for a morning meeting at a women's shelter. A few brush strokes, then letting her lustrous hair hang loose around her shoulders. Maggie placed the .38 in her purse, grabbed a sweater from the closet and followed the fragrance of coffee into the kitchen. She poured the coffee into a

Styrofoam cup and after locking the door, carried it to her car. By the time she cleared I-20, the headache was less intense, but unremitting.

Maggie felt a pang of reproach as she turned into the shelter's parking lot. It had been more than two weeks since her previous visit to OverReach and the offer from Alice Fogleman. The visit was on Thursday, after a rainy morning of grocery shopping with Pixie and Imogene. Over the weekend she had made a decision to accept the job offer and, as promised, she notified Alice Fogleman on Monday. A few days later she received a call from Personnel, a request to come by and sign her contract. Maggie was surprised, since she would counsel without compensation, and this: she had never signed a contract with The Shelter in Dallas. Maggie dragged her feet; she didn't see her first patient until next month. So what's the rush?

Late Friday afternoon, before Carl arrived with the lasagna, she received another call, but this one carried an impression of urgency. Fogleman wanted to talk with her about a very important matter, which for privacy reasons needed to be discussed in the director's office. A face-to-face meeting was absolutely necessary. While Fogleman gave no details, the exigent tone of her voice got Maggie's attention, and she had made an appointment for the very next day.

Maggie locked the car and took the steps to the wide veranda. She heard the noise overhead. She knew it was a private plane cleared to land at the Camden Airport. The Delta morning flights had come and gone hours ago. She pushed through the oak door and into the Spartan reception room. Madeline in her pink smock was at her desk—texting on her iPhone, the laptop pushed aside, oblivious to the visitor.

Maggie cleared her throat. "Madeline . . . it is Madeline?"

The receptionist looked up. "How can I help you?" No inflection. No warmth. The sound of a robotic female voice.

"I have an appointment with Mrs. Fogleman."

"Let me check." She picked up the phone and punched the extension.

Maggie was incredulous. Two visits, and she had yet to hear a "good morning" or a simple greeting. While the red hair and green eyes were appealing, *polite* was not in Madeline's vocabulary, and Maggie wondered how she kept her job. Maybe nepotism was at work.

Madeline placed the receiver in the cradle and retrieved the key from her desk drawer. She unlocked the security door leading to the interior of the two-story Colonial and stepped aside. "You remember the way?"

Maggie nodded, holding her tongue. It was no time (nor was it appropriate) for a lecture on courtesy and civility. But she would mention it to Fogleman.

The director's office door was open. As on the previous visit, Fogleman stood at the window, with its picturesque view of the placid waters of the bayou and the bald cypress flourishing at the water's edge. A tap on the door frame got her attention.

"Oh, hi, Mrs. McFarland . . ."

"Maggie, please."

"Then I'm Alice," she laughed and pointed to the armchair.

Maggie took a seat and put her purse on the floor.

The director, in khakis and a sweatshirt, circled the chair and closed the door before returning to her desk. She wore no makeup, only lip gloss and her auburn hair in a low twist ponytail.

Saturday casual. Maggie wished she had done the same.

"Thanks for coming on such short notice."

"My pleasure . . . I need to sign the contract while I'm here."

Fogleman shuffled the papers on her desk. "Here it is," she said and passed a copy to Maggie. "It's a simple document, only a couple of pages. The stipulations are those we discussed: three days a week, flexible hours, and your compensation . . ." Alice shook her head and broke a hard-to-believe-smile. " . . . a dollar per annum. After our session here, you can look it over, and unless there's an objection, sign the original."

Maggie scanned the first page and then put the contract in her lap. "There was something else you wanted to discuss?"

"During your earlier visit, I mentioned that OverReach received funds from several sources, but most of our support comes from the Armstead Foundation. We are deeply indebted to Mr. Armstead and his family for their financial commitment, for without their largess, OverReach would struggle to survive."

Fogleman fingered her lower lip, her eyes narrowed. "A.B. called me yesterday, before eight o'clock, and needed a favor. Something he had never done before. It seems Robbie Armstead, the son of his younger brother, has a problem with depression and drugs—marijuana for sure, maybe hard drugs as well. He added the boy was in trouble, but gave no details."

Maggie felt her neck muscles tighten; she knew where this was going.

"A.B. insisted Robbie needs counseling and wants it done here." She paused and looked Maggie in the eye. "And he wants you to be the boy's counselor."

"Why me?" Maggie asked. "He doesn't know me from Adam's house cat."

"Mr. Armstead does his homework. It's one of the reasons he's been successful." Fogleman opened a manila folder and checked the names on a sheet of note paper. "He personally checked your references, including Dr. Dwayne Walker, your mentor at the University, who gave you a glowing report—as did several of The Shelter's directors for whom you worked. He is convinced you are highly qualified and, I might add, the right gender to counsel Robbie Armstead. Incidentally, he had met your late husband for whom he had enormous respect several times. So he feels a connection with you."

"Alice, I appreciate the kind words, but if the boy is depressed with drugs in the mix, he needs a psychiatrist. He'll probably need medication, which I can't prescribe. OverReach has its own on-call psychiatrist, so why not use him?"

Fogleman shook her head vigorously. "I posed the same question during my conversation with Mr. Armstead. 'No, No, No,' is all I got. He is adamant and only wants Margaret McFarland. Now he realizes you don't have an obligation to accept the assignment, but . . ." She reached over and tapped the phone. " . . . he was very emotional, something I'd not heard before."

"I don't know, Alice." Maggie grimaced. "I need a few days to think it over."

"Reasonable . . . very reasonable. After all, you're going from retirement to a complex and who-knows-what kind of case."

Maggie translated the clumsy phrase. It was synonymous with *challenging.*

Fogleman half-stood, leaning with both hands on the desk. “One other thing: A.B. mentioned the construction of a second safe house in Dallas—Plano, actually. He plans to make a sizable contribution in your husband’s name.”

Maggie waved both hands frantically. “Jack wouldn’t want that. He tried to keep his own gifts anonymous.”

“It’s not a bribe, Maggie. He just happens to know the wonderful influence Mr. McFarland had on the Metroplex, as well as your dedication and good works at The Shelter. Maybe a plaque in the reception area, but nothing bold or ostentatious.”

Maggie frowned. “Something else to consider,” she said, again rubbing the muscles in back of her neck.

“Let me know when you make a decision about the boy. While there’s no deadline, it sounds like Robbie Armstead needs help ASAP.”

“I understand.”

“Mr. Armstead is available if you would like to speak with him directly.”

Without thinking, Maggie put the contract on the desk and lifted herself from the chair. “You’ve conveyed his message.” When she reached the door, she turned and said, “I’ll be in touch.”

On the way out, Maggie passed the reception desk. Madeline was preoccupied, her face buried in the laptop, the iPhone in easy reach. No goodbyes, but none were expected. Maggie chided herself for failing to mention the ill-mannered receptionist to Fogleman. The request to counsel Robbie Armstead had gotten her full attention, and Madeline was temporarily forgotten. Next time, she would file her complaint.

During the drive home, Maggie wished Jack was with her. He was always able to find solutions for difficult problems. She remembered how often he made tough decisions with calmness and circumspection. Aside from raw intelligence, he was a genius at logical reasoning and critical thinking. She was sure he would give her sage advice and settle her uncertainty. It was only one of the many ways she missed him. While her life with Jack McFarland had ended, he was still lodged in her bank of memories. And now and then, in her dreams . . . sweet dreams, all of them.

Before the entrance ramp to I-20, she put on her dark glasses to cut the glare from the overhead sun. Maggie pulled down the visor and readjusted her glasses. An accident on the Interstate brought traffic to a standstill. Maggie waited patiently behind a Ford pickup, rolled down her window, and thought about Mr. Armstead's request. Depression and drug addiction were common psychiatric problems. But his comment that 'Robbie is in trouble' raised a red flag. What kind of trouble? Was the "trouble" connected to his depression and/or drugs? No details were given. Not even an inference. She conjured up a half-dozen scenarios in her mind. A waste of time. No need to speculate, since she wasn't sure a psychologist should handle a patient with so much putative pathology. She needed a sounding board and would call Carl, with whom she was comfortable and could safely confide. The connection would have to wait, since Carl had an early morning golf game and an afternoon meeting with Bailey Grant to plan their trip to the trailer park and a dicey visit with the potheads, carrying a warrant to search the premises. Her efforts to dissuade Carl were like whistling in the wind. Despite Jack's Christian orthodoxy, Maggie was only "religious" at the edges. But she would say a prayer for Carl's safety and count on seeing him for their Sunday golf game; then was time enough for a serious discussion.

Maggie, lost in concentration, had not realized the Ford pickup was moving. A horn sounded. Not a tap. An incensed driver in a black Camry sat on his horn. She checked her rear view mirror and waved an apology through the open window. For her trouble, she got a scowl and the one-finger salute. Maggie let it go, thinking there were a lot of angry people in the world. The face of Randy Bynum flashed by . . . again.

The plan for lunch at The Sandwich Shoppe was scraped and Maggie, suddenly exhausted, settled for a coffee and pastry at Starbucks. After turning onto Lamy Lane, she noticed a foreign car of some kind, maybe a Porsche, parked in front of the Kalils', her across-the-street neighbors. A man wearing a fedora and sunglasses sat behind the wheel. Once inside the house, Maggie hurried to the foyer and its view of the street. Cal Kalil had just opened the car door and settled in the passenger's seat. Obviously the stranger was a friend or family member. Bynum didn't drive a Porsche and wouldn't make his move in broad daylight. But when she saw the stranger, Bynum in disguise had crossed her mind. Maggie let out a breath of frustration. She hated to admit that paranoia had breached her defenses, and she needed to shore up her moxie. Maggie kicked off her shoes and stretched out on the sofa, a pillow beneath her head, and fell asleep.

CHAPTER 26

WHEN MAGGIE AWOKE, she sat up and checked her watch, drew strands of hair from her face. Despite a two-hour nap, the nagging headache was unabated. She opened a drawer beneath the kitchen counter and took out the Advil. When had she taken the last dose? Maggie counted the hours with her fingers, dropped the bottle in the drawer and settled for two Tylenols, which she washed down with a glass of milk. After wetting her face at the kitchen sink, she went out on the deck and leaned on the railing, her spirits buoyed by the signs of a nascent spring. The grass had a hint of green, or was it her imagination? The two Bradford pears bloomed in white profusion, as if they had just weathered a heavy snowfall. A Cardinal settled on the feeder Maggie had hung from the limb of a sweet gum, and spring roses climbed the trellis beside the basement window. Maggie looked at the gas grill and wished Carl was here. While she might need a wrap as the late afternoon cooled, it was idyllic for a cookout with a friend, someone special. It was also a reminder for Maggie to worry about the drug raid. Despite her entreaty, Carl was determined to join the sheriff's war party. While she believed the role of Trappers in the Joslyn murder was unlikely, still, it was Carl's idea and the reason for his inclusion. Maggie looked at the gas grill one last time before leaving the deck. Her stomach growled; she had eaten very little, only the pastry from Starbucks. Maybe a big, fat hamburger from the grill would help her headache.

When she went inside, Maggie realized she had not picked up the mail. She walked to the entry hall and looked through a sidelight. The street was lifeless . . . deserted. Despite the jitters, Maggie scooted down the driveway to the curbside mailbox. She bundled the mail, hurried back into the house and bolted the door.

She went into her work room (the spare bedroom) and sat at her desk. She turned on the lamp and began to separate the mail; some bills, a few circulars, and the usual flyers from fitness centers and pizza parlors. And another invitation to Carefree Living, a retirement home with so many amenities that it made growing old sound like fun. All were filed in the wicker wastebasket. There were only two letters—one from the Richland Parish Tax commissioner regarding her ad valorum taxes; the other, a smaller envelope which bore no return address but was postmarked Tyler, Texas.

Maggie felt her heart skip a beat; another message from Randy Bynum. How far was Tyler from Dallas? She'd have to look it up. After opening the envelope, she pulled out a card similar to the others. On the front was a picture of Bugs Bunny wearing outlandish glasses and eating a carrot, with the tag line: I'LL BE SEEING YOU. Inside the card was blank, other than for the same handwritten block letters.

BUT WHEN?
AND WHERE?

Maggie took the card into the kitchen and poured herself a glass of wine, headache be damned. She made a patty from the fresh ground sirloin she had put in the fridge yesterday and placed it on a dinner plate. She sliced a juicy tomato and a Vidalia onion she'd gotten from the Farmer's Market. After lighting the gas grill, Maggie took the plate and the card from Bynum onto the deck. She used a metal spatula to place the patty on the grill and then closed the lid.

She leaned on the deck railing and reread the card. Was there anything she could do, other than wait? Bynum clearly had the advantage; she was on the defensive. Were there other options that might change the odds? She was tired of being vigilant—Carl's admonition—and a prisoner in her own home. Maggie admitted with a wry smile that she had more locks and bolts on her doors and windows than the city jail. An exaggeration, of course; but still, it was disconcerting when spooked by a Porsche that belonged to a neighbor's friend.

A light went on in Maggie's head. Maybe she could draw him out. How? Well, she would have to think about that. Unless she was mistaken, it would level the playing field if she suggested the time and location. She knew Bynum was aggressive, which ratcheted up the risk, but it was imperative to prove his threats were real and provide evidence that nailed him as an irrefutable stalker.

"Oops," Maggie said as she lifted the lid and salvaged the well-done hamburger. She scooped it onto the plate and went back to the kitchen, where she constructed a hamburger that would put The Blue Light and their "world-famous hamburgers" to shame. She added potato chips from a bag in the pantry, along with a slice of dill pickle and some ripe olives. She carried the plate and her wine glass outside, settling into a canvas chair. Serenity . . . she loved it. Overhead a red-tailed hawk glided across a seamless blue sky as the setting sun painted the horizon with vivid colors.

After her meal, Maggie planned to spend a quiet night at home, some of it devoted to formulating a scheme that would set a trap for Randy Bynum. Maybe she could finish *The Bridge of Sighs.* Russo was her favorite author—well, one of her favorites. She would select something classical from her stack of CDs, perhaps Rachmaninoff or the New York Philharmonic. While a good book and classical music had their appeal, she had the worry of unfinished business. Her concern for Carl was irrepressible, and she felt his participation in the Trappers' raid was jejune. If Bailey Grant needed backup, he could have used another of his deputies or borrowed Dray Moody, who knew more about the trailer park than any member of either department. Carl was not a cop, never had been, and being deputized didn't make it so. Despite Bailey's assurances, Maggie knew that confronting dopers was not child's play, and Carl could easily get hurt. While he had promised to call on his return to the Annex, she knew if all went well, it would be around midnight, since the sheriff wanted to arrive at party time—ten o'clock or later. Just thinking about the possibilities put her nerves on edge.

She wanted to talk with Carl about her plan for Bynum, and the weighty request of A.B. Armstead that she, not the psychiatrist, counsel his nephew. Carl was her sounding board, much needed, since Robbie Armstead's problems seemed well beyond the bounds of a psychologist. She had promised Alice Fogleman an answer in "a few days." She also needed to sign the contract, which she had forgotten and left on Alice's desk. Unless the raid at Trappers turned sour, she could have a conversation with Carl tomorrow about these matters after their golf game. Nevertheless, these intrusions had spoiled the contentment of a splendid spring evening.

Carl pulled into the parking deck behind the Annex a little before six. While the raid was scheduled for much later, Bailey wanted to discuss the mission in infinite detail, certain he had covered every contingency. The sheriff's compulsive personality was an asset in situations that carried even low levels of risk. Carl had often heard Bailey's mantra—*details, details, details*—during his last few years in the D. A.'s office. He believed it was another reason for Bailey's success and his record-setting re-election, voted by his peers as the best sheriff in North Louisiana.

Carl made his way to the Annex and found Spook at the security desk, reading a dog-eared paperback. He stopped and gave the guard a waggish grin. "Got the weekend duty?"

Spook put the book away and stood up. "Lost Eloise last week. Guess you heard." He shook his head and dropped his eyes to the floor. "Carbon monoxide got her. Faulty heating system, and the woman spent too much time in her small laundry room. If she'd opened the window or walked outside for a breath of fresh air . . ." His face clouded, betraying the grievous loss of his friend.

"We know heart attacks and strokes are common killers. But carbon monoxide . . ." Carl threw out both arms as if to ask, who can explain it?

"The service has hired a replacement, Ned Bowen. Know 'im?"

Carl shook his head.

"He'll start next week, which is why I'm here on a beautiful Saturday."

Carl reached over and cuffed his shoulder. "Take it easy, Spook. I'm on my way to meet with the sheriff."

Spook picked up his book and waved him on.

Carl took a right turn, followed the corridor to the sheriff's department and pushed open the glass doors. The reception area was empty; Rose Marie, who worked a half-day on Saturdays, was long gone. Carl tracked the scent of fresh brewed coffee into Bailey's office. The sheriff looked his way and pointed to the multi-cup coffee maker. "Help yourself."

Carl poured a cup and took a seat in the cane-bottom chair. "Who else is part of this mission?"

"Walt Whiteside, one of my deputies."

Carl didn't recognize the name. "Must be a new recruit."

The sheriff rocked back in his swivel, his dark eyes widened with satisfaction. "Walt had a distinguished Army career. Discharged with an enviable record, including a Bronze Star for valor during the Gulf War. He returned home to Camden and joined us a few months ago. A great addition to our department." Bailey looked at the wall clock and said, "He'll be here shortly."

Carl crossed his legs and held the cup in his lap. "Do we know who rents the stoners' trailer?"

"I had DMV check their database for motorcycle licenses and gave them the trailer park address. Bingo . . . a match."

"So you have the name."

Bailey moved up in his swivel and reached for his notes. "Mickey Randle, age twenty-six, brown eyes, six feet, one hundred and seventy pounds." Bailey looked up and added, "And we got his picture . . ." The sheriff's lively eyes could not hide the irony. " . . . from an expired license."

"Expired, huh? Sounds like more problems for Mickey Randle."

"No priors. A bit of a surprise, but we'll see."

Carl thought about his ten years as the district attorney for the Richland and Morehouse parishes. There were countless times when the record of a driver's license or information from the parish tax commissioner assisted in an investigation. Of course, there were always those shrewd criminals who tried to outsmart the cops by using stolen cars—or even easier, stolen plates. He remembered a few instances in which the perpetrators had the audacity to rent a car using fake credentials and credit cards. Rental agents rarely took the time to examine the picture on the driver's license; something the miscreants counted on. Some were good with disguise. A fedora worn low on the forehead and a pair of dark glasses shadowed the face and made identification unlikely. Fortunately, Mickey Randle was just a kid flouting the law, but without the cunning or intent of the criminal mind. But Carl was old enough to know there was no guarantee that unbridled behavior at Randle's age would not morph into something more pernicious. It was another subject to discuss with Maggie.

"So what's the plan?" Carl asked. "Or should we wait on your deputy?"

Bailey eyed the clock again and frowned. "Not like Walt. I'll track him down if he's not here pretty soon."

Bailey refilled his coffee mug and stood by the window with its view of the river. While sunlight waltzed on the water, the wind picked up and dark clouds gathered beyond West Camden. "Hope the wind pushes the rain to the south. Don't want anything to interrupt Mickey's party."

Carl half-turned with his arm over the back of the chair. "The plan, Bailey . . . ?"

"We'll confront Mickey and voice the complaints."

"Which are?"

"Disturbing the peace, smoking dope, and driving a motorcycle without a license. All illegal in the Pelican State."

"Witnesses?"

"I've spoken to Bernice Majors, who Dray Moody interviewed at length when he reconnoitered the trailer park. She and her neighbor have agreed to testify to the wild parties and loud music, and the endangerment from the motorcycle races down Trappers Road. Last Saturday night, Ms. Majors' grandson, Matt, went uninvited and spoke with Mickey Randle about the loud music, which Ms. Majors swears can be heard all the way to Old North Road. He asked if Randle would turn down the volume so their neighbors could sleep. Civil tone. Reasonable request."

"And?"

"Several of Mickey's friend joined him—strength in numbers—and told Matt to 'get the hell off Mick's property.'" Bailey took another look out the window. No pedestrians on the sidewalks, a smattering of cars on South Grand. "Matt, not looking for trouble, walked back to his grandmother's trailer and gave her his report. No luck with the music, but from where Matt had been standing, he saw three or four partygoers smoking pot. A light haze of smoke hung over the room and wafted through the open door. It had an odor like burning leaves. He would swear to it, under oath, if it came to that."

Carl finished his coffee and tossed the plastic cup in the wastebasket. "Last summer, you led the drug bust at Trappers. Any connection with Randle and his friends?"

Bailey returned to his chair and settled in. "Nope, but Trappers seems to draw the stoners like flies to honey."

"I seem to remember, one or two got prison time."

Bailey nodded. "Only two. Minimum security, out in three months. The others got community service; a slap on the wrist."

"I'm surprised they got off so easy. The state has some tough drug laws. If I remember correctly, it's five years for possession, second offense."

"Well, several factors were in play with these bikers. This was their first offense, users only, agreed to three months of rehab, appeared contrite in court, and a judge who cut them some slack."

"You still plan to search Randle's trailer?"

"Absolutely." Bailey opened a desk drawer and pulled out the warrant. "Got authorization right here."

A knock on the jamb got their attention. A big man in a khaki uniform filled the doorway. "Sorry I'm late, Sheriff."

"Have a seat, Walt." Another look at the wall clock. "We've got plenty of time."

Carl stood and introduced himself. He got a firm handshake before the deputy took his seat. The floor boards beneath the carpet complained. Carl thought of his favorite TV rerun—just a flicker of memory—and found the image amusing. This former member of Delta Force with a buzz cut and bulging biceps was the antithesis of Barney Fife.

Carl figured some in Camden would wonder why Whiteside had left the Army and signed on with local law enforcement. Carl had asked Bailey that very same question and received a credible answer: Like

Ray Graves, Walt wanted to come home. He was born and raised in Camden, and his aging parents (his father had Parkinson's disease with motor impairment and the pill-rolling tremor) needed him. But after a year of "care and support," he wanted, in addition, something to fill his day. Bailey had added, "Our lucky break."

After a few minutes of small talk, the sheriff got down to business. He spent the next half hour laying out in detail the plans for the Trappers' raid. He covered all contingencies and expressed with firm resolve the need to avoid the mistake made in the drug bust a year ago. A failure to get the names of at least six of the partygoers, an omission that gave them a free pass. A short question-and-answer period followed.

Carl asked, "Why the two cruisers?"

"Safety in numbers."

Walt waved one of his huge hands. "I'm good."

"Okay, then let's meet here at 10:30. When we get to Trappers, the party will be in full swing." The sheriff hesitated and glanced at both men. "Just the way we want it."

Bailey was pleased. The winds had shifted and pushed the rain to the south. Overhead a few stars dared to speckle the night sky, while clouds covered the moon. It was dark as a tomb until a car heading for Camden head-lighted Old North Road. The sheriff checked his rear view mirror; Whiteside, in the second vehicle, was on his tail.

They passed the Chevron station and convenience store. "Keep your eyes open, Carl. Trappers Road is unmarked, hard to find. Moody said it's past that gas station, less than a quarter mile."

"My night vision is shot to hell. Probably need to get my cataracts out."

"It might help your golf game," Bailey ribbed.

"Think I'll call Dr. Brownlee on Monday and set up an appointment."

Bailey stared hard to his left. "Moody also mentioned a sign at the entrance to Trappers Road, but it's so weather-worn, he had trouble reading it in broad daylight." The sheriff slowed to a crawl since there was no northbound traffic, other than Walt's cruiser—at least not that he could see.

"I should have better recall," Carl said. "All those trips to the Indian mound."

Bailey laughed. "What was that . . . sixty years ago?"

"Sounds about right," he admitted. "Where did the years go?"

Bailey said nothing. He was fixed on finding Trappers Road.

"And file this away, Bailey: The older you get, the faster time flies."

Preoccupied, he ignored Carl's musings. "There it is," Bailey said, letting out a deep breath. He had caught a dim view of the sign in the reflective light of a car heading south.

He flicked the turn signal and crossed the highway onto the dirt and gravel bridge. He was grateful Moody had warned him about the jerry-built bridge in advance. Namely, it was narrow, without guard rails, and if the driver was careless, the car could end up in the drainage ditch.

Bailey could see the reflection in his side view mirror. His deputy had made the turn and followed him into the trailer park. There were lights in the windows of only two trailers. Otherwise the park was dark and ghostly quiet. No loud music. No signs of a party, wild or otherwise. The cruisers passed the laundry shed and avoided most of the pot holes in the asphalt road. Bailey knew it ended in a cul-de-sac and that Randle's trailer rested on a cement pad near the dead end.

They parked in the clearing next to a late model Honda Accord with Louisiana plates. Walt recorded the numbers in a small notebook and called it in. Then he followed instructions: remain in the clearing, a lookout for any activity along Trappers Road or around Randle's trailer.

Bailey and Carl, each with a flashlight, crossed the road and into the yard . . . strips of dead grass. A motorcycle on its kickstand was parked beside the trailer. A curtain filtered dim light through one of the oval windows. Bailey stopped at the front steps and took Carl's arm. "Hold on."

He swept a beam of light over the trailer and the pint-sized yard but saw nothing of interest. Bailey held his breath and listened, his free hand cupped to his ear. Soundless; quiet as a cemetery. "So what do you think?"

"Someone tipped them off," Carl said.

"Maybe the gang went to the beach. About time for spring break."

"Explain the motorcycle." Carl pointed in its general direction.

"Okay, they had their reasons and took the weekend off."

Carl shook his head. "According to Moody, they party every weekend."

"A waste of time speculating," Bailey said as he took the three steps of stacked concrete blocks to the front door. "Let's talk to Mickey and check it out."

Bailey rapped on the jamb. From inside, they heard a dog barking. The door opened and backlighted a young man who fit the DMV's description, and who quieted the dog that had begun to growl.

"Mickey Randle?"

"Just call me Mick," he said with a smirk.

Bailey flashed his badge and canted his head in Carl's direction. "This is Mr. Sweeny, the former D.A. of Richland Parish."

Nothing registered on Randle's face. "So, what's the big deal?"

Bailey replaced the badge in his back pocket, figuring Carl was right—a tipoff. Randle expected the visit. "We've gotten several complaints. 'Rowdy parties and loud music' was the way your neighbors put it. Officially, you're accused of 'disturbing the peace.'"

"A little music . . . c'mon!" His lips curled into a sneer.

Bailey leaned forward. "Listen carefully, Mick. "This is an official warning. If it happens again, I'll bring the troops, seal off Trappers Road, arrest you and your buddies and haul your ass to the Parish jail. Got it?"

Mick shrugged it off.

"Let's hear it." Bailey raised his voice, almost a shout.

"I got it," he said, the words dripping with contempt.

The sheriff pulled the warrant from his jacket pocket. "The second complaint is far more serious. Witnesses will testify that some of your hell-raisers are pot smokers, which in this state is illegal. A stiff penalty, Mick. Six months of prison time for smoking weed, five to ten years for selling hard drugs." Bailey gave him the warrant.

Randle, unfazed, took a quick look and handed it back. "Too dark . . . can't read it."

"It's a search warrant, Mick. If you'll move, we're going to check out your trailer."

Mickey stepped aside. "Be my guest," he said, an invitation seeping sarcasm. "Just don't mess up the place."

Bailey had checked. The trailers were 15' by 60', a snug 900 square feet of living space. The sitting room was dimly lit by a table lamp and a muted color TV. For the first time, both Bailey and Carl saw a human form lying on the sofa with his eyes closed. The sheriff turned around, but Randle had disappeared into the kitchen. "Guess we'd better wake him up."

Carl leaned down and tapped a shoulder. A young man—Mick's age, maybe a little younger—with long hair and a cleft chin sat up and rubbed his eyes. He appeared calm; neither startled nor annoyed by the abrupt awakening.

"You have a name?" Carl asked.

"Robbie Armstead," he said, looking at the floor.

"Any kin to A.B. Armstead?"

"My uncle," he said softly, barely audible.

"Is Mickey Randle a friend?"

Robbie nodded. "Sometimes he loans me his car."

"The Honda out front?"

"Mick prefers the Harley, and I get to use the Honda."

Carl straightened up. "Hang around, Robbie. We may have a few more questions."

"I'll be here." He lay back on the sofa and drifted off.

"I think sleep's got him," Bailey said. "Now, let's get to work."

After turning on all the lights, Carl checked on Mickey, who sat on a kitchen stool and sulked, a can of beer in one hand and a cigarette in the other.

Bailey divided the floor plan into two sections. He would take the bedroom and bath, while Carl checked the kitchen and living room. The search was tedious and time-consuming. They found nothing. Not even a speck of dirt. Only some dirty clothes piled in the bedroom closet. The place had been scrubbed clean. Even the rooms smelled of air freshener. Not a hint of the weed anywhere.

Robbie was still asleep as Carl and Bailey walked back to the kitchen.

"Satisfied?" Mick asked

"We're leaving, but we'll be back. Count on it," Bailey said.

"Harassment. Better talk to my lawyer."

"You do that, Mick. Maybe next time we'll meet in Municipal Court." Bailey stopped short. "By the way, you own any arrowheads?"

"Nope."

"Any of your friends collect arrowheads?"

"How the hell would I know? "

"The Indian mound is less than a hundred yards from here. And you never check it out, looking for arrowheads."

"Never!" He clenched his fists as he spat out the answer.

Carl saw the anger in his eyes. Through his own vast experience dealing with the whole spectrum of criminal behavior, he believed the eyes were a telltale sign; often the pathway to the soul.

The sheriff tugged on Carl's jacket sleeve. "Mickey's wound pretty tight."

"Like a ticking time bomb."

"Let's go. We're done here, for the time being."

CHAPTER 27

NORTHEAST LOUISIANA, WHILE PART of America's growing secular society, struggled to preserve its strong Protestant traditions—one of which was the sanctity of Sunday. A storied past when commerce was closed, government offices were shuttered, and church bells rang, a clarion call to Sunday worship. Families gathered around the dining room table, highlighted by "happy talk" and a sumptuous meal. Often a picnic, if weather permitted. While the churches maintained a strong presence in Camden, exemplified by Reverend Rhea Joslyn's impact on the Southside, many commercial establishments were open on Sunday, business as usual.

After their golf game, Maggie took Carl aside. She looked at him with those vivid blue eyes and made an admission: She urgently needed his input. Bynum and Armstead were unsettled issues that had to be addressed. Since she respected Carl's advice, it would weigh heavily on any decision she might make.

Carl suggested an early dinner; say around six, at the Blue Light, one of the few restaurants that remained open on Sunday night. The Club was an option, but the grill and dining room were noisy and privacy was an illusion. He had too many gregarious friends, and Maggie drew men to their table like honeybees to wildflowers. He checked the clock above the door to the Pro Shop. He could drive home, shower, change clothes, and take a nap on the sofa before it was time to pick up Maggie.

The Blue Light was a free-standing stucco building a block off Louisville, a locally owned variant of T.G.I. Friday. The signature: a blue-and-white striped awning over the entrance. Dark vinyl booths lined both sidewalls, each with a cordless lamp. Tables for four were covered with a blue tablecloth, and Bentwood chairs encircled a square bar. The Sunday liquor law was a local option, and Camden chose to allow the sale of beer and wine. The floor was made of wood planks and the walls were unadorned. Two big-screen TVs hung high above the back bar, angled for easy viewing. The music from wall-mounted speakers was a mix of country and rock ‘n roll, but muted on Sundays. It was a blessing for those who wanted meaningful conversation, not the least of whom was Maggie McFarland.

A hostess led Maggie and Carl to a booth and handed each a menu. Maggie scanned the room; maybe a half dozen diners. A young waitress with ordinary looks wore a pencil skirt and a blue-and-white stripped soccer shirt. She greeted them with a rehearsed smile and took their order: cheeseburgers and fries; Maggie a Diet Coke, Carl a Coors Lite. She picked up the menus and headed for the kitchen, her sandals flapping on the wooden floor.

Maggie placed the napkin in her lap and rested both arms on the table. Distracted, she rearranged the bowl of artificial sweeteners and the salt and pepper shakers. “I’m not sure where to start,” she said.

Carl raised a hand. “First, a compliment . . .” He canted his head toward the three men at the bar. “ . . . they think I’m taking my daughter to dinner.”

“It’s your imagination.” Maggie placed her hand on his. “But you’re a dear man, Carl Sweeny.”

He noticed she had worn the ring, which pleased him. It was one of those times when Carl thought maybe . . . just maybe . . . her feelings for him had taken a step forward, into something consequential and ongoing. He reengaged. “I’m here to help, wherever you start.”

Maggie removed the card from her purse and slipped it across the table. “Another message from my good friend Randy Bynum,” she said tongue-in-cheek.

Carl checked the postmark. “Tyler?” He rubbed his chin while reflecting. “East Texas, right?”

Maggie nodded. “Tyler’s a nice town, ’bout a hundred miles, maybe a little less, east of Dallas and just off I-20.”

"Why Tyler? That's a three-hour drive, round trip."

"Direct Energy has customers in Tyler. Maybe it was a business trip and a good place to mail the card. Or an associate had the appointment in Tyler and did him the favor." Maggie shrugged. "Who knows?"

"The loon has gone to a lot of trouble to avoid a Dallas mailing. Guess he thinks it'll provide an alibi if the game he's playing backfires."

Maggie sipped her water and dabbed her lips with the napkin. "It's one of the things I wanted to talk about . . ."

"Bynum, the stalker," he interrupted.

A weary nod. "I'm tired of having a target on my back, always looking over my shoulder, furtive glances even in the middle of the day, and carrying the .38 everywhere I go, which makes me feel like a modern-day Belle Starr without the buckskin and boots." Maggie stopped long enough to take a deep breath and let it out slowly. "He has the advantage, Carl. The time and place—well, it's his call. Meanwhile, I'm supposed to stay alert and bolt the doors. Not fair. I want to lure him out. At least that would put us on a level playing field "

Carl understood her concern and the cause for worry. No one knew how long Bynum would continue to send the cards and make the phone calls. It was a progression: a tease, a taunt, a threat . . . but at some point, he would make it personal. That was the psycho's end game: to torture and kill, up close and in-your-face. But Carl was sure that Bynum, with his picture plastered all over Camden, would not chance a daylight visit. Rather, he'd come under the cover of darkness and in disguise . . . a baseball cap, glasses, facial hair, a limp, even crutches; something outrageous. Maggie was right. She was at a tactical disadvantage, not knowing when he would make his move. He also agreed there was merit in a plan to draw him out. But how? It was something he needed to discuss with Bailey, even Sheriff Clancy in Dallas. Any plan would make Maggie the "bait" and put her at risk, but no greater risk than waiting for Bynum to strike at the time and place of his own choosing.

Carl saw the waitress with a tray of food heading their way. "Do you have a plan?"

Maggie shook her head. "I thought, together, we could devise a way to coax him, like a fly into a spider's web."

The waitress placed the food and drinks on the table. "Can I get you anything else?"

""We're good. Thanks."

She tucked the tray beneath her arm and wandered back to her station.

"We'll get Bailey and Clancy involved. Put our heads together and come up with a game plan."

She reached across the table and squeezed his hand. "Thanks, Carl. I just want to end the madness."

"I'll get the ball rolling and contact Bailey tomorrow."

During the meal, there was a lull in the conversation. Neither ate more than half their cheeseburger. The discussion of Randy Bynum had blunted their appetites.

Maggie slipped out of the booth. "Be right back. Need more advice . . . another matter."

Carl pushed his plate away and sipped his beer. He tried to think of some way to get Maggie relief from Bynum's malevolence that followed her like the scent of her own perfume. Maggie was no shrinking violet, he was sure of that, but the constant vigilance and inordinate security measures extracted a price, both emotional and physical. He had also dismissed his own intervention—a flight to Dallas and a hard-nosed visit with Bynum. It was the world he'd lived in for ten years. But Lee Clancy had done that, only to find Bynum in adamant denial. The sheriff was stymied without the facts and/or evidence necessary for a search warrant or an arrest. Anonymous phone calls and unsigned greeting cards with their sinister messages were forms of stalking, but without Bynum's imprint, none of it rose to the level of probable cause. So Carl chose to stay in Camden, close to Maggie, reminding her often to bolt the doors.

By the time Maggie returned, the waitress had cleared the table and brought another round of drinks. She picked up her can of Diet Coke and leaned against the corner of the booth.

"You had something else on your mind," Carl said.

"Yesterday, despite a miserable headache, I drove out to OverReach."

"I'm listening."

"Alice Fogleman called Friday and asked to see me in her office as soon as possible. She said it was urgent, a word she repeated several times."

"Let me guess: she made a request that gave you heartburn."

A faint smile through tight lips. "Carl, I know you're smart, but I didn't know you were a mind reader."

"Not really," he said. "Why else would Alice ask for an urgent meeting, unless she needed a favor?"

"It was a troubling request and the reason I wanted your opinion."

"Is she making a last-ditch effort to pressure you into a full-time position?"

Maggie shook her head. 'No, no, it's much more important than that."

He drummed the table with his thumb. "Okay, give me the facts."

Maggie knew that Carl was aware of the Armstead connection to OverReach. He had served on the Board and probably had interacted with A.B. Armstead over the years. But Ronnie Armstead was the problem, and she explained the reason for her dilemma. Armstead had insisted that she, Margaret McFarland, counsel his nephew. After hearing of Robbie's depression and drug use, she felt inadequate. The young man needed a top-notch psychiatrist who could provide psychotherapy and prescribe medication if needed. Maggie stated her feelings succinctly: it was neither fair to her (nor any psychologist), nor would it benefit the patient. Fogleman had made the same argument with Armstead, but her words had fallen on deaf ears.

Carl took a swig of beer and processed the facts as Maggie had laid them out.

"Have you signed the contract?"

"I had planned to sign when I was there yesterday. But the Armstead request threw me for a loop, and I left the papers on Fogleman's desk unsigned."

"Okay, how 'bout this? Since you haven't signed your contract, you have no legal obligation to honor Armstead's request."

Maggie waved her hand through the air as if she were erasing a blackboard. "I can't do that, Carl. If I offend Mr. Armstead, it may have a chilling effect on OverReach . . . those unintended consequences you talk about." She stopped and shook her head. "No, I can't use the contract as a way to sidestep his request."

Carl nibbled his lower lip thoughtfully. "Then try this approach . . ."

"That's why I need you," she said, reaching over and taking his hand.

"Agree to counsel Robbie. Hear him out. After three or four sessions, you may be surprised at how well you are handling his problems. Conversely, if you're hitting a brick wall, speak with Mr. Armstead in person and explain the need for referral to the best psychiatrist in the state." Carl raised both arms, as if he were giving a benediction. "How does that sound?"

"Reasonable."

"Oh, by the way, I met your prospective client at Trappers last night."

"You're joking."

Carl shook his head. "I'm dead serious. Someone had tipped off the stoners. When we drove into the trailer park it was quiet, not a sound.

"And Robbie . . . where was he?"

"Bailey knew upfront that a goof-off named Mickey Randle rented the last in a long line of trailers and hosted the party-goers. An enabler . . . probably selling the stuff. Last night we checked him out and found nothing but a smartass with a big mouth. He identified his visitor as Robbie Armstead, who was asleep on the sofa. Either too much vodka or too much pot."

"Did you smell anything?"

Carl nodded. "Air freshener. They knew we were coming and had cleaned up the place. The rooms were spotless." A pause as he drained the can of Coors. "One other thing: Bailey asked about the arrowheads. Of course, Randle acted as if it was a stupid question. Neither he nor anyone he knew collected crap like that . . . his words."

"I guess the salient question is why was Robbie Armstead hanging out with a pothead?"

"Maybe you'll get the answer during one of your sessions."

It was dark when Carl pulled into the driveway. He walked Maggie to the porch; the outside lights were off. While unlikely, he wondered if she had forgotten to flip the switch before locking the front door. Carl had not paid attention and, of course, there was light from the setting sun when he picked her up. But Maggie always turned the outside lights on if there was a chance of getting home after dark.

Carl looked warily in all directions, but the darkness was deep and foreboding. Stratus clouds, remnants of Saturday's warm-weather front (the chill was back again), dimmed the illumination from a half-moon and a scattering of stars. A wall light on each side of the door was enclosed by frosted glass in a bronze frame. Carl opened the glass panes—both light bulbs were missing. "You've had a visitor," he said, unable to hide his grave concern.

Maggie unlocked the door, punched off the alarm system and turned on the living room lights. "Bynum's in town. Think it's part of his little game, or something more ominous?"

"I suspect it's another calling card; a reminder that you're still in his crosshairs."

"Let's go inside," she muttered.

"Just long enough to check the house."

"Want some coffee?"

"No thanks. You're tired. Kinda bushed myself."

Maggie waited at the front door until Carl was satisfied the house was secure. "I'll take care of the porch lights tomorrow," he said.

"Thanks for dinner and your wise counsel."

"Good night, Maggie." He held her close and felt her press against him, molding her body into his. Carl felt the flush in his face and a carnal stirring that had lain dormant for a very long time. He yearned for intimacy with Maggie, a woman he loved as he'd loved no other. But he knew that would have to wait. He settled for a passionate kiss and another good night. He heard the lock click and waited until she turned off the living room lights.

CHAPTER 28

MONDAY MORNING, ON THE WAY to the Annex, Carl stopped at Starbucks for coffee. Work traffic was lighter than usual and the sweater-weather ideal. Sunlight splashed the windshield and caused him to squint, miffed that he'd lost his dark glasses over the weekend. He turned off Calypso into the parking garage and followed the blue awning into the lobby of the Annex. Spook, dependable as Big Ben, was at the security desk. With the loss of Eloise, he was doing overtime. He wondered why Ned Bowen, the new recruit, was not available. But Carl was in no mood for morbid conversation, so he slowed his pace, waved a good-morning and kept moving.

Rose Marie, in a tan pants suit and a green satin blouse, was at her computer when he came through the glass doors.

"Hello, Carl." She came around her desk and gave him a hug.

"Hi, Rose." He stepped back and gave her the once-over. "I like your outfit. Good with the eyes and gives the place a little pizzazz."

"Thanks." A half-bow. "Now, what brings you in so early on a Monday morning?"

"Is Bailey available?"

She looked over the top of her desk; a red light was blinking. "He's on the phone. Shouldn't be long."

Before Carl took a seat, the office door opened and Bailey in uniform stepped out. "Mornin' Carl, come on back."

Carl blew Rose a kiss and followed the sheriff into his inner sanctum.

"Have a seat. I see you have coffee."

Carl sat in a chair near the desk. "I wanted to return the badge, since I'm no longer a deputy." He leaned forward and placed it on the desk. "But the real reason I'm here is to talk about Maggie."

"Another message from Bynum?"

"'Fraid so. A card in the mail Saturday." Carl's expression turned somber. He recounted the events of Sunday evening and the missing porch lights. Vandalism was a possibility. More likely, Bynum was in town. "It's wearing on Maggie, on guard all the time, and she wants to draw him out and end his vendetta, one way or the other."

"How does she propose to do that?" he asked.

"Not a clue. That's why she came to me. And I, in turn, have come to you."

"I'd like to help, but . . ."

"Think about it. Call Clancy and get him involved. He has a personal stake in keeping Maggie safe. Between the three of us, we should be able to devise a scheme that will make it happen."

"Clancy made it clear in our last conversation that he'd do anything within his power to help Mrs. McFarland."

"Jack, the husband, cast a long shadow across the Metroplex and earned an enormous amount of respect. Whether it was admiration for Jack's good works and philanthropy, or Lee felt an obligation, maybe owed him a favor—whatever the reason, Jack, and by extension Maggie, won a special place in the heart of Lee Clancy."

"I'll call this afternoon."

"How 'bout a follow-up in a week and see what we've got?"

Bailey checked his desk calendar. "I'll try to set a date when I talk to Lee."

"The sooner the better," Carl said.

Rose knocked, entered and asked if either cared for coffee. Head shakes gave her the answer. "You know how to hurt a girl's feelings," she moaned. Puckered lips. A pout. A pivot and she was gone.

"You'll miss her," Carl said. "She brightens up this rather drab office. You may have to surrender and hang some pictures."

Bailey looked around the room, the four walls, and broke a smile. "I like drab."

Carl shrugged and stood to leave. "Any plans for Mickey Randle?"

Bailey placed both elbows on the desk, his chin rested on clenched fists. "I've assigned a deputy to drive by Randle's trailer every Friday and Saturday nights. He'll call if he spots any action or suspicious activity. But I suspect Randle and his friends will lay low for a few weeks, or more likely, move the party to another location."

"How 'bout the expired license?"

"I ran into Dray Moody and he's rattling Randle's cage in the Joslyn investigation, using the expired license and uninsured Harley as leverage. No need to double down, a waste of assets. Dray can handle it."

"Good. If both agencies keep the heat on Randle, sooner or later a snitch will call looking for a deal."

"I hope you're right," Bailey said. "I remember the Trappers raid a year ago, and I'd like to avoid another ugly confrontation."

Carl leaned on the back of his chair. "One other thing and I'll get out of your hair. Saturday night, Randle's only guest was Robbie Armstead. You heard Robbie mention his uncle, A.B. Armstead."

Bailey nodded. "What's the point?"

"Armstead, who underwrites OverReach, the woman's shelter, called Alice Fogleman, the director, and demanded counseling for Robbie. He said the boy had problems with depression and drugs. Needed help." Carl hesitated and straightened up. "And here's the kicker: he wants Maggie to counsel the boy, though she is neither qualified nor has she signed her contract with OverReach. But Armstead carries a big stick and wields enormous influence, overriding Fogleman's objections and engaging Maggie. She's considering a proposal that I believe Armstead will accept."

"Which is what?"

Carl descried the terms of the agreement he had suggested on Sunday. "While her sessions with Robbie are confidential, over time, something useful may unfold."

"As in Robbie, the informant?" Bailey asked, perceiving the irony.

"Maybe he'll give you Mickey Randle and the names of the potheads." Carl turned to leave. "Keep me posted."

Rose was on the phone as he passed her desk. He stopped long enough to plant a kiss on her cheek. "Next time, I'll get my coffee here," he mouthed, grinning.

She covered the speaker with her hand. "Shoo, Carl Sweeny."

Dallas, Tuesday, March 27th, 2012

Jim and June Underwood lived on Mesa Drive, next door to Randy Bynum. Jim, a strapping six-footer, worked for a top-tier accounting firm in downtown Plano. After the two children left home, both students at the University of Texas, June returned to teaching the third grade at Booker Elementary, only a short commute from Mesa Drive. The Underwoods treasured their privacy and Bea Simpson, three houses down, summed it up:

Pleasant, yes; neighborly, not so much. When either Jim or June saw Randy Bynum over the boundary hedge or at his street-side mailbox, they waved, but not a word had passed between them.

After the evening meal, Jim pitched in and loaded the dishwasher and cleaned the kitchen counters. June inventoried the fridge and made a grocery list for her mid-week after-school visit to Kroger's. Both were avid readers and enjoyed an occasional movie, but they were neither club members (Jim played golf on a public course) nor supporters of the fine arts. Both were active members of St. Matthews Catholic Church, a sanctuary from the secular world which neither embraced.

They had just settled into their comfortable chairs with their books: June favored fiction and had just started John Hart's *Iron House,* while Jim hoped to finish Isaacson's *Steve Jobs.* The nights were still cool, no need for A/C or the whirr of the attic fan. Mesa Drive was a half-mile from the noise of a heavily traveled U.S. 75. It was a quiet street, one of the features that factored in their decision to buy the house. They savored the stillness that enveloped the neighborhood. Occasionally, the yelps of a coyote or a dog baying at the moon would break the silence. But tonight was different—alarmingly different.

Jim placed the book in his lap, removed his glasses and rubbed his eyes. He stifled a yawn and checked the clock on the mantle. "It's almost eleven, June. Are you ready to turn in?"

Before she could answer, a blood-curdling scream came out of the night. Another followed . . . a long, chilling cry.

Jim went to the window and heaved a heavy sigh. "Bynum's at it again."

June slipped out of her chair. "I'll call 911."

The operator answered, "What's the problem?"

"Domestic violence at 623 Mesa Drive in Plano. The Bynum residence."

"Your name, please."

"June Underwood, a next-door neighbor. Bynum's done this before. One day he'll kill the woman."

"Did you see anything?"

"No, but we heard the screams. He's probably beating the daylights out of his live-in girlfriend."

The operator promised to send a cop car to that address and added, "He may want to speak with you."

June placed the wall phone in its cradle and poured herself a glass of milk. "I'm going upstairs and take a tub bath," she said, massaging her shoulders.

Jim gave her a good night kiss, then went back to the window. He leaned against the frame with its view of Bynum's front porch and lighted entryway. While waiting for the cop car, he listened; nothing but the baying hound. He wondered if the young woman had survived the beating.

In the distance he saw the flashing light bars of a Plano police cruiser. Good response time, he thought, five minutes right on the nose. He followed the cruiser down Mesa and up Bynum's driveway.

Jim watched the officer follow the walkway to the front door and saw him rap the jamb. The cop took out his notebook and waited. But not for long; a woman opened the door. Jim was sure it was the girlfriend, since she was backlighted by lamps in the entryway. He tried to read the cop's body language, but there was little animation. He probably asked several standard questions, which the woman answered as if nothing had happened. It was the pattern of the past—the women (there had been more than a few) took a beating but refused to bring charges at the risk of Bynum's death threat. Jim knew it didn't take a genius to understand the dynamics of the assault and the victim's fear of a more brutal reprisal.

The officer extended his arms as if to say: You need help, but our hands are tied until you ask for help, He pointed to her face. Jim was sure it was swollen and battered like the others, a bloody mess that makeup could not hide. The cop closed his note pad and spoke some final words. Surely a caveat: call us if you change your mind. He tipped his visor and returned to his cruiser. Much to Jim's surprise, the cruiser backed down the driveway into Mesa, passed his place, and headed for U.S. 75. He was relieved, since he was in no mood for conversation. What he really wanted was to go next door and beat the stuffing out of Randy Bynum.

The following evening

Lee Clancy left his office Wednesday night, a little after eight. Dusk had folded into darkness. Bynum should be home. For some time he had planned to have a no-nonsense face-to-face with Randy Bynum, and the Monday afternoon phone call from Bailey Grant provided the catalyst. He had also received a copy of Sergeant Ewing's report, the officer who responded to last night's 911 call: domestic violence at 623 Mesa Drive. Clancy figured it was the opportune time to pay Mr. Bynum a visit. He also wanted to see the victim and the trauma she sustained, but without a warrant, that was unlikely.

As he drove the four-lane, he thought about Bailey Grant's request. He understood Maggie's misery; the constant vigilance would wear anyone down. He remembered an old truism: *dripping water wears away the stone*. Maggie wanted closure and believed her odds improved if she could draw Bynum out and deal with him on her terms. Clancy conceded her point and promised Bailey he would put on his thinking cap and await his call. But of this he was sure: He'd do everything in his power to keep Maggie safe, even if it meant extreme measures. He owed Jack McFarland that, and a great deal more.

Clancy parked at the curb and crossed the yard to the front of the house. There was a car in the driveway with the imprint of Direct Energy on the front door panels. Bynum was home. He removed his badge from his belt and rang the bell. The porch light came on and the door swung open. Clancy was surprised, since Bynum was much bigger than the poster picture he'd sent to Camden three weeks ago had suggested. A full head of hair, but the face was indistinct in the pale porch light.

"Lee Clancy, Sheriff's Department, Dallas County." He held up his badge, close enough for Bynum to see it.

"Welcome, Sheriff. What brings you to Plano?" He sounded as friendly and inviting as a church greeter. Not a hint of tremor or stutter in his voice.

"I'd like to speak with Ms. Crowley, Cathy Crowley. A police officer answered a 911 call last night at this address and spoke with her."

"Sorry, Sheriff, she's not available."

"Officer Ewing described the young woman as badly battered and unwilling to answer his questions." Clancy stepped closer; he wanted a better look at Bynum.

"An unfortunate accident, Sheriff. She tripped and took a terrible tumble down a flight of stairs."

"You can skip the bullshit, Bynum. Last night was the fourth time in the past eighteen months the Plano police have responded to a 911 call from the Underwoods." He pointed to the house beyond the boundary hedge.

Bynum ignored the accusation. "Did you know, Sheriff, that more than half the accidents in this great country of ours occur in the home?" He opened his arms and cocked his head, as if he'd made his point. "It's a fact," he said for emphasis. "Accidents happen."

Clancy decided to move on to another subject, the real reason he was here. "Since Ms. Crowley is not available, I'd like to ask about someone else with whom we share a mutual interest:"

Bynum's shoulders sagged beneath the weight of Clancy's probing, but he refused to wilt. He sighed agreeably. "Ask away, Sheriff."

"You know her. Name's Margaret McFarland, formerly of Dallas."

"I met her once, a while back. Seemed like a nice lady."

Clancy tipped his Stetson back and moved in a step closer. "Do you know the penalty for second-degree aggravated battery?"

"Don't know. Don't care."

"Fifteen years in prison. Angola's a hellhole. Not sure a good-looking white boy would survive six months."

"Come on, Sheriff. You're wasting my time." He started to close the door.

Clancy realized he'd pushed the right button and put a large boot on the threshold. "Do you know the penalty for premeditated murder?" He didn't wait for an answer. "Life in prison without parole. Give it some thought, Bynum."

"You must be crazy, I hardly know the woman."

"For what it's worth, should any harm come to Mrs. McFarland, don't worry about Angola, I'll take care of you myself. Do I make myself clear?"

"Vigilante justice, is that it, Sheriff?" A sardonic snicker. "Back to the days of Jesse James and Billy the Kid." A hand to the mouth covered another snicker. "Is that what you're saying to an innocent man?"

Clancy got in his face, so close he could smell Bynum's cigarette breath. "Consider it a warning—leave the woman alone. Got it?" The order was crystal clear and delivered with a cutting edge.

Bynum slammed the door shut.

Clancy heard the lock click. As he walked back to his car, he noticed the lights were on in the Underwoods' residence. They may have felt like informants, a part of the drama, since according to the records they had heard the screams and made all the 911 calls. He opened his car door; a last look at the Bynum house. His gut told him this was not his last visit. Some people would be intimidated by a stern warning from the formidable sheriff of Dallas County. Clancy doubted Bynum was one of them.

During the drive home, Lee remembered with clarity his obligation to Jack McFarland. 1978, thirty-four years ago, after a decade-long tenure as a deputy, he decided to run for the office of sheriff. His opponent was an entrenched incumbent. Family and friends offered their support—but none, not a single one, gave him a Chinaman's chance. A month before the election, he received a substantial contribution from McFarland and Associates. A copy of a letter McFarland had sent to a number of the Metroplex's "movers and shakers" was enclosed. It announced the unwavering support of Lee Clancy. He had done due diligence and was certain Clancy was the man for the job. McFarland solicited their participation in the election process, along with their vote. The money poured in, and an ad blitz made Lee Clancy a household name. The election was close but the victory was sweet. Without McFarland's advocacy, there would have been no fairy-tale ending. But most memorable were McFarland's comments: no attack ads; the incumbent has flaws, let the people decide. And this . . . my support is unconditional; there is no quid quo pro. Above, his distinctive signature: "Dio sia con te." (God be with you.)

It was a debt he could not pay, even if Jack were still alive. But his widow, Maggie, was very much alive, and she knew Lee Clancy was a trusted friend, ready to help if help was needed. Now Bynum afforded him the opportunity to satisfy part of the debt.

Clancy planned to retire at year's end. He'd had a successful career that validated Jack's faith in him so long ago. Neutralizing Bynum and removing the dread and danger that had become Maggie's inseparable companions would be the perfect denouement. But there was work to do. He would make the phone call to Bailey Grant first thing tomorrow morning.

CHAPTER 29

Dallas, March 29th, 2012

CATHY CROWLEY STOOD IN FRONT of the bathroom mirror. It had been thirty-six hours since Randy had punched her with his fist, slammed her against the wall, and kicked her in the side for good measure. She could still hear glass shatter, and in her mind's eye see the overturned furniture . . . her own personal war zone. Cathy felt waves of nausea as she examined her reflection—her face bruised and swollen, blood crusted beneath her nose, her right eye only a slit. Cathy knew from Randy's previous assaults it would take some time for the swelling to subside and for her body to heal. Since it had happened before, it would happen again. "So why am I still here?" she asked her reflection. Easy answer: Randy threatened to kill me if I tried to run away. Another long look at her battered face, long enough for Cathy to reach a decision: she had to get away from the man she had met by chance at O'Grady's Bar and Grill in downtown Plano three weeks ago. He seemed to be the consummate gentleman, a good-looking guy and generous to a fault (or so it seemed). Several dinners later, she had moved in with Randy Bynum. *Fools rush in where angels fear to tread* flashed before her. For some reason, Alexander Pope and her twelfth grade English class surfaced. Now she must leave, and without a trace. But how? She had no money other than pocket change, maybe enough to fill up the Civic. Randy had the key to her car; she had lost her job at Pizza Hut (corporate office in Plano), and there was no family to call. Her mother had died of lupus ten years ago, and her detached father remarried and moved to South Florida. Her stepmother, who was only a few years older, resented her youthful good looks and let Cathy know after the marriage to expect nothing more than an arm's-length relationship. As she applied makeup to mask some of the facial trauma, she considered her assets, not the least of which was a car key in a magnetic case attached to the underside of the Civic's left rear fender. One suitcase would hold all the clothes she needed. Her mother's jewelry (aTag Heuer watch, a diamond mounted engagement ring and a gold locket) was insurance, although it would break her heart to pawn any of them.

Cathy went to the bedroom window and looked out. Bright sunlight greeted her and boosted her spirits. Since Randy occasionally came home for lunch, she needed to get moving. She checked her purse and found a twenty and some loose change. While she packed, she considered location. Where would she go, and in which direction? She didn't care, but a large city was essential, since it provided anonymity and more job opportunities. And more apt to afford temporary shelter, like the YWCA or a home for battered women. She pulled up her mental map: Houston to the south; Atlanta to the east; Oklahoma City to the north; all possibilities. Cathy figured if she didn't know until she turned off Mesa Drive, then Randy wouldn't know.

Before leaving, she left a note on the kitchen table. A feel-good decision effected a crooked smile, well worth the shooting pain into her jaw.

Randy, I'm gone for good. Catch me if you can, you scumbag.
My parting advice: get help before you end up in a psycho ward,
or worse still, a cell in Huntsville. Okay, I was the fool, the foil,
the punching bag. Now, thank God, you're out of my life forever.
Goodbye, you sicko. Or are you the Devil's disciple?

Cathy packed the car, slipped into the driver's seat and keyed the ignition. As she drove away, she chose the direction that would carry her far from Dallas. It was the most important decision she'd ever made. The stakes were high, her life in the balance, but she never looked back

Camden

Thursday morning, Maggie picked up Pixie and Imogene at eleven o'clock and took them grocery shopping at Safeway. It had become a part of her weekly routine. Thursday was scratched, already taken, when she chose her three work days at OverReach. While it took two hours out of her morning, shopping in slow motion, she relaxed and enjoyed their company—especially Pixie, who had a sense of deadpan humor not unlike Groucho Marx. Of course the two old spinsters were frail and unable to drive, but their minds were nimble and razor-sharp. Maggie's reward was a sense of satisfaction that she felt each Thursday after she'd carried the bags of groceries inside and set them on the kitchen counter. She had once asked herself, what would Jack have done were he the next-door neighbor? Easy. Jack would have put a car and chauffer at their disposal every Thursday. She was sure that some of his inherent goodness and generosity had spilled over into her life, and for that she was grateful.

Maggie was fascinated by her elderly neighbors. Each leaned on the other. It was a true symbiotic relationship. Maggie wondered if either could survive without the other. Pixie had more than her share of grit and aggression. She also had a way with words, better able to express herself. Imogene was reserved and would be lost without her sister, who anchored their lives. Had either gotten close to marriage? Maggie only knew they were school teachers, but she was curious, and one day at the propitious moment, she would pop the question.

There was enough time before her meeting with Alice Fogleman for Maggie to have a sandwich, freshen up, and check her answering machine. There was a message from Carl saying he would drop by around four, if that was convenient. He had some news of interest. Maggie found her cell and hit redial; the call went to voice mail. She left her reply: "Hi, I'd like to hear the news and hope it's good news, for a change. My appointment at OverReach is at two; should be home in plenty of time. Bye."

Maggie pulled into a parking space in front of the white Colonial with its six Tuscan columns. She crossed the veranda and entered the austere reception room. Madeline looked up from her computer and pointed to the security door. "It's unlocked."

Maggie refused to let an impolite receptionist spoil her visit. She gave Madeline a hard stare before she opened the door that emptied into the long hallway. As usual, the interior was quiet, only the hum of a vacuum cleaner from somewhere upstairs. While she had not seen it, Maggie wondered if there was an elevator, since the second floor provided bed and board for women who needed temporary shelter.

Maggie was surprised to see Alice Fogleman standing in her office doorway with a worried look. She wore a short-sleeved, plain cotton dress. Make up covered the small scar on her forehead. Clear polish on her nails, a recent manicure; and her hair, the last time in a ponytail, now hung loose around her shoulders.

"Hello, Maggie. Come in," she said, pointing to the armchair.

"Hi, Alice, I like your dress. Yellow is my favorite color."

"Thanks. The weather has warmed a bit, so I broke out my spring wardrobe knowing full well that with Easter just around the corner, there'll be another cold spell before we can put our winter wraps away."

Maggie scooted her chair closer to the desk. "First, I want to apologize for the delay in getting back to you."

"It wasn't pressing."

"To be honest, I agonized over my decision, but it's finalized. I'll agree to counsel Robbie."

Alice let out a huge sigh of relief. "A.B. called early this morning and wanted to know if I'd heard from you. And if I hadn't, why not?

He was a bit agitated, but calmed down when I mentioned our meeting and a promise to call him this afternoon."

Maggie gave her the terms of the agreement. If there was progress after three sessions, she would continue to work with him. Otherwise, she would refer Robbie to a highly respected psychiatrist. Maggie added, "I know Mr. Armstead cares about his nephew and is genuinely concerned about Robbie's mental health and his bohemian life style. At the same time, I have reservations about my ability to deal with what sounds like some serious pathology. But I'm willing to give it my best effort. When you speak to Mr. Armstead, please make it clear, the agreement is non-negotiable."

"I think A.B. will be pleased. He knows that Robbie needs help and is anxious to get the ball rolling."

"Contractually, I begin working on the first Tuesday after Easter."

Alice looked at her desk calendar. "Tuesday, April the 10th."

"Since there seems to be a sense of urgency, I'll see Robbie next Wednesday."

"Will one o'clock work for you? Don't want to make it too early."

Maggie leaned back and thought for a few seconds. "One o'clock is fine. But tell Mr. Armstead he or a family member must get Robbie here next Wednesday, and on time."

"That won't be a problem," Alice said confidently.

"Guess I'd better sign that contract," Maggie said.

Alice opened a desk drawer, removed the document and slipped it across her desk. She handed Maggie a pen and a key to the security door. "You've read it, but if you want . . ."

"I'm good." After putting on her glasses, she changed the starting date to April 4th, initialed the change and signed the contract.

Alice leaned over the desk and handed her a copy. "For your records."

"Call me if there's a problem with the appointment."

"Of course. And we're delighted to have you join the OverReach family."

"It's my pleasure," Maggie said. She placed the copy of the contract and the key in her purse.

When she passed the reception desk, Madeline was still immersed in her laptop. No words were exchanged; a subject she had once again forgotten to discuss with Alice. She figured the forgetfulness must be Freudian (meaningful error) as she drove away from the Colonial and headed for home.

Carl had parked his car at the curb. His presence nearby mitigated the threat of Randy Bynum. Maggie pulled into the garage and walked back to the street. No sign of Carl; maybe he had decided to visit the Sweeneys. She picked up the mail, retraced her steps and closed the garage door. Once inside, she kicked off her shoes, went to her desk and checked the small stack of mail: only more promos, a wedding invitation, the daughter of an old friend from Dallas, and her Camden Bank statement. There was nothing from Bynum, which was no surprise since she received his last card five days ago. He seemed to have a timeline for his postings and phone calls. She wondered if he had set the date to end the mind games and make his move.

Maggie was startled by the doorbell. She was mad at herself for the involuntary reaction. It wasn't a mystery—the Bynum threat had put her steady nerves on edge, an admission she hated to make. She had been fiercely independent after leaving Rutledge, still a teenager. Her Las Vegas experience, interacting with men of every stripe, had made her tough and gutsy; qualities attenuated by her move to Dallas and her life with Jack McFarland. Her disquiet was the reason she had asked Carl to design a plan of entrapment. Again she thought of the spider web, the perfect metaphor.

Maggie knew that implementing a plan was one thing, pulling it off was another. She recalled from graduate school that the intelligence quotient of psychopaths fell along the entire spectrum: some bright, some much less gifted, some in the lower percentiles. High-profile cases like Ted Bundy and the Zodiac Killer suggested all psychopaths were highly intelligent. Not the case. While there were slight differences of opinion among the savants, Maggie concluded the I.Q. spread was close to that of the general population. Based on Rita's comments and Bynum's work record at Direct Energy, she believed Randy was well above average intelligence, and it would not be easy to outsmart him.

She walked to the entryway and checked the sidelight before opening the door.

Carl stood there holding a brown bag.

"A bottle of wine," he said and stepped inside.

"How are the Sweenys?"

"They're good. Edith said to tell you hello."

Maggie looked at her watch. "Maybe a little early for . . ."

"It needs to cool. A burgundy, Pinot Noir, your favorite."

She reached for his shirt, pulled him close and kissed him. "You know the way to a girl's heart," she said. "Better put the wine in the fridge."

The show of affection caused Carl's heart to accelerate and filled him with breathtaking bliss.

"What's the news of interest?" she asked.

After putting the wine away, he joined her at the kitchen table. "Clancy called Bailey this morning and gave him the rundown on his confrontation with Bynum. ." Carl recounted the Underwoods' 911 call and Clancy's brash encounter. "The sheriff hoped intimidation might scare him off, but he wouldn't bet on it."

Maggie shook her head in disbelief. "Only a week after Rita disappears, Randy charms another young woman who's frightened by his death threats and becomes docile and submissive. I've heard the story countless times during my counseling at The Shelter. These women are afraid to leave and have no place to hide." Maggie sighed despairingly. "Predators like Randy need a doormat, preferably a live-in, to release some of their pent-up anger. According to Rita, it's part of sexual foreplay. Once the physical abuse ends, Randy becomes contrite, begs for forgiveness and sweet talks her right into bed."

"I dealt with a few cases in which the abuser carried out his threat. All are serving life sentences without parole at Angola . . . that is, if they've survived that cesspool."

"Has Bailey or Lee come up with a plan to draw Bynum out of the shadows?"

“Not yet, but it’s still on the table.”

Maggie reached over and patted his hand. “Now, on a more pleasant subject.” She moved closer and rested both arms on the table. “I took Pixie and Imogene to Safeway this morning. While there, I did a little grocery shopping of my own.”

Carl folded his hands on the table and made a confession. “I suppose at some subliminal level the wine was a bribe, hoping for an invitation.”

‘I’m glad you’re here, Carl. I may have bought the filets for the same reason—hoping you would stay for dinner. ”

He dropped his head, as if he were searching for the right words. After an unbroken silence, he looked up and said evenly, “I love you, Maggie. There’s no place I’d rather be than here with you.”

Maggie went to the fridge and removed the wine. She uncorked the bottle and half-filled two wine glasses. She brought them back to the table and reclaimed her chair. She took a swallow and dabbed her lips with a paper napkin. She had used the time to consider a response. “Carl. You are my best friend. I enjoy just being together. And I’m grateful for your care and concern for me. I believe we share many of the same values and interests, but . . . there has to be a feeling . . .” She paused and pointed to her heart. “I confess that feeling has deepened with each passing day. It really has. But do I love you, Carl?” She extended her arms toward him, as if to draw him to her. “Just a little more time.”

“As I said before, I’m a patient man. Meanwhile, I hope we can share more time together.” He cupped his hand and muffled a chuckle. “I’m in desperate need of a golf instructor. How much do you charge?”

A Cheshire cat grin. “Probably more than you can afford.”

Carl shrugged and picked up his glass. “To the beautiful *Annabel Lee.”*

“A poetry lover in the D.A.’s office,” she said gleefully. “When did your love affair begin?”

“It started in college. I fell in love with the nineteenth century lyrical poets. Poe and *Annabel Lee* followed me through two marriages and left me brooding about those failures.”

“The real world is just so different, Carl. Not all hearts and flowers.”

“I lived in the real world for a lot of years. But poetry was my retreat.” He closed his eyes and quoted the first stanza from memory:

It was many and many a year ago,
In a kingdom by the sea,
That a maiden there lived whom you may know
By the name of Annabelle Lee,
And this maiden she lived with no other thought
Than to love and be loved by me.

“The real world, Carl.” She refilled his wine glass. “Better light the grill.”

CHAPTER 30

Dallas

RANDY BYNUM LEFT DIRECT ENERGY a little before six o'clock. It was a twenty-minute drive from the office park to his place on Mesa Drive. He figured Cathy would have dinner ready around seven; enough time to stop at O'Grady's for a drink. He had put in a long day at the office and felt the fatigue settle in the muscles of his arms and shoulders. He needed a couple of drinks, that magic elixir which allayed the tension and temporarily pushed his problems into oblivion. Like most addicts, he blocked out the role of alcohol in feeding his dark side and its role in triggering his bent for violence.

O'Grady's was a block off K Avenue, just another five minutes of travel time. Dinner could wait, and Cathy wasn't going anywhere with her car key locked in his glove compartment.

The sun was near the horizon when Randy pulled into O'Grady's lot. The Bar and Grill was crowded as usual. No surprise, since it sat near the center of Plano's main mercantile area and served drinks at reasonable prices. The steady drone of human voices filled the room. A flat TV hung above the back bar, muted, as a tape of the Dow's final numbers moved across the screen. Every table in the room was taken, and clusters of patrons stood close to the large windows with their angled view of K Avenue.

Randy stood just inside the paneled-glass door and scanned the room. A stroke of luck: a gray-haired gentleman slipped off his bar stool, put on his straw hat, retrieved his cane and with his jacket in the crook of his arm, waved to the bartender and limped toward the exit. Randy wasted no time, almost knocking down a waitress in a rush to grab the seat near the end of the bar. He found himself between a stockbroker (a guess) with his face buried in the WSJ, and a nurse or medical tech (presumably), in green scrubs, mesmerized by a good-looking guy next to her that Randy figured was a doctor. The Medical Center on West Fifteenth St. was only a short distance away. Since he was in no mood for conversation, Randy was glad his bar-mates were engrossed in their own tightly circumscribed worlds.

Randy, half-standing, waved vigorously to get Beckham's attention, but the bartender had his hands full. Not one empty bar stool. As a regular at O'Grady's, he had gotten to know Beckham and wondered why he had not parlayed his good looks and friendly manner into a more lucrative job. Only having a high school education may have held him down. Always neat and dapper, not a hair out of place, and with a pencil-thin mustache, he could have stepped out of a Don Ameche movie.

Without asking, Beckham set a Scotch on the rocks and a bowl of peanuts in front of him. For the next half hour, he munched peanuts and sipped the Scotch. The stockbroker tucked the paper beneath his arm, slipped off the stool and bumped Randy's shoulder on his way out.

"Hey, goddamn it, watch where you're going." The reprimand was loud and acerbic.

The broker stopped, slapped the folded paper against his free hand and gave Randy a stare, hard as a blue agate. The room went quiet as a wild-west saloon when a gunslinger walked in.

Randy wiped the splash of Scotch from his shirt with a paper napkin. "Let's hear an apology, you asshole," he shouted.

Beckham caught the broker's eye and canted his head toward the front door. The young man nodded and walked out of the bar. Then Beckham turned to Randy, a scowl that got his attention. "Settle down or I'll throw your ass out . . . understand?

"Yeah, I'm okay." He pointed to the wet spot on his shirt and shook his head. "The SOB didn't say a thing. No apology. Nothing."

During the brief verbal skirmish, the nurse and her friend had paid their tab and left O'Grady's. Most of the bar stools were available. Randy crunched the ice in his empty glass and let his anger simmer down. He gave Beckham a limp apology and ordered another drink, wondering if Cathy had dinner ready. She was not much of a cook, but she made up for it in other ways.

He moped over his drink until it was gone and ordered another. Randy had heard that alcohol tamped down a man's libido. Not so with him—it only fueled his sex drive, almost drove him crazy. He checked his watch; dinner was ready, but dinner could wait. Cathy was flexible; she knew the drill.

Beckham placed another drink in from of him. "You driving?"

"Sure." He held out both hands. "Steady as a rock."

"Three's the limit. Understand?"

"Got it."

The crowd at O'Grady's had thinned out. "Where's that pretty woman you brought in here a few times? Haven't seen her lately."

"You mean Cathy?"

"Yeah, that's the one."

"She's around." Randy stirred his drink with a swivel. "I still see her occasionally."

"She looked like a winner. Hope you didn't screw it up."

"I'm on overload at the office. Had to cut back on playtime."

Beckham fingered his mustache. "Keeping your priorities straight, huh?"

"I need a paycheck," Randy said and drained his glass.

Beckham wiped the mahogany counter and refilled the bowl of peanuts. "Bring Cathy with you the next time."

"Yeah, sure, Beck, I'll do that, just for you." Randy slipped off the stool, dropped a twenty and a ten on the counter, and started for the door.

A little wobbly, Beckham noticed. "Drive carefully."

When Randy Bynum pulled into his driveway, he knew something was wrong. The house was dark. He opened the garage door with the remote; the Civic was missing. Despite his alcoholic haze, he knew Cathy was gone. The anger begin to build. He'd kill the bitch if he could find her. He slammed his car door shut and dashed to the stoop. He keyed the front door, stepped inside and flipped the light switch.

The only sound was the ticking of a grandfather clock that stood like a sentry in the entryway. He headed for the kitchen and half-filed a six-ounce glass with Dewar's and one ice cube. With drink in hand, he toured the house, staring with the upstairs bedroom. Some of her clothes were in the closet, and knick-knacks which she had brought from her apartment were still scattered about. Bynum felt the flush of anger in his cheeks and nursed his drink as he checked the rest of the house. Nothing was missing or out of place. When he returned to the kitchen and refilled his glass, he saw the note on the table. He sat down and read it, following a finger that tracked the words. It unleashed his rage, like feeding a dead caribou to a pack of wolves. And the name-calling raised the level to a boiling point, a simmering volcano about to erupt.

"Bitch," he shouted to an empty kitchen and furiously threw his drink across the room, glass shattering on the far wall. He poured another drink and walked outside. Down the street a dog howled, a frightful sound that only layered his anger. He was never a dog lover, having been bitten by a stray as an eight-year-old walking home from school. The dog was never found, and he became a pin cushion—anti-rabies shots, a lot of them, for a month. The memory was still fresh and painful. Bynum bellowed, "Come down here, you mangy cur, and I'll put you out of your misery."

He sat in a lawn chair near the back door and gulped his drink He tossed his glass and covered his face with his hands. He had to do something, or he'd go crazy. Find Cathy, or take his Glock 23 and twelve-gauge shotgun to South Ashford with its all-night strip joints and a haven for drug pushers, and do some real damage. What irony, he thought: a service to humanity. He leaned back and looked at a dark sky. His blood level of alcohol had reached an emotional peak and began a slow descent.

Lights were on in the Underwood residence. Maybe one of his neighbors saw Cathy leave—or better yet, she may have talked with them about her leaving. He needed to know where she was going, and they might have the answer. He damn well planned to find out. Only one image mollified some of the anger: his hands around Cathy's neck, squeezing the life out of her. Choking was such a clean kill and oh, so personal.

Bynum took the short cut and squeezed through a narrow space in the boundary hedge. While next-door neighbors for five years, it was the first time he had been on the Underwoods' property. It could just as well have been Switzerland or some foreign country. He cut across the neatly manicured lawn (unlike his own), mounted the steps and rang the bell.

The porch light came on and the door opened. Jim Underwood, built like an NFL linebacker, filled the frame. "Whatta you want, Bynum?" he growled.

"I know it's late, but I can't find Cathy and I wondered if you or June had spoken to her recently."

Jim folded his Popeye-like arms across his chest and shook his head.

"Did either of you see her today?"

Another head shake.

"I'm afraid she's gone . . ."

"Don't blame her. We heard the screams"

"I want her back, Jim. I love the woman."

"What a strange way of showing it. You beat the daylights out of her. Maybe you need help."

Bynum took a step back. "I didn't come here for a lecture. Just wanted to ask a simple question."

"I don't have the answer, but if I did, you wouldn't hear it from me."

"Thanks for nothing." He spit on the steps and walked away.

"She's gone, Bynum. You'll never see her again."

A salvo of expletives before Bynum wedged his way through the boundary hedge.

Underwood shouted a final rejoinder: "Get some help, Bynum. You're one sick puppy."

Bynum stumbled up the back steps, scraping his knee on the brick, and hobbled into the kitchen. The bottle of Dewar's was empty. No liquor anywhere, no beer in the fridge. He slammed the refrigerator door shut and tossed the empty bottle into the back yard. He felt out of breath and sat at the kitchen table to recover. He pulled a pack of Marlboros from his shirt pocket, lit a cigarette with his silver Ronson lighter, a gift from Rita, and considered his options. While his rage had begun to subside, like an ebb tide that follows a beach-battering storm, he still needed to vent and relieve the tightness in his chest. He looked at the lighter—only a glint of silver in the dim kitchen light, but thoughts of Rita reignited the torment that racked his brain, and a gigantic wave of anger crashed over him. He reminded himself that Rita would still be here if not for that meddling McFarland bitch. But she would pay the ultimate price. He had the plan and needed to speed up the process. He would use the pay phone at the Greyhound bus terminal in Plano.

Camden

Carl had grilled the steaks. Maggie rated them better than The Rendezvous and Ruth's Chris Steak House. He had left around ten; it had been a long day for both of them. But another pleasant evening and Maggie admitted that she, more than ever, relished his company. While Carl may have been a take-no-prisoners kind of litigator and a tough D.A., he had a gentle side. *Annabelle Lee,* she thought. A poetry lover, a soft spot . . . who would have guessed?

Despite some self-imposed resistance, her feeling of affection for Carl Sweeny had grown inexorably over the past month. Was it akin to *love?* Well, she had experienced it before, falling in love with Jack McFarland, a man she loved dearly. Some of those same feelings were tugging at Maggie's heartstrings this very Thursday night. With him she felt comfortable and safe, even with Bynum lurking . . . out there, somewhere. She thought about the emerald ring and considered it a gesture of generosity and affection. He was like Jack in so many ways, and she wondered how a woman who came out of rural Texas an impoverished teenager, and survived her meretricious behavior in Las Vegas, could be loved by two exceptional men, their lives worthy of emulation. She would see Carl again on Saturday evening, with plans to drive to Benton and have dinner with Sam and Jane at her favorite restaurant, *The Place Where Louie Dwells.* She hoped Rufus was still at the stand-up piano running the keys. With any luck at all, Gertrude would be MIA.

Maggie made the rounds to be sure all the doors were locked. In the kitchen, she poured herself a glass of milk and carried it into the bedroom. She took a swallow and placed the glass on the bedside table. She removed the .38 from her purse and placed it in the table's drawer. It was all part of her nightly ritual. After she undressed, she slipped on the oversized golf shirt and went to the bathroom. But she was too tired to shower. That could wait until morning. After brushing her teeth and a perfunctory face wash, she climbed into bed with Russo's *That Old Cape Magic.* Maggie eyes grew heavy, and after only a few pages, the book slipped from her hands and she dropped like a feather into the arms of Morpheus.

The phone rang and shook Maggie from a sound sleep. The clock on the night table read 3:05. She sat on the side of the bed and let the phone ring, hoping it was a wrong number. But she knew, intuitively, it was another call from the stalker.

With her heart pounding, she picked up the receiver. "Hello."

"I'm here." Only two words, but filled with menace.

"What do you want at this ungodly hour?"

"A reminder: your time is almost up."

Maggie was now wide awake. "Randy, are you drunk?"

"The wrong question, McFarland."

"And the right question?"

"How much time do I have?"

"Okay, how much?"

"Very little. In fact, I may be across the street as we speak."

"Tell you what, Randy, I'll unlock the front door and you can come pay me a visit. We'll sit down and talk this out. How 'bout it?"

"I'm not stupid, McFarland. When I strike, you won't see it coming. And it's coming . . . soon."

Maggie reached into the drawer for the gun. She checked to be sure the safety was on. "You remember Sheriff Clancy"?"

Silence, only background noise. Pay phones, once ubiquitous, had been phased out with rare exceptions. Maggie figured he was at one of the airports or bus terminals.

"I told you once before if you touched me, you were a dead man. Remember?" She waited for a response, but there was only heavy breathing. "Lee Clancy won't wait for your trial, not even an arraignment. He'll take you down before you see the inside of a courtroom."

A cackle. "Don't count on it. I can handle Clancy." Another cackle. "Two for the price of one."

"Nothing you do will bring Rita back." Maggie knew that attempts at persuasion were a waste of time. A psychopath like Randy shunned logic and compromise, since he was locked into a warped sense of revenge, no matter the price tag. She was the object of his malevolence, and that's how it would play out.

"You'd better sleep with one eye open, you rich bitch," he said, followed by maniacal laughter. It reminded Maggie of some old horror movies she had seen with Dell on Saturdays in Odessa.

Before she could make a caustic reply, the line went dead. Maggie felt foolish, carrying the gun and checking the deserted street. The houses she could see through the sidelight, the Kahlils' and the O'Malleys', were dark. She doubted Randy was in Camden, since his job at Direct Energy should keep him in Plano. But there was the possibility he'd called in sick, giving him a long weekend. She remembered the cautionary aphorism: *Better safe than sorry*. So she checked, feeling a bit foolish. The front door was bolt-locked and the burglar alarm was set, its red light glowing. Satisfied, she went back to bed and with surprising ease fell asleep, the gun beneath her pillow.

CHAPTER 31

ON FRIDAY MORNING, DRAY MOODY arrived at The Schulze a little before eight. He took the stairs to his cubicle on the second floor. Just enough time to grab a cup of coffee and review his notes before the meeting with Captain Graves. He noticed the office door was open, which meant Graves was at his desk and ready to begin. Dray buttoned his grey seersucker coat and reworked the knot in his maroon tie. Since the weather had warmed, Dray had stored his cashmere sweaters in his mother's cedar closet. With his hands full—coffee cup and notebook—he headed for the open door and tapped the frame with his shoe.

The captain looked up and waved him in. "Close the door and we'll get started."

Dray took a seat and placed his cup on the floor beside his chair.

Graves was in uniform, his hat on a wall rack. He stood and took off his coat, hanging it on the back of his chair. "May as well get comfortable."

Dray nodded his approbation and opened his notebook.

The captain leaned both arms on the desk and made eye contact. "I want an update on the Rhea Joslyn homicide. Have you made any progress?" He didn't wait for an answer before adding, "The press and some of Rhea's church members are still breathing down my neck."

Dray cleared his throat. "Let me begin with what we know."

Graves nodded.

"First, money was the motive. What we don't have, I'm sad to say, are witnesses or a weapon. Nor do we know if the perp shot the preacher with intent or if it was accidental."

"Go on."

"Second, the perp was local, not a stranger passing through Camden. To rob a church office implies the perp is somehow church-connected or had second-hand knowledge of the pastor's fund." Dray stopped long enough to shuffle through his notes. "I interviewed at length twelve church members, all of whom were charter members of Southside. One of those conversations may have provided some insight."

Graves leaned back, hands behind his head. "And what might that be?"

"Mr. Arnie Preston, who owns *Kill the Critters: Pest Control*, mentioned the chairman of the finance committee . . ."

"So?"

"He has a son with a drug problem."

"One of a growing number, unfortunately," Graves said.

The detective picked up his coffee, drained the cup, and tossed it in the wastebasket beside the desk. "I thought Mr. Preston was rather perceptive by implying the drug users as a group should be looked at. One among them needs money to feed his habit and is desperate enough to commit a felony. And I might add, so loopy that he would rob a church office."

"I thought Bailey Grant had been working that angle with the stoners on Trappers Road."

"His objective was a drug bust, not Rhea's killer."

"Too bad his raid fizzled."

"Someone leaked the sheriff's plan and Mickey Randle, the stoner's lead dog, cleared everyone out and cleaned up the place. 'Spotless' was the way Grant described it."

"The stoners have abandoned Trappers?"

Dray nodded. "I spoke again to Bernice Majors, one of the trailer tenants, and she said it's as quiet and peaceful as Sunrise Cemetery. Translation: they've moved their fun and games to another location."

"And where might that be?"

"Just up the road, Morehouse Parish, out of Sheriff Grant's jurisdiction." Dray felt the buzz, since a homicide investigation had no such limitations. "Randle still lives in the trailer at Trappers, and I plan an early morning visit."

Captain Graves had heard enough to reach a tentative conclusion. The local drug activity seemed to coalesce around Mickey Randle. While the odds were small, it was possible the shooter came from within the group of stoners. It was not a promising lead, but it was all they had. “Bring Randle downtown for your interrogation. Voluntary, of course. If he refuses, isolate him in the trailer and ask the hard questions.”

“Tomorrow morning; seven should be early enough,” Dray chuckled.

“Take him a cup of Starbucks. It’ll soften him up, just your friendly cop.”

“There’s one other piece of evidence,” Dray said.

Graves opened a desk drawer, reached in, and held up the arrowhead. “Are you referring to this?”

Dray nodded. “It’s almost a certainty the shooter dropped the arrowhead during the confrontation with Rhea.”

“Can we make a connection of any kind?” Graves asked.

“Mr. Sweeny noted the old Indian mound was within shouting distance of Trappers.”

“Dubious, at best.”

Dray shrugged. “But possible.”

Graves walked over to the coffee bar and refilled his cup. “I think Bailey talked with Randle about the arrowhead Saturday night. Of course, the bozo denied owning an arrowhead or knowing anyone who collected arrowheads.”

“Come on, Captain, he’s not going to say, ‘Yep, one of my friends lost his arrowhead. Must have dropped it in the preacher’s office.’”

The captain nodded his concurrence. “Call me if you strike gold tomorrow; otherwise I’ll talk with you Monday.”

Dray lifted himself out of the chair and shook the captain’s hand. “I believe we’re getting warm.”

“How’s your intuition?”

Dray rocked both hands. “About fifty-fifty.”

“Not bad.” The keen eyes beamed encouragement. “Good luck.”

Dray turned to leave. “I’ll keep you posted.”

“Oh, one other thing,” Graves said and handed Dray the arrowhead. “Return this to Sergeant Blanchard in the evidence room.”

Saturday required an early start if he rolled into Trapper's by seven o'clock. Dray had set the alarm for 5:30, enough time to shave and dress, and to get his mother up and ready for the day. The stroke five years ago was devastating, paralyzing her right side, impairing her speech . . . what was called an expressive aphasia. According to her neurologist, his mother could understand his questions but could not formulate answers. It was as if the neural pathway that carried the answers was blocked or broken. After several months of rehab, Mable Moody regained some use of her right arm and leg. Therapy also strengthened her left side, and she learned to write (barely legible) with her left hand. Her verbal communications were limited to pointing, mimicry, a written word or two, and halting incoherent sentences. Dray had hired Nell Dillon to help, a woman strong enough to transfer his mother to the wheelchair and drive her to therapy. Nell was available on an as-needed basis; perfect for Dray, who worked odd hours. Whatever progress his mother had made, Nell deserved most of the credit.

Each morning he allocated an hour to getting Mabel dressed, fed and medicated. In some ways she had become self-sufficient. She brushed her teeth while seated. With her left hand she could change the TV channel, handle a fork and spoon, and control her motorized wheelchair. The neurologist told Dray his mother had maxed out, but physical therapy once a week was worth the time and effort . . . massage and range of motion to keep her joints limber and her muscles toned. They stopped out-patient therapy after three sessions, when Dray realized he and Nell could handle the therapy at home and avoid the hassle of travel and parking.

Dray pushed his mother into the den, a TV tray beside her chair. He reminded her that Nell would fix her lunch and stay until he got home. Dray kissed her on the cheek and left through the kitchen door, locking it behind him.

Dawn broke over Camden, assuring Dray of clear skies and a dandy day. After the stop at Starbucks, he turned on the radio, the dial set on KNOB, a pop station headlining The Mills Brothers and their up-tempo "standard," *Shine little glow worm, glimmer, glimmer* . . . It was toe-tapping time all the way up Old North Road.

He wondered if Bernice Majors was awake at this early hour. Probably not; too early for a courtesy call. He passed the Chevron station, which was open, two cars parked at the convenience store. Dray slowed and caught a glimpse of the weather-beaten sign which marked the entrance to the trailer park. He crossed the jerry-built bridge and drove to the end of the asphalt strip. No lights in any of the trailers. He was right; Bernice was still snoozing. He hoped REM sleep brought her pleasant dreams.

He backed into the clearing and turned off the engine. There were no other cars parked nearby. No sign of the Honda Accord. No light in the windows. He saw the motorcycle on its kickstand beside the trailer and figured Mickey Randle was home . . . sound asleep.

Dray stepped out of his car, stopping long enough to button his coat, brush a hand through his thinning hair and reassuringly pat his holstered gun. Satisfied, he picked up the cups of coffee and crossed the road. From somewhere nearby a rooster crowed.

Dray placed the cups on the top step and circled the trailer. Nothing, other than grass stains on his seersucker pants. He'd picked up the suit yesterday from the cleaners, but Dray refused to let a weedy yard, wet from an overnight shower, distract him or rattle his composure.

He knocked on the trailer's door and waited. He reached for the leather wallet in his coat pocket, removed his badge and clipped it to his belt.

Dray knocked again . . . harder. He heard nothing inside the trailer.

He pounded the wood door with a closed fist, loud enough to wake the dead. Finally, footsteps. The door opened halfway.

"Mornin', Mickey."

"Who the hell are you?" Randle opened the door all the way and leaned on the frame; his shoulders sagged. In boxer shorts and a rumpled T-shirt, he swiped dishelmed hair from his eyes still heavy with sleep.

"My name is Detective Dray Moody from the Camden Police Department, homicide division." He opened his coat and exposed his badge, then reached down for the coffee and passed a cup to Randle. "It'll pick you up."

The young man rubbed the stubble on his chin and looked at the cup of Starbucks with ambivalence. “Homicide? I ain’t killed nobody.”

Dray gave him a look of reassurance. “Just a few questions, that’s all.”

“First the sheriff and now the police. What the hell’s going on?” he asked, half-shouting.

“This is not about a little weed or disturbing the peace. That’s between you and the sheriff. I’m investigating the murder of Rhea Joslyn.” Dray pointed a finger skyward. “You know who I’m talking about?”

“Read about it in the paper.”

“You’re not a suspect, Mick. So jump in your jeans, and we’ll go downtown and have a friendly conversation.”

“Whoa!” Mick was now fully awake. “Unless you have a warrant, I’m not going anywhere.”

“How ’bout this . . .” Dray took a step closer to the threshold, holding his cup against his chest. “You have six unpaid parking tickets, an expired driver’s license, and no motorcycle or car insurance. Your penalty will be several hundred dollars . . . minimum.” He pushed the front door the rest of the way, fully open. “Here’s the deal: I’ll get your penalties revoked and the record expunged in exchange for thirty minutes of your time.”

“Come on in.”

Dray stepped inside. “You still must renew the license and get your insurance, which may take some time. I’ll mark my calendar and check with you in three weeks. If you are non-compliant, the sweet deal is off the table. Understood?”

“I got it,” he said as he led Dray into the kitchen and pointed to a small table and two plastic chairs. “I’ll be right back.”

Dray took a seat and looked around. He remembered Bailey’s comment after their failed raid: *I’d give ’em the Good House Keeping award.* No medals this morning. The sink was full of unwashed dishes and the linoleum floor needed a good scrubbing. A bundle of dirty clothes leaned against the refrigerator, which Dray assumed Mick would carry, in his own sweet time, to the laundry shed. He took a few deep breaths and caught the odor of stale air and something else: a spicy smell, unlike tobacco, which Dray knew was the scent of pot.

While the party-goers had moved to another location, someone, probably Mickey, had smoked marijuana in the trailer last night.

Dray wanted no diversions while honing in on the homicide. He would steer clear of any drug talk, leaving the stoner problem with the sheriff. Still, if Mickey thought moving beyond the reach of Sheriff Grant would stop the harassment, he was wrong. Sheriffs don't live in a vacuum. Bailey had already put Al Clark, the sheriff of Morehouse Parish, on alert and faxed Clark his reports. Grant had underlined the name "Mickey Randle," who among the group of stoners was an organizer, an enabler, a user and probably a dealer. Dray had done business with Sheriff Clark, an ex-Marine, during two separate homicide investigations and considered him tough as nails and tenacious as a bloodhound. It was only a matter of time before Randle's weekend parties were over in Morehouse Parish, and the party-goers, like gypsies, were on the move.

Mickey had put on a pair of well-worn jeans and a yellow T-shirt with the Harley-Davison symbol above the pocket. He wore scuffed loafers without socks and had hand-combed his hair. He dropped a pack of Marlboros, a Bic lighter and the cup of coffee on the kitchen table, sat down and lit a cigarette, curling gray smoke toward the low ceiling.

"Let's get started." Dray finished off his coffee and tossed the cup into a near-full waste basket. "A hypothetical question . . ." He waited for a comment of some kind, but none was forthcoming. "Let's suppose a preacher was murdered in her office, like Reverend Joslyn. Who would do that?"

Mick tapped his head. "A nut case."

"How about someone on medication or drugs?"

"Yeah, that too." He took a long drag off the cigarette and dropped it into his near-empty cup.

"Whatta you make of someone robbing a church office?"

"Stupid or crazy, one or the other." He fingered another cigarette from the pack and lit up. "If it was my thing, I sure as hell wouldn't target a church when the 7-Eleven is right down the street."

Dray felt he had disarmed Mick, since there had been no change in his facial expression and his answers seemed spontaneous. He decided a ploy to keep the interview civil and constructive: a little misdirection. "Ever go to church, Mick?"

"Naw, don't fancy that stuff."

"But you feel sorry for the preacher?'

"Hell yes, anybody in their right mind would feel for the lady."

"Okay, Mick, here's where we need your help." Dray leaned on the table and made eye contact. "We believe the shooter may have been a doper desperate for money." Dray paused for effect. "Help me here. Do you know of anyone, say, among the party-goers, who might fit the description?"

For the first time Mick's eyes narrowed and his expression changed . . . sullen, almost a scowl. "No fucking way, Jose."

Dray raised a hand like a guard at a school crossing. "Hold on, Mick. Think about it. No skin off your nose and vindication for the lady preacher."

Mickey shook his head, but said nothing. He blew more smoke at the ceiling.

"An agreement is a two-way street. I'm forgiving probably three or four hundred dollars in fines, wiping your record clean. May put in a good word with the sheriff, but you're not giving me the time of day." Dray reached across the table and squeezed his arm. "That's not the way it works, my friend."

Mickey jerked his arm away and gave Dray a baleful stare. "I'll think about it."

"I want the name of every party-goer, with a comment—your comment—beside each name. After I receive the list, I'll begin the process of revocation."

"Whatever you say, Detective." His upper lip curled in distain.

Dray backed away from the table, scraping the linoleum. "I'll let myself out." He stopped at the threshold and half-turned. "Remember, you have three weeks to renew your license and reinstate your insurance. I'll not forget."

"Next time you drop by, make it around eleven. Some people like to sleep in," Mick said with a smirk.

After Dray left Trappers, he stopped for gas at the Chevron station and a coffee at the check-out counter. During the drive to The Schulze, he wondered if the interview with Mickey Randle had been a waste of time. But, maybe not. He and the captain had agreed, while a long shot, it was possible a drug user was the shooter. They had no other suspects and nothing else made sense. Then, there was the arrowhead in Rhea's office: a coincidence or a connection? A curio or a rabbit's foot?

Dray knew Mickey was hostile toward law enforcement in general but hoped his offer would buy his cooperation. Would Mick come up with something evidentiary? "Fat chance," Dray muttered. "But you never know," he added. "Might get lucky, like winning the lottery."

CHAPTER 32

CARL PICKED UP MAGGIE as planned. They were to meet Sam in Benton at seven o'clock, forewarned to expect a big crowd at *Louie's* on Saturday night. Maggie suggested they leave Camden early; enough time for a casual tour of the Colby campus.

It was late afternoon when Carl drove across the Louisville Bridge and onto I-20 West. He put on his dark glasses and pulled the visor down to shade his eyes from a blood-red sun in slow descent.

Carl broke the silence. "Do you know what makes me happy?"

"Breaking ninety from the blue tees," she said with a lighthearted laugh.

"Yeah, that too."

"Do I get another guess?"

"Sure."

"Hmmm, let's see." She rested her chin, Rodin-like, on a folded hand. "You bought an IPO that'll make you millions." She muffled a chuckle with a fist over her mouth.

"I missed that chance with Tesla Motors. Had my order in for five thousand shares and cancelled at the last minute."

"I give up," she said. "What makes Carl Sweeny happy?"

He stole a look into those stunning blue eyes. "You . . . you've made the colors brighter, the birdsong sweeter, and filled the hollows of my heart."

"Mr. District Attorney, ever the poet." She reached over and caressed his cheek. "I have feelings as well. But later; we'll talk about that later."

Carl broke what seemed another interminable silence. "I'm looking forward to meeting Sam. The two of you seem to have an open and well-connected relationship. You have been his guardian angel, and more so during the ten years without Jack's exemplary presence. Sam has received a child's ultimate gift: your unconditional love. He, in turn, has become a man of character with a bright future who can express his love for you unabashedly." Carl spoke with candor and clarity, not unlike his closing argument in a high-profile trial.

Maggie's eyes brimmed. She found a Kleenex in her purse and dabbed the moist lids. Too emotional to speak, she folded her hands in her lap.

"Your good fortune brings up another subject, one I should have told you about weeks ago."

Maggie half-turned in her seat, seeing him in profile. "If it's a secret, I'd like to share it."

"No, no, it's not a secret. I guess you'd say it's more of a disappointment."

"Sometimes it helps to talk about it." She caressed his cheek again. "Do I sound like a nosy psychologist?"

"Maggie, I have a daughter . . ."

"Oh, Carl, why haven't you told me?"

Carl shrugged. "We've never been close," he said ruefully. "I'm afraid I failed as a father."

Maggie looked out the window as she processed this revelation. The Acura streamed past one of the weathered clapboard churches she had seen on her earlier visits to Benton. She reached over and squeezed his arm. "Tell me all about her, Carl."

He chewed on his lower lip, deciding where to begin; a starting point to recount plaintive memories. "Meg is thirty-eight, and fortunately inherited her mother's good looks." He hesitated; a side-glance.

"Go on," she said.

"She graduated cum laude from Sophie Newcomb, then sailed through med school and a pediatric residence."

"And . . . ?"

"She met Carlton Chapman, a urology resident at Charity. They fell madly in love and were married after a short courtship. When Carlton finished his residence, they moved to San Diego and joined a large specialty practice in Chula Vista."

"And they've been there ever since?"

Carl nodded. “Almost ten years and I’ve only seen her twice.”

Maggie wanted to know the reason for the disconnect. She had heard the disappointment in his voice. As a psychologist, the need to know was compelling—and since he was more, much more, than a friend, she wanted to understand the dynamics of the emotional separation. There was always a reason, although it was sometimes opaque. Surely the divorce played a role. Who was to blame for the loss of her mother? The blame game in a suicide is problematic, but Carl was the convenient fall guy, since it occurred after he remarried. Perhaps Megan saw the marriage as the salient reason, or at least the catalyst, for her mother’s suicide. Then there’s the gene pool. She remembered a wise man’s adage: *Blood kin does not guarantee affection or even friendship.* It was clear that Megan had created space by moving to the West Coast. But who had created the dissonance? That was the sixty-four dollar question, the one she had to ask.

“Do you know the reason for the separation?”

Carl shook his head. “I love Meg and told her so. Abby dished out the discipline, which spared me that unpleasantness. I wish I’d spent more time with Meg when she was a child, but I was trying to build a law practice and working sixty to eighty hours a week. On reflection, it’s really my only regret.”

Maggie closed her eyes and let her mind reel back to her years in Rutledge. She had ample cause to feel alienated and resentful. Escape from the house of horrors was her only viable option. She wondered how Megan, a child of privilege with decent parents, would unfold had she grown up in her shoes, walking to school on that dirt road in sun-baked Rutledge.

“When did you last hear from Meg?” While she wanted to know more about this filial detachment, Maggie was hesitant, knowing the subject made Carl wistful. She didn’t want to spoil the evening.

He slowed the Acura as they approached the Welcome to Benton sign. “I only hear from her on special occasions . . . Father’s Day, a birthday, Christmas, either a card or an email. The notes are brief, nothing about her life in California. I assume she and Carlton have a busy practice and a solid marriage. But that’s an assumption on my part. I figure if there were a major crisis, I’d hear of it.”

"Any children?"

"It's the ultimate irony; a pediatrician in a childless marriage."

All at once, there were signs for the upcoming exits, including one in bold print, black on white: **VISIT COLBY COLLEGE.** Carl exited onto a surface street that wound through an area of upscale homes before passing the Colby campus. "Years ago, I tried to break down the barriers that kept us apart, but she thwarted every attempt. Finally, I accepted our detachment and hoped for the best. It's not what I want, but it is what it is." Carl sighed deeply. "Maybe someday it will change."

After a drive-around tour of the Colby campus, Carl drove back to town and found a pay-to-park lot only two blocks from *Louie's*. Sam stood in the shade near the front door of the restaurant, a leg propped against the stucco. He saw them coming and waved a welcome. After one of his bear hugs, Maggie took a deep breath and made the introductions. The two men shook hands. Carl believed eye contact and a firm handshake were markers of a man who was self-assured and comfortable in his own skin. Sam qualified; he had his mother's blue eyes, and his large hands delivered a bone-cracking grip.

"I've heard good things about you," Carl said.

San looked at his mother and smiled. "She may be a little biased."

"A mother's prerogative," Carl said. "Let's go in and get acquainted."

They passed through the swinging doors into a long, narrow room, dimly lit by wall sconces. An upright piano stood in the far corner with Rufus at the keyboard, a nimbus of smoke around his head from the ever-present cigarette as fingers danced over the keys, a jazz rendition of *Night Train.* But Rufus' improvisations, not the riffs, took front and center. The threesome chose a table in the middle of the room and tuned out the ambient noise when the piano man stopped playing.

A waitress appeared, filled the water glasses, took their orders and hurried back to the kitchen. "College student," Sam said. "She took my English Lit course last semester. The class read most of the works of

Graham Greene. At the end of the term, we took a vote of their favorite. Would you like to guess?"

"*The Power and the Glory,*" Carl said.

"Nope. Mom, your turn."

Maggie rubbed her chin thoughtfully. "I'll say *The Heart of the Matter.* Surely I'm right. It was his magnum opus."

Sam shook his head and laughed heartily. "An overwhelming majority voted for . . . are you ready for this?" He tapped the table with his spoon, a weak imitation of a drum roll. "*The End of the Affair* got sixty percent of the vote, and surprisingly, *Brighton Rock* took second place. But you know what I'm most proud of?" he asked rhetorically. "Those kids will always remember the Whiskey Priest and Maurice Bendrix, and the meaningful messages they conveyed."

"It sounds like you chose the right profession," Carl said. "I can hear the excitement in your voice when you talk about a great writer like Greene and how his works came alive for those young people."

"It's wonderful you love what you do and still have the time to be creative." Maggie, the proud mother, patted his hand.

Carl sipped his water and wiped his mouth with a paper napkin. He looked at Sam and said, "I'm sorry Jane's not feeling well. I was looking forward to meeting her."

Sam stared at the ceiling and rolled his eyes. "I'm never sure whether her complaints are real or an excuse."

Maggie sat facing the piano, her back to the saloon doors. She reached across the table and took Sam's hand. "The pregnancy . . ."

"The baby's fine." A frown formed on his handsome face. "Jane's mother calls every day, the puppeteer pulling the strings. And if she had her way, the marriage would implode." Sam leaned back in his chair and looked at Carl. "Of course, the baby changes everything. I'm guessing that Gertrude will be less inclined to sack the marriage." Sam threw up both arms in apology. "Sorry, Carl, I didn't mean to burden you with my officious mother-in-law."

"It's okay, Sam, wish I could help."

Maggie chose another subject, knowing further discussion of Sam's marriage would put a damper on the evening. "I told Carl all about your novel, Sam. So how's it going?"

Sam's face lit up, as if his mother had flipped the light switch. "Good, really good. But book-length fiction takes time . . . a lot of time. Unlike Stephen King, I can't turn out two thousand words a day. I'm happy with five hundred . . . on a good day."

"You're young, the best days ahead. My advice: keep at it and you'll succeed." Carl leaned in Sam's direction. "I'm putting my order in as of now for the first copy . . . signed, of course."

Sam laughed. "Just hang around a couple of years, and it's a deal." Another bone-cracking handshake.

"Carl, he's here!" Her shriek turned heads at nearby tables.

Carl was nonplussed; the outburst was unlike Maggie. But he saw the look of shock and surprise on her face. "Who's here? What are you talking about?"

She pointed. "In the corner, across from the piano."

Both men strained to see a man sitting alone, sipping a drink, seemingly caught up in the music.

"It's Bynum." She turned to Sam. "Randy Bynum, the stalker. Strange coincidence, wouldn't you say?"

Carl turned his chair and started to get up. "I'll have a little chat with Mr. Bynum."

"Don't, Carl! Please don't. It'll only fan the madness."

He stood for a moment, vacillating, and then slipped back into his chair. He could not ignore Maggie's plea.

Sam stared in Bynum's direction, as if he considered a confrontation.

Her hand on Sam's arm was a restraint. "He'll put on his sanctimonious face . . . that's what the psychopath does. And then he'll ask, what's illegal about dinner at *Louie's?* After all, he was just passing through Benton; Direct Energy has business in Jackson."

"I could challenge him on the cards and phone calls." The dim light in *Louie's* could not hide the flush of anger on Carl's neck and cheeks.

"Settle down, Carl." She held his hand, pulled him closer to her. "Surely you know, as a former district attorney, his answer to your accusation."

Carl conceded and pressed his glass of ice water against his hot cheek.

"Just two words . . . right?"

He nodded.

"*Prove it.* Then the sicko would laugh in your face."

"You're so sensible, Maggie. We did agree there is nothing on the mailings that connects them to Bynum. And the phone calls were made from pay phones, so there's no record. And the fact he's here tonight might be pure coincidence, a business trip; just passing through. And we only have your word that he threatened to kill you. Rita heard the warning, but she's irretrievable, well hidden by the Battered Women's Protection Program. So it's his word against yours. A stalker for sure, but way short of *probable cause,* and with what we have it would never make it to a grand jury."

Sam checked on Rufus, who was still tickling the keys. He looked pensively at his mother. "He's gone. Guess he made his point."

After a gourmet meal and warm goodbyes, Carl and Maggie drove back to Camden. "I should have mentioned Bynum's last phone call," Maggie said diffidently.

"Recent?"

"Early Friday morning, and unlike previous calls, we had a conversation . . . of sorts."

Carl pulled into the driveway on Lamy Lane and turned off the ignition. "Did he have something to say, or was it just another scare tactic?'

Maggie noticed a car parked in front of the Kahlils', but it was too dark to tell if there were occupants. A light was on in the Kahlils' living room and the blinds were open, which suggested the car belonged to a guest or family member. Maggie was irked that once again, she let a benign night scene conjure up shadows of suspicion.

"Bynum, did he have anything to say?" Carl asked . . . again.

"Oh, sorry, sometimes my mind wanders." She felt the gun through the soft leather of her purse and found it reassuring. "He said, in so many words, my time was about up."

"I wonder if he made the call from Camden."

Maggie shook her head. "Don't think so. Probably a pay phone in one of the Dallas airports. Lots of background noise. Easy drive to Camden on Saturday, then followed us to *Louie's* and slipped in unnoticed."

Carl walked her to the front door, the wall lights were on. He took her in his arms; a good night kiss. "It was a real treat to meet Sam, and I hope there'll be many more occasions."

"You did seem to hit it off. Maybe we can get Sam and Jane to Camden. He'd love to play a round of golf and have a nice dinner at the Rendezvous."

"Handicap?"

"He carries a three . . ."

"You're kidding!"

Maggie keyed the lock. "Jack was a scratch."

Carl shook his head, incredulous, as Maggie stepped inside.

"Lock up tight. I know I sound like a broken record, but be careful until we bring Bynum down."

Carl waited until he heard the lock click and a light went on in the entryway before leaving the porch. There were worry lines in his face; Bynum was out there lurking . . . somewhere . . . closer than before. And his pattern of behavior carried ominous overtones. Yet law enforcement was helpless unless Bynum made a fatal mistake or, Heaven forbid, he should carry out his hate-filled vendetta.

CHAPTER 33

Wednesday, April 4th

WHEN MAGGIE AWOKE, sunlight filtered through the blinds, the clock on the bedside table read 8:15. She lay in bed, stretched and yawned and wished Carl was with her. If that were so, Maggie was sure she'd smell the aroma of fresh-brewed coffee and hear breakfast clatter in the kitchen. It was a fantasy. She last saw him Saturday night and looked forward to their lunch date at the Blue Light after her session with Robbie Armstead. Missing him meant something, and it didn't take a master's degree in psychology to figure it out. A dummy could do it. How lucky could she get? To hit the mega-jackpot not once, but twice.

She fluffed her pillows and settled back, comfortable and content. There was plenty of time to dress, pick up her coffee, and keep her appointment at OverReach.

The past few days were uneventful, other than for two phone calls. Late Sunday night, Pixie, who had become her watchdog, buzzed her cell with one of her astute and disturbing observations: the prowler was back, and she wanted to be certain Maggie had bolted the doors and set the alarm. Maggie was sure the intruder was Bynum. He was in Benton, at *Louie's* Saturday night; doing reconnaissance (again) late Sunday before driving to Plano; and back at his work desk with time to spare. While it made sense, Maggie found it troubling and felt Bynum's plan was about to play out . . . and soon.

The second call Monday, late afternoon, was from Lee Clancy. He mentioned his recent visit to Mesa Drive and his in-your-face conversation with Randy Bynum. He described to her his attempt at intimidation, which rolled off Bynum like water off a duck's back. But Lee admitted "Mr. Cool's" reaction was not unexpected. During his thirty-year career in law enforcement, he had seen a number of psychopaths undergo withering questioning without breaking a sweat. He supposed it was part of their aberrant nature, the way they were wired.

He then gave Maggie the real reason for his call, which she processed with her eyes closed. She knew Clancy had been keeping a check on Bynum from the day of Rita's admission to The Shelter and the venomous threat to Maggie's safety. What she didn't know until the phone call was the lowdown on his son-in-law, Bruce Holloway, an executive at Direct Energy and Clancy's conduit for the travel schedule and other intelligence regarding Randy Bynum. Bruce had just told Clancy that Bynum had started a two-week vacation. No one in Holloway's network knew where he was going, or with whom. Maggie remembered the sheriff's advice as she opened her eyes and stared at the ceiling. "Take extra precautions; two weeks is a large window through which he could climb and make his move."

Maggie was sure that Lee was a true friend and would do all within his power to ensure her safety and well-being. During Jack's last agonizing days, his body riddled with metastatic disease, she had heard Lee make that very promise—words Jack understood, that brought a faint smile to his hollowed-out face. But the present threat, dealing with Bynum's malicious intent, Clancy was limited by location—two hundred and fifty miles from Camden, center stage for the stalker.

Maggie sat on the side of her bed and considered her ties with Lee Clancy. She believed most friendships were as fragile as butterfly's wings. Like gossamer, easily disrupted. A misunderstanding or a new address or a loss of some mutual interest may cause friendships to flounder and friends to go their separate ways. Maggie thought of them as casual friends or acquaintances, and she had lots of them in Dallas and had cultivated a few during her short stay in Camden. Ed and Edith came to mind. But the genuine article, a true-blue friend, was loyal, warm-hearted and enduring. And on the darkest night, a light that may flicker but never goes out. She remembered Jack's maxim: *To have two or three steadfast friends in a lifetime is a man or woman's good fortune.* She was blessed; Lee Clancy was one of them.

Maggie's consultation room at OverReach was half the size of Alice Fogleman's office. But it had two windows with a wide view of the bayou. Spare furnishings, only two arm chairs with beige cushions which faced each other a few feet apart. While the floors were hardwood, the chairs sat on a multi-colored area rug. Maggie felt an intimate setting was important in advancing a confidential conversation. A decorative vase filled with daffodils and branches of forsythia rested on a side table nestled between the two windows.

Maggie arrived a half-hour early and went directly to her room and closed the door. She had thought long and hard about the wisest approach to Robbie Armstead, often mulling over her options with the first cup of coffee. Now Maggie needed some time to review her tactics and put those thoughts in order. She knew the first five minutes, including the introductions, could make or break the chance for success.

She had dressed conservatively, a short-sleeved blue dress with a high collar, the hem just below the knee. She wore no makeup other than lip gloss and a light application of mascara (eye contact was an important tool), no jewelry other than her Rolex, and hair pulled back in a chignon. Maggie wanted no distractions, either in the room or on her person.

A knock on the door interrupted her pondering. The door opened without invitation, and Alice Fogleman led A.B. Armstead into the room and made the introductions. Everyone remained standing as Armstead surveyed the room before his probing eyes settled on the attractive Maggie McFarland.

Armstead was short, stout and bald, but exuded the Hollywood charm of Darryl Zanuck and the business confidence of Donald Trump. His physical appearance was not what Maggie expected, certainly not the stereotype of the alpha male. Jack, and now Carl, had set that standard.

"Where is Robbie?" Maggie asked.

"He's with Madeline. I wanted to speak with you privately." He looked at Alice as if she was exempt from the privacy rule.

Armstead stood, his arms folded. "Would you care to have a seat?'

"No, I'm fine," Maggie said.

Alice moved to one of the windows and looked out, removing herself from the stream of conversation.

Armstead leaned on the back of a chair. "Robbie is a fine boy, Ms. McFarland. But he has problems . . . even a layman can see that. My brother and his wife are distraught and asked my advice. Robbie needs help, and I believe he can find it with you. I wanted to thank you for taking on this assignment. A note or phone call seemed inadequate, so I'm here in person."

"I appreciate your confidence, and I'll do my best to help your nephew. However, as I stated upfront, if after several sessions we're not moving the ball, then I'll refer him to Dr. Edwin Edwards, one of the best psychiatrists in the state."

"I understand. Nevertheless, something tells me . . ." He stopped long enough to tap his forehead. " . . . you're absolutely the right therapist for Robbie."

Maggie summoned a smile. "We'll see."

"Goodbye, Ms. McFarland, and thanks again."

Alice Fogleman nodded to Maggie and followed Armstead, with his short quick steps, out the door.

Alice Fogleman returned with Robbie Armstead in tow. "This is Ms. McFarland, Robbie. She's your counselor and here to help you." She nudged him toward the chair.

Maggie gave him an amiable greeting. "Glad to meet you, Robbie."

The young man stood with his head down, as if he were spellbound by the colors in the area rug.

"Have a seat, Robbie. Let's get acquainted."

It took another nudge from Alice before Robbie dropped into the chair. She waved to Maggie and backed out of the room.

Robbie wore khaki pants, freshly pressed, and a gray T-shirt with TIGERS stamped in purple across the front. His long hair had been washed, brushed and tied in a ponytail. Maggie had read Bailey Grant's description of Robbie Armstead: *disheveled,* an observation made during the failed drug raid on Trappers Road. It was clear his uncle had cleaned him up. She also made a mental note of Robbie's general appearance: thin as a reed, and at least a foot taller than his uncle. She wondered who gave him his height. Just a guess: his mother.

Maggie waited for more than a minute, letting the silence settle over the room like dust motes. It set the mood for the first session, a device she'd used successfully during her long tenure at The Shelter. No accusations. No police-style interrogation. No patronizing. Rather, Maggie spoke evenly, hoping to bring Robbie into her domain without resistance. In the past, this empathetic approach had been effective in forming a workable relationship and, in time, opening a free-flowing line of communication.

Maggie wanted Robbie to look up of his own accord. But he was the perfect picture of dejection—slumped in his chair, his eyes glassy and downcast. "Robbie, I'd like to establish some ground rules as a starting point," she said firmly. "First, our conversations are private. Anything you tell me is confidential. I'll share information with your uncle—or anyone else—only with your permission. What's said in this room is privileged, just between the two of us. Is that understood?"

Robbie looked up and nodded.

"Second and most important, I'm here to help. In order to do that, you need to trust me, open up and let me explore your world. I am neither a mind-reader nor a magician, which means I need to befriend the real Robbie Armstead if we're going to make a difference in your life."

Robbie looked up again . . . briefly.

For the next twenty minutes, Maggie pitched softball questions: What's your favorite movie? What kind of music do you like? Was computer science your best subject in school? Who is your closest friend? There were others, simple questions; get-acquainted kind of questions. None were meant to intimidate or accuse or stir negative emotions. She wanted him comfortable and communicative.

Robbie's answers were either a head nod or monosyllabic. The sheriff had described Robbie in his Trappers' report as *taciturn*, but added a disclaimer: he may have been under the influence of dope or alcohol. If that was the case, Maggie thought Grant's observation was meaningless. However, a caveat from Alice Fogleman was more telling: "Conversation won't come easy. According to his uncle, Robbie is and always has been a young man of few words." Maggie had counseled taciturn clients before and knew that patience was the key that unlocked the door to revelatory speech.

Maggie moved to one of the windows, her back to Robbie. A black man was pole fishing the sun-drenched waters, his boat anchored beneath the overhang of a bald cypress. She watched the fisherman check his line and bait his hook (either a worm or a cricket) before she half-turned and re-engaged her client. The juxtaposition of the serene fisherman and the inner turmoil of Robbie Armstead was striking. It was times like this that Maggie wished she were a visual artist and could put the contrast on canvas.

"Robbie," she began again . . . lightly. "Your family is concerned about your welfare; not just the weight loss, but the lethargy and lack of initiative. Or as your uncle put it, 'He's dragging his tail, running on fumes, and that's not the real Robbie.'" She stepped back to her chair, still standing, looked down on the dispirited young man, and spoke in her most persuasive voice. "Robbie, tell me how you feel."

"I'm . . . I'm okay," he said without looking up.

"How much weight have you lost?" There were no more softball questions.

A shrug of indifference.

"Robbie, I can't help if you run and hide." A purposeful pause. "I'll ask again. The weight loss . . . how much?" Maggie kept her tone tempered.

He rubbed both hands over his face, as if searching for an answer. "Twenty pounds . . . more or less."

"Do you know the reason for the weight loss?"

"Just lost my appetite," he said. For the first time, the answer came quickly.

Maggie was surprised and hoped it was a sign of progress. She shifted in her chair and crossed her legs, lady-like. "You dropped out of L.S.U. after your freshman year. There must have been a reason." She held out her arms like a supplicant pleading for a full accounting.

Robbie raised his head. "I tried to adjust . . . Lord knows I tried . . . but it didn't work. I told my dad I'd join the Army before going back to college."

Real progress, she thought. "You're how old?"

"Twenty-three next month."

Maggie did the math with her fingers. "You've been out of school for more than three years, correct?"

Robbie sat upright in his chair. "I guess . . ."

"Doing what?"

"Working for my uncle."

"Doing what?" she asked again.

"For a year, I was part of the cleaning crew. The six-story high-rise in West Camden, headquarters for Armstead Industries. Well, I was part of the crew that cleaned the building. Worked nights. Slept days. I think my dad figured hard labor would send me back to college."

"And . . . ?"

"It didn't work, so A.B. moved me upstairs to accounting. An intern, really. But I was computer savvy and good at math, so they figured it was the shoe that fit."

Maggie looked at her watch; ten minutes left in the session. "How long did you work for your uncle?"

Robbie slumped back in his chair and broke eye contact. "'Til I got sick."

"And when was that?"

"Last November . . ." He stopped and scratched his chin. " . . . Thanksgiving, maybe . . . yeah, around Thanksgiving."

Maggie counted the months and held up four fingers. "How've you spent your time?"

Robbie leaned forward, elbows on his thighs. "Takin' it easy." The heavy silence weighed on him. "Hangin' out, you know, with friends."

"Is Mickey Randle a friend?" It was a question she had not planned to ask, at least not during the first session.

For the first time Robbie's face showed some animation, although Maggie wasn't sure if it was shame or vexation. "One of 'em. He lets me borrow his Honda."

Maggie decided not to go there. Not enough time to transition her inquiries into depression and drugs. Those two subjects would have to wait until later. In addition, she had a feeling, only intuitive (but based on a world of experience), that some strong emotion, probably guilt, was weighing him down. But that too was for another time.

Maggie stood up and said, “We’ve made a good start, Robbie.” She reached for his hand as he lifted himself from his chair, and walked him to the door. “I’ll see you next Wednesday, same time.”

Only a head shake. No goodbye.

Alice Fogleman was waiting in the hallway and escorted Robbie to his car.

Maggie went back to the window; the fisherman had pulled up anchor and left the shade of the bald cypress. She hoped he had caught a few bream and at least one big catfish. Maggie deferred any in-depth assessment of the meeting with Robbie Armstead, although she believed the session was constructive and an inchoate connection had been made. A crack, however small, formed near the rock-hard fault line of his psyche. It was a slender cord of encouragement, but Maggie knew only more time together would unravel the emotional entanglements. To her surprise, she relished the challenge.

When Maggie arrived at The Blue Light, she spotted Carl’s Acura and nosed into a parking space beside him. She was a few minutes late for their lunch date, but he had been warned in advance there might be a delay if Fogleman or even Armstead wanted to “know how it went.” Fortunately, she only had a brief conversation with Alice about Robbie’s return visit the following Wednesday.

Her cell phone chirped as she turned off the ignition. She dug it out of her purse; Maggie recognized the area code. She still had friends in Dallas, but wondered who would call mid-week and at lunchtime. (She had checked the dashboard clock.) Maggie answered with a frosty “Hello,” something she would regret, even though the car was attic-hot with the A/C off and she was late for lunch.

“Hi, Maggie. Lee Clancy here. Did I catch you at a bad time?”

Maggie felt her cheeks color, a blush of reproach. “No, no, Lee, good to hear from you.”

“I wanted to give you an update on Bynum.”

Maggie rolled her window down, but the warm humid air offered no relief. “The last bit of news was your call Monday. If memory serves, Bynum was taking a two-week vacation, but no one at Direct Energy knew where he was headed."

"I drove by his house Monday night, but there were no signs of life. No lights inside, the doors and windows were locked, and his car's gone. Don't think there's any question, he left Plano. Yesterday I asked Bruce to check his sources again, hoping someone might have an idea where Bynum planned to spend his vacation. One of the executive VPs, mentioned Bynum's mother who lives in Santa Fe, and that could be his destination. Bruce checked it out; in fact, he spoke with Mrs. Bynum by phone. He described her as pleasant, widowed, and works as a volunteer in the hospital gift shop, but she hadn't heard from Randy in over a month."

"She knows Randy's a problem," Maggie said. "I suspect there were episodes of bad behavior during his pre-teen years. One doesn't grow into a psychopath overnight. While expressions of violence and malevolence may appear later in life, the template was always there."

"I'm still surprised he doesn't have a criminal record," Lee said. "I've double-checked the national database, and he's clean."

"He's one of the smart ones, Lee. And as you know, they come in different shapes and sizes. Ted Bundy prototypes are rare birds." Maggie was uncomfortable, sweat trickling down her back.

"I suspect he's headed your way," Lee said.

"You're probably right. In fact, he may be sitting in this very parking lot. But, in a way, I've taken your advice and I'm more than ready for a showdown."

"We'll keep our eyes open on this end—and you, as I said before, be vigilant. Don't take foolish chances. And keep that .38 with you at all times. Use it, if necessary."

"Thanks for calling, Lee, I appreciate your concern."

"If you need me . . . well, you have my number."

Maggie closed her phone and dropped it in her purse. She opened the glove compartment, picked up the gun and ran her hand down the barrel. Felling more secure, she replaced the gun and relocked the compartment. Maggie wiped the beads of perspiration from her forehead with a Kleenex before she set the door lock, stepped outside beneath a blazing sun and sidled between cars to the entrance of The Blue Light.

The restaurant was almost full when Maggie stepped inside. On opening the heavy glass door, she felt a blast of cool air, which was a welcome reprieve. The hot weather was unexpected, a pre-Easter surprise. She spotted Carl in one of the vinyl booths waving her over. The smooth sounds of Rodney Atkins (Take a Back Road) flowed from the wall speakers and put a bounce in her step, even though the lyrics were muted by the rattle of dishes and the drone of the lunch crowd.

"I'm sorry I'm late." Maggie reached over and gave his hand a squeeze.

"No apology necessary. I'm good for the day."

"I got a call from Lee just as I turned off the ignition." She gave him a what-could-I-do shrug.

"I hope the sheriff had some good news."

"Not really." She recounted her conversation with Lee Clancy. "Apparently Bynum left town without tipping his hand. Neither co-workers at Direct Energy nor his next-door neighbors have a clue."

A waitress appeared and took their order. Business-like, she poured water into their blue-stemmed glasses and hurried away.

Maggie was thirsty and drank lustily. She dabbed her lips with a paper napkin and leaned against the corner of the booth. "The real reason for Lee's call was a reminder: to be . . . how did he put it?" She thought for a moment, and then snapped her fingers. "Vigilant, that's it. Be vigilant. He's worried . . ."

"I'm worried." Cal frowned. "Bynum's out there; we know he was in Benton Saturday night, but what the hell is he doing?"

"Playing his little game, keeping me on edge," Maggie said. "Waiting for the right time to make his move."

"It's frustrating to sit and wait . . . and worry. And vexing that two of the best sherriffs in the state and a retired D.A. can't come up with a plan to entrap the creep."

"Let's forget Bynum for now and enjoy our lunch," Maggie said.

The waitress in her slim-fitting skirt and soccer shirt brought their order: Caesar salads with slices of chicken breast and glasses of iced tea. "Anything else?" she asked before stepping back from the booth.

"We're good, thank you," Carl said.

"Our waitress . . . not the friendly type," Maggie said as she emptied a packet of sweetener into her glass of tea.

Carl nodded absently. "How did your session with Robbie Armstead go?"

"It went well."

"Will you see him again?"

"Next Wednesday, same time."

"I know the questions and answers are privileged, but I'm hoping you can help the boy." He put his folk down and sipped his tea. "I've known the Armstead family for a lot of years and admire their hard-earned success. They're good people, strong Camden loyalists, and their charity has endowed numerous worthy causes, OverReach among them."

"Alice told me A.B. was Rhea Joslyn's biggest contributor; two million for construction of the sanctuary."

"He's a charter member of Southside Methodist, and I think he's chairman of the Board." Carl pushed his salad bowl aside and rested his arms on the Formica. "This Sunday is Easter. I'd like to attend Southside to pay homage to Rhea. How 'bout it?"

"I'd like that, Carl. I remember when Jack and I were members of Preston Hollow UMC, Easter Sunday, the senior pastor would welcome an overflow congregation and always add, 'To those of you I'll not see again for a year, I wish you a Merry Christmas.' A bit corny, but it never failed to get a laugh. I guess humor is a tactful way to make a point of reproval."

The waitress passed their booth without a word, stopping long enough to leave the check.

Maggie caught Carl's look of annoyance, the petulant toss of his head. "Let's cut her some slack. She's probably working two stations, or just having a bad day."

His pique morphed into a halfhearted concession. "You're such a kind and forgiving person, Maggie. It's one of the things I love about you . . . one of many."

“And you, Carl Sweeney, always the gentleman, may have won this maiden’s hand.” A highly charged pause. “And her heart.”

He felt his own heart pounding in his chest. “Do you mean it, Maggie?”

She locked his gaze with those knock-out blue eyes and reached for his hand. “So close, Carl. Oh, so close.”

.

CHAPTER 34

ON GOOD FRIDAY, gunshots rang out at the end of Trappers Road.

Bernice Majors was washing dishes at the kitchen sink when she heard the explosions. Startled, she went to the window that overlooked the asphalt road in time to see a black sedan speed by, bouncing wildly over potholes, heading for the exit on Old North Road.

Bernice dialed 911, gave the operator her name and address, and described the exigent circumstances; the need for police and medics. When the operator asked if she had observed any of the commotion, Bernice insisted "seeing" wasn't necessary. There had been trouble in that area of the park in the past, drug problems, and she'd heard multiple gunshots. "We're wasting valuable time," she admonished the operator.

After hanging up the phone, she opened a kitchen drawer and shuffled its contents until she found the card. It was the business card Dray Moody had given her on his visit three weeks ago. She punched in the numbers; the call went to voice mail. She delivered the message with a sense of urgency and hoped Detective Moody would check his cell with dispatch and respond. Bernice knew she'd feel more comfortable with the homicide detective who had ingratiated himself during his earlier visit; his familiarity would put her at ease.

She draped her apron over a kitchen chair and went outside, looking down Trappers Road. The row of mobile homes sat side by side, at an angle that blocked her view of Randle's trailer. She stepped cautiously to the edge of the asphalt; the road was desolate, empty all the way to the cul-de-sac. Bernice felt chill bumps in the uncanny silence, until the wail of sirens rent the afternoon air. She hoped Dray Moody was on his way.

Bernice saw the flashing light bars after the vehicles passed the Chevron station and followed the two Crown Vics and an EMS ambulance as they rolled past, all the way to the end of Trappers Road. It was only a matter of minutes before an unmarked police car (no lights or sirens) traversed the bridge and parked in the clearing across from her trailer.

Bernice let out a sigh of relief when she saw Dray Moody, dressed in brown seersucker, step out of the car and cross the road.

"Afternoon," he said pleasantly.

She grabbed his hand, a firm grip. "I'm glad you got my message."

He canted his head in the direction of the dead end. "What's going on? Any idea?"

Bernice looked at her watch, then at Moody. "A half hour ago, there were gunshots, a lot of 'em." She thumbed the direction from which the shots were fired.

Moody took a long look in that direction. "If I had to guess, I'd say it's drug-related and the action is in Mickey Randle's neighborhood."

"It had to happen, sooner or later. Those party-goers were shameless hedonists. Smoking dope; maybe Randle was a supplier, just flaunting it as if it were nothing more than a pastime, like a cold beer and a game of ping pong."

Moody stepped back and looked carefully at the trailers on both sides of Bernice Majors' well-kept yard. There was a car in the clearing, but neither of her next-door neighbors had ventured outside. Maybe they were frightened. Or hearing impaired. Or were half-asleep and thought the gunshots were fireworks. Only Bernice reacted appropriately—no surprise to Moody, based on the impression she'd made during his previous visit.

"I saw the getaway car," Bernice volunteered.

"The getaway . . ."

"Well, the shooting stopped and this car flew by my window like a bat out of hell. So I assumed someone was in a hurry to leave Trappers."

"Did you get a description, or was it moving too fast?"

“A black four-door sedan . . . that’s about it.” There was a trace of disappointment in her voice, as if she had let Moody down.

“Anything else, like tinted windows or the color of the license plate?”

Bernice closed her eyes and revisited those fleeting seconds. “The car hit a big pothole. Thought it might’ve busted an axle. But no, it kept right on going.” Bernice kept her eyes closed, concentrating. “Oh, one other thing, roof racks.”

“To mount a canoe or surfboard?”

Now wide-eyed. “Exactly,” she said.

“You saw the driver . . . right?”

“Briefly,” Bernice said. “And a form in the passenger seat. So there were two of ’em. At least two.”

“Good eyes,” Moody said with a muted hand-clap.

“20/25 on my last exam.”

Dray Moody took another long look down Trappers road, the cul-de-sac blocked by the EMS ambulance parked near the dead end, its light bar still flashing. He hand-scrubbed his face and muttered his frustration.

“Aren’t you gonna go and check it out?”

Moody recovered his remarkable composure. He removed his coat and let it hang in the crook of his arm. “Can’t do it.”

“Why not?” she asked, bemused.

The detective grimaced, as if the answer was painful. “It’s all about boundaries . . . legal limits.”

Bernice looked even more muddled.

“A crime, any crime, committed outside the city of Camden falls in the sheriff’s jurisdiction. Whatever happened at the end of the road . . .” He turned his head and looked that way. “ . . . is Bailey Grant’s responsibility. While we have a working relationship with the sheriff’s department, we try not to overstep our legal authority.”

“Then how do you explain your visit a few weeks ago?”

“It was part of an investigation; a homicide that occurred in Camden.” He paused and extended his arms. “Understand the difference?”

Bernice nodded. “So the murder of Rhea Joslyn allows you to go wherever the trail takes you?”

“You got it,” he said. “But I’d still like to see for myself what’s happened down there.” A gesture toward the EMS ambulance.

“Sorry I called. Hope it wasn’t too much of an inconvenience.”

“You were just being a good citizen. Be sure to pass along your observations to Sheriff Grant.” Moody re-crossed the road and stopped, turned back. “Have a good Easter. Hope it cools down.”

She watched him go, all the way to Old North Road. A last look in the vicinity of Mickey Randle’s trailer before Bernice returned to the kitchen and a sink full of dishes.

The EMS vehicle drove south after crossing the improvised bridge and headed for home, the fire station on Calypso Street. A customized GMC Savana van waited in a northbound lane for the ambulance to make the turn onto Old North Road.

After a thorough assessment of the crime scene, the sheriff had put in a call to Dr. Nathan Swanson, the county medical examiner, and his assistant Nanette Hawthorn, a forensic photographer. Nat Swanson heard the urgency in the sheriff’s voice, and it meant one thing: he’d find one or more dead bodies. After a bumpy ride down Trappers Road, he parked near the dead end and observed the yellow tape that cordoned off Mickey Randle’s trailer home. Two Crown Vics were parked in the clearing and Bailey Grant leaned on one of the front fenders, his knee bent, the heel of his boot hooked on the bumper. After a careful check of the perimeter, two deputies rounded the trailer just as Dr. Swanson killed the engine and stepped out of the van.

Bailey knew the parish was blessed to have an M.E. the caliber of Dr. Swanson, whom he considered one of local law enforcement’s greatest assets. Nat completed a pathology residency at Tulane; Board certified. After a short tenure in academic medicine, he went back to school (his words) and spent two years in forensic pathology. He retired a full professor at the age of sixty-two and returned to Camden, where he was born and raised. Gentle persuasion by the mayor, an old boyhood friend, and Camden's low homicide rate brought him out of a short retirement and provided the parish with one of the most respected M.E. s in the state.

Dr. Swanson convinced Nan Hawthorn, whom he had met during her training at Charity, to join him in Camden. Nan was driven and she accepted his offer on the condition that she could also freelance—unless, of course, they were involved in an active homicide. Not yet thirty, Nan was single and totally committed to her craft.

The sheriff greeted Swanson with a firm handshake and a look of relief. He introduced his deputies, Walt Whitehead and Cleve Dewberry, to the pathologist. Nan, lithe and comely even in her green scrubs, got more than her share of attention.

The sheriff looked at Randle's trailer and shook his head. "Not a pretty picture."

"They rarely are," Swanson said. He pulled out his notebook and ballpoint pen. "Tell me what you know."

"First, some background." The sheriff recounted the failed drug bust two weeks earlier. However, he still believed the wild weekend parties about which the neighbors complained were fueled by marijuana, and it's likely meth was in the mix.

"So you get a 911 this afternoon?"

"Yep! One of the tenants heard the gunshots and put in the call."

"We were here in twenty minutes and secured the crime scene. We found three dead bodies—one of them is Mickey Randle, face-up on the kitchen floor in a pool of blood."

"You recognized him?" Swanson asked.

"We became acquainted during the botched drug raid."

The M.E. jotted the name in his notebook. "And the other two?"

"One in the bedroom and one on the sofa. I'd say . . . mid-twenties, probably friends or clients of Randle."

"Names?"

"I'll let you get the IDs. We couldn't reach their wallets, too much blood."

"Any witnesses?"

"Nope."

How 'bout the 911 caller?"

“Ms. Bernice Majors, just down the road. The operator reported Ms. Majors heard the gunshots but couldn’t see their location. Those trailers are set on concrete pads, side by side. She can’t see much of the road from her kitchen window. But she may have seen the getaway car. I’ll speak with her on my way out.”

“Anything else?”

“After we determined the three were goners, their bodies riddled with bullets, we checked all the rooms. The place looked like a war zone. I’m thinking assassination rather than simple homicide.”

“Sounds like it.” Another notation.

“After a walk-through, we enclosed the perimeter and waited for you.” The sheriff turned back toward the trailer, a flickering finger gesture. “Nat, it’s all yours.”

“I’ll give you a call when we finish here and complete the autopsies.” Swanson put the notebook away and motioned Nan, a canvas bag looped over her shoulder, to get started. They ducked under the yellow tape and passed the motorcycle, stopping long enough for Nan to set her camera and take pictures of the Harley Davison and shots of the trailer.

“You should hear from me Tuesday of next week . . . at least some preliminary results,” Swanson said from across the road.

The sheriff leaned on the top of the open car door. “Thanks, Nat, Sorry to get you out on Easter weekend.”

Swanson gave him a dismissive wave before putting on latex gloves and entering the trailer.

“Hold on, Walt.” The sheriff rolled down his window and spoke to Cleve. “I don’t think the shooters—there had to be more than one—will come back. There’s really no reason, since they completed their mission. But we need to hang around as long as Dr. Swanson and Ms. Hawthorn are on the property. So, keep your eyes open until they’re done and headed back to town.”

Cleve reached for a pack of Marlboros in his shirt pocket. “How ’bout the bodies?”

"Swanson will handle that. I suspect he's already made the call."

Walt eased the car out of the clearing and onto the road.

"Stop at the Majors trailer."

"Which one? They all look alike."

"Over there." The sheriff pointed to a trailer with a manicured lawn. "I'd heard she's the only tenant who takes pride in her yard; even grows her own flowers."

"Need me?" Walt asked.

"Naw, I'll only be a few minutes. But you'd better park in the clearing."

Bailey climbed out of the cruiser and strolled over cut fescue, still green despite winter's chill. His boots clacked on the cypress deck, and he stopped to admire the potted flowers. He removed his Stetson and rapped on the front door. While he waited, Bailey wondered if Nat had enough light—the sun was just above the tree line—to make his observations, collect blood samples, and anything else of evidentiary value. He was sure that neither lengthening shadows nor fading sun would affect Nan's photographs.

The front door swung open, Bernice Majors holding the door knob as if for support. "Hello, Sheriff."

"Afternoon, Ms. Majors."

"I saw your cruiser from my kitchen window."

"I'm glad to meet you," Bailey said, a gentleman's greeting. "You are the good citizen who reported the gunshots a short time ago. I wonder if you'd answer a few questions."

Bernice leaned wearily against the doorframe. "Look, Sheriff, I'm awfully tired and I've already told my story."

Bailey showed surprise.

"Detective Moody was here . . ."

"Dray Moody?" Bailey interrupted.

Bernice nodded. "After the 911, I called his cell. He'd paid me a visit a few weeks ago, part of the Rhea Joslyn investigation. A real nice man; left his business card. When I asked this afternoon why he wasn't lending you a hand, he said something about boundaries . . . and the gunshots were in your jurisdiction."

“Sounds like Moody. He gathers the facts but won’t step over the line.”

Her shoulders sagged, and her eyes had lost their luster. “Sheriff, I didn’t see much, but Detective Moody asked a lot of questions and I did my best to give honest answers. I’m sure he’ll remember every bit of our back-and-forth. Couldn’t you get that from him?” She looked at the threshold, embarrassed, knowing her reticence displeased him. “Next time, I’ll be feeling better and will invite you in for a visit and a cup of coffee.”

Bailey slapped his thigh with his Stetson. “I’d like that, Ms. Majors. Hope you’re feeling better real soon, and thanks for your time.” He took a step back and nodded at the geraniums. “Beautiful flowers,”

The compliment lifted her spirits . . . a little.

Bailey walked into a deserted department and turned on the lights. Rose Marie was done for the day, her desk tidy as usual. His cell chirped before he reached his office. He checked CID: Dr. Nat Swanson. He settled into his swivel and opened the phone. “How’d it go?”

“The three bodies are in the morgue. I’ll start the autopsies tomorrow.”

“Identification?”

“Mickey Randle, of course. The other two only had driver’s licenses. Both twenty-five, both from Farmersville; a Ronald Smallwood and a John Hix.” Nat paused and cleared his throat. “I don’t envy you informing the families.”

“They may be hard to find on Easter weekend. But we’ll persevere.”

“When you contact the families, ask someone to come down and make a formal identification.”

“Did you find anything of value?”

Nat shook his head. “Just bullet holes and pools of blood around the victims. They left nothing, not even a measly cigarette butt. I dug a deformed 9mm out of the wall in the living room. Semiautomatic hand guns would explain the spray of so much ammo. We dusted the place, got lots of pictures, bagged some fibers, but I don't expect to uncover anything helpful."

"Still looks like an assassination, and I'm betting Randle was the target."

"I agree, this was no run-of the-mill-homicide. It was a massacre with enough firepower to take out a goon squad. If Randle owned a gun, he didn't have time to defend himself. The shooters walked in unexpected and started firing. Professionals, for sure. My guess: they were out-of-towners."

"Drugs are the centerpiece, the common denominator."

"Could be, but that's your job, Bailey. I'll have more for you on Tuesday."

"Thanks a lot, Nat. Happy Easter."

CHAPTER 35

Easter Sunday

WHEN THE SERVICE ENDED, an overflow crowd poured through the exits of Southside Methodist. Carl took Maggie's hand and led her through the jam-packed parking lot. Late-comers had settled for the side streets in a neighborhood like Bertha and Jessie Franklin, blocks from the sanctuary. Most of the houses that lined those streets were small wood-frames with front porches for rocking. Some yard flowers: golden daffodils and multi-colored crocuses in full bloom, a paean to spring.

It was a glorious sun-lit morning, the perfect setting to celebrate the resurrection of Jesus. The bishop had assigned the church a new senior pastor—not an easy decision, since it required a special talent to fill Rhea Joslyn's shoes. Maggie was impressed by the traditional order of worship and the fifty-member choir. The young preacher's Easter message was spot-on, and the ecstasy of Easter swept over the congregants like a bracing March wind. The grand finale, Handel's Hallelujah Chorus, always stirred Maggie's heart, and her eyes brimmed with tears. If there was a Heaven, a subject she continued to wrestle with, then Rhea Joslyn was smiling.

It was a conversation she'd had with Jack on more than one occasion. Maggie had always envied his unshakable certainty that life was a continuum and death only a way station for the rest of the journey. When pressed for proof, he would smile and quote Paschal: *The heart has its reasons the mind cannot know;* or Kierkegaard: *It's a leap of faith,* or another savant. It had been ten years, and Jack's last days still haunted and intrigued her. His body ravished by disease while she watched him writhe in pain until the morphine kicked in. She had seen suffering on his face, but never a trace of angst or fear. To the contrary, as his life unraveled, he faced the inevitable with equanimity, as if he welcomed it. But she remembered with clarity those last few minutes; lifting a finger to beckon her close, then a whisper. *It's so beautiful.* His chest heaved as he took his last breath. She had wondered countless times: what had he seen? *Something . . . so beautiful.* Was he delusional? Drug-induced, perhaps? Or was it a snapshot of the Heaven he had earnestly believed in, a preview of *the rest of the journey*? For Maggie, Easter was the wellspring, a reminder of her own quest to find the answer to the overriding question: is life a dead-end street or the beginning of *something . . . so beautiful.*

"What time are we expected?" Carl asked as they crossed the river.

"I told Sam it might be a little after one." Maggie checked her watch. "I figured the church crowd would slow us down."

"Is Gertrude joining us?"

"I think she's preparing the meal and choreographing the entertainment."

"An Easter egg hunt?" Carl snickered, unable to restrain himself.

"Pin the tail on the bunny," Maggie added, amused. "With Gertrude, who knows?"

Carl shook his head. "A mother-in-law may be an asset or a liability. Supportive without hovering, or a control freak, still tethered to her daughter. That can divide loyalties and put a terrible strain on the marriage." Carl glanced at Maggie. "I speak from experience, having been down that road."

"Sam can handle it," Maggie said. "I'm sure of it."

Carl got the message: *Change the subject.*

It was an easy drive to Benton, an Interstate all the way. A bright mid-day sun colored the sky cornflower blue. The Acura rolled smoothly past one of the clapboard churches, cars and pickup trucks filled a vacant lot adjacent to the cemetery, a service still in progress. As they passed a stretch of woodland, a deer loped across the road. Carl hit the brakes hard, almost a collision. The frightened deer scampered through the eastbound lanes and into the brush.

Maggie folded her hands prayerfully. "Thank God there was no one behind you."

Carl checked his rear view mirror and breathed a sigh of relief. "Maybe it was an Easter dispensation for all the good works you've done."

Maggie ignored the compliment, reached over and rested her hand on Carl's shoulder. "Where were we before the distraction?"

"Roads," Carl said. "I'd been down that road," he repeated.

"Right . . . roads are a reminder. Where is Randy Bynum?"

Carl shrugged. "We saw him a week ago at *Louie's.*"

"According to Lee, that was the beginning of his two-week vacation."

"So it's been a week and nary a word. Not a card or a phone call." Maggie moved her seat back and stretched her legs. "Pixie buzzed me this morning. She and Imogene have become my lookouts. They sit on their back porch after dark and keep an eye out for intruders. They've spotted a prowler . . . probably Bynum . . . on two occasions, but nothing in the past week."

"He's tracking us," Carl said. "He may have been at the church service this morning; in disguise, of course."

Maggie looked at him and frowned. "I think he gets his kicks out of 'playing the game,' and if this is all prelude, he won't make his big move until next weekend."

Carl rubbed the small scar on his cheek. "No later than next Saturday night, and early enough to make the five hour drive to Plano and devise an alibi."

Maggie changed the subject. "How did you get that?" She reached over and touched the scar, which she'd hardly noticed before.

Carl laughed lightly at himself. "I was in the second grade and walked to school every day. I saved time if I cut through Mrs. Tally's backyard. Unbeknownst to me, she put up a barbed wire fence without a warning. She never said a word—no yelling, like 'get outta my yard, you little twerp' . . . nothing. The next day, on the way to school, I was in a footrace with Billy, my best friend, and looked back as I crossed Mrs. Tally's yard. The wire clipped my cheek and blood ran down my shirt and onto my pants. It scared the heck out of Billy's mother, who was at the kitchen window and saw my bloody face as I ran through her yard heading for home. And that's how I acquired the name 'Scarface,' thanks to an early thirties movie by the same name, refueled by Al Pacino in a remake in the early eighties."

"Oh, Carl, you can hardly see it." She rubbed a finger over it again. "I love it, Carl. It gives you an identity. Someone special."

Carl hoped those words had *special* meaning. Her love would make him the happiest man in the world.

Carl took the first Benton exit; four lanes, a boulevard that ran through residential neighborhoods and past Colby College. The campus was deserted. Nothing stirred. "I guess the kids are home for the Easter holidays," Maggie said.

"Great trees," Carl said, pointing to the towering live oaks that lined the median.

"Take a right at Sycamore, which runs along the western fringe of the campus. The college received a gift—twenty acres—a few years ago, from an anonymous donor. The parcel adjacent to the campus will be used for new construction. The eight acres across Sycamore is restricted by residential zoning, Rather than a confrontation with Benton's zoning board, bungalows were constructed and offered to faculty members at very affordable rates. The bungalows are small, but roomy enough for the two of them. And the rental is month to month, so there's no long-term commitment."

Carl got the picture: cookie-cutter bungalows on small lots and a sidewalk that ran the length of the street. The look-a-likes were of wood-stone construction, painted white, with wraparound verandas and low-pitched roofs. "Which one?" he asked.

Gertrude gave the order; Jane must stay out of the kitchen and sit in the family room with Sam and her guests. She was in charge of the dinner, having selected the menu and prepared the meal. Despite Jane's feeble protests, her mother insisted on a buffet rather than a formal seating. The dining table was too small to accommodate five people. Everyone could serve his or her own plate and find a comfortable seat in the family room. Gertrude had prepared an urn of coffee and a pitcher of tea, which sat on the marble-top table between the windows.

Jane had offered little resistance, since her domineering mother always—without exception—made the family decisions. The dynamics of the mother-daughter relationship never changed, even though Jane was twenty-six years old, married and pregnant. Jane, like her father, capitulated, rather than challenge Gertrude and face the inevitable rancor that flowed when anyone opposed her. Jane was resigned; it would always be that way. She was glad that Sam, although he felt Gertrude's negative vibes, was civil and respectful, the mark of a man who was self-assured and fiercely independent. It made her love him even more.

From her easy chair, Maggie had a direct line of vision into the dining area and Gertrude bobbing in and out, loading the table with food. She was a tall woman with red hair and a pointed chin. For some odd reason, the shape of her face reminded Maggie of triangles and Mr. Griffin, her high school math teacher, who had taught her more about trigonometry than she needed to know. But Maggie would never forget Mr. Griffin's prosthetic grey-green eye, the same color as Gertrude's.

She wondered where her boundless energy came from. Gertrude was in charge and shooed anyone out of the kitchen who offered to help. Maggie leaned back in her chair and sipped a glass of white wine, fascinated by Gertrude's spirited movements. Maybe she'd reset her metabolic rate, which would also explain the reason Gertrude was thin as a rail—a bit too thin for a woman in her mid-fifties and looking at the autumn of her life.

After the meal, Gertrude served coffee from the urn and passed the sugar bowl and creamer on a small silver tray. "I enjoyed the buffet," Maggie said as she stirred sugar into her coffee. "The tenderloin was cooked to perfection. You would qualify as the queen of the kitchen in the *brigade de cuisine.*"

A nod of acknowledgement, then Gertrude moved a few steps to serve Carl and Jane, seated on the sofa engaged in cordial conversation.

San stood at the door to the entry hall and waited until he caught his mother's eye. Maggie got the message. She put her coffee cup on a side table, slipped out of her chair and crossed the room. He led her down the short hallway and into an empty bedroom. "Are you okay, Mom?" he asked after closing the door.

'I'm fine, Sam."

"Just wanted to be sure." He gave her a worried look. "My level of concern went sky-high Saturday night."

"Spotting Bynum at *Louie's?"*

Sam grimaced. "It's obvious he's dangerous and bent on hurting you . . . or something a lot worse." He scratched his head as if confused. "Why can't Sheriff Grant or Captain Graves put an end to the harassment?"

"Dinner at *Louie's* is not a crime, even though he was there for a reason." She stopped and pointed at her chest . . . *moi.* "Of course, Bynum would swear it was simply coincidence."

"How 'bout this?" Sam removed an envelope from his pants pocket and handed it to her.

"Where did you get it?"

"I found it by the front door when I went out for the morning paper."

"Bynum." The envelope was blank, no address. "And hand-delivered, no less."

"Mom, he's stalking you. The cards and phone calls are his bizarre reminders. For all we know, he may be watching us as we speak." Sam took a few short steps and closed the Venetian blinds.

"I don't think he'll hang around, since Carl's with me." Maggie removed the card. On the front, another cartoonish figure: a bald-headed man in prison stripes, his long nose pressed against the bars of his jail cell. Inside, a hand-printed message, the same large block letters: **ONLY PRISONERS ON DEATH ROW KNOW WHEN THEY WILL EAT THEIR LAST MEAL**

Maggie held up the card. "If you discount *Louie's*, I've not seen or heard from Bynum for a while, other than one of his spooky phone calls in the middle of the night. He's playing a game, Sam, a dangerous game, and no matter how it plays out, it's a game with a tragic ending. Not unlike your world of Shakespeare."

Sam shook his head vigorously. "Mom, you can't sit around and wait for this asshole to strike."

"No one in law enforcement has devised a plan to neutralize Bynum. So I formulated my own. Sheriff Clancy, whom I spoke with recently, believes Bynum will make a move before his vacation runs out this Sunday. I'll be ready." She stood on tiptoe and kissed him on the cheek. "Don't worry. I'm a big girl, Sam, and your father taught me well."

"Before we join 'the maddening crowd,' may I ask you a personal question?"

"Of course, Sam."

"I really like Mr. Sweeny and wondered about your relationship. Just good friends, or something more?"

Maggie sat on the edge of the bed and looked up at her son. "When your father died, I was sure there'd never be another man in my life. A friend, maybe, but nothing more. Your father set a very high bar, a man of immense integrity. I sometimes wondered where all his goodness came from." She stopped long enough to wipe her eyes. "Does Carl meet the standard? Probably not, but in some ways he reminds me of your father."

Sam knelt down and looked her in the eye. "Does Carl brighten your day? Share your interests? Is he considerate and kind?"

Silence.

"Well . . ."

Maggie nodded and wiped her eyes again.

Sam placed his hand on her knee. "Mom, are you in love with Carl Sweeny?" He waved all ten fingers as if coaxing an answer.

"It's been evolving slowly . . ."

"Your affection for Carl?"

She nodded again. "I unwittingly let him steal my heart."

Sam stood up and lifted Maggie off the bed. "If he makes you happy and keeps you safe, I'm behind you all the way, and I'm sure those are my father's sentiments as well."

"He's a good man, Sam." Her voice was soft and tender.

"I sure hope he stays close with this psycho on the loose."

"Guess we'd better socialize, before Gertrude gets curious."

"Gertrude, curious . . . ?" Sam chuckled. "Of course she's curious. That's a given, as certain as the sun rises and the sun sets."

Late afternoon, after a round of hugs, Carl and Maggie left the bungalow on Sycamore and took the surface streets to the Interstate. Maggie had a lot on her mind. Another message from Bynum was her primary concern. All indicators pointed to next weekend as when the stalker would make his move. Lee Clancy had referred to Bynum's vacation, which ended next Sunday, as his "window of opportunity." And the latest card, which suggested that only a death-row inmate knew the time of his last meal. She thought the inference was pretty clear and suspected another note, maybe a menu, a day or two before the drama played out. Would Bynum be so bold? Maggie understood that "daring" was part of the excitement. The cards and phone calls and sightings were each a thrill. Layers of thrills, culminating in the "killer thrill," and in the case of the sexual predator: physical gratification. Rita's confessions and her description of Bynum's sexual fetishes and aberrant behavior made Maggie believe that Randy Bynum's reprisal would make sadistic sex a part of the finale, before the hunting knife to the heart. Maggie had done the research: a gun was unlikely; a six-inch blade was the weapon of choice. Silent. Deadly.

She remembered Sam's petition: *You're crazy about Carl and he's head-over-heels in love with you. Why not invite him to spend the nights on Lamy Lane, at least until this matter is settled? Whether you share a bed is your decision, but having him there is added security. Makes sense to me.* But Maggie had a plan to deal with Bynum, and it required she spend her nights alone. She didn't want to spook Bynum. It was time to end the madness, one way or another.

It was almost dark when Carl pulled into the driveway. On the porch, he gave her a good night kiss and the usual reminder to lock up tight.

He started to leave; it had been a long day. He did a quick turn-around and reached into his pants pocket. "Something special." He handed her a folded email.

Maggie stepped back, beside the porch light, and unfolded the printout.

"It came this morning . . . from Meg."

Maggie read the short message aloud:

Hi, Dad,

A bit of news. I'm twenty-two weeks pregnant. . Thought you'd like to know.

Mother and baby (a girl) are fine.

Meg

Maggie reached for his hand and tugged him into a snug embrace. "Oh, Carl," she said, stepping back. "The news is a Godsend, another Easter blessing."

"I'm happy for Meg . . . and Carlton." He took Maggie's hand. "And another miracle for me."

Maggie dug the key from her purse. "I already have her name."

"What might that be?"

"Hope. Hope Chapman . . . it has a nice ring to it."

Carl laughed. "Where did that come from . . . out of thin air?"

"No, not at all. Hope is an expectation, to bring you and Meg together. She'll bridge the divide that's kept you apart."

"Nothing would please me more."

She keyed the lock and stepped inside. "Call me tomorrow, Carl."

"Goodnight, Maggie."

Once the entry hall light went on, he walked to his car and drove away filled with conflicting emotions. He was delighted by the news from San Diego and would send Meg his love and congratulations tomorrow. And he was overjoyed as Maggie moved ever closer, their relationship merging like two free-flowing streams into a single channel. But there was worry . . . real, legitimate worry. Bynum was out there, somewhere, and about to make his move. But when? And how? Carl didn't have the answers.

CHAPTER 36

ON TUESDAY MORNING, BAILEY GRANT left the Annex mid-morning, spoke to Rose Marie on his way out, and drove to St. Francis. The weather was summer-warm, lots of sunshine, although rain was in the forecast. The sheriff took a side-street entrance to the hospital and parked the cruiser in the back lot. He hurried through the ER to a flight of stairs. The morgue and Nat Swanson's office were in the basement, with its cinder block walls and thin industrial carpet. The walls were bare, colorless. No windows, only artificial light. And as spectral quiet as a haunted house. Bailey had been in Swanson's morbid realm many times and had the same recurring thought: Poe would be at home here.

He found Nat in his office, the door open. The pathologist sat at his metal desk, entranced by the slide beneath his microscope. He looked up and pointed Bailey to the only other chair in the room. "A surgical specimen," he said, removing the slide and putting it in a cardboard holder.

"How was Easter?" Bailey asked.

"Busy." His brow wrinkled into a frown.

"At Trappers you said you'd have the Mickey Randle report, at least most of it, by today."

Nat took off his glasses, cleaned them with a tissue and laid them on the desk. "We completed the three autopsies, but found nothing relevant. Those kids were peppered with bullets—9mm Parabellum. Never had a chance." He paused and shook his head, as if appalled by the folly of it all. "There were a couple of incidental findings: Hix had a small ventricular septal defect, which he could live with, and Smallwood had syndactyly."

"What?"

"Webbing of the toes of his left foot. An anomaly, totally benign."

"Anything else?"

"The fibers we collected came from the living room carpet, and the only prints were those of the victims." Nat bent forward, arms on the desk. "Here's how I see it: the killers came unannounced, gloved and capped, shoe covers like A/C technicians, and shot up the place. Since there is only one exit from the trailer park, they made sure their job was clean and quick. In and out; less than five minutes would be my guess."

"I assume the pools of blood belonged to the victims."

"Yep, all nine samples. Toxicology is pending."

"The odds of finding the killers aren't good. We have no weapon, no witnesses, no prints . . . but motive, maybe. Sure smells drug-related."

"A supplier and an unpaid debt would be one scenario."

"Or Randle talked too much, and it was a way to shut him down. As for Smallwood and Hix, well . . . wrong place, wrong time. An assassin leaves no witnesses."

Nat turned off the ring light and moved the microscope aside. "Sorry I haven't been much help. I doubt toxicology will be helpful, but I'll send you the report."

"Thanks." Bailey started to stand. "Oh, by the way, I spoke to the parents of Smallwood and Hix. That part of the job is never easy. Mandy Hix became so hysterical, her husband took her to the ER."

"Randle's uncle came by this morning and made the ID. He was very phlegmatic, as if Mickey was a stranger and his violent death came as no surprise."

Bailey stopped at the door. "Thanks, Nat. Too bad the shooters left nothing behind." He put on his Stetson, tipped it back. "I guess a cigarette butt or a matchbook with a logo would've been too much to hope for."

"The place was clean." Nat lowered his voice, but was unable to hide his disappointment. "They made sure of that. Only the bullets. And a 9mm is as ubiquitous as Coke and Pepsi."

"Gotta go . . ."

"One other suggestion, Bailey. You might consider getting the Feds involved in the investigation. If this is drug connected, the shooters may have been from out of state, or even Mexico. I think the DEA would love to jump in."

"Good idea." Bailey doffed his Stetson. "See ya, Nat."

Maggie awoke early Wednesday morning with Robbie Armstead on her mind.

She made a pot of coffee and returned to the bathroom to brush her teeth and wash the sleep from her eyes. Maggie slipped on her short silk robe, a present from Jane and Sam, her last Christmas in Dallas. She looked out the bedside window and remembered vaguely the heavy rain that pounded the house. Water still clung to the glass, but the skies had cleared and the early morning augured more sunshine. Barefoot, she padded back to the kitchen, filled a mug with fresh brewed coffee and sat at the kitchen table.

Maggie opened the notebook and reread comments and key words she had jotted down after the first session with Robbie Armstead. *Rapport.* She felt they had formed a favorable relationship, which was crucial for moving forward. *Opened up.* Toward the end of the session Robbie had talked more, which was a good thing. She needed answers, and only Robbie and an unimpeded line of communication could provide them. Near the bottom of the page, Maggie had scribbled a name: *Mickey Randle???* It was a subject she intended to explore. Robbie had a connection with Randle, and she wanted to know how that relationship played a part, if at all, in his life. She wondered if the events of Good Friday might color his description of their putative friendship. How about the funeral tomorrow? Would he attend? If so, how would the anticipation impact their session at OverReach?

At the very bottom of the page, Maggie had printed, on a slant, *Honda.*

Is he still driving the Honda? (He had mentioned the car voluntarily during their first session.) Or had Randle's brother reclaimed it? If she knew more about Randle and his family, it might clarify Robbie's connection. And the Honda might be the key to opening that door.

Carl had given her a full report on the assassination of Randle, Hix and Smallwood on Good Friday. Investigators from the DEA had been summoned by the sheriff and would take charge of the investigation. Drugs and their toxic fallout were a subject that required a candid discussion, since Maggie knew from her world of experience that depression—and Robbie was depressed—is triggered and/or exacerbated by a number of factors, including grief, guilt, failures, a profound loss, traumas (physical and emotional), and of course, mind-altering drugs.

The wall phone rang and interrupted her ponderings. Maggie wondered who would call at this early hour. Only a few steps away, she reached for the handset.

"Hello, Maggie. It's me. Hope I didn't wake you."

"No, no . . . I've had my first cup of coffee."

"We're still keeping a check on your place. Every night we sit on the back porch like two old sentries, but no signs of the prowler. Maybe he's gone for good."

"I hope you're right, Pixie, but my instincts tell a different story. He's out there, lurking, waiting for the time to strike."

"Remember, I've got a twelve-gauge in my hall closet if you'd like to have it."

"Thanks, Pixie, but I'm good."

"Are we on for tomorrow?" she asked. "Running low on milk and cereal."

"Absolutely, unless you're wary of a woman with a target on her back."

Pixie cackled. "Honey, at my age, nothing frightens me. If Count Dracula knocked on the door, I'd invite him in and offer him a glass of wine. Besides, the folks at Safeway would worry if we don't show for our Thursday shopping."

"The usual time, Pixie, and thanks for your concern."

Maggie replaced the phone and retrieved her mug. After a refill, she crossed the short hall to her bedroom and turned on the radio, a classical music station. She recognized the symphony: the *Adagietto of Mahler's Fifth,* which she had heard for the first time as a teenager when her mother tuned in to the funeral of Robert Kennedy. It was also one of Jack's legacies: cultivating her taste for the symphonic music of Beethoven,

Schubert, (his *Unfinished Symphony,* her favorite) and other greats. While she had plenty of time before her eleven o'clock appointment, she sat on the love seat, sipped her coffee and let the music wash over her as if she were sitting in a summer rain.

When she finished her coffee, Maggie decided to shower and dress. She chose the same blue cotton fabric with the high collar and black patent leather flats. She brushed her thick, lustrous hair and let it hang loose around her shoulders, again forgoing makeup and jewelry other than her watch.

She transferred the .38 from the night table to her purse. It was a reminder that Bynum's vacation ended in four days, and if Lee Clancy was right, Bynum would make his move before that narrow window closed on Sunday at midnight. If logic followed, Bynum needed to be at his desk at Direct Energy on Monday morning. The drama's finale was imminent.

The washroom door opened into the garage. It was the way she entered her car. After she started the engine and hit the lock button, she opened the garage door with the remote. It was Carl's suggestion, and he insisted that it was a prudent precaution. Who knew if Bynum might seize the opportunity of exposure if she got in her car through an open garage door? It only heightened Maggie's feeling of restraint, another check on her freedom of movement. She followed Carl's advice, since she was sure Bynum's vendetta was about to end, one way or the other.

After the garage door opened, she checked her rear view mirror before backing down the driveway. Lamy Lane was deserted. No cars on the street. Not a soul in sight. She shifted to drive and, with a premonition about the session with Robbie Armstead, left the neighborhood and followed her mental map to the women's shelter.

Maggie pulled into OverReach and parked near the entrance. She transferred the .38 to the glove compartment, locked the car and went inside. Madeline, as usual, was buried in her laptop, but looked up and said a diffident, "Good morning."

An improvement. Maggie wondered if others had spoken to Alice about the icy front desk, and whether Madeline had received a reprimand. She unlocked the security door and went directly to her consultation room. Only twenty minutes to organize her thoughts, although Robbie had been on her mind for the past several days.

At exactly eleven o'clock, she heard the rap and looked up. Robbie was standing alone in the doorway, hands stuffed in the pockets of his chinos. Another L.S.U. T-shirt, dark yellow, with TIGERS screen printed across the front. Today he wore a plastic lanyard, school colors, around his neck. His hair was combed back and his face clean-shaven, very presentable—A.B. Armstead at work. But Robbie's shoulders slumped and his eyes had found the floor. Maggie suspected that Mickey Randle's violent death had deepened Robbie's depression.

"Come in, Robbie. I've looked forward to our visit," Maggie said cheerfully and pointed to the arm chair.

He moved slowly, as if each step was an effort, like walking in sludge. After sitting down, his head drooped, his eyes fixed on the multi-colored rug. Not a greeting. Not a word. No animation other than fingering the plastic around his neck.

Maggie let the silence hang suspended while she reconsidered her line of questions. While Robbie was withdrawn a week ago, he had opened up as the session progressed and she was encouraged, even optimistic. But today was different. He had lost the color in his cheeks and appeared thinner than before. He was listless, shackled by inertia. Maggie had seen countless cases of depression during her career and felt qualified to make an assessment. This one was grave and worrisome; Robbie had fallen into an even darker place over the course of a few days. It again raised the question in her mind about the death of Mickey Randle and how that played into the psyche of Robbie Armstead. She glanced at her notebook and put it aside. If after the morning session he failed to show signs of assuagement, she'd make the referral.

"Robbie, how do you feel?" she asked.

A head shake, nothing more.

"Last week I promised our conversations were private, nothing left this room without your permission. Do you remember, Robbie?"

A nod. No eye contact.

"I also said it was important for us to have a conversation. Otherwise I would be of little help. Remember?"

"Sure." He leaned heavily on the padded arms of the chair, eyes still downcast.

Maggie had questions she intended to ask, but the assassination of Mickey Randle and its effects on Robbie altered her approach. She was sure something had jolted Robbie since his initial visit, and the most plausible explanation was the death of Randle. Maggie realized that the subject was problematic and she needed to tread lightly. The funeral, scheduled for one o'clock tomorrow, was another issue that had to be addressed. Would he attend? And if so, why? But Maggie knew the most effective way to enter the world of Mickey Randle and Robbie Armstead was gently.

Maggie moved her chair closer and asked, "Robbie, were you and Mickey friends?"

He looked up briefly. "Kinda . . . I guess."

"Good friends?"

"He let me use his Honda."

Maggie was happy to get a declarative sentence. "It's no secret that Mickey hosted weekend parties, and the neighbors complained about the loud music and the scent of weed so thick it drifted through the park. The sheriff believes Mickey used and sold marijuana, and other hard drugs as well." Maggie stopped long enough for Robbie to digest the charge. "Were you a user?" she asked uneasily, as if skating on thin ice.

He hesitated; eyes back to the floor. "Yes'm." Almost a whisper.

"Did you buy your weed from Mickey?"

A soft sibilant, "Sure."

"How 'bout other drugs?"

His eyes left the floor and went to the ceiling.

She waited, but got no answer. "Be truthful, Robbie. It's important, since a drug, almost any drug, can affect the way you feel."

He brought his hand to his face to hide the shame. "Meth a few times, but I never touched the other stuff."

"Crack cocaine?"

"Never!"

"Would you call Mickey a drug dealer?"

"Big time."

"What happened if you couldn't pay up front?"

Robbie straightened up and looked at her for the first time. "Pressure, lots of pressure. When I was delinquent a couple of times, he threatened to tell my folks; strong-arm tactics if necessary, anything to get his money." Robbie twisted the lanyard until it was taut and reddened his neck. "I was desperate but always beat his deadline."

Maggie started to ask how he got the money, but demurred. "I thought you were friends."

"He could turn on a dime. One day a threat to pay up and the next, offering me the Honda."

Maggie was gratified (and surprised) that he had become more forthcoming, but the dejection never left his deep-set eyes. His face was wooden and Maggie felt a pang of regret, even self-reproach, for surrendering to A.B. Armstead in the first place. The change in Robbie s demeanor over the past week was unmistakable. Robbie needed the counsel of a high-end professional like Dr. Edwards.

Maggie looked at her watch. Only fifteen minutes into the session. While she had made the decision to transfer Robbie into more capable hands, there were still questions of interest. He had begun to open up, which might afford the opportunity to get additional background. But Maggie knew that it required tact, avoiding the hurtful words that would shut him down or deepen the shadows that followed him. Since a question might cause unintended damage, she would be circumspect.

"Robbie, is there anything you'd like to tell me?"

"Like what?"

"Oh, say a problem with someone in the family, or someone at the workplace. How 'bout losing a girlfriend, or an old friend from your short time at L.S.U.?" Maggie extended her arms, as if coaxing an answer. "If you have a grievance or feel the sting of betrayal, it helps to talk it out . . . get it off your chest. You always feel better by sharing the load with someone else."

Robbie threw his head back and closed his eyes. "Does guilt count?"

"Of course. Guilt may be the heaviest burden of all."

Maggie waited, hoping they were on fertile ground and that Robbie would say more.

Only silence. His face clouded and tears streamed down his cheeks.

"Can you talk about it?" she asked.

He shook his head vigorously and clasped his hands over his face. "I wanna go home."

Maggie moved her chair closer and handed him a Kleenex. "Take a few minutes to gather yourself, then I'll walk you to your car." She handed him another tissue.

"Are you going to Mickey's service tomorrow?" Maggie thought changing the subject was a good idea.

"Yeah . . . I guess."

Maggie steepled her chin. "You still have the Honda?"

"Yes'm."

"How did that happen?"

"Mick's brother told me to keep it for a few weeks. He knows my old Camry is falling apart."

"Do you think Mickey had an ulterior motive?"

Robbie looked up, puzzled.

"To use the car. It seems mighty generous, but maybe he had a reason."

"Like what?" Robbie wiped his nose with a tissue.

"Maybe he wanted to keep you quiet and on his buyer's list. Should your uncle, with connections downstate, discover Mickey's drug operation, it would not bode well. He considered A.B. Armstead a more dangerous avenger than even the sheriff. "

Robbie shrugged indifferently.

Maggie reached for his hand and led him down the hall. "I have a friend, a very wise man that I want you to see. Ms. Fogleman will notify your uncle, and then she'll set up an appointment with Dr. Edwards. I hope no later than Saturday."

Maggie stood at the front entrance and watched him drive away. When she returned to her office, she opened her notebook and entered only one word: *Guilt.* That brief discussion had elicited real emotion, the only time in either session he had cried. She had not laid the groundwork that allowed her to broach the subject of suicide, but it was a gut feeling that she tried unsuccessfully to allay. She hoped Dr. Edwards could work a miracle.

CHAPTER 37

Friday evening

EARLIER IN THE WEEK, Maggie had spoken to Chris Markos about this once-in-a-lifetime occasion. She pre-ordered the dinner: eight-ounce tenderloins, au gratin potatoes, and the house salad with Chris' secret dressing. She asked him to select a bottle of his best red wine and prepare the dessert . . . a pastry chef's surprise. Maggie had looked around the spacious room and pointed to a table well past the rock fountain and koi pond. Chris understood the reason—a little more privacy—and promised her the table for the evening.

It was almost dark when Maggie and Carl left Lamy Lane. Dinner at *The Rendezvous.* A birthday celebration . . . the big 7-0.

"I missed seeing you yesterday," Carl said as he turned north onto Stoop Road.

"It was much busier than I'd planned."

"Like what?" He gave her a sidelong glance.

"Well, let's see. I still take Pixie and Imogene to Safeway every Thursday morning. They're very frugal shoppers, so it takes a while. And they move like two tortoises, which at their age is expected, but it's very slow going. After I unload the groceries and get Pixie and Imogene safely inside, it's time for a late lunch."

Carl braked for a red light at the center of Camden. "I called mid-afternoon, but you were on the go . . . somewhere." He eased the Acura across Main Street, then two blocks north to the Illinois Central tracks.

"I had a message from Alice Fogleman when I got home. She had talked with A.B. Armstead and explained the reasons for Robbie's referral to Dr. Edwards. But Armstead wanted to talk with me. So we arranged a meeting at OverReach where I expressed my grave concern for Robbie, who had grown more depressed during the short time between visits, perhaps darkened by Randle's murder. The referral to Dr. Edwards was imperative."

"Any pushback from A.B.?" he asked as they bumped over the rails.

"No. He finally, though reluctantly, acquiesced."

"Did Robbie attend Randle's graveside service?"

"According to Armstead, Robbie was there, along with Randle's brother and some of Randle's friends. Of course, I worry the burial will only deepen Robbie's depression. During our Wednesday session, I advised him to finesse the funeral." She paused, her voice softened. "He didn't listen, or maybe he was too self-absorbed to even hear me."

"When is the consultation with Edwards?" Carl turned off Louisville and onto the circular drive of *The Rendezvous.*

"That's what killed the afternoon. Alice had been unable to contact Dr. Edwards, so I spent the rest of the day chasing him down and filling him in. He agreed, based on my narrative, that Robbie needed help—maybe hospitalization. He'll make that determination when he sees him Saturday."

"You have been a busy girl," Carl said as he eased past the green awning and stopped at the valet parking stand. He handed the keys to a peppy young man, took Maggie's arm and escorted her into the restaurant.

It was no surprise to either of them that the elegant dining room was full.

Maggie looked around, but there were no signs of Chris. The host stand was vacant. She wondered who checked reservations and greeted the guests. Out of the corner of her eye she caught a hand-wave near the back of the room. Ed and Edith were there, seated, early arrivals.

Maggie took Carl's hand and led him through the maze of diners, past the rock fountain. When they reached the table, there were handshakes and hugs all around. Maggie was pleased to see Edith more cheerful, like her old convivial self . . . the life of the party. It had been a month since their gloomy lunch at *Renee's Tea Room*, and she suspected Edith had finally taken Dr. Greene's pep talk to heart. Ed, on the other hand, had digested his diagnosis with aplomb, and if it worried him he kept it under wraps. Everyone appeared to be in good spirits, the perfect setting for a celebration.

A waiter with a broad smile appeared table-side, holding a napkin-wrapped bottle of chilled champagne. "My name is Walter. and I'll be serving you this evening. Unfortunately, Mr. Marcos is under the weather and asked me, on his behalf, to extend birthday greetings to Mr. Sweeney." He carefully worked the cork from the bottle's neck and poured the pink liquid into fluted glasses. "Compliments of Mr. Marcos, the best champagne in our wine cellar; a rosé from Jura in Eastern France." After serving, he placed the bottle in a table-side ice bucket. "Your dinner has been pre-ordered, so I'll give you enough time to enjoy your drinks and celebrate this special occasion." Like an illusionist, he was gone.

Edith lifted her glass and made a toast: "Long live Carl Sweeny."

A clink of glasses. The pink champagne went down easy.

Ed spoke up. "Seventy, huh? Guess you've joined the over-the-hill gang."

"No, no," Maggie insisted. "I know you're kidding, Ed, but seventy, if healthy, can be the continuance of a productive life."

"Proof, please," he asked with a playful grin.

"Okay, Tolstoy was seventy-eight when he published *Resurrection*—which, by the way, is my favorite Russian novel. Monet was in his early eighties and still working on his *Weeping Willow* series, and Sibelius, the Finnish composer, was an old man who tried, though unsuccessfully, to finish his *Eighth Symphony.* So you see . . ." She stopped and looked up into Carl's dazzled eyes. " . . . Carl has so much to anticipate; the future beckons."

"Is she amazing or what?" Carl asked, canting his head in Maggie's direction.

"That . . . and more," Ed conceded.

Edith gave polite applause. "Maggie, you are remarkable."

"But here's another thing," Ed said, pointing to Carl across the table. "You owe me, big time—well, Edith anyway, since she was the matchmaker."

Maggie wanted to steer the conversation in another direction and handed Carl his birthday card.

He slipped it out of its cover. A traditional greeting on the front; a note inside:

Happy birthday, Carl
Your gift's at the club, a new set of PING irons.
Charlie McInnis and your friend Ed made the selection.
Guaranteed to improve your game.
May this be the best year ever.
Love, Maggie

Carl felt that blissful feeling swell within him, as if his chest might explode. He read it again: *Love, Maggie.*

Nothing could have made him happier. Just two words . . . the consummate gift.

After a sumptuous meal, Walter cleared the table and removed the ice bucket and the empty bottle of champagne. He returned with a three-layer chocolate cake with fudge filling and creamy chocolate icing. A single white candle stood in the center of the cake. Walter handed the cake cutter to Maggie and lit the candle. A second waiter appeared with coffee. "Enjoy," Walter said. A half-bow, and both men backed away.

"Where are my candles?" Carl asked.

"It might be a little crowded," Edith said with a straight face.

Maggie urged him to make a wish and blow out the candle. She had the cake cutter at the ready.

Ed spoke up. "Several years ago, my daughter made me a birthday cake with only one candle. I asked Carl's question: where are my candles?" Ed paused for comic relief. "My nine-year-old granddaughter had the answer: 'Grandpa, we didn't want to start a bonfire.'"

Everyone laughed, relaxed by champagne and congenial company.

Maggie realized as they left the restaurant that Randy Bynum had never crossed her mind. Not once. Inside, she was too engrossed by the festive party and the affability of friends. Outside, it was dark and foreboding. Bynum was back, at least in her conscious mind. Maggie also remembered her plan, well-conceived—waiting for Bynum to make his move. Tonight? Possible, if Clancy's projection was on target. Bynum's vacation timeline ended on Sunday. Closing in, for sure. Maggie took Carl's arm and snuggled close while they waited for their car.

Carl turned into the driveway and cut the engine. Across the street, the Kahlils' porch light was on. Overhead a half-moon nestled in a black velvet sky. It was bright enough for Carl to scan the immediate neighborhood as he took Maggie's hand and walked her to the porch.

"I worry about you, Maggie. Bynum is out there with a madman's obsession."

She reached for the lapels of his coat, pulled him toward her and gave him a passionate kiss. Maggie broke the embrace, but held onto his hands and looked into his eyes. "Don't spoil your birthday with worry, Carl. I'll be okay." On tiptoe, she kissed him again.

"Why don't I stay with you?" He looked down, as if embarrassed. "I'll sleep on the sofa."

"No, not tonight. Bynum won't make a move if you're here." She was adamant, no room for argument.

"Are you sure?"

She rested her head against his chest. "Carl, I've handled men like Bynum before . . . all those years at *The Shelter*. I need closure, and that will happen only if Bynum thinks I'm alone and vulnerable."

Carl felt helpless, like a Luna moth flitting aimlessly around a wall light. "Where is your gun?"

"On my bedside table, loaded, all six chambers."

Still holding her close, he kissed her forehead. “I wish you’d let me stay.”

Maggie stepped back “No, Carl, I have to do it my way. Okay?”

He let out a deep breath of concession. “Lock up tight, please. If anything happened to you, I don’t know what . . .”

Maggie put a finger to his lips. “”Shush . . . don’t worry, Carl. Go home and get some sleep. Call me tomorrow and we’ll make a plan. Maybe hamburgers on the grill, and I’ll have Robbie’s report from Dr. Edwards.”

“I love you, Maggie. Don’t ever forget that.”

“And you’re my sweetheart, Carl Sweeny.” She turned and unlocked the front door.

“Oh, and thanks for the birthday dinner and all the trappings. It was the best of the best.”

She blew him a kiss and opened the door.

As always, he waited until he heard the lock click and the entry hall light went on. Reluctantly, he returned to his car, lowered his window, and drove away with the wind in his face. Leaving Lamy Lane, he heard the ominous howl of some wild thing, probably a coyote in the nearby woods. Another predator, he surmised as he drove down a dark and forbidding Stoop Road.

Her phone rang just as Maggie stepped inside. After bolting the door, she hurried to the kitchen, flipped the light switch and answered the call.

“Hi Maggie, it’s me, Pixie.”

“Are you all right?” Maggie dreaded the odds—an emergency, one of the old ladies had fallen, a broken a hip or something more serious.

“We’re fine for two old coots. But I called about your prowler.”

“My prowler?” It took her a few seconds to find clarity; too much champagne.

“Yep, he’s back. Snooping around ’bout an hour ago.”

Maggie felt her heart accelerate. A final reconnaissance before the assault. What was his weapon of choice: a knife, a gun, or a garrote?

And he would carry duct tape and ligatures, since sexual abuse was surely a part of his plan. The odds were heavily weighted in favor of rape, since past psychopathic behavior, which Maggie had studied for years, suggested violent sex was often the prelude to murder.

"Thanks, Pixie, but I'm in lockdown and the alarm is set."

"Honey, double-check those doors and windows before you retire. And remember, I have a shotgun, and if you say the word, I'll blow his ass all the way to Morehouse Parish."

Ninety pounds of grit and that twelve-gauge shotgun . . . Maggie had to smile. "Let's hope that's not necessary." She knew the recoil would send Pixie—well, she didn't want to think about it. "Thanks again. Talk to you tomorrow." She replaced the phone in its cradle, kicked off her shoes and followed a trail of intuition into her bedroom. Today was Bynum's appointed time. She was sure of it.

She revisited her plan: the house is dark, except the entry hall, which backlights anyone standing in the bedroom's doorway. Those double doors swing inward, and one has to step into the room to see the bed on the right and the love seat against a side wall on the left. The blinds are drawn; the room is dark as a dungeon. A bolster is placed under the bed covers next to the window, which gives the vague appearance of a bulky form. A wig is stuffed with bubble wrap, the stuffing faces the window. Enough light leaks through one of the blinds to give the impression . . . a bed and a body. The night light in the bathroom is unplugged. A flashlight fits snug between the cushions of the love seat. A hand towel hangs on the arm. The .38 and cell phone rest in her lap.

Maggie, her instincts on high alert, believed this was the night, although Saturday was still possible. Pixie's call confirmed Bynum was prowling the neighborhood, so she would prepare as if his strike-date was imminent.

After Maggie undressed, she put on her gym shorts, Carl's golf shirt and sockless tennis shoes. She carried a water glass into the master bath and went through her nightly routine. After putting on her silk robe, she checked the clock on the bedside table—almost midnight. With a mix of trepidation and resolve, she began the process of setting the trap.

She hit the entry hall switch and stood at a sidelight in full view, hoping he was out there watching. She unlocked the bolt and disarmed the alarm. Maggie was certain Bynum could pick the second lock, a push-button knob, and it was important for him to feel that he was "breaking in" rather than being suckered. She wasn't sure how Bynum would have deactivated the burglar alarm, but it was a non-issue, since she had turned it off. On the way to the kitchen, she unlocked the doors to the basement and the garage. It was important that Bynum have easy access.

She went back to the bedroom and left the doors slightly ajar, which allowed a ribbon of light from the entry hall. Maggie settled into the far corner of the love seat, the gun and cell phone within easy reach. While calm and in control, her palms were moist and she wiped them with the hand towel.

Maggie was weary; a long day, a birthday dinner with more champagne than she intended to drink, and the unshakable concern for Robbie Armstead. Her eyes were heavy, and she fell like a rock into a deep sleep.

Maggie awakened with a start, but heard nothing; the bedroom doors were as she had left them. She chided herself for falling asleep and wished she had brought a thermos of coffee. Across the room, the clock read 2:35. The extended nap only seemed like minutes, not an ill-advised two hours. She knew a vigil was essential for success. So Maggie willed herself to stay awake, and hoped Bynum would choose tonight to seek his revenge and end the insanity.

Maggie didn't have to wait much longer. Within the hour she sensed his presence, although she'd heard nothing other than the thrum of the A/C compressor outside her window. The bedroom doors slowly opened. She reached for the .38 and leaned against the far corner of the love seat. She felt her heart accelerate, a surge of adrenaline, as she watched him move to the foot of the bed, enough light to catch the glint of the blade.

"Get up, you bitch." The command was harsh and frightening.

It was too dark for Maggie to see Bynum waving the knife in one hand and holding the ligature in the other, allowing it to drop to its full length.

“It’s playtime, McFarland, and this is my nipple-knife.” A cackle. “Just relax and enjoy it; my going-away present, so to speak. Otherwise, with your body, it would be such a waste.” Another cackle. “Don’t you agree?”

Silence.

“Get up, you bitch. We’re wasting time.”

The silence lingered.

“Don’t fight me, or I’ll tie you up. Won’t matter to me. I’ll get it one way or the other.” He licked his lips and whirled the ligature around as if it were a toy. It was a minute or more before Bynum intuited the deception. He walked to the side of the bed and threw back the covers. Enraged, he drove a gash into the wig, scattering bubble wrap in all directions. He stood up and looked around, trying to process this unexpected development. Where was she? Was someone with her? How had he allowed himself to be set up, trapped like a fly in a black widow’s web?

“Turn on the lamp, Randy. I’m over here,” she said evenly from across the room.

Stunned and befuddled, he turned on the light. He saw her clearly but was unable to organize his thoughts. Confusion had usurped logic and reason. Instead he acted out of primal instinct, and with the knife in the kill position moved toward her. “Playing games again,” he snapped, drooling venom like water from a leaky faucet. “I wondered where you were hiding . . . you meddling bitch.”

Maggie sat in plain view, wanting to be seen. “Don’t come any closer, Randy.” She pointed the gun. “Put the knife down!”

Bynum, only a few feet from the love seat, took another step. A mistake.

Maggie leaned on the arm of the sofa and fired the .38. The bullet ripped through Bynum’s right shoulder and lodged in the wall between the two windows.

Bynum howled with pain and let the knife fall to the carpet. He crumbled to his knees, blood trickling down his right arm. “Goddammit, you crazy bitch!” He reached for the knife with his left hand and tried to stand up.

“Don’t do it, Randy. I’ll defend myself and won’t aim for your shoulder. She tossed him the hand towel.

He dropped back to the sitting position and covered the entry wound with the towel. Bynum, still filled with rage, had trouble defining his options. He was able to pick up the knife with his right hand despite the searing pain in his shoulder.

“You have two choices, Randy.”

He looked at her, his eyes glazed, as if he wanted nothing more than to plunge the serrated blade into her chest and turn it violently. He wished Rita were here watching.

“Actions have consequences, Randy. Move a foot closer and I’ll blow you away.” Maggie kept the gun steady, ready to fire. “If you move back a bit, I’ll call 911 and you’ll walk out of here alive. Your choice. Think it over.”

Before the words left Maggie’s mouth, he lunged at her, his wounded arm extended.

Maggie fired. The bullet found his chest, penetrated his heart and sheared the aorta.

The awkward arc of the knife slashed the love seat as he fell. Bynum’s head brushed her leg. He was dead before he hit the floor, face down.

With sweaty palms, Maggie checked his carotid pulses. There were none. She fumbled for her cell phone and punched in Carl’s number. Maggie figured he was a sound sleeper, but the delay caused her some fleeting concern.

He answered on the fifth ring.

“Carl, I need you.”

“Are you okay?”

She hesitated. “Bynum is dead . . . lying on my bedroom floor.”

“Stay calm, Maggie, I’ll be there in ten.”

Maggie, dry-eyed, looked at Randy Bynum and breathed a sigh of relief. The nightmare had finally ended.

CHAPTER 38

Same night

IT WAS 4 A.M. and Robbie Armstead had not slept. He lay in bed, moving closer to the edge of a bottomless abyss. He had made a decision. It was time to take that first step, despite the enervation that pulled at him like an ocean's undertow. He dressed quietly, stuck the folded missive in his pants pocket and slipped out the kitchen door. He fired up the Honda and headed across town for Lamy Lane. Other than for the "plan," his mind was as empty as a bucket in a dry well. His eyes saw nothing but the strip of asphalt that carried him from his home—always a sanctuary—for the last time. Yet he felt nothing, nor did he see the large possum in the middle of the road. How could he not see the dead marsupial? An easy answer: abstracted. Ms. McFarland had said depression pushes everything inside, while everything outside is monochromatic and lifeless. The things that matter evaporate like chimney smoke into a meaningless void.

Last night before going to bed, he reread the letter written earlier that same evening, which he intended to leave in Ms. McFarland's mailbox. Consumed by malaise, the writing required an inordinate amount of time and effort. But Robbie was in no hurry, and it was his last chance to set the record straight.

Dear Ms. McFarland, I want to share with you some things which I was unable to express at OverReach. You mentioned that guilt often made depression worse. Well, guilt is eating me alive. While you are not a priest, I have a confession. I killed Rhea Joslyn. It was not my intent. I was high on crystal meth and the gun went off accidentally. I needed the money for my habit, and my plan was simple: get the money and run. In my wildest dreams, I would never harm anyone, much less a nice lady like Reverend Joslyn. But what's done is done. After our last session, I considered my options. Either go to the police with this confession, or drop off the edge of the cliff and escape the dark despair that owns me.

I checked Louisiana law on the internet and found the penalty for armed robbery, even without intent to fire your weapon, is life without parole. A plea bargain might be possible since I have negotiable information—namely, I know who killed Mick Randle. I overheard a phone conversation one night in Mick's trailer. Still, the best deal would mean ten to fifteen years in prison, minimum, and I'd rather be dead.

I'm enclosing the name of Mick's killer with the hope you'll pass it along to the authorities. Background: Mick was into drugs big-time as a user and a dealer. While cannabis was the most popular drug, he pushed large amounts of cocaine, heroin and crystal meth. His supplier was CARLOS TORRES, head of the Gulf cartel headquartered in Matamoros, a city of some size and across the river from Brownsville, Texas. Mick made the mistake of a partial payment on one delivery and Torres went ballistic. He gave Mick two weeks to settle up, a warning Mick should have taken seriously. I can't swear Torres fired the shot that killed Mick, but if not, he ordered the assassination. Mick's phone records should support my charge. This may be of more interest to the Feds than to local law enforcement. Mr. Sweeny should know how best to disseminate this information. I hope it will help put pressure on Torres and the cartel; a business that has ruined countless lives, including my own.

I appreciate your counseling, Ms. McFarland, but unfortunately, my problems are beyond repair. And that's okay, since every life has a beginning and an end. The sixty-four dollar question: Is there a forgiving God? Guess I'll soon know the truth. What better place to find the answer than a mountaintop with its scenic view of the river?

Robbie Armstead

As soon as Robbie made the turn into Lamy Lane, he noticed, with the help of sodium lamps, unusual activity at the end of the street. The cluster of cars, one with a spinning light bar, meant the police were involved. Robbie wondered if trouble had occurred at the McFarland residence. If so, he hoped she was safe and unharmed.

He parked at the curb near the end of the first block and walked the rest of the way. While it was drudgery, Robbie wanted to deliver the letter without being seen. Otherwise there would be questions; after all, the police were here, even though the flashing light bar had been turned off. *Why is a twenty-something from the other side of town at a crime scene at 4:30 in the morning?* Robbie knew that question would pop up like a jack-in-the-box, the question he didn't want to answer. Nor did he want the delay of an interrogation. He had a critical deadline.

Robbie stood in darkness beside the trunk of a beech with leafless limbs. All the cars appeared empty, including the medical examiner's SUV and the Camden cop car. He saw no signs of the officer or the coroner and figured everyone was inside the well-lighted McFarland residence. With the stealth of a cat burglar, he tiptoed to the mailbox and opened the lid. He put the folded note paper inside, along with a black flint arrowhead, and then closed the box. Satisfied that his delivery went unnoticed, Robbie stuffed his hands in his pants pockets and with hunched shoulders headed back to the Honda.

Robbie had a plan, a destination. The surreal scene at the McFarland residence was quickly forgotten. He left curiosity and concern behind in the shadow of the beech tree. Nearby, a dog yelped, a fearful sound, just as he reached the car.

For Robbie, there was no reluctance, no looking back, as he drove to the trailer park off Old North Road. It was an easy drive and required no concentration. He had made the trip many times; the route as familiar as the back of his hand. While Robbie was immersed in inertia, the mission remained clear. He had no intention of turning back. In truth, he felt a compelling need to move ahead.

At this hour, there was only a rare headlight in the southbound lane. Robbie drove cautiously; a conversation with the State Highway Patrol was not an option. He kept both hands on the steering wheel, his eyes fixed on the black median strip in front of him. He failed to notice the shadowy Chevron station, shut down for the night. After crossing the makeshift bridge, he followed Trappers Road past darkened trailers and the dull glow of the laundry shed. He parked in the clearing across from Mick's vacant trailer and opened the glove compartment. He removed the .22 and a small flashlight, then dropped the keys inside and clicked it shut. Robbie stepped out of the car, placed the .22 in the waistband of his khakis and quietly closed the car door.

He crossed the cul-de-sac, turned on the flashlight and found the worn-down, weedy footpath which led to the Indian mound and the river beyond. Overhead, a half-moon shone like quicksilver high in the night sky, as if impaled there. When he reached the chain link fence that enclosed the mound, he could read the *NO TREPASSING* sign without the flashlight. Robbie knew that while the moon would wane, dawn was less than an hour away. Perfect timing, just as he'd planned. He climbed the fence, which he had done before, and dropped onto a thick carpet of Bermuda grass.

This was his second home, almost as if he belonged here, from the day he found his first arrowhead. He had done the research, fascinated by the history of the nearby Poverty Point mounds, which archeologists had shown to be older than Stonehenge and the Maya pyramids. The Camden mound was constructed of dirt and packed clay; grassed over in the early twentieth century. In reality, there was a cluster of six conical mounds connected by ridges, the center mound reaching a height of fifty feet. From the river, the mounds appeared as one; from overhead, as an oval formation. To the locals, the ancient earthworks were simply an Indian mound, a historic site owned by the state.

Within the enclosure, Robbie trudged along a walkway of cypress planks to the tallest, steep-sloped mound. There were no steps or ladders. But he had climbed the mound before, and the night was no impediment. When he reached the top he was breathing hard. The mound tapered, and there was a small, flat area at its crown. Robbie sat down and leaned back on his elbows. He scanned the night sky filled with star-lit constellations; below, only a few hundred yards away, the river shimmered with moonlight. This was where he wanted to spend his last night. Drugs and depression had stolen his dreams and drowned him in an impervious darkness; they crushed his will to live. Then there was the homicide, albeit unintentional. The best Robbie could hope for, even with a negotiated plea deal, was a long sentence with the possibility of parole. Winn Correctional, a medium security prison, was not on the table. Armed robbery and murder meant Angola, the notorious state penitentiary. Robbie had thought it through—Angola was not an option.

To the east, a narrow band of pink defined the horizon. Daybreak. Robbie took the gun from his waistband and ran a finger over the hard, cold metal of the barrel. He opened the cylinder and fed a hollow point bullet into an empty chamber. He clicked the cylinder shut. Robbie said a silent prayer and took one last look at the heavens, growing ever brighter, before he pulled the trigger.

The explosion scattered a flock of crows cawing from their roost in a nearby river birch. Two fishermen close to the riverbank were distracted briefly, but only shrugged and continued to drift downriver.

Bernice Majors was awake, but heard nothing. Trappers Park was morbidly quiet. She lay in bed as dawn seeped through the cracks in her window shade and thought about the tragedy that had occurred in Mickey Randle's trailer on Good Friday. A vestige of violence still hovered over the park, slipping through the fissures and beneath the door of her trailer, invading her space. Something was wrong in her tightly circumscribed world. She could neither see nor hear it, but the feeling was intense. The next day Bernice got the appalling news of the suicide, a call from Dray Moody. She replaced the wall phone and leaned disheartened on the kitchen counter. Her prayer for peace and benevolence was only a pipe dream.

The ghosts of the hunter-gatherers who built the earthworks five thousand years ago loomed over those mounds, and the lifeless body of Robbie Armstead.

CHAPTER 39

MAGGIE SAT AT THE KITCHEN table and waited. Carl had said he'd be there in ten, but she knew it would take twenty, minimum, even without the traffic. She had swapped the silk robe for a flannel bathrobe that fell below the knee. She needed more cover for the gym shorts and golf shirt. The house would be full of cops, homicide detectives, and the medical examiner (among others) within the hour. The silk was a bit too provocative. She turned on the overhead light. Nothing else was touched or altered. Bynum remained face down on the bedroom carpet. She had checked his carotids, but otherwise the body lay as it fell . . . undisturbed. She walked around Bynum, avoiding small pools of blood, through the double doors and into the dim-lit entry hall. The front door stood open, and she chose not to close it. Carl was on his way, and she wanted him to see firsthand the recent break-in by this psycho who had stalked her for weeks. Maggie tapped the table with her fingers, anxious to see him. Carl was more than a man who had captured her heart; he was her fount of comfort and security. There was one other certainty: two gunshots, explosions that should have awakened everyone on Lamy Lane. She was surprised that Pixie hadn't called.

Maggie was calm, her hands steady. She had just killed a man, but she felt no remorse. It was self-defense . . . wasn't it? Yes, she had set him up, but for almost two months he had taunted and mocked her with cards and phone calls. On two occasions he had been spotted prowling her property in the dead of night. Stalking her. She remembered the night at *Louie's*. His intent was clear—frighten her with threats until, in his warped mind, time ran out, and then he would kill her. While she had taken a life, there was no feeling of compunction or the slightest twinge of contrition. Ironically, it was this insensitivity that troubled her and as in the past, she wondered why it was so. Had vestiges of growing up in Rutledge and working Las Vegas survived for four decades, hidden in some dark crevice of the mind?

This was not the first time. She had killed another man indirectly. She clearly remembered the sordid scenario that occurred a very long time ago. Maggie had been in Las Vegas less than a year when a one-time john by the name of Rollie Bannister, with a Carson City address, began stalking her. He kept his distance but followed her everywhere, often parking for hours across the street from her Desert Sky apartment. Letters and lewd phone calls followed. After several weeks, they took on an air of menace. Maggie wondered if she had insulted him in some way during their fee-for-service encounter. Or had she made, inadvertently, a disparaging remark that set him off.

Banister was an amputee—left leg, at the knee—with a carrot top and an acne-scarred face. She remembered him, but could not recall anything "off limits" during their two hours together at the hotel. But Maggie had learned early on that some of her clients were indubitably weird. She figured Mr. Bannister was one of them.

A late-night phone call from Bannister was the tipping point. The words were still embedded in her long-term memory. "You're the best sex I've ever had. I'm coming over for more. Resist at your own peril." The phone line went dead, and Maggie's heart started to pound. She got up, bolted the door and put in a call to Frankie at The Capri. She gave him the name and the gist of the phone call. She heard the anger in his voice—harming "one of his girls" was met with harsh and swift reprisals. He assured her Speck would be at the apartment in ten minutes and he, Frankie, would take care of Mr. Bannister. Maggie hoped Frankie would just scare him off, but she had heard the stories. A phone call from Frankie to his father, mob boss Joe Agosto, and Bannister would disappear. A month passed, no sign of Bannister. She checked with information in Carson City, but there was no listing for a Rollie Bannister. No surprise. Maggie believed he was buried deep in the scorching Nevada desert.

She had shot and killed Randy Bynum. When Maggie left Las Vegas many years ago, Rollie Bannister was presumed dead and she was responsible. Had she not made the phone call to Frankie and set the wheels in motion? Then, as now, the salient question: was self-defense justification? Legally, yes; morally, she was not so sure.

Maggie heard a car pull into the driveway. She hoped it was Carl. The house was wide open; anyone could walk in. She turned her chair, an angle that allowed her to see him standing just outside the bedroom where he could scan the room without crossing the threshold. As a former D.A., he would not run the risk of contaminating the murder scene. His arrival brought Maggie relief and eased the tension in her tightly drawn muscles.

He came into the kitchen with a look of concern, kissed her lightly and sat down across from her. Carl left home in a hurry. Stubble covered his face, and his hair was more unruly than usual. He had put on a pair of wrinkled khakis, a black turtleneck sweater, and loafers without socks. He reached across the table and took her hand. "Are you okay?"

Maggie nodded. Despite the frightening experience, she appeared calm as a millpond. No one would guess, from her imperturbable appearance, that she had just shot and killed a man.

A second question followed: "How did it happen?"

She gave him the short version, admitting she had set the trap and Bynum had taken the bait. Not too different from placing a mouse trap at the most suitable location and baiting it with a cube of cheese. "I was tired of looking over my shoulder, not knowing when Bynum would strike. So I devised my own strategic plan."

"A classic case of justifiable homicide." He leaned back in his chair and swept a hand through his hair." I've called Dray Moody, who'll be in charge of the investigation. I gave him some background on the phone, but he'll want to ask questions. So be prepared for an interrogation downtown. Meanwhile, Dray has called Dr. Swanson, the M.E., who'll notify Nanette Hawthorne, his forensic tech and photographer. The swarm of investigators will arrive shortly."

"Nothing you've said is a stunner. I expect the police to ask questions, and the sooner the better. I want to get Bynum out of my life." She paused and patted his hand. "Out of our lives, forever."

Later, much later, Maggie realized that Carl's predictions were spot-on. The front of the house was cordoned off with yellow crime scene tape by two Camden police officers. Dr. Swanson got a briefing from Dray Moody, who was the first to arrive. The M.E. made a cursory examination of the body and the well-lighted bedroom. He stepped into the bathroom, but found nothing of interest. After removing the bullet from the wallboard, he placed it in his coat pocket. Nan Hawthorne took a dozen pictures, including the gash in the loveseat, and collected random samples of dried blood. She placed Maggie's gun and Bynum's knife in evidence bags and tucked them in her satchel. They were in and out in less than an hour. The two policemen rolled the body onto a stretcher and carried it to Swanson's SUV for transport to the city morgue and a pending autopsy. Meanwhile, Dray Moody got the basic facts from Maggie at the kitchen table, but he needed an official interrogation downtown. After all, a man had been shot, even though Cleve Barnes, the D.A., would strongly consider it justified. Meanwhile, Dray had to get the facts. All of them. His report to the D.A, must be factual and detailed, since it might save her a trip to the Annex and more questions from Mr. Barnes. She remembered he tittered and said, "No cuffs; Mr. Sweeney can drive you to the station." While his bit of humor surprised her, she was grateful for the courtesy. Having Carl with her would make the ordeal much easier. And he had been a mentor to Barnes during his last few years in the D.A.'s office. She knew the interrogations and the publicity, especially the front page of the *Camden Crier,* were part of the cost of defending herself. Bynum tried to kill her, and the gruesome drama that just played out in her bedroom was irrefutable proof.

The chirp of her cell phone awoke Maggie from a sound sleep. She sat on the side of the bed and opened the phone. A quick glance at the clock read 11:10. A patch of carpet near the palladium window was ribbed with sunlight. It was another glorious spring day after a ghastly night. It took a few seconds before she could clear her head and answer.

"Maggie, this is Alice. Are you all right?"

A yawn. "I'm okay, but it was a long night," she said without embellishment.

“I’m sorry to disturb you, Maggie, especially on Saturday, but it’s important.”

“I’m awake now.” Maggie stifled another yawn. “I’m listening.”

“Would you meet me at OverReach after lunch, say, around one o’clock? I have some news that I’d prefer to discuss in person.”

“Sure, I’ll be there.” Maggie hesitated before adding, “I have some news of my own.”

Alice didn’t probe. “I’ll see you at one. Mr. Armstead may join us.”

Maggie started to ask, “Why Armstead?” But Alice had closed her phone.

She fluffed her pillows and lay back, enough time to consider every aspect of the Bynum encounter and the enormous relief she felt in knowing the danger had passed. The two hours in the interview room at the Annex were no cup of tea. It was a small space, stuffy and windowless. Her chair was bolted to the floor, which Carl later explained kept the camera on her during the interview.

Dray Moody was gracious and allowed Carl to sit with her during the process. He offered coffee, which she politely refused.

Moody hoped to get her comfortable with a few easy questions. But he shifted gears quickly and asked for a full recounting of her relationship with Randy Bynum. She complied, beginning with the trip to Dallas in February to rescues Rita Bynum from her violent and abusive husband. Randy was enraged and demanded Rita’s return or else. She sliced a finger across her throat, from ear to ear, to make the point of Bynum’s lethal intent.

Maggie let the narrative unfold, step by step, culminating in the house invasion and the assault. She had been stalked since early February and was prepared for the confrontation. She started to raise a relevant legal question: “Do I not have the right to defend myself?” But she had second thoughts and didn’t ask. Moody was letting her swim in calm waters. There was so need to make waves.

Detective Moody asked more than his quota of questions, at least in Maggie’s opinion. Many of them were immaterial or had been asked before. Throughout the long session, she remained poised and answered truthfully, carefully avoiding gratuitous addendums. She had stated the bare facts, and they should lead Moody to only one conclusion: justifiable homicide.

Home at seven in the morning. Four hours of sleep in her guest bedroom. Carl had begged her to stay with him until they could replace the carpet and make the repairs. When she demurred, he replaced the front door in its frame . . . a temporary fix.

Maggie was crazy about the guy. He had been a solid pillar of support, and during the interrogation he had remained silent, but spoke to her with his eyes or the squeeze of his hand.

"Get up and get moving," she muttered. Maggie had spent more time ruminating than she'd intended. First things first: a trip to the kitchen to brew a pot of coffee. Next, a hot shower to loosen muscles still taut from the stress and pressure of the past twelve hours. She dried off with one of her fluffy towels and put on her robe. Little makeup as usual, her hair pulled back in a ponytail.

She made her first post-Bynum trip to the master bedroom and across the blood-stained carpet, surprised that it evoked no emotion. It was necessary, since she needed to access the closet. She chose tan slacks and a cotton sweater the color of Bahamian waters that matched the ribbon in her hair. An afterthought: she opened her jewel box, removed the emerald and slipped it on her ring finger. Maggie took a last look in the mirror; satisfied, she headed back to the kitchen.

She poured coffee into a Styrofoam cup and carried it to her car. She checked the dashboard clock as she drove away. No need to hurry, there was enough time to make the appointment. She relished the release from Bynum's vindictive threats, free from the worry that had hung over her like the sword of Damocles. Almost euphoric, she lowered her window. Fresh air and the scent of jasmine filled the car.

Maggie had given little thought to Alice's phone call, which had awakened her from a sound sleep. After all, her mind was overloaded from last night's horrors and the tension-filled interrogation at the Schulze building. The reason for the call—well, she'd know soon enough. She turned into the OverReach driveway and parked out front. There was no one at the reception desk. Maybe Madeline or her Saturday fill-in had taken a lunch break. Maggie unlocked the security door and headed straight for Alice Fogleman's office, stopping at the threshold. Alice, as on her previous visits, stood at the window that overlooked the bald cypress and the sun-splashed bayou.

She spoke evenly, without turning away. "Robbie is dead."

"Oh, no!" Maggie exclaimed. Momentarily dizzy, she leaned against the doorframe, her eyes moist. "How did it happen?" she asked as tears trickled down her cheeks.

"He shot himself," she said calmly.

"Alice, please sit down and tell me what happened." Maggie dropped into the arm chair and wiped her eyes.

Alice left the window unwillingly, as if the view held the answer to Robbie's troubled life. Solemn and dry-eyed, she returned to her desk.

Amid the mournful silence, Maggie felt an unspeakable sadness and struggled for composure. "Alice, talk to me, please! What happened?"

Alice rested her arms on the desk, her face as stoic as Zeno. "Robbie left a note on his pillow. His mother found it this morning. He thanked his mom and dad for their love and support, and asked their forgiveness for his delinquent and shameful behavior." Alice walked around the desk and sat on the front edge. "Robbie made the decision because . . . his words . . . *the darkness devoured me.*"

Maggie was choked with emotion. She took a Kleenex from her purse and wiped her eyes again. "Who found him?"

"In the note he alluded to a 'second home.' That's where they could find him."

"I don't get it," Maggie said.

"A.B. figured it out. He knew Robbie's love of arrowheads and Indian lore, put two and two together, used his connections to borrow the sheriff department's helicopter. The pilot spotted the body atop one of the Indian mounds. A paramedic scaled the mound and confirmed Robbie's death. The helicopter lifted the body and the gun off the mound, reeled the rescue basket into the copter and landed on the roof of St. Francis. Dr. Swanson was in the hospital, which made the transfer of the body quick and easy."

Maggie looked dispirited. "I let him down, Alice. If I had . . ."

"Don't beat yourself up, Maggie. Robbie made the decisions that shaped his life. In all fairness, during most of those years he was plagued by depression, and it was the demon that killed him."

"Time of death? Any idea?" Maggie wondered if it could have occurred close to the time of Bynum's break-in.

"The paramedic reported early rigor mortis. Swanson set the time between four and six this morning."

"He waited until daybreak," Maggie said. "Only a guess, but I believe it was important for Robbie to witness another sunrise."

"We'll never know, will we?"

"I suppose not." Maggie started to stand. "I thought Mr. Armstead was joining us."

Alice reached for a note near her office phone. "He called with apologies. There are decisions to be made; a flurry of activity, as you might imagine, and the family looks to A.B. for guidance and advice." Alice checked the note. "He asked me to convey his appreciation for your commitment to

OverReach, and for your genuine interest in helping Robbie."

"I wish I'd done more. . . . and sooner." Maggie started for the door.

"You mentioned you had some news," Alice said to her back.

Maggie stopped at the door and turned around. "I'm really tired, Alice. It's been a long twenty-four hours. Read about it in the Sunday *Crier.* It'll be a front page story." She gave Alice a half-hearted wave and left the office.

On the drive home, Maggie had a lot on her mind. What would Cleve Barnes' disposition be after getting Dray Moody's report? Would there be another interrogation? It was clearly self-defense, but she had baited Bynum. Was that a form of entrapment? And then there was Robbie. Did she bear any of the responsibility for his suicide? If she had refused Mr. Armstead's request and referred Robbie directly to Dr. Edwards, would that have made a difference? It was a vexing question, and she would never know the answer with certainty. She needed sleep and planned to bed down on the sofa when she got home. She expected Carl around five—hamburgers on the grill, away from the noise, time to relax, just the two of them and the shadow of the Chinese elm. She checked the clock; enough time for a long nap. That is, if she could turn off the glut of thoughts and questions and the self-reproach that spun like a top in her head.

CHAPTER 40

MAGGIE LEANED ON THE RAILING and sipped her glass of red wine. While there was still some sunlight, the Chinese elm cast a shadow across one end of the deck. She heard Carl make his way through the house and glanced at her watch: five o'clock, on the nose. Carl was punctual, a trait she could count on. She wondered if it was a compulsion, always on time, or if ten years in the D.A.'s office had something to do with it. *Time is of the essence* was one of his oft-used maxims.

"Best-looking legs in Richland Parish." A school boy's snicker. "I'm not kidding."

She turned around and patted the plaid Bermudas with her free hand. "It seemed a good choice for the warm weather." Maggie put her glass on the railing and reached out to him, rewarded with a warm embrace and a delicious kiss.

"Are you okay?" he asked, still holding her. "It was a long, nerve-rattling night."

She stepped back and picked up her glass. "I was calm and under control until this morning, when I got the news of Robbie Armstead's suicide."

"I heard," Carl said. "Bailey called and broke the news."

"I wish I could have done more," she lamented. "It's heartbreaking when death takes one so young."

"Don't play the blame game, Maggie. You tried to help, but I wonder if anyone could have saved Robbie. Mix drugs and depression . . . well, you're playing with fire."

"That's what Alice said, in so many words, trying to assuage my remorse."

Carl went back to the kitchen and poured himself a glass of Zinfandel, although he doubted if this California wine would find a place in Chris Marcos' wine cellar. He picked up an envelope off the granite countertop and returned to the deck.

"I parked at the curb and got the mail. Most of it looked like junk mail, with one exception." He handed her a letter marked: *Ms. McFarland . . . PERSONAL.* No stamps. Hand delivered.

Maggie took the envelope and unsealed it. She removed the folded notepaper and saw Robbie's signature. "I'd like to read this. So why don't you light the grill and make the hamburgers? The fixings are in the fridge."

"Just call me Chef Prudhomme." Carl chuckled and doubled back to the kitchen.

Maggie pulled a patio chair into the shade and sat down. After reading the letter, she dropped it in her lap and stared ruefully into the distant tree- line. Robbie had answered some important questions. His confession brought closure to the death of Rhea Joslyn. Maggie was certain, as Robbie admitted in his letter, that guilt subdued him. Psychology 101: blend guilt with drugs and depression, and you've got a lethal potion.

She picked up the letter and read it again. She realized that Robbie had chosen her to make his confession and release the information regarding Mickey Randle's assassination. He knew she would give the letter to Carl Sweeney, who would pass Robbie's confession to the Camden police and the name of Carlos Torres to the Feds, along with the information he'd enclosed. Robbie knew Carl had the connections, and she was simply a reliable conduit.

Lost in thought, Maggie did not hear Carl approach until he tapped her on the shoulder. "I meant to give this to you earlier." He handed her the arrowhead. "It was in the box along with the mail."

She took the arrowhead, and in turn gave him the letter. "I want you to read Robbie's confessions."

Carl unfolded the note paper but waited for her reaction to the Indian relic.

She fingered the arrowhead, turned it over, and felt the sharp point against her skin.

"Why?" she asked, returning the black flint.

"Maybe a talisman. Robbie was into Indian legends."

Possible," Maggie said without much conviction.

"How 'bout this? It was a clue . . ."

"To what?" she interrupted.

"To the Indian mound, the place he planned to take his life."

Maggie gave him a dismissive wave and snapped her fingers. "Remember the Franklins found an arrowhead in Rhea Joslyn's office the night of the murder?"

"I should remember. Bertha Franklin gave me the arrowhead, which I in turn gave to Bailey the morning of the funeral."

'Okay, then maybe this arrowhead was meant to validate his confession."

Carl shook his head. "It could be any of the three, or none of the above. I guess we'll never know for sure." He tapped the arrowhead on the aluminum arm of his chair. "I'll pass it along."

Her chair scraped the wooden deck as she stood holding her empty wine glass. "Why don't you read the letter while I make the coffee and toss the salad?"

After they finished eating, Maggie and Carl sat in the patio chairs and soaked up the silence as twilight faded into darkness, a silence broken only by a cool breeze that rustled the young leaves of the Chinese elm. It was still too early for the chirp of crickets and the clicking call of cicadas. Overhead, galaxies glittered like shiny spangles, and the moon began its steady climb into the night sky.

"When will it end?" she asked.

"Soon."

"How soon?"

He heard the weariness in her voice. It was not unexpected after riding an emotional rollercoaster for a very long time.

"A week at most," he said firmly, hoping to lift her spirits.

Maggie sipped her coffee. "Will I be charged?"

"For what?" he chortled. "There's no law against self-defense."

"I set him up, Carl."

"But only after he'd stalked you for two months."

Maggie looked up at the star-flecked sky. "It's so beautiful out here. And to have someone I care about." She reached over and tugged at his arm. "I just want to be free of Bynum, who is still a pebble in my shoe, and somehow find the rationale to nullify my role in Robbie's suicide."

"Listen, Maggie, I talked with Cleve late this afternoon. He's already received a call from Dray Moody, but he needs the official written report, which Moody promised was forthcoming." Carl reached for his mug on the deck's railing. "I decided, rather than wait, to give him an up-close and personal version of Bynum's menace with the expressed intent to kill. Cleve listened patiently to my narrative, even asked a few questions. While he could make no comments on the matter, he promised to expedite the process. As an old prosecutor and D.A., I am ninety-nine percent certain there will be no further interrogations, no grand jury, and no charge other than justifiable homicide. It expunges the record, and you walk away as free as a bird."

"Do you really believe that, Carl?"

"Absolutely, without a doubt."

"I hope you're right." Maggie took his mug and went inside. She put on a sweater and refilled the mugs. She backed out the kitchen door and handed Carl his coffee. "I'll come to terms with Robbie," she said, sitting down in her chair. "I'd grown fond of him in such a short time. It made the loss more painful and raised questions about our interaction during those final days. Could I have saved him? Done something different? Called Dr. Edwards sooner?" She shook her head dejectedly.

Carl let the rhetorical questions fade into the gentle night. Then he turned his chair toward her and held up the letter. "I'll make copies . . . one for Captain Graves, which should bring closure to the Joslyn matter, and one for the sheriff, who in turn will contact the DEA regarding Torres." He gently slapped the arm of her chair with the folded notepaper. "Okay with you?"

"Of course. It's what Robbie wanted."

Carl put the missive away, shifting gears. "I have a suggestion . . . a proposition, really."

"What's on your mind?" She managed a thin smile.

"Let's get away after the dust settles."

"You mean after Barnes' decision and Robbie's funeral?"

Carl nodded. "Wherever you'd like to go. San Francisco, Dorado Beach, Paris . . . you pick the place."

"New Orleans. It's been ages since I was there. While recovery from Katrina is still a work in progress, New Orleans is an adventure."

"Good choice. And we could invite Ed and Edith . . ."

"No, no, Carl." She raised her hands, as if pushing the suggestion away. "Just us. Just the two of us."

He felt his heart pound in his chest. He loved this woman, and there was nothing in the world he would cherish more than spending time with her, anywhere . . . just the two of them.

"Are you sure?" He paused for effect. "Paris is still an option."

Maggie shook her head. "I want to have coffee and beignets at the Cafe du Monde, antique shop the French Quarter, and listen to authentic jazz at Preservation Hall."

"And don't forget the D-Day Museum, or Jackson Square with its mimes and magicians."

"Maybe we'll have one of the artists who are usually there paint a portrait of us."

The both laughed.

"You'll love the Maison de Ville on Toulouse St. with Royal around the corner. It's an old-world hotel, with suites that overlook an enchanting courtyard and its three-tiered fountain. With luck, I'll reserve room nine . . ."

"What's special about nine?" she cut in, her curiosity piqued.

"Tennessee Williams rented that room and finished, in my opinion, his masterpiece: *A Streetcar Named Desire."*

"Sounds heavenly, Carl. Let's plan on it."

"When I was in New Orleans on a case some years ago, I stayed at the boutique hotel. My sweetest memory was an early evening, sitting in the courtyard with a glass of Sazerac, enjoying the piped-in music of the brass marching bands before a short walk to Antoine's for dinner. An epicurean's delight, I might add."

The chair groaned when she moved over and sat in his lap. Maggie wrapped her arms around his neck and kissed him, overwhelmed by a swell of passion she had not felt since Jack was alive. She leaned back and rested her head against his chest. “You know something?” she asked softly.

He kissed her forehead. “Nope, no idea.”

“You are my best friend, Carl.” She snuggled closer. “My staunch supporter—reliable, considerate, generous . . . and much more. I never dreamed it would happen again, but the heart has a way of sending unforeseen messages.” Maggie lifted her head and looked up at him. “I love you, Carl Sweeney. Let’s go to New Orleans and celebrate.”

He held her tight and wondered if his heart could handle the boundless joy that he felt. It was a transforming moment, for sure. But how should he respond to her declaration? The words came after a flash of inspiration. “Maggie, remember awhile back I told you about a college English requirement, and for some crazy reason I chose English poets? Nineteenth century, and Browning was my favorite. Among his many poems—I can’t tell you why—I still remember *Pippa’s Song.*” He tapped his temple. “I think it’s still there.”

“Carl Sweeny, the tough and fearless district attorney . . . a romanticist.” She stroked his cheek softly. “I can’t believe it, but I’d like to hear it,”

He crossed his fingers and held them up. “Okay, here goes: *The year’s at the spring/And days at the morn/Morning’s at seven/The hillside’s dew-pearl’d/The lark’s on the wing/The snail’s on the thorn/God’s in His heaven/All’s right with the world.*

“Browning was wrong, Carl. There’s much wrong with the world, then and now.”

The darkness hid his blissful smile. “My world, Maggie. All’s right in my world. And you’ve made it so.”

On the drive home, Carl felt the wonder that engulfed him. Still, he saw the irony. After he and Beth parted ways, he learned to live alone and accepted solitude as his lifelong companion. Despite the effort of friends, and those wretched blind dates, he was not looking for another woman in his life. Then it happened, out of the blue—a Saturday night dinner with Edith and Ed, who happened to invite their new neighbor.

She was attractive, engaging, and featured an easy smile. Unknowingly, she pulled him in with the ease of a fisherman reeling in a silver shiner. Morning coffee at Starbucks, and Carl knew he had fallen hard for this bewitching woman. Then the question flashed like neon: Would he be more than a friend to Maggie McFarland? Carl remembered in infinite detail the small steps they had taken which moved the relationship forward. His formula was simple: thoughtful, respectful, and supportive, never invading her space without invitation. Progress was slow, but Carl was undaunted, hoping for the day when her feelings matched his own.

Carl turned into his driveway and cut the engine. He stared at the sky through the open window. Tonight it had happened, beneath a million stars—his most fervent wish had come true. She had said the words that brought warmth to his heart and made his eyes brim with tears. How do you explain it? Something magical? Perhaps a miracle. Maybe the transforming grace of a loving Father. He stepped out of the car, looked up to the heavens, and offered a prayer of thanksgiving.

Carl went inside and headed for his study. He popped in his favorite tape, kicked off his shoes, and settled on the sofa as pleasing sounds floated across the room.

I will find you in the morning sun/And when the night is new,
I'll be looking at the moon/But I'll be seeing you.

Relaxed, he lay back and drifted down into a peaceful sleep. As always, sweet dreams of Maggie.

Carl Sweeny was a happy man.

CPSIA information can be obtained
at www.ICGtesting.com
Printed in the USA
FFOW02n2312280515
13773FF